Rise Of The Alpha

By Cassie Lein & Bre Rose

Beyond The Pack Series Book 1

Cover Design and Paperback Wrap by Sugarbaby Designs

Proofreading and Editing by Shayna Turpin

ARC and E Book Formatting by Bre Rose

Paperback Formatting by Bre Rose

To all the women who want a ferret in the streets
and a Bone Crusher in the sheets.

Blurb

THE FOLLOWING HAS BEEN INSTILLED IN ME FROM THE DAY I WAS BORN...

1) Our pack is the best

2) Everyone else is inferior and beneath us.

3) Women are purely for producing powerful male pups and sexual gratification

I hate it, the whole mentality of the Exodus Pack repulses me.

When a rare opportunity presents itself to escape the confines and everyday scrutiny of the pack I loathe, I pounce on it.

I'm immersed in a world filled with every type of supernatural being imaginable.

A place where I can be free in who I am and who I want to be.

Finding love in the strangest of places, some new to even me.

But one spell changes everything, sending my life into chaos.

Now I'm in demand even more than before, wanted by those who only seek to abuse the power I can give them.

Will love prevail, or will evil snuff it out before it can really even begi*n?*

Author's Note and Content Warning

This is a dark Why Choose Paranormal Romance. Our characters will not have to choose between their love interests. This story will contain a FF relationship within the group as well as both females will be with the others members. Rise of the Alpha will have a building harem that will not be complete in the first book This is the first book in a series and will end on a cliffhanger, however the series will end in a HEA.

Please note this story will contain triggering elements to include but not be limited to:

Familial Abuse, Explicit content, Sexual Abuse, Cult like Ideals, Miscommunication, Kidnapping and drugging

If any of these are triggering for you then please do not read we value your mental health more. Also if you do not like a dash of comedy with your darkness this is not for you. Thank you for taking the time to read our first co-write baby together. We enjoyed all the late night calls as does our cellular phone service.

If you are good with all the above then happy reading and I am ready for all the screams at the end. Happy reading. If any errors are found while reading please reach out to me brereseauthor@gmail.com or send a message to either myself or my PA, Shayna Turpin. Sending them directly to us allows for a quicker and smoother correction process without causing disruptions for others in reading and enjoying the book

Rise of the Alpha Playlist

I Wanna Be Your Slave - Maneskin

Daisy - Ashniko

Thinking With My Dick - Kevin Gates

Girlfight - Brooke Valentine

Down With the Sickness - Disturbed

Still Counting - Volbeat

Not Your Barbie Girl - Ava Max

Ava - Natalie Jane

Toxic - 2WEI

Rabbit Hole - Qveen Herby

Like a Villain - Bad Omens

I'll Make You Love Me - Kat Leon

Mad Hatter - Melanie Martinez

Prologue
Magnolia

Being part of a pack was supposed to be the greatest thing. Loyalty above all to your pack and, most importantly, the Alpha. Twice a year, packs across the United States came together with the ultimate goal of finding their mate. But when you are part of the Exodus Pack, you can forget that happening. We never leave pack grounds, our mate bonds are formed from blood and tears and with members of Exodus only!

Unfortunately, I was born into a pack of bigoted elitists. Their mindset, drilled into them for longer than I can remember, is that they're far superior to all others. We're preached to, from the time we're pups and no longer suckling on our mother's tit, that other packs are weak because they're impure from breeding with other weaker wolves or even worse, they're blasphemous and allow other species to live with them.

Our pack was large, however, low in females. About sixty years ago, our former Alpha instituted a rule that all females would take multiple mates, which is still in effect to this day. Each year, when a female turns twenty-one, a battle is held. Every eligible non-mated male wolf has the opportunity to submit his name to fight for the right to own her bond. The males then battle, to submission or death, for the female. If no males come forward for the female, then a random draw takes place, and she receives only one mate, as she is deemed undesirable and unlikely to produce a powerful offspring. The rumors often whispered are that the males that are chosen abuse their females and only want her to ensure the continuation of their wolf line. They belittle their mate and beat her but always ensured they never hurt the pup she could be carrying. In my opinion, the female is the poor unfortunate soul in that mating. For the female who has many suitors, she gets the top four candidates after a battle in the pit.

My mother once told me a story about when she was a young woman. She had found the man she wanted to be mated to. He was loving and kind, everything the men of the Exodus pack weren't. Much to her dismay, she was sought after by others. Three beta wolves had long wanted her and saw this as their chance to take her, they didn't care she had already chosen a mate. Since they were of high standing, my mother was given to them. This broke my mother's heart, but she swore her love to only one man, the one she wanted. Her mates now knew her heart belonged to another, and it infuriated them. Her love, the man she wanted, was killed by a rogue wolf while on a hunt. My mother often secretly questioned if it was really my father and her other mates, but feared what would happen if she ever questioned it. My mother became a sullen woman. After enduring their abuse and finding out she was pregnant with me, she made the hard decision to become the compliant wolf her mates wanted her to be. She spilled her story and her fear of what would happen to me when I came of age one night, which I never forgot.

I just turned eighteen, and I know this isn't the life, or the pack, for me, but I'm bound to it. I want a chance to experience life, to live normally without their watchful eyes on me twenty-four hours a day. So, a year ago, unbeknownst to my father, I applied to colleges outside of our state. I was accepted to not one but three, and I want to attend the one the farthest away, Arcayne University in Albany, New York. The best thing about this college, and what I hoped would seal the deal with my father, was that it's a school strictly for supernaturals.

It took six months, but after constant pleading and finally promising I would no longer fight the mating challenge, he gave in. He gave me stipulations though. The obvious no dating, because, as I said before if you aren't from our pack, you are considered low status. I also have to come home for every holiday break and one weekend a month. The condition I fought the most, but was the dealbreaker for my father, is that I have to be here next summer for the ranking ceremony. During the summer of your nineteenth year, you are tested to determine if you're an Alpha, Beta, Delta, Omega, or subordinate wolf. This determines not only your importance to the pack, but helps draw in your potential suitors. My father has suspicions I'm a Beta and is hoping I will attract the interest of the Alpha's son and his Betas. My father is giddy at the thought of a pairing between them and me and the status it will bring to him.

"Magnolia... Magnolia... Magnolia Holloway." Finally, I realize that my father's been calling my name, and by him including our last name, I know he's gotten angrier since I ignored him the first few times.

"Yes, Father," I meekly respond, keeping my head bowed to him the way he expects. God, I can't wait until I don't have to keep up this fucking weak ass persona. Another reason I'm ready to get away from this pack. Women are considered defenseless; only good for fucking, cooking, and bearing pups.

"Where the fuck is your head? The Alpha is coming over today to discuss you going away to college and his son's potential interest in you," he tells me, as a malicious smirk crosses his face. My father has been practically giddy since he found out the Alpha is thinking of me as a potential mate for his son.

There it is. I finally get why he relented so easily. The Alpha's mate is required to be educated, and able to mingle with the wives of other Alphas in surrounding packs. But this level of interest is fucking news to me.

"What are you talking about, Father? His son is interested in me? We've never even talked," I ask curiously. I have caught his and his Betas' lustful stares at me, but they've never taken the opportunity to even say hello.

"Of course, they would be. Especially, since I've let it be known we expect you to be a powerful Beta. What better pairing for a mate could there be other than an Alpha?" He laughs before continuing. "And there hasn't been a female Alpha in this pack for more than two hundred years. At this point, an Alpha female being born would be an actual miracle."

Knowing I need to play the game to keep him happy so I can get the hell out of here, I answer the way I've been trained. "Yes, sir. I'm very lucky to have such desired pack members thinking about bonding with me. I will make you proud."

"Go clean up and put on a dress. I expect you to look presentable when they arrive. The Alpha has never let a female leave pack lands, not even his wife, she was educated by a pack teacher. He wants to confirm that my conditions meet his expectations as well as let you know his. Also, he wants to ensure you understand how considerate he's being in allowing you to go." I hurriedly race up the stairs to do as my father ordered. Getting out of this hellhole is number one on my list, and I'll do whatever it takes to guarantee it happens.

The Alpha shows up about an hour later with his wife. She keeps her head held low not even looking at my father unless he speaks to her, which is only to greet her at the door. Women should be seen and not heard. Quiet unless spoken to. The only times we've really heard the Alpha's luna speak is at higher pack functions and only to wives of higher ranking wolves. He sits on the couch across from my father, who sits in the recliner. I cautiously moved pass them both, opting to sit alone on the ottoman. I clamp my knees together and cross my feet at the heels, lying my clasped hands in my lap, like the studious daughter I am. Well, more like my father has made me be, and unfortunately, until I am free from here, it is a charade I have to keep up.

The Alpha agrees with my father's stipulations, but he has some of his own as well. I have to earn a degree in a field of his choosing, and with the potential of being his son's mate, I had to study Political Science. I let out an internal groan of repulsion along with my wolf. Is it worth studying something so insanely boring to be free from here?? Fuck yes, it is.

The night ends, and I'm on cloud nine. Now, all I can do is count the days until I can be out of here and free, even if that freedom has a time stamp on it.

Magnolia

Today is the day. The day I get the freedom I've wanted for so long. I already shipped a box of my larger items last week, which included all my school supplies, comforter, toiletries, and some clothing, to the school. The notification came yesterday that it had been delivered and placed in my room, ready for when I arrive. When I saw the school offered such a service, I booked that shit immediately. Surprisingly, even my father thought it was a good idea and paid for the shipping. Since I'm flying to New York, I don't want to have to take more than my two suitcases and a carry-on bag with me.

Jumping out of bed, I quickly dress and pick up my luggage before bounding down the staircase to the living room. Sitting everything by the door before heading to the kitchen for some breakfast. I should've known my mother would be here, preparing her last meal for me before I leave. She is busily placing food on my plate while I take a seat at the table.

Taking a moment, I sit and gaze at her. She's always said how she wanted nothing more than to be a wife and mother. She seems to love the way of the pack and her role in it. I often wish I could feel the same way, but I don't. Sometimes I wonder if she suffers from Stockholm syndrome after years of being forced to behave a certain way. I want the feeling of belonging but being equal like the stories I've read in secret about the other packs in the world. I know I will never find it here as much as I long to, it's why I want to see the world and what is out there.

For as long as I can remember, it's always been the three of us. A month before I was born, a rogue Dire wolf killed my mother's other two mates, and as a slap in our face, the

Stonehaven Pack offered him asylum. When she heard I was going to a school where I could be exposed to others from that pack, she feared something would happen to me.

"Good morning, Momma. I'm really gonna miss this when I'm gone. There's no way the cafeteria at the college has anything on your cooking." It's honestly one of the two things I'll miss, her and her food.

"I'm going to miss you so much, baby." She quickly turns and heads back to the sink, busying herself with the dishes, but I can hear her muffled sobs. She had slipped a note into my room last night, leaving it on my desk for me. She encouraged me to do as my father and the Alpha wish. She is terrified of what could happen to me if I were to step out of line, even though she wishes for me to run as far from this pack as I can. I knew if my father ever saw the words she wrote he'd kill her, so I ripped it up, then burned the small pieces.

I rush through eating, struggling with the emotions I'm feeling, hearing her cry. Wanting to be here for her and also to get the fuck out of here as fast as I can. Thankfully, the second option wins out as I hear my dad descending the stairs.

"Magnolia, are you ready? We need to head to the airport," he calls out as I hear his feet hit the last step, before walking across the room to the desk, where I hear shuffling papers.

"Yeah, Dad. I'll be right there." Standing, I pick my plate up, take a few steps over to the sink, and set it on the counter before facing Mom and wrapping my arms around her. I squeeze her tightly, inhaling her scent, memorizing it to comfort me while I'm gone.

"Call me when you get there," she whispers, shifting her stance as she returns to washing the dishes. Releasing my hold on her, I step back before hurriedly turning and rushing to the living room, ready to begin my journey.

My father's already headed out the door, leaving all my suitcases and carry-on bag for me to take to the car myself. Shrugging my shoulders, I make my way over and begin to strategically place my bags on top of each other, so I can have the straps all together and lug them out the door. Oh, look, my dad did help, he popped the fucking trunk. *Asshole.*

Quiet tension fills the ride to the airport. I keep having a nagging feeling in my gut that my freedom is about to be ripped away from me before I even have a chance to taste it. Instead of taking the airport exit for the parking garage, my father pulls up to the drop-off lane, comes to a stop, and places the car in park. He sits there for a moment, his knuckles turning white as he grips the steering wheel.

He turns to look at me but only for a brief moment before turning his head to gaze aimlessly out the car window. "You are to carry yourself in a manner befitting a member of the Exodus Pack. No dating or fraternizing with any other packs. You are to remember ours is superior. You have a chance to be mated to the next Alpha and his Betas. Do not, under any condition, embarrass our family. I will send you the information for your plane ticket for your weekend visit. Now go before you miss your flight," he says coldly, not once looking back at me.

Opening the door, I step out, placing my feet on the pavement that will lead me to my temporary freedom. Hearing him pop the trunk, I head to the rear of the car and pull out my bags. I've barely closed it before he's pulling away, back into the flow of traffic. Taking a deep breath, I remind myself I'm so close to being out of this town and once again, fight with my bags as I head inside and beeline straight to the ticket counter.

The flight was smooth, minus the twenty minutes mid-flight where we hit a hefty amount of turbulence. A wave of motion sickness hit a few people, and thank fuck I wasn't one of the poor unfortunate souls seated by them.

The pilot taxis into our terminal, and we all eagerly await to disembark the plane. Thankfully, the wait isn't too long, and ten minutes later, I'm standing, reaching up, and grasping the handle of my bag. As I try to pull it from the overhead compartment, I smell the most delicious scent. An *Alpha Wolf*, from the amount of power that's emitting from whoever it is. Looking around, I try to search for the source of the scent, but with the cluster of people pushing their way forward, eager to exit the plane, I can't find the wolf. But god, the scent is intoxicating, sending a wave of arousal straight to my center.

Pulling myself together, I get my bag down, apologize to the people behind me for holding them up, and head to the plane's exit. I opt to wait for some of the people to clear out from around the baggage claim area before heading over and collecting my bags, making sure to secure a luggage cart before heading out to hail a cab. Luck is with me today, and there is a line of three waiting outside. I head for the first one in line and give him the address to the dorm I'm staying in. Thankfully, he loads the bags in the trunk for me, so I climb into the backseat. I pull out my phone, sending a text to Mom to let her know I arrived, and that I'm still in one piece.

Riding through the city, I gawk out the window, broadcasting to everyone that I'm a tourist. But I don't even care, this town is gorgeous. The buildings look like some you would find in a gothic-themed movie, and I'm living for it. I keep noticing the driver glancing up into the rearview mirror, staring intently at me and following my every move.

"First time here?" he asks, his voice raspy, like someone who's smoked cigarettes since he was a child.

"Yeah, freshman year."

"Well, we're about to pull onto campus. You'll want to be sure to catch a glimpse of the statues at the gate," he tells me, which piques my interest.

I look up just in time to see the large wrought iron gate that's currently wide open with two large ass gargoyle statues, sitting on either side of the fence. All I can imagine is them coming to life at night, and just by chance, getting to catch a peek of them shifting. I plan to visit the gates every night to see if it happens. I mean supernaturals are real, even though humans are oblivious to them, so they could be real gargoyles.

We make several turns going deeper and deeper into campus before finally coming to a stop in front of my dorm; Salvatore Hall. I open the door, stepping out slowly as I scan the area, taking in each and every detail, while the cab driver unloads my luggage.

"You're all set," he tells me, as I quickly reach into my purse and pull out a fifty and hand it over to him. "Keep the change and thank you."

Once again, I load my bags up, so I can lug them inside to the reception desk to sign for my room key. Lucky for me, there's only one person in line, and they have just finished.

Stepping up to the desk, I see an older woman with graying hair. She has moon-shaped glasses perched low on her nose. The family photo sitting on her desk points to her being an ostrich shifter. She's sitting in a chair in the middle, surrounded by children and young ostriches. Thanks to the few books on other supernaturals that I was able to get a hold of, I am confident in my deduction and delighted to meet a new kind of shifter.

"Hi, I'm here for my room key, Magnolia Holloway." She flips through a file folder to her right and pulls out a paper with a key attached to it. She has me sign the paper after showing my ID, proving my identity, then hands me the key and sends me on my way. Before I turn to go, I ask if there is an elevator. She nods and throws her hand out, pointing to the left. Following her finger, I see a little sign marked "elevator".

Hallelujah!! I don't have to lug this shit up three flights of stairs. Making my way to the elevator, I stop in front of it and press the up button, waiting for the doors to open before I step inside, dragging my luggage along with me.

Looking over my dorm assignment, I look at my roommate's information again while the elevator jerks into movement and heads up. Wylla Michaelson. Her name is beautiful, I wonder what she's like. I really hope she's nice and not a snob like the bitches in my pack. The elevator comes to an abrupt stop and the door slides open. I move quickly, stepping out of the doors with my bags before they have a chance to close on me.

Eighties music is blaring, and I have to admit, I love the music choice, being a huge fan of it myself. As I make my way down the hallway toward my assigned room, the music gets louder and louder, until I find the source of it coming from the room I'm assigned to. Room 312.

Opening the door, I see a girl with long, colorful hair. She's standing with her back to me. Some of the most beautiful, intricate artwork covers her skin that's visible, and I immediately feel relieved. We're going to be the best of friends.

Almost as if she senses me, she turns, and I'm overwhelmed by her beauty. I've always been attracted to females, but I've never acted on any of my feelings; it would never be accepted by my father or the pack. But the sight of her has me salivating.

Wylla

I'm standing at my bed, sorting my clothes as I unpack when I hear the door to my room opening, and the most delectable scent fills my senses. I continue to go about my business since the easiest way to know the intentions of a fellow supernatural is to give them your back. Right away, you know if they are a friend or foe by what they do. An enemy would take advantage of a turned back and immediately attack, while a friend would not. Whoever opened the door has finally decided to step inside the room, but they've not moved farther than a few feet over the threshold.

Turning around to face my guest, I'm shocked into silence. Standing before me, looking like an afternoon snack, is the most stunning creature I've ever laid eyes on. She's about the same height as me at five-foot-eight with the most amazing shade of light gray and white shoulder-length hair. Hazel eyes stare back at me, and damn if she doesn't have the smoothest, creamiest skin I've ever seen. I step forward and stick my hand out to introduce myself.

"Hey, I'm Wylla. Are you my roommate?" *Please, goddess, let this woman be my roommate.*

"Ummm," she stutters out, stepping a little farther into the room. "Hey. Yeah, this is my room, so I guess that makes you my roommate, Wylla. I'm Magnolia." She takes my hand. I watch her eyes move slowly, dragging her gaze down my body from my eyes to my toes, clearly checking me out.

"Well, Magz–yeah, I'm not doing Magnolia. I can already tell we're gonna be besties, so Magz it will be. I was just unpacking. Why don't you put your stuff over there, and we'll unpack together and chat? Then we can get food or something and really get to know each other better. Sound good?" I toss her a wink.

She nods at me, moving her bag to the other side of the room. We unpack our clothes and chat about general things like what we're majoring in and if we know anyone else on campus. Just the normal idle chit-chat people do when they first meet. I'm finished before her, so I slide my bag under my bed and head over to help her unpack. She brought a whole hell of a lot more than me.

"Goddess, woman, did you bring your entire house with you?" I ask, picking up a picture of three sexy but dickish looking men. She takes the picture from me and throws it in the trash can next to the nightstand.

"No, I actually only packed the stuff in the bags you saw me wheel in here. The rest is all things my father thought I would need. Obviously, I didn't need everything he thought I did."

"Ohhhh, a daddy's girl; okay, I can get behind that. What's his name? Is he sexy?" I ask her as she makes a gagging noise and covers her mouth with one hand.

"What the hell? No, he's not sexy. He's my dad, and he's a right asshole. I had to beg, borrow, and steal just to come to this school. Hell, I even had to pick a major my Alpha approved of, which I need to figure out how to change. No way am I ever going to be a Political Science major. I want to get a psychology degree," she tells me as she shoves some clothes in the dresser.

"Okay, so not a daddy's girl, got it. Do you have any family or friends here? You're not giving me much here, Magz, and I'm just trying to get to know my new bestie better."

"You have no idea who or what I am, do you? I thought you knew and were just getting your kicks off playing me, or trying to get more information on my life back home." She's looking at me like I've missed some big announcement about who the hell I'm rooming with. I mean, who could she possibly be? Lucifer's daughter? I look at her with one eyebrow raised and shake my head.

"I have no idea, but please enlighten me."

Sighing loudly, she throws her empty bag under her bed like I did and sits down. "Okay, well, first things first, I'm a wolf, in case you didn't know or couldn't tell. I'm from the Exodus Pack."

"What the fuck?" I gasp and tense up at her admission. Holy Shit, my roommate is from the wolf cult! *This is insane!* I'm not sure if that's really how they are, but my grandmother always said the Exodus Pack was evil and to not fraternize with any of them if the opportunity ever arose. Which it hasn't since they never leave their pack, especially the females if everything I've read and Grandmother told me is true. She looks normal though, so maybe what I've heard is false? Looking at her stunned, I let her continue.

"My dad's a Beta and the right-hand man to the pack Alpha. I'm sure you've heard of our pack. We don't socialize, and I know there have been articles on how we live. No, I'm not ready to get into all that. Just know some of the things those articles say are true and some are very false. I'll tell you when I'm ready and trust you more, I promise."

Magz is staring at me, waiting for me to say something, nervously rocking back and forth from foot to foot, chewing on her bottom lip. Her eyes get glassy, and she looks like she's about to fall apart. I need to quickly reassure her I would never judge her or anyone based on where they come from. Collecting my thoughts, I shrug, trying to keep it together for her.

"Umm, okay, cool, I've heard of your pack. So you're right, it's mostly bad things. I won't lie to you, but I also won't push you to tell me more cause that's not what besties do. Right? Right! So I'm a witch and a necromancer. Yeah, that's right, baby, I'm a black magic witch. Ummm, don't be scared. I dabble, but besides necromancy, I don't do much dark magic." I laugh and toss a wink at her, hoping to lighten the impact of what I've just told her. It normally sends people running in fear.

She laughs, surprising the shit out of me. Yeah, we're going to be besties. We continue to make more idle chit-chat and order a pizza. I bust out a bottle of Moscato I smuggled in with me, take a swig, and pass it to her. She stares at it like I just gave her poison, slowly lifting it to her lips, and taking a small sip before passing it back. We both take a seat on the floor, while we bullshit back and forth, waiting for the pizza to arrive.

We somehow managed to eat almost an entire large pizza ourselves, and now we're lying on my bed with drunken giggles, continuing to get to know each other. Magz rolls onto her left side and faces me as she reaches out and runs her finger down my arm, tracing along the outline of the tattoos I have there. Both my arms have full sleeves, so she's tracing my sheaf of wheat and my crows perched on a large pair of scissors.

"These are amazing, Wylla. I've always wanted a tattoo, but it's forbidden in my pack for women to mark their bodies with anything other than a true mate's bond mark. But that will never happen since the female population declined and we no longer have mate bonds in our pack. You have so many, and they're all, from what I can see, unique pieces of art. I'm jealous," she tells me, still running her fingers up and down my arm.

Goddess above, this woman is tempting me, and I don't think she even knows it. I wish we'd covered what her sexuality is when we were in the 'getting to know each other' phase tonight. I'm proud to be openly bisexual. However, being raised so sheltered and close-minded, I don't know how Magz will react to that knowledge. Being uncomfortable in my own skin or sexuality because of someone else's bigotry and narrow-mindedness is something I refuse to feel.

"Idea!" I shout, startling her a bit. "What if your first act of defiance is to get some ink? I know a guy, and he could totally get you in right away. Come on! What do ya say? It can be small and easily covered, so daddy dearest never knows."

She nervously looks at me, then bites that bottom lip between her teeth again. I'm sure she's going to tell me no and shut down the rest of our night. However, she surprises the hell out of me.

"Fuck it! Text him right now! Definitely don't want small, though. I want it to take up a good majority of my bicep. A woman and wolf howling at the moon together. Just the outline, no color." She's talking fast, her words running together so that I have to listen hard to decipher them. She's super excited about giving her dad a big 'screw you'.

I reach back, pick my phone up from the nightstand and text my guy. I tell him exactly what she wants, that we need to have it done as soon as possible and the cost doesn't matter. *I'm going to treat my new best friend to a 'welcome to the real world' gift.* I no sooner set my phone down and it pings, telling me he's responded. I read the message and reply.

"Next Saturday, so a week from today. Seven PM, you're in, and he's going to send me a sketch later this week for you to check out and make any changes or additions. Does that work?"

She eagerly nods her head at me and whispers how exciting yet terrifying this all is. Before placing my phone down, I notice it's close to two in the afternoon and we have been chatting most of the day. We make plans to go to the freshman mixer tonight and to walk her to the guidance office to change her major and schedule first thing in the morning. I laugh evilly to myself, I'm already corrupting my sweet, naive roommate. *We'll just have to work around her Alpha and dad's demands.*

Before I know it, Magz is sound asleep. She was telling me about her favorite movie *Crybaby* one minute and out cold the next. I lie here thinking about how easily she embraced the idea of getting a tattoo and how I can't wait to see what other things I can show her this year.

Closing my eyes and hoping to catch a few hours as well, I feel an arm and leg fling over me. I tense up and gaze over at Magz; she's full-on cuddling with me. Now that I'm totally wrapped up in her limbs, I have no intentions of moving. *It's gonna be a long fucking year if this bed situation is a foreshadowing of our friendship.* My eyes slowly close and I drift off to sleep. Visions of me and Magz together fill my mind.

Wylla

I wake up and immediately know I'm alone in my bed. "Good afternoon, Goddess," I say, stretching as I look up at the Hecate tapestry hanging to the right of my bed. I sit up and take a look around our small dorm room. Magz is nowhere to be seen. *Where the hell did my sweet girl go?*

Getting up, I grab my toiletries from the three-tier rolling cart we've set our bathroom necessities on. Heading out, I close our door and head to the communal bathroom. Stepping inside, I see I'm the only one in here at the moment, so I head straight to the closest sink. Setting down my bag, I pull out my electric toothbrush. Squeezing some toothpaste on it, I turn it on, and it springs to life, making a vibrating humming noise. As I get to work scrubbing my teeth my brain begins to think of the oddest shit.

I wonder if my sweet girl will mind this noise from another one of my special gadgets. HA!

Finished with my teeth, I splash some water on my face before lathering it up with my papaya scented face wash. I rinse off my face and pat it dry with a hand towel before quickly running a brush through my rainbow-colored locks. Happy with my after nap look, I give myself a wink in the mirror and gather my shit and head back to our room.

Putting my toiletry bag back on the cart and throwing the towel in our hamper next to the door, I grab my yoga mat from the top of our closet and lay it out on our floor. Starting in the mountain pose, my feet are together with big toes touching and my arms at my sides but palms up. *I am enough. I have enough.* I hold that until I switch to the downward dog; my feet hip-width apart and bending my knees to lift my hips towards the ceiling. *No one can make me act out of character.*

Stepping my feet forward, I inhale and lift my right leg up. Taking another deep breath, I hop off my left foot so both my feet are now off the mat. Bringing my left heel close to my ass, I balance and cross my legs above me. *I accept my emotions and let them move through me.* Once I'm done with my affirmations in this pose, I slowly bring my legs down and straight out in front of me while sitting on my mat.

Sitting up tall, I flex my feet and inhale, sending my arms straight up to the sky. On the exhale, I reach my hands toward my toes, folding my body forward, relaxing my head and neck. I hold this for five minutes while I slowly breathe in and out. *I use my voice to speak up for myself and others.*

It's been a few hours, and I still haven't seen or heard a peep from Magz. I thought we had a great time earlier today, but now, she's just dipped out. *Maybe she didn't enjoy this morning as much as I did.*

Trying not to focus on my missing roommate, I sit at my desk, open a drawer and pull out my tarot cards and notebook. The best way to journal my intentions is by using my deck. Setting the deck on my desk and taking a deep breath, I close my eyes and focus only on the present. I push all the mundane thoughts from my head and center myself, then ask myself what my intention is at this moment. *Magz.*

Magnolia. I say her name, then grab my favorite purple pen and write the date and her name in my journal.

Taking the deck, I flip through it, thinking only of her, while I sift through the cards, splitting them into two piles. One that resonates with my intention and one that doesn't. Once I've sorted the entire deck, I pick up the pile of resonating cards, laying them all out and letting them just speak to me. I'm not sure why I keep focusing on the Tower card. Almost like it's calling out to me. Strangely, it just doesn't give anything close to the vibes I felt from Magz. It's so contradictory to the woman I met and hung out with earlier. Picking it up, I choose that as my card; it doesn't have to make sense to me right away, that's part of the magic.

The Tower card symbolizes sudden change, chaos, burn this shit to the ground type of stuff. This isn't the card I wanted to pull when thinking of my new friend. *Fucking hell, this is bad.* Once you select a card, there is no way to change it. Just as I'm about to display the card and start to journal my thoughts about it and why it resonated with Magz, there's a knock on our door.

Standing up and quickly putting my things away, annoyed I'm being interrupted and loudly voicing that to whoever is on the other side, I storm over to the door and fling it open. Standing there with his fist still in the knock position is a delightful specimen of a man. *Did they let any unattractive people in the school this year?* He's every bit of six-foot-four inches and muscular as hell, with black hair buzzed short on the side, with the top long and slicked to the side. He's had his barber shave a defined line on the left side of his head, distinguishing the buzzed section from the longer. Tattoos cover his forearms and biceps. Large brown eyes look back at me as he takes the hand frozen in mid-air and rubs the back of his head.

"How can I help you? Well, besides the obvious," I ask, giving him a cocky little smirk.

"I'm Jude, in the room right above you; four twelve. We got a package delivered to our room this morning for a Magnolia Holloway. We figured we'd check the room with the closest numbers to ours before we turn it over to Security. Is that you?" he asks.

I take the package from him, and he quirks an eyebrow at me but lets me have it without issue. I walk over to Magz's bed and set the package down, then turn back to face the sex on a stick in front of me.

"Magz is my roommate. She got here this morning, and I'm not quite sure where she's at right now. We took a nap, and when I woke up, her little ass was MIA. But I'll put it there on her bed for when she comes back," I tell him and gesture for him to take a seat in the desk chair I just vacated. He ignores me and just leans against the door frame.

"So Jude, are you going to the Freshman Mixer tonight?" I ask, hoping he says yes, so we have some eye candy.

"Fuck no!" he fires out instantly.

I walk over to him and run my finger down his chest. "Such a shame. Magz and I—I'm Wylla, by the way—will be there. We were looking forward to hanging out and maybe even dancing with a guy such as yourself."

I give him a little shove and close the door with a wink, laughing when I hear him groan as he walks away from our room. I look over at the box he brought and wonder what Magz could possibly have delivered that wouldn't already be in the million things she brought with her. Then again, if her dad sent most of it without her knowing, this might be another daddy surprise package. Which reminds me, I walk over to the trash can, take out the picture she threw away and shove it into the back of our closet.

Maybe my girl has a little love triangle back home, and these fellas broke her heart or she broke theirs. I'll save the picture in case she wants it later.

I'm sitting back at my desk with my light-up, makeup mirror set up on the desk. There has still been no sign of Magz, and I'm starting to worry. Wanting to distract myself, I decided to do my makeup and hope to Goddess she comes back so we can still go to the mixer together.

After priming my face, I apply my foundation, which is one of the lightest shades I can find. Having such creamy light skin is common among my coven, but it makes makeup and the summer sun a nightmare. The amount of sunscreen I go through is insane! I contour my nose to give myself a more slender, defined look that I like and throw some subtle contour on my cheeks.

Picking up my favorite bronzer, *Dr. Pepp,* I dab it on my cheeks, chin, and forehead, so I have some color. Then taking my blush, *Meet me at Rose,* I swipe some across my nose and cheeks. The last step before I can move on to the eyes is the highlight. I grab the *Tickle My Pickle. The name always makes me giggle.* I brush a little right at the corner of my eyes on the zygomatic bone and a little bit on the very tip of my nose.

Onto the windows of my soul - the eyes. Of course, I like when they match my soul, so black it is. My soul isn't actually black, but I like to joke that it is, especially when it comes to makeup, because I'm constantly asked why it's so dark.

After rubbing some black shadow on my eyelids, I dab my brush in a charcoal-like color and blend that out towards the outer corner of my eyelid. Taking my eyeliner, I draw a perfect line on each upper lid from the inner corner to the outer corner, giving me the best wing I've seen in a while before smudging the lower liner down just a bit to give me the smoky eye look I love. I then swipe some mascara on my lashes and take my trusty lipstick, *Soulless,* and apply it to my lips.

Finished, I look in the mirror and blow myself a kiss. *Fuck, I'm hot.* Black eyes, black lipstick, and rainbow hair make perfect sense. I quickly put my hair up in two little space buns, so I look like a sexy, gothic alien and call it a day for the hair and makeup. Now, I just need to pick my outfit. I want to wait for Magz to come back, so she can help me. It's been hours.

Where the fuck is she?

Magnolia

My eyes slowly flutter open, and I instantly notice three things: my pussy aching with need, my body burning up, and a weight sitting on my chest. Casting a glance to my left, I see Wylla nestled up close to me with her hand resting on my left tit as she gropes it. Her touch is sending waves of electricity all over my body and beelining right to my core, already wet with desire.

All my life, well, at least since my hormones couldn't be ignored any longer, I knew I was attracted to both males and females. I love the contrast between the soft feminine body and the muscular, masculine body. My pack's views on sexuality are very bigoted, and if I'd ever acted on those desires, it would have ended disastrously. I still craved both sexes but suppressed my body's lustful desires. It was easier and less heartache to just go along with the status quo of the pack. But fuck, this beautiful woman has those emotions and feelings breaking through. My nipples are pebbled under her touch, and all I want is to feel her mouth on mine.

I need to get out of here and clear my mind, figure out what the hell I'm going to do. I gingerly reach up and grasp her hand in mine, lifting it off my chest, and shimmy my body out from under her. Once I'm out of her reach, I pull my pillow down and place her arm on it. She instinctively cuddles into it. Fuck, if she isn't adorable with her pouty lips and the little bit of drool leaking from them. Her shirt has shifted, giving an ample view of her breast. All I want to do is lean over and pop her stiff nipple in my mouth.

What the fuck is happening to me? This is more intense than I've ever felt before.

Knowing I need to shift and let my wolf out, I don't even bother changing. Tiptoeing over to the door, I open it and step out into the hallway before closing it behind me. I scurry down the hallway toward the stairs, not wanting to wait for the elevator. Needing desperately to get out of here and run. When I arrived at the dorm earlier this morning, I caught sight of the wooded area behind the building and my wolf screamed to be let free to roam. I promised she could run later and placated her longing to be free with the excitement of seeing our room and meeting our roommate. If only I knew then the instant attraction I would have to her.

Exiting the building, I turn to the left and head around to the back of it, straight for the treeline. Walking into the woods, I feel all the stress from my pack slowly rolling off of me as I inhale the scent of my new home, my new running grounds. I keep walking deeper and deeper until I find the perfect tree to stash my clothes in. I step behind it and slowly begin to remove my shoes and socks, followed by my shirt and shorts until I'm left standing in just my matching lacey, hunter-green bra and panties. Reaching behind my back, I unhook my bra, allowing the straps to fall down my arms before removing it, folding it up, and laying it on top of my other clothes. Lastly, the panties come off. I pick up everything and set them safely in the nook at the base of the tree.

Stretching my arms above my head, I prepare for the shift. Other females in my pack spoke horror stories about their shift. Not wanting to appear different from them, I lied and told my own horror stories. Every time I did, my wolf would howl in laughter. Truth was, the shift was invigorating, my body craved the change, and my wolf eased me through it. I felt every bone break and morph, but there was never pain. Often, I felt like an outcast because of it. *Time to run!* My wolf calls. *Yes, it is.* Calling the shift, I feel the bones in my body begin to break and shift, molding into their new form. My mouth and nose enlarge and begin to stretch out into a strong muzzle. My legs buckle and elongate until I'm dropping down to the ground on all fours. Sitting back on her hind legs my wolf turns her snout up to the sky and lets out an ear-piercing howl before standing and taking off in a mad dash deeper into the woods. I've always stood out in my pack, being the only full white wolf. I often wondered how it happened with my father's wolf being jet black and my mother's brown.

We've been running for about thirty minutes when it hits us. The delicious smell of cedarwood, the same scent from the airplane. We're drawn to it, our body craving to be wrapped in the smell, letting it take over every inch of us. My wolf changes direction, sniffing the air, following the scent as anxiousness sets in, wondering who it is and why we're so drawn to it.

Each time I think we've caught up to the owner of the scent, it disappears again until finally it's gone. Not even a trace, like it disappeared into thin air. My wolf begins to whine at the loss of the intoxicating scent. *We will find who the scent belongs to, just be patient. They have to go to school here.* I tell my wolf as I call for the shift to return to human form.

I stretch my arms above my head once I've shifted back. Looking around, I see a large oak tree standing in front of me. The exposed roots above ground weave together in a way that makes a chair-like area for me, so I don't have to sit on the cool ground. Moving over, I slowly lower my body, allowing it to relax against the roots.

My body is still thrumming with need. My hands automatically move to my stomach as my legs spread open, allowing my right hand to roam lower, sliding down my stomach until it cups my sex. Strumming my finger back and forth across my clit, electricity pulses through me as I think of my rainbow-haired roommate. Visions fill my mind as I imagine her naked, legs spread, and her pretty pink pussy on display for me. I begin to rub tight circles on my little nub, then slide my fingers through my wet folds, all the way to my opening. Firmly placing the heel of my palm on my clit, I apply pressure as I allow two of my fingers to slip inside my tight hole, pumping in and out.

I take my other hand and begin to knead my aching tits, rolling my pebbled nipples between my fingers as I feel my orgasm building. I should be afraid of someone stumbling on me, seeing me in my vulnerable state, but I don't fucking care. I long for the day someone else brings me to orgasm instead of just my fingers. My mind brings forth the sounds of Wylla's moans as I imagine licking up and down her clit as she rides my mouth, but it's not her moans getting louder, it's mine. The way she seemed to glow with joy when she saw me like she was actually excited to meet me, not like others who wanted to know me merely for the status they could gain. Her pert tits as her nipples pebbled against her tight shirt had me wanting to take them in my mouth, even though I'd never done it before. I begin to pump my fingers faster. Imagining her naked in front of me as I take my tongue and lick up the length of her delicious pink pussy.

Chasing the orgasm that's building, I start to rub my clit almost violently until my orgasm explodes from me. Throwing my head back in ecstasy as lights dance behind my eyes, I ride out the waves of pleasure rippling across my body.

When the final waves of pleasure leave my body, I open my eyes, glance above me, and spot the cutest sight. A small animal, almost rat-like in looks, is perched on one of the branches. Its fur is brown and tan. Actually, no, the coloring is so light it's hard to tell. It may be white. After studying the animal longer, I realize it's a ferret. The little cutie is laying on the lowest hanging limb, staring right at me, almost like it understands exactly what I was doing. God, I feel embarrassed now.

I close my legs, sit up taller, and try to coax the animal to me. "Come here, little guy, or girl," I sing-song to it. Then the damndest thing happens. The little creature scurries down the branches and right into my lap. Scooping it up into my arms, I bring it close to my chest. I gently stroke his head as he begins to lick the fingers that were just knuckle-deep in my pussy, and still covered with all my juices.

"You know, you caught me at a very vulnerable moment." I start talking to the ferret like he understands what I'm saying. He continues to lick at my fingers, and I allow myself to relax back further against the tree.

"Do you have a name? No. Okay, I think I'm going to call you Snuggles. Because you are so soft and cute and I could see myself snuggling with you. You're probably wondering why I'm out here and why I was masturbating. Well, I'm attracted to my roommate, and I don't know how to handle these feelings. I mean, I like guys, but I like girls too, it just wasn't allowed in my pack. We fell asleep on the bed together, and when I woke up, she had a hand holding my tit, and I was on fire. What should I do? Snuggle with her? Should I tell her? Should I fight what I'm feeling?"

I must be crazy. Sitting here talking to a ferret who has no clue what I'm saying. But the way he's looking at me with those sweet chocolate eyes has me rethinking it. I sit there for a while longer in silence, just stroking him as he starts to lick my skin, getting eerily close to my nipple, and I know it's time to cut my visit short and head back. Wylla and I have plans for the freshman mixer tonight, and I still need to get dressed.

I stand with the ferret in my hand, before turning and placing him in the spot I just vacated. I call my wolf forward, shifting before racing back through the woods toward the dorm.

Climbing the stairs slowly, I begin to psych myself up to see Wylla again. I stop at our door, taking a deep breath before opening it and stepping inside. The gorgeous sight before me steals my breath. Wylla's seated at her vanity, her hair up in two little space buns, and damn, if she didn't just blow herself a kiss. She turns to see me, jumping up and running to me frantically.

"Where the hell have you been, Magz? I woke up, and you were gone, no note, nothing. What the fuck?" She pulls me into her arms, hugging me so tight I can barely breathe.

"Wylla! Air!" Sensing what I mean, she lets go, taking me by my hands and pulling me over to her bed. Once we're there, she flops down, pulling me down beside her.

I begin to worry my lip. Shit, do I tell her what's really wrong? What if my thoughts disgust her?

"I'm sorry, my wolf just wanted to run, and I caught a familiar scent from the airport and was chasing it around the woods. Never found it though. Then I shifted back and just enjoyed the beauty of the day under an oak tree, where I found the cutest little ferret of all things." Not all lies, I just omitted the part about being attracted to her and, oh yeah, masturbating to visions of her.

"Well, while you were busy fondling some random animal in the forest, you missed the hunk of a man who delivered a package for you. Lucky for us, he lives right above us. I tried to talk him into going to the mixer tonight, but he declined." She gestures towards the package on my bed.

Standing slowly, I step over to my bed and gaze down at it. Definitely not something I sent, and the label is clearly in my father's handwriting.

"From the look on your face, I take it you didn't send it," Wylla asks, stepping up behind me and placing her hand on my shoulder. My stomach quivers in excitement.

This girl is going to be the death of me. How am I gonna make it through this year?

"Not to be an insensitive bitch and all, but what's inside?" she asks, egging me on to open it.

I take hold of the strip of tape on the edge, pulling it back enough that I can rip the strip open. Once the tape is off, I open the flaps and peer inside. There's a plane ticket. Picking it up, I notice the date is for the last weekend of the month. I place it on the bed before pulling out the books below it. The first is the history and hierarchy of all wolf packs, and the second is about the role of the Alpha's Luna. Asshole, I couldn't get the smallest of breaks from his plans. I chuck the books down on the bed, then flop down on it myself, knocking the empty box onto the floor.

"What are these books for?" she asks, sitting down beside me, as she picks them up and flips through them.

"My pack has fewer females than males. So my father has this grand plan that next summer at the ranking ceremony I will be ranked a Beta, making me a prime match for the Alpha's son and his Betas."

Before I can finish, she cuts in, "Why the Betas?"

"Like I said, we have fewer females than males, so when we are matched for mating, we are paired up with units of three to four males. My father hopes I'll mate with the future Alpha, thus gaining him more status and power. It's a barbaric ritual. Women have no say and often are tortured by the men they do mate with." I let out a deep sigh, knowing what fate lies before me.

"And what if you aren't a Beta, then what?"

"Fuck if I know, but I'm sure it won't be enjoyable. I wish there was a way I could find out before then."

"What if we could!" Wylla exclaims. "Just hear me out. What if I could find a spell that would reveal what you are before then? Would that help?"

"Do you really think you could do that?" I mean, do I want to know? It would be nice just to have the option.

"I don't know, let me do some research. But first, we have a mixer to attend, and you need to shower, babe. You fucking stink, and then we need to pick out some killer outfits. So chop chop." She laughs as she heads over to her closet and starts flipping through the clothes.

I step over to my dresser, pick up my shower caddy along with a towel and robe, and head toward the door.

She called me babe. Stop it, Magnolia Holloway, don't read more into it than what it is.

Jude

I'm headed back up to the room I share with my two best friends. We've been friends since we were kids when we all ended up at the same supe camp. Our parents sent us away for two months that summer so we could get a handle on our abilities. Up until then we knew each other from school but didn't hang in the same groups, since we were different types of supernaturals. We're all close in age, and this is our first year here at Arcayne University. Technically, Z and I could've started earlier, but we made a pact that we would start together. So now that Blaine is nineteen, here we are.

Holy fucking macaroni... our downstairs neighbor is sexy as hell. I wasn't expecting that at all. I thought I'd quickly run that package down to the neighbors and come right back. I didn't expect the door to be opened by a little, rainbow-haired, sex goddess with what seemed like a carefree attitude. She swung open the door, looking unimpressed as I told her about the package. She took the package from me and placed it on the bed, then slammed the door in my face.

Such a fucking turn-on.

Getting back to my dorm room, I open the door, walk straight to my bed, and flop backward, sighing loudly. Right away, Blaine and Z take their gaming headsets off and ask me what's up.

Groaning, I start telling them about the adventure of meeting Wylla. "Bros, I took that package to the room below us, right? Okay, so I knock on the door, and I hear some bitching about being interrupted, and I'm instantly thinking like 'fuck, the downstairs neighbor is a bitch, right? We're gonna get so many complaints for being loud when we party. This year's gonna suck big time.'"

They nod their heads in unison at me, so I continue, "Okay, so then the door flies open, and standing in front of me is the sexiest piece of ass I've ever seen. She was all of five-foot-six, with light gray eyes, and rainbow-colored hair. She's also covered in grayscale tattoos and has a fucking septum piercing. She's fucking hot and will be starring in all my filthy dreams."

"Did you get a pic of her or does she have a *SupeChat* profile?" Blaine asks, his interest piqued at her description.

"No pic, sorry, man. No clue about social media, but we could look. She did say she was going to the mixer tonight with her roommate and asked if I was going, which I told her there was no way in hell. Then get this, she walked her two fingers right up my chest and said 'what a shame, we'd love to dance with a guy like you,' I literally almost came in my fucking pants."

They're both laughing and cracking jokes about the whole interaction. They're lucky we're best friends or I'd punch the shit out of both of them.

"Blaine, man, are you still going to the mixer?"

"Yeah, let me guess, you want to change your mind about tagging along now?" he quickly asks me before pausing a moment to take the win while Z isn't paying attention to the game they are playing.

"Hell yeah, I am. I'm going to go and find that little sex goddess, and I fucking pray her roommate is just as sexy. We could make a Jude sandwich tonight," I say as I throw a wink at my friends.

They both roll their eyes at me, then Z sighs and says, "It must be a requirement to be hot as hell to get into the university." Blaine and I both stare at him questioningly. *Guess I wasn't the only one to find a hottie.*

"So speaking of hotties, I was in the woods today in my shifted form. I just needed to shift since it's been a while and I thought the woods, especially how deep I was, would've been safe from prying eyes," he whispers the last part.

"Zeke! You know we don't care what your shifted form is. You need to stop being so embarrassed about it. Not like you had a fucking choice in the matter, man. Own that shit," Blaine scolds him, and I nod my head in agreement

Z just shrugs. "Anyway, I was just rolling in some leaves letting my animal stretch his legs when this pure white wolf came barrelling into the clearing. The wolf shifted into the most beautiful woman I'd ever seen. I quickly scurried up the tree and hid on the branch above her."

We both start to interrupt him, wanting more details on what she looked like. But Z doesn't let us, he shushes us both before continuing.

"Get this, she's naked as the day she was born since she just shifted, whatever, no biggie. But then she walked over to the tree I was in, sat at the bottom, and played herself like a well-tuned instrument. After she came, she noticed me watching her and called me to come to her. Of course, I fucking listened, and she picked me up and nestled me into her tits, stroking me and telling me all about her crush on her roommate."

We're both staring at him wide-eyed because no fucking way he's telling the truth. Who would pick up another shifter and hold them? That's not quite "normal" for supernaturals.

"It gets better, or well at least for me, it did. As she was petting me and telling me about her crush, I licked the leftover cream off her fingers. Guys, she tasted like fucking heaven. Then, when she was finished sharing her drama with me, she put me down, said bye, shifted back, and was gone. I had such a fucking hard-on as I walked back here to our room."

Blaine is howling in laughter, and I join him because this is fucking epic. I can't believe Z was bold enough to lick the female's fingers. I can't believe she let him. When I pull myself together, I tell him I think he is full of shit.

"Z, there is no way in hell another shifter would let you do that. Hell, you're making it sound almost as if she didn't even know you were one. She'd have to have been raised under a rock not to recognize what you really are. But I'll give you props, that's a damn good story," I jokingly confront him.

"No man, I swear it. She must not know about all the shifters. Believe me, I was just as shocked as you. No one has ever just picked me up and held me. The way her juice smelled on her fingers as they stroked me, I couldn't help myself. I had to taste it. I'll prove it to you assholes, I'll go to the mixer and point her out to you guys if she's there."

"DEAL!" Blaine and I say in unison.

Blaine

My dad had messaged me last night as soon as he heard through the wolf's grapevine that the Exodus Pack had sent a wolf to Arcayne University this year. The first wolf they've let attend in over seventy-five years, according to my dad. We've all grown up hearing stories of the Exodus Pack, but most of us have never met a wolf that actually was a part of it. Their pack is extremely closed off and secretive. They don't mate with wolves from outside their pack, and I heard that each female wolf takes multiple mates, which isn't totally unheard of for supernaturals. However, we've heard gossip saying none of those pairings are mate bonds, but the results of some battle royale males have for certain females. I'm not sure if all that's true since we've not met an Exodus wolf, but I'm hoping that changes tonight.

If I could meet this male and get friendly with him, it would really secure my place as the Stonehaven Alpha Heir. Making an ally of the Exodus Pack would be unheard of. Maybe they're not as bad as people claim, and this guy and I could become friends. I'm assuming they sent a male since they don't ever let women leave, let alone advance their studies. Women are, from what I hear, only used for homemaking and reproducing. Which can't possibly be right because female wolves especially are getting rarer and well, you're supposed to love and care for your female like she's the most special creature there ever was. It has to be their Alpha's son that's come here, it's the only possibility.

That doesn't matter, though, I have to find this wolf and make an alliance. Our pack has been an outsider among the others ever since my dad made the decision to allow other shifters to settle on our lands. Since that decision, other packs have thought of us as being weak. We're one of the larger packs in the country. *The* largest if they'd count our non-wolf members. We opened our lands to other species by application and interview only. We don't just take any and every shifter. We make sure we take those who truly want to better our world and rid it of bigotry.

You fill out an application, then my dad sorts through them. If you make it past that round, the next step is meeting with him and the Stoneridge board we voted in to help with the integration. If you are selected after the interview, you're given a ninety-day trial, and if it doesn't work, you're asked to leave immediately. We've had hundreds of applicants and have accepted and welcomed ten other supe types to our land.

The Rodriguez family, which is Z, his parents, and his baby sister Eliza. Then there is, of course, Jude, his dad, and older brother, Magnus; the Goodmans. We have the singular Dire wolf; the family of black bears and some Hawk shifters.

A coven of witches also recently applied, the *Samara Coven* to be exact. I'm not familiar with them, but apparently, they were given a vision from the Goddess that they needed to be within our pack lands. They wouldn't specify more than that until they were approved. My dad and the board met and let them through to the interview process. He said their application was actually pretty impressive. The only thing they mentioned that raised a little bit of a question was that they have one younger member of the coven who has ties to the *Matilda Coven*. The *Matilda Coven* is known to be ruthless in all things. The leaders of the *Samara Coven* have agreed to an interview in two weeks when their youngest member with the *Matilda* ties can meet via video chat since they're apparently here at this school.

My dad asked if I could investigate this young witch, but I told him I was busy looking into the Exodus wolf. Then I let it slip that when I arrived on the plane, I caught the scent of the most delightful creature. The way I was drawn to this scent has me thinking the owner is my mate bond. It was sweet and had my mouth watering, but I was off the plane before I could search for the owner. My father had a driver waiting for me; having set up a meeting between me and the Dean. The Dean wanted to make sure this new Exodus Pack wolf and I would have no '*issues*'. While en route, I got the call that the Dean needed to cancel due to personal issues. *There goes my chance at solidifying who the Exodus wolf is.*

The guys and I spent the rest of the afternoon ribbing each other and scouring the *SupeChat* looking for them, with no luck. Who doesn't have a *SupeChat?* Jude starts going on about what he's going to wear tonight. Fucker should've been born a girl, he's such a prima-donna.

"I'm going to go grab a shower," Z says, grabbing a pile of clothes and taking them with him.

As soon as he is out the door, Jude starts laughing, "Fifty bucks he's gonna rub one out to that wolf girl."

"Why would I take a bet on something like that when I know I'm gonna lose? I'm gonna give him about twenty minutes to rub that monster cock of his, then I'm gonna take a shower too."

After thirty minutes, I showered quickly. Hurrying through my bathroom routine, I slid on a dark wash pair of jeans and a light gray Henley, pulled on my black lace-up boots, and quickly ran some hair wax through my short, shaggy brown hair and called it a day.

Forty minutes later, I'm dressed and ready for this mixer, just waiting for fucking Jude to move his ass. He has to make sure every strand of his black hair is in its perfect place. Z, like me, just showered and changed into fresh jeans and a Henley.

I have one mission tonight. *Okay, maybe two.* Find information on this Exodus wolf, if not meet him myself, and see if the scent from the plane is anywhere in the vicinity. While I'd like to meet these hotties from Z and Jude's day, securing this alliance is my priority, then maybe meeting who I think might be my mate.

Jude comes storming out of his closet, whining about not having anything to wear to impress Sex Sprinkle Barbie from earlier. No, I'm not exaggerating, he literally called her that. He settles for a pair of light wash distressed jeans and a black curved hem t-shirt. He gels his hair, so it stays exactly how he wants it. Before we walk out the door, he pumps a little lust into the room, along with freshening his personal scent with some extra desire.

Fucking incubus, tonight is going to be interesting, to say the least.

Magnolia

As we walk down the cobblestone sidewalk leading from our dorm to the quad in the center of the campus where the mixer is being held, I'm fully regretting my decision to let Wylla dress me. It took her a whole ten minutes of looking through my clothing to throw her hands in the air with an audible sigh of frustration. Storming across the room to her closet, she began flipping through her clothes, mumbling under her breath about how she needed to take a bitch shopping for something not so '*Little House on the Prairie*'.

She has me dressed in a skin-tight black dress with a single strap that wraps around my left shoulder. The front plunges down into a deep 'V' ending right between my tits. Thank god for being blessed with perky breasts because there is no way in hell I'm able to wear a bra with this. Then to top it all off, it has cut-outs all along the sides. I keep reaching down, tugging on the bottom of the dress as it rides up my thighs, and with it stopping just under my ass cheeks, I'll be giving everyone here a show. Being naked in front of others when you shift is one thing, but to be on display just for the pure hell of it is a totally different entity altogether.

"Stop fidgeting, you look hot as hell. A tasty little snack for the people here," she snaps at me as she slaps my hand away from where I'm pulling on the dress. My vagina feels like it's on display for the world, and all I can hear is my father's harsh voice in my head reminding me not to embarrass him or the pack.

"Easy for you to say." Pouting, I turn my head to gaze at her. She's dressed in some black denim booty shorts that mold to her ass, allowing just a tease of her cheeks that are peeking out the bottom. Her boots come up to her knees, leaving the ripped fishnet stockings she wears to show off her exposed thighs. The ripped, crop top band tee is the icing on her outfit. Her hair is down, hanging in wavy rainbow curls that flow down her back to just above her ass. "Some of us are dressed more comfortably than others," I say, rolling my eyes.

She steps closer to me, linking her arm through mine, and goosebumps rush to the surface of my skin. God, her touch thrills me in a way no one ever has before. My thong is already sopping wet from the excitement of her touch. *Fuck me!* How am I going to make it with my hormones going crazy over her? Hell, I don't even know if she feels the same. Yeah, she's made slight innuendos about her sexual orientation, but that doesn't mean shit.

Not to mention, she's already talking about the guy who lives above us. He's more her speed than a virgin who's never even been kissed before. I don't know what type of warning my father sent out, but every male in the pack was scared to even get close to me, let alone be caught kissing me.

The thumping bass becomes louder as we get closer to the quad. The amount of people here is mind-boggling. I can feel my nerves rising, and I'm already regretting coming tonight. I just want to turn and run as fast as I can back to the dorms.

Wylla unlinks our arms and grabs me by the hand, pulling me along faster toward the partying crowd. I look like a duck out of water trying not to fall in the six-inch heels she made me wear. It's fucking lucky that we not only wear the same size in clothes but shoes as well.

"Slow down, Wylla, or I'm going to bust my ass!" I call out to her, barely getting it out through the laughter.

"Nope, no time for that. I've got me a hottie to find, and some drinking to do," she sings out to the beat of the music.

Yep, there's absolutely no way I can compete with what she all but described as a sex god. He could have her screaming seven ways to Sunday as she orgasms, and I wouldn't even know where to start. I know how to flick my own bean, but what would I do with a guy or a girl? Groaning, I move faster to keep up with her, and within a couple of minutes, we're breaching the outer limits of the quad.

People are crowded around a makeshift dance floor, where bodies are writhing together in vulgar movements. I'm frozen in place, both in shock and awe at the same time. How amazing it must be, to be this free with who you are.

"Let's get something to drink. What do you want?" Wylla asks excitedly.

"Pepsi will be fine, or water," I rattle off to her, still taking in the bodies intertwined on the dance floor. Scanning the area, I see multiple couples engaged in different stages of making out.

"You're fucking with me, right?" Shock is written all over her face. "I ask what you want and your answer is water. I'm sorry, Pepsi or water. Bitch, I meant alcohol. We're partying, not at a nunnery."

"I'm sorry, I've never really drank. It was forbidden. The only times I was allowed to have anything alcoholic was at pack functions, and it was only a single glass of red wine."

Her face changes from shock to sadness, to fury. "Fuck your pack. Tonight we drink, we dance, and whatever else the goddess deems fit to happen. Stay here, *I'll be back*," she says in her best *Terminator* voice as she skips off.

My eyes keep roaming the crowd, wondering if the owner of the scent I've smelled twice now is going to be here. I lift my nose to the wind, but nothing. About five minutes later, I see Wylla, holding two shots in her hand, parting the crowd as she walks, almost as if she had some magical control over them. There's a lanky boy in glasses, with tousled black hair following close behind with two beers firmly grasped in one hand while he's holding what looks like more shots in the other. His eyes are firmly planted on her ass that's swaying back and forth.

"I got us shots!!" she squeals out loudly when she gets closer, which has me shaking my head and wondering what the hell she's about to get us into.

She speeds up, rushing towards me, stopping just before barrelling right into me. "Here's our first shot," extending her arm out to hand me the small cup with a brown liquid inside of it. Reaching out, I take it from her hand, bringing it up to my nose, inhaling deeply. Just the smell alone has me almost gagging.

"What is this?" I quickly ask, my stomach already turning before even tasting it.

"Crown Apple, don't knock it till you try it," she exclaims, raising her hand with the cup. "Let's toast. Go for it, Magz." Lifting my cup in the air, I decide to say fuck it and enjoy the night. "To the men we may meet tonight." I tap my cup against hers, lowering it to my lips to swallow it down.

"Or women," Wylla quickly says with a giggle before downing her shot.

She reaches back to the boy still captivated by her and takes the two shots he was holding. "Now for a little something different, *Sambuca*." She hands one of the cups to me before bringing the one in her hand to her lips, tossing her head back, and drinking.

Lifting the cup, the smell of black licorice overtakes me. "To freedom and new experiences." I toast again before swallowing the rich liquor.

"You have been so sweet, Chad, now run along." She takes the two bottles of beer, Busch Light and Budlight, from him before giving him a flirty wink and shooing him away.

"You are such a tease, using him like that." I give her a gentle shoulder bump as I turn back to the dance floor and the bodies gyrating against each other.

"Please, I made his night. Now he can go back to all his friends and tell them how he got to see me shake my ass in front of him across the quad. Win for me, I didn't have to carry all this on my own." She barely finishes when the song changes over to "*Daisy*" by Ashnikko. She reaches out, takes my free hand, and drags me out into the sea of people on the dance floor.

"Wylla, stop, I can't dance," I plead with her.

"Biotch, please, all you need to do is let loose and allow the music to overtake you. Sway with the beat," she screams out over the pulse of the music.

She takes my free hand, spins me around, and pulls me back tight against her body before moving her hand down to my hip and gripping it, placing the arm that's holding her beer over my shoulder. Her hips begin to sway behind me, gyrating to the beat of the music, begging mine to move in sync with hers.

My body immediately responds to her touch, my nipples pebbling and rubbing against the material of the dress, alerting anyone who looks at me of my arousal. Her hand slowly slips lower down my hip, moving closer towards the front of my body, her fingertips trailing along the area so close to my pussy. A soft moan escapes my lips, as her grip tightens.

My emotions are overloaded. I'm so confused by this beautiful woman. But does she feel the same? Is she telling me something with her touch or am I overthinking it? The song ends as another upbeat song with a salsa beat starts up. Knowing I need to break free from this hold she has on me, I quickly speak, "Another shot?"

"Hell yeah!" she fires back as she leads me off the dance floor. Lo and behold standing there at the edge of the floor, waiting, two shots in hand is her admirer from earlier.

"Thank you, Chad," comes from her seductively, as she takes the shots from him, handing one to me. Leaning into him, she places a kiss on his cheek, a move that instantly makes a bolt of jealousy hit me that I can't explain. My wolf growls at the show of affection between them. "You can go now." She turns to me, smiling from ear to ear before a frown takes over as she looks at me. "What's wrong, Magz?" she asks, concern etched on her face.

What's wrong? If only I could tell her, express these overwhelming feelings I have for her. But instead, I shake it off, plastering a smile on my face, "Nothing, just wish I was a better dancer. Maybe this shot will help." We both fall into laughter as I take the cup of liquid courage from her.

"To the best girls' night ever!" She lifts her cup, toasting, before we both swallow down the harsh liquid. A different one this time. I really think I'm going to have a hangover tomorrow.

"Well, hello neighbor," comes from behind us, in a deep, playful voice. We both turn in unison, and my breath is taken at the God standing before me. "Well, if it isn't the hot guy from upstairs. Thought you weren't coming," she purrs, as her eyes drag up and down the length of his body.

He's tall with black hair that's cut close on the side and longer on the top, styled to perfection. What I can see of his arms, left exposed from the dark t-shirt he's wearing, are covered in tattoos. His jeans fit him like a glove and damn if he isn't sporting a massive bulge in the front. He reminds me of a young Aaron Kwok.

He just shrugs, tossing us both a wink, very aware of the way each of us was taking in his body. "Well, I couldn't pass up a chance to meet your elusive roommate, Magnolia, right?"

Hearing my name quickly pulls me out of my sex god induced haze. Sex wafts off him in a way I can't even explain.

"Well, this would be her," she pulls me in closer to her. "Magz, meet... I'm sorry, what was your name again?" Damn if she doesn't have this flirting shit down to a T. But why am I not having feelings of jealousy like I did earlier with Chad?

"Oh, so we're gonna play it like that, are we Rainbow Sprite? It's a pleasure to meet you, Magnolia. Your name is far too beautiful to shorten, but not nearly as gorgeous as you are. I'm Jude, and if you ever need anything, I'm right on top of you," he says as I feel the sexual tension in the area rise, a cacophony of moans is elicited from the group behind us as they begin to grind on each other.

My head begins to whip around, soaking everything in and confused at the same time. "He's some type of sex demon. I picked up on the lust earlier today when he dropped off your package. My guess is Incubus," Wylla explains as Jude gets a shit-ass grin on his face.

"Very good, Rainbow. What are you ladies drinking?"

"Oh, just a little of this and a lot of that!" Wylla laughs.

"Are you here all alone?" I ask, shocked by how easily I spoke to him.

"Nope, came with my roommates. They're both off looking for some wolf Blaine's trying to meet. We split up. I chose the more enjoyable option, looking for the two of you, and I think I'm the winner tonight."

Heat burns straight to my core. I feel drawn to this man, more than just the sexual lust he's letting off in waves. My body doesn't know how to deal with my attraction to not only my roommate but now the guy who lives in our dorm. Plus, I still can't find the person who owns the scent that's lived in my mind rent-free since the first time I smelled it.

The conversation continues about random shit and the upcoming school year. He steps closer and closer into our bubble, maneuvering his body between us until his shoulders are flush with one of ours.

Feeling like my body is on fire, and my heart is about to beat out of my chest just from the touches both of them are giving me tonight. I need to get away, just for a minute to regroup.

"Hey, guys, I'm going to run to the bathroom. Be back in a bit," I tell them, before turning and hurrying off. It takes me about five minutes and two stops to ask for directions, but I finally find it and head inside.

There's a cluster of girls standing in front of the mirror, primping and talking about some guys they were hoping to run into tonight. I smile awkwardly, quickly passing them, opening a stall door, and stepping inside.

Relieving myself, I hear the door open and close as the giggling girls leave. Taking a deep breath, I open the stall door, step out to the sink, and wash my hands. Bracing myself on the sink, I stare at my reflection in the mirror, already looking so different from the girl who arrived here this morning.

Okay, Magnolia, get it together. You need to control these hormones. You cannot fall for your roommate, the hot neighbor, and whoever owns that scent. Your father would snatch you out of this school in a heartbeat and take you back to the pack. After giving myself a mental pep talk, I know it's time to head back out.

Swinging open the bathroom door, I step outside and barrel right into a wall. The force so hard, and already off balance on these ridiculous heels, I feel myself fall. But instead of hitting the ground, two massive hands grab me, keeping me upright as I regain my composure.

Looking up, I see the most stunning man, with chocolate eyes that call out a sense of familiarity to me.

"Thank you, I'm—" I tell him, still drawn to those eyes that see through my soul. I never get to finish, though, before he curtly cuts me off.

"Next time, watch where you're going," he gruffly says, his face reddening, before he turns and storms off into the crowd.

What an asshole!

I'm still caught off guard by his rudeness when I rejoin Wylla and Jude, who are laughing and carrying on right where I left them by the dance floor.

Zeke

Running into her tonight was not in my plans. Leaving the bathroom and seeing her again caught me off guard. The way she looked at me like she knew me, still has my heart beating frantically. I was such an ass, instead of just saying 'excuse me' I acted like a fucking dick.

Damn, she's just as fucking beautiful now as she was earlier today. I wanted to be with her, hell, my ferret was clawing at me to shift. He wanted nothing more than to be curled up against her body as she stroked him. But that would never happen. Once she found out I was nothing but a measly ferret shifter, a prey animal she would never want to be with us. Not to mention the fact that she spilled her guts to me while I licked her sweet juices from her fingers.

I rushed back across the quad to where I left Blaine, who was growing more pissed by the minute about not finding the Exodus Pack wolf. I see him standing by the bar, the slutty fairy that's been trying her hardest to get him to notice her, still there. My movement quickens, cutting the remaining distance between us.

"Fuck off, slut. He doesn't want you!" I bark out at her, causing her to jump in fear. Tears stream down her face as she scurries off into the crowd.

"What crawled up your ass?" Blaine laughs, fucker knows he's glad I got rid of her.

"I ran into the chick from the woods I told you about. Acted like a dumbass and was a grade-A prick to her. It's for the best. She'd never be interested once she found out."

"You need to get over it. We don't care what your shifted form is. You've proven with every cage match you've fought in that you can beat the living fuck out of anyone. You're a ferret, own the badass shifter you are," he lectures me for the millionth time.

He's right about one thing. I'm a beast in the ring. Hell, just last week I took down two dragons. Whoever said they were one of the fiercest shifters in the world fucking needs their heads examined. But I hate talking about me, and he knows it. So I switch quickly to a subject that'll get him going.

"Did you find the Exodus Wolf or get confirmation on who it is?"

"No, it's like it's being kept top secret. No photo, nothing to identify who it is. What the hell is wrong with this school? Couldn't they put out a freshman registry with a name, picture, supe type, and pack or coven? You know, all the basic shit someone should know?"

His face reddens the angrier he gets, lessening to some degree how bad I feel about being rude to my white wolf. "Seen Jude anywhere?" He'd taken off about ten minutes after we arrived, wanting to find the girls from downstairs.

"Nah, but let's go find him and see if he found our neighbors. I'm curious if the one is as hot as he keeps going on about. Let's check out the dance floor. You know he's probably there showing off his *Magic Mike* moves, especially if he got tired of looking for the girls."

He pushes off the bar, and we head through the crowd, heading to the center where the dance floor was set up and the music is the loudest. It's still crazy how people quickly move out of his way when they see the future Alpha of the Stonehaven pack moving toward them.

As the dance floor comes into view, I see Jude. "There he is," I tell Blaine as I reach out and point him out.

"Fuck me! If they look as hot from the front as they do from the back, his ass better be sharing them," exclaims Blaine with a guttural groan.

Casting my gaze off Jude, who had been my center of attention, I see the two girls with him. One with rainbow-colored hair just as he described, with a banging ass body. But it's the one on the opposite side of him that has my heart plummeting. The girl has gray shoulder-length hair, and I don't even have to see her face to know who it is. It's her, my white wolf. Fucking no chance in hell of me being with her now that she's met Jude. Who would want a ferret when they could have an Incubus? A man literally built for sex. Looking to my left, I see Blaine, and he's zoned in on them as well. Fuck, he's drooling over them. Yep, it's a done deal. With an Alpha Wolf and Incubus sex machine, the lowly puny ferret won't have a chance. There's no way in hell I can walk over there and be near her, especially after how I treated her.

"Blaine... Blaine... Earth to Blaine... Are you in there? Fuck this shit, I'm going back to the room," I bark out gruffly when the fucker ignores me. I take one final look at the woman who captured my heart today before turning and leaving. Passing by the makeshift tent set up as one of the many bars, I reach over the counter, grabbing a bottle of Jim Beam. The asswipe behind the counter goes to say something before I cut a glare at him and throw up a middle finger.

The rest of my plans tonight include getting fucking plastered and forgetting everything. I hope like hell this liquor helps me fight this pull I feel for my white wolf. I open the bottle, taking a long swig of the brown liquid, a slight burn to my throat as it slides down.

Blaine

Well, fuck me. There's that mouth watering scent again; cotton candy. Smells so sweet, I feel like I could get a toothache just from inhaling it.

Looking around, I'm trying to find who this scent belongs to. I will figure out who they are tonight. There won't be any escaping me this time. Finding the Exodus Pack wolf was a huge fucking bust. Not one sign of him anywhere, and when I asked some fellow wolves at the mixer, they all gawked at me like they had no fucking clue what I was going on about.

The holier-than-thou attitude must apply to attending parties at school as well, I guess. The wolf is probably locked up in their private room, reading a 'how to be a douche' handbook and eating caviar. Entitled ass bastard.

So my mission has now changed from finding the pompous ass to searching for who smells like the tastiest treat I might ever have. I'm positive the scent is pulling at me so hard because of who the owner of it is - *my mate.*

After Zeke meets back up with me at the bar, we talk for a few minutes before Z asks if I've seen Jude anywhere.

"Nah, but let's go find him and see if he found our neighbors. I'm curious if the one is as hot as he keeps going on about. Let's check out the dance floor. You know he's probably there showing off his Magic Mike moves, especially if he got tired of looking for the girls."

I push off the bar, and we head through the crowd, heading to the center where the dance floor was set up and the music is the loudest.The scent is stronger the closer we get to the mass of writhing bodies in the middle of the quad. Then Zeke points to the opposite side of the dance floor, where my gaze lands on Jude and the two smoking hot babes he's chatting with.

"Fuck me! If they look as hot from the front as they do from the back, his ass better be sharing them," I exclaim.

The closer we get to Jude and his two new friends, the more I'm salivating. The scent belongs to one of those two ladies. I see the rainbow-haired girl Jude mentioned lives below us, and she's sexy as hell. However, the one with the gray hair has an ass that has me ready to bow down and worship her like the goddess she is.

Totally ignoring Zeke beside me and what he's saying, I am hook, line, and sinker, already obsessed with this beauty. The DJ switches the song over to *Thinkin' With My Dick* by Kevin Gates. Right now, the song is accurate. Since I'm rock hard staring at who, I'm pretty sure, is my mate. The pull towards her is like nothing I have ever felt before. *Holy fuck! It's her!*

As I approach, I see Jude grab the girls' hands and lead them to the dance floor. My wolf is clawing at me to be free. Screaming *MINE... MATE.* This has never happened to me before. My wolf has been silent any other time we've seen a female wolf. My wolf's rage only intensifies when we see Jude sandwiched between the two girls dancing.

Jude, the fucking horny bastard that he is, is oblivious to what is happening right next to him. He turns around and grabs my mystery girl, pulling her back against his very obvious hard cock. Her eyes are closed, and she's just moving to the music, looking like a free fucking spirit. Our neighbor, who's now behind him, is laughing her ass off. Screaming 'hell, yeah' and grinding her pussy against Jude's ass.

I'm going to snap Jude's neck for grinding on my mate like that. I'm crossing the dance floor before I even realize I'm moving. The only thought on my mind is my mate and the man, my friend, touching her. Jude's going to wish he kept his hands to himself tonight. My wolf is in control right now, and I'm barely holding off his shift. Just as I'm almost to them, the girl with the whitish gray hair opens her eyes, and they immediately lock with mine, staring right into my soul.

Our gazes are locked together, neither one of us willing to break the stare off we seem to be having. My mouth is watering and my cock is tingling at being this close to her. I can practically taste the sugar spun treat in my mouth. I turn to tell Zeke I found the scent I've been unable to stop thinking about, but he's gone. *What the fuck? Where did he go?*

Her eyes widen as she continues to stare at me before finally mouthing, "You!"

Magnolia

"*Mate,"* my wolf calls out with longing.

This can't be! I've finally found the owner of the amazing cedarwood scent that's been haunting me since this morning on the plane. But my mate?

True mates were a children's fairy tale in our pack, and even though I often dreamed of having one, that's all I thought it was. A dream. It was a known fact when the female population declined, the mate bond disappeared.

Shit! Shit! Shit! My father's going to kill me. He'll pull me from the school before I even get the chance to attend one class. How in the heavens can this be?

I'm so lost in my thoughts, listening to my wolf screaming that *she found her mate*, I don't even notice how close he's moved towards me until his lips slam down on mine as he growls out, "*Mate*".

No! I can't! Using all my force, I reach my arms up between our bodies, placing the palms of my hands firmly on his chest, and push. Strength fills my body, and I'm able to knock him back so hard he stumbles, barely catching his balance.

Tears fill my eyes. So much has happened today. I'm overwhelmed, and I can't deal. Turning to a stunned Wylla, I whisper with a creaky voice, "I'm getting out of here. I'll see you later." Then I run, as fast as I can, on the damn heels she has me wearing, straight for the wood line.

I constantly check over my shoulder, but he doesn't follow. Maybe my wolf is wrong. Shouldn't he have followed me?

"Not wrong. Mate. Our Mate. Need him," she whines.

Trying to console her, I remind her the mate bond doesn't exist. We can't be with anyone or we will lose our freedom. What little we have anyways. Once I'm covered by the wood line, I take off my clothes, place my shoes and panties inside my dress, and do my best to turn it into a bag to hold my items. Once I've done that, I allow my wolf to come forward.

My wolf picks up the dress holding the rest of my things in her mouth and takes off in a sprint. I let my wolf run the distance back to my dorm as I try to clear my head. Needless to say, I resolved nothing, and I'm just as confused now as I was earlier.

My wolf begs to return to the dance and claim our mate, but I deny her that chance, pushing her closer to our dorm. Once we reach the edge of the wood line, I shift back and quickly dress.

God, I hope I haven't scared Wylla off from being my friend. Fuck, how am I going to handle my attraction to her, the mystery man outside the bathroom, the upstairs neighbor, and now a fucking mate?

I have to keep this from my father. One slip of the tongue, and he'll have me packed and out of here before I could even blink. My heart begins to race with all the what-ifs.

Stepping up to my dorm building, it feels like a ghost town. Nobody is hanging around like they were earlier. I guess they're all at the mixer. The spotlights shine an eerie light down on the front of the entrance doors, casting an ominous glow. If I were scared easily, this would appear to be a haunted house and one I would run from without hesitation.

A large shadow comes across the building, causing me to jump in place. A gust of wind flows over me, and I have to look twice, even rubbing my eyes, because it looks like a huge bird of some type flying overhead.

Taking off at a run, I cross the short distance from the woods to the doors, grabbing hold of the handles and flinging them open. Once I'm inside and safe from whatever was flying around, I bend over, placing my hands on my knees, and begin to take deep breaths, trying to calm myself.

This has to be a damn dream; there is no way any of this can actually be happening. Any minute, I'm going to wake up and be in my bed at home, prepared to move to campus. This is all a result of my nerves and excitement. Just a dream.

Reaching down, I take my fingers and pinch my forearm, over and over. Each time triggering pain, but not waking me from this nightmare I've found myself in.

Fuckitty! Fuck! Fuck!

Okay, it's fine, Magnolia. You just need a plan. This is a big school. I can avoid the wolf whose scent makes my core pool with desire, even the asshole who clearly wants nothing to do with me. Hell, I can even run in the opposite direction when I see the hot guy from upstairs. The only downfall to the plan is if he hangs around Wylla. He did seem attracted to her, so that'll make it harder to ignore him. The worst would be having to watch him and her together when all I want to do is crawl in between them. Yeah, that will prove a little harder to avoid.

Choosing to skip the elevator, I take the stairs. No way do I want to be cramped inside a tiny box with anyone right now. Slowly climbing, I make my way up the three flights of stairs to our floor before opening the door and stepping into the vacant hallway.

There's no noise, not even a soft humming of music. Clearly, everyone is out and having fun. Not me, I ran from a man who called me his mate, my hot roommate, and an even sexier neighbor. I craved the solitude I hoped my room would provide. It's only when I get to the door to our room, I remember the one small flaw in my plan. *Wylla has the key to the room since she has pockets.*

Sighing deeply, I lean my back against the wall and slide to the floor. Stretching my legs out and crossing my feet, I close my eyes. Nothing I can do but wait, especially since there was no one at the desk when I came in. I just pray she comes back alone and not with him.

Wylla

What the fuck is happening? One minute Magz and I are dancing with the hot as fuck demon from upstairs and the next, she's running from the quad like her ass is on fire.

I'm pissed off as I glare at the guy who kissed her before she took off. I pull away from Jude and storm towards him. Slamming both my palms into his shoulders, I shove him backward.

"What the fuck did you do?" I scream at him.

He is wide-eyed and looks like he's in agony. *What the fuck is this guy's deal?*

Taking no chances of him lying to me, I cast a quick truth spell, "*Truthio!*"

He looks at me shocked and hottie demon man is yelling, "*What the fuck,*" at me.

Grabbing them both by their arms, I drag them off the dance floor with me and away from the loud ass crowd to a semi-secluded spot. Now that I can hear myself think, I turn on both of them, rage coursing through my blood.

"Tell me what happened. Do you often assault women by kissing them without consent?" I demand.

"What? No! Fuck no! I've been smelling this scent all day, at the airport, and in the woods outside of campus. It was stronger at the party tonight. My friend, Z, and I, I'm Blaine by the way, were looking for this asshole," he points to Jude. "When the scent got so strong, I could practically taste it. Then I saw him," he gestures towards my hottie demon, "dancing with you two, and I honestly wasn't sure which one of you smelled so fuckable. But then that girl turned around, and my wolf screamed at me, *Mate.*"

I whisper, "Oh, fuck," but neither of them hears me, and I give the wolf a go-on hand gesture.

"With my wolf riding me so hard, I couldn't get a handle on him quick enough and instincts had me kissing my mate. I didn't expect her to reject me so publicly, especially after dancing so sexily with my roommate, of all people." The last part coming out like a kicked puppy. *HA! No pun intended, but that's funny shit. Kicked puppy? He's a wolf.*

"Well, fuck me. No wonder she took off," I say, pacing a few steps back and forth. Trying to grasp everything Blaine just told me.

"This is a huge fucking mess. FUCK!" I yell to no one in particular.

"What are we missing here, Rainbow?" Jude asks.

"Yeah, I wanna know what's happening with my mate," Blaine growls, his chest puffing out in anger.

"Buckle up, sexy demon man and growly puppy. Magnolia is my roommate and my own proclaimed bestie. She just arrived this morning and from the very little amount she's told me about her..." I pause for a minute before continuing, "Let's just say this little turn of events isn't going to be good for her."

"That's bullshit! Finding your mate is the best thing that can happen to a supe. We all know that," Blaine interrupts all pissy.

"Bingo!" I say, giving him the gun fingers. "However, I bet those supes don't have a dad who has controlled every aspect of their lives. They also don't have archaic ass rules and guidelines for their hierarchy members. Especially the women."

Blaine's eyes and mouth are wide open. He gasps, "No!"

"If you just guessed that my bestie is part of the Exodus Pack, you'd be right, mutt. She was allowed here by her dad and Alpha as long as she majored in something they could find useful, and she comes home on a schedule. There's more I'm sure, but I've only known her a day, so she hasn't told me everything yet," I tell them.

Jude is staring at Blaine in confusion. Blaine is just glaring at me before he storms off toward the large oak tree a few yards away and punches it. Jude runs over to him and yanks him back away from the poor tree. "*Reparo,*" I whisper to the tree. Should help fix the splinters the wolf just created with his fists.

"The hell, man. What's the deal?" Jude yells as he's wrestling a very pissed-off Blaine.

"You're a moron, dude. I just told you guys about this pack tonight in our room before we came here. I was interested in forming an alliance with the Alpha. FUUUUCK!" he yells exasperatedly as he runs a hand down his face.

"I knew the Exodus Alpha allowed a pack member to attend this year. I thought for sure it would be his son. Why was she allowed? They NEVER let female members leave pack lands," he asks me.

"She could only come as it was believed she will be a Beta and then she'll become the mate to the Alpha's son and his Betas," I tell him what she told me when she got her package from her dad earlier. "They literally picked a major that would be beneficial for a Luna to have."

Blaine is staring at me confused like I just spoke gibberish to him.

"What do you mean she *will be a Beta*? Wolves' designations reveal at puberty and she's a grown ass woman?" he tells us.

"What I understand from Magz, is her pack suppresses their designations until they're nineteen. We spoke right before we came tonight about looking for a spell to reverse whatever suppresses it from happening as young teens. Now, enough chit-chat with you two sexy bastards. I have to go find my girl," I tell them, and without waiting another second, I turn on my heel and book ass toward our room. I hope my girl is there and I can help her.

Before I get too far from the guys, I focus on Blaine. "*Reverso.*" I don't need him spilling the truth to every soul he meets from now until whenever I remember to reverse the truth spell I cast. So I do it now before I forget.

Now, back to the main event. Getting to Magz as fast as I can.

Blaine

Shocked is an understatement of how I'm feeling. I'm fucking reeling from what Wylla just told me. She hurried off to find Magnolia and left me in a cloud of rainbow dust. I felt the witch bitch reverse her little truth spell while we were standing in the open field still. Jude is just standing there, looking at me, baffled at what the fuck we were just told.

Heading back to the dorm together Jude told me her name. *Magnolia, it tastes delicious as it rolls off my tongue.* Getting to our dorm building, I freeze in shock as I stand outside the door. *I have a mate.* Jude snaps his fingers in my face. Finally, out of my head, we walk up to our room.

Mate, I have a mate. Well, if she accepts me, that is. It's not looking great for me since she ran out of the mixer like her ass was on fire. I thought she was rejecting me, *my heart shattering into a million pieces,* but after her roommate gave us a proper tongue lashing, *which we fucking deserved*, I understood more about what was happening.

I need her out of that pack. *No, I want her out of the pack.* There is no way my mate is involved in the wolf cult. *No fucking way! Even if she rejects me in the end, I will long for her for the rest of my days.* My wolf won't let me love another after finding our mate. So at the very least, I'm going to make sure she lives a long and prosperous life. Which won't happen if she stays in the Exodus Pack.

Storming into our room, Z is laying on his bed just staring at the ceiling with his headphones on. I'm pissed. He left me without a word tonight. When I needed him, he was gone. *Fucking asshole! I'd never desert him like that.* I pick a pillow up off my bed and throw it at him. It smacks him in the face, and he jolts up in a fighting stance. Throwing off his headphones, he looks at us, confusion on his face when he sees my peeved expression.

"What the fuck?" comes from him in a mocking tone.

He doesn't seem to pick up on how pissed off I am at him. His punk ass left me to deal with the aftermath of meeting my mate alone, Jude was no fucking help either. Hell, I feel like ripping him to shreds for touching my mate the way he did.

"We need to talk right the fuck now. You left and shit hit the fucking fan," I growl at him. My body is wrought with fury, and at this moment, it's directed solely at him.

He sits up on his bed, getting more comfortable. "What the fuck happened? It's only been like an hour since I left. What could have happened in that short amount of time? Shit. I had to go; I was dealing with my own issue."

It's Jude who answers me. "I found the neighbor girls and was dancing with them. Then dark and broody here showed up and apparently found his mate and pissed her off; Magnolia, that's the neighbor girl who was missing, by the way, all in one fell swoop. He kissed her, and she shoved him away and ran off, crying. A real Casanova."

"Shut the fuck up! This is fucking serious, Jude!" I interrupt, yelling at him.

Z looks back and forth between the two of us, confused, before he asks.

"You have a mate? You kissed her? Which girl is this? Dammit, I leave you two alone for an hour and you come back mated?"

"You would know if you stayed around. Wylla is the hottie with the tight ass body and all the tattoos. Magnolia is the hot as fuck, gray-haired girl," Jude tells him.

"Watch your fucking mouth. That's my mate you're talking about," I grit out through clenched teeth. He's walking a thin line after the way he danced with her already, having his hands all over her body, one meant for me and my wolf. Add in his fucking mouth and he's about to get an ass beating.

Jude just falls back on his bed laughing, rolling side to side as he basks in his amusement at the fucked up situation. Z then takes a huge inhale of breath before putting a hand to his temple. *This can't be good.* He looks pained before he even opens his mouth.

"Well then, you won't like what I'm about to say. I'm only telling you this since we've been friends for years. Brothers really. My girl from the woods. Your mate, they're one and the same." His eyes are downcast at the last part; the fucker can't even look me in the eye. He knows he's in the wrong.

HELL. FUCKING. NO!

Jude's laughter becomes hysterical as he rolls off the bed and falls on the floor, holding his stomach. He's laughing so hard that his skin, which is usually a light fawn, is turning blue from him trying to catch his breath. Z tries to go on, but before he can even utter another syllable, I'm on him, punching him in his lying fucking mouth. Blood drips from the split in his lip. *MINE!* My wolf is snarling and snapping his teeth, wanting to rip Zeke's throat out.

"You tasted my mate's pussy before I did? You nestled those perfect tits before me? She doesn't even know your kind of shifter exists!" *Hell, I'm still trying to understand how she doesn't, but it must have something to do with what Wylla said about her.* "I'll fucking kill you!" I roar at him. My body is vibrating in rage. I'm barely controlling my wolf's need to shift at the moment.

We wrestle around on the ground for a bit before Z gets me in a restraint hold. My back is to his chest, as his legs are wrapped around me, pinning me, unable to escape. He's speaking rapidly to me, his tone firm but full of remorse.

"Oh, it was all fine and dandy when she wasn't your mate. You laughed if I recall. For the record, I liked her, but when I saw you staring at her tonight, I knew I didn't stand a chance. That's why I left so quickly. Fuck you, man, for thinking I'd betray you like that and for busting my lip."

I shrug and give him a fake apology. *We're shifters; we heal quickly.* He releases me, and I spin around, going to punch his smug fucking face again. Pausing for a moment to stand up, I try to remind myself that this is one of my best fucking friends. My eyes never leave his and seeing the tortured look on his face, I know he's punished himself enough already.

"Fine, I don't like it, but you didn't know, and I didn't know she was my mate yet. Fuck, this is a mess."

"What happened to make her run out on you after finding out that you're mates? I thought wolves were ecstatic when finding the one they were destined to be with?" Z asks as he sits back on his bed. He looks pained to even ask that, but he's trying to make the best of this situation, same as me. I take a seat in the computer chair next to his bed, while Jude is sitting on the floor with his back against the bed, just watching the show. *Bastard.*

I tell him the whole thing from start to finish. How I kissed her, and she ran out, Wylla dragging us from the mixer and spelling me, the Exodus Pack, and what Wylla knew about her roommate. Z rubs a hand down his face after staring at me in shock.

"Fuck, dude, this is serious. We have to get her out of that pack," Zeke says. The tone of his voice tells me he's just as serious as I am about getting her away from that pack of crazies.

I sigh loudly and agree, but how am I supposed to do that when she won't even talk to me? We chat a little longer about the mixer and the girls. It's well into the early morning by the time we are slowing down the conversation and yawning in exhaustion.

"We should come at this in the morning with fresh eyes," suggests Jude.

We agree and get into our beds to try to get some shuteye. Before I fall asleep, I need to say one more thing.

"Zeke?"

"Yeah, man?" he replies.

"I'm sorry I split your lip. My wolf is just riding me hard, and he's getting harder to control. Any female would be lucky to have you by their side," I tell him, and mean every word.

"Thanks, man. It's okay, I've gotten worse in the cages," he says with a chuckle.

With that, I close my eyes and fall asleep thinking about a gray-haired vixen riding my cock like a jockey and her being round with my child. Tomorrow will be better. I just know it. Wylla will have spoken to her, and she might be ready to talk to me. *We can only hope.*

Magnolia

I'm just dozing off when I hear the dinging of the elevator doors as they open. Lifting my head and glancing to the right, I see Wylla stepping out. Her eyes are down-turned as she bites her lip. She still hasn't noticed me as she turns and makes her way to our room. I just sit here, my throat tight, afraid to make a sound. I don't know why, other than she probably thinks I'm a fool from the way I acted earlier.

It doesn't help that whenever I'm around this goddess of a woman, I can't fucking think straight. In my head, I can be big and bad, expressing how I feel. But that's the thing, I could never be that way at home; I had to suppress my emotions and be the dutiful daughter who follows all the rules. In other words, be meek and not be heard. I don't want to be that way anymore. I want the powerful person inside of me to be set free.

She takes a moment to look up, her eyes laser-focused on me. "What the fuck are you doing out here?" she whispers-shouts at me, no doubt trying not to wake anyone who may be in their rooms.

Standing slowly, I look at her and let out a laugh. "Well, let's see, you have the room key and I don't know how to pick locks. So the hallway it was. I haven't been here too long, maybe thirty minutes or so. What are you doing here? I thought you'd still be with the neighbor." She moves to the door, pulls the key from her pocket, and places it in the lock, opening it.

"Bish, please. You're my girl. Chicks before dicks," comes from her with a wink as she steps inside the room.

"Aww, I feel so loved," I tell her, placing my hand over my heart in fake adoration.

"You are," Wylla says so softly, if not for my wolf's hearing, I never would have heard it.

This woman has me so confused with her comments. It's bad enough I don't even know how to process what I'm feeling for all these people I've met today. Fuck, is it possible to be drawn to different people, so intensely you want all of them with every fiber of your being?

I close the door behind me as I step inside the room. Turning around, I catch Wylla mid-change. Her bare back is to me. Her shorts drop to the floor as she stands there in her fuschia-colored thong. She has her juicy ass on full display for me. I bite down on my lip, needing to hold back the groan that wants to escape my mouth.

She turns around as she slips her nightgown over her head, exposing her rose-colored nipples that had been covered by her clothing. After a minute I look up and catch her staring at me with curiosity filling her eyes. *Fuck, did she catch me staring? Is she upset about it? Does she hate me? She's gonna want a new roommate.*

So many thoughts are racing through my mind that I can't focus on one long enough to plan an answer.

"Magz, are you okay? Is the shit that happened earlier still bothering you?"

"Umm..." I stammer out, not sure what to say or how she'll react.

"No! Stop right da fuck there," she orders, stomping her foot on the ground before making her way over to me, taking my hand in hers, leading me over to her bed, and sitting me down.

Fuck, her hands are so fucking soft, and when she touches me, I swear it feels like a heat wave rolling across my skin.

"Now spill it, or I'm gonna make you."

"Fuck, I don't even know how to start. It's just that everything has been so much. New place, new people. Meeting that wolf who says he's my mate, and as much as I hate it, my wolf felt the pull to him and he's so fucking hot. Then there's this mystery guy I ran into by the bathroom and there's a pull to him. Then, when I was dancing with you and the hot guy upstairs, all I could think about was being between the two of you as we made out. Fuck, how can I be attracted to you and them? And now all I'm worried about is how this is going to affect us." Looking over at Wylla, I see her frozen with a blank expression on her face.

"You were worried about how this would affect me and you. You're attracted to me and them?" Her voice is husky as she speaks and scoots closer to me.

The impact of her question comes barreling into me like a wrecking ball. See, this is what I get for opening my mouth when I'm so emotionally overwhelmed.

"Oh my goddess, Wylla. I'm so sorry. I shouldn't have word vomited that out to you. It's just I know you don't feel the same way. I heard how you were talking about Jude and the way you two were tonight; I could tell there's tension between the two of you." She just stares at me. Nothing, not a word or even a noise comes out of her. Fuck, I've ruined this friendship before it flourished.

She scoots even closer to me, our thighs now grazing each other as she angles her body toward me. She reaches up, takes the strands of hair that have fallen into my face, and pushes them behind my ear before placing her hand on the side of my head, pulling me into her as she places her lips on mine and kisses me softly. Her tongue dances along the seam of my lips, begging for me to open them, which I do. She deepens the kiss as her tongue caresses mine.

My hand instinctively moves up, cradling the side of her face as we continue to kiss like we are starved for each other until she slowly pulls away. She moves her hand down the side of my face so that she can glide the pad of her thumb over my lips.

"Does that feel like I don't feel the same? I've been attracted to you since the moment you stepped into this room."

I'm awestruck. She leans back into me, wrapping her arms around me as she gives me a passionate kiss. My arms go around her, and we fall back onto the bed. I can't get over how amazing she feels in my arms and how great she tastes.

I'm so lost in her mango scent. My legs wrap around her as she moves on top of me in between my thighs. Her hand moves down, cupping my tit, and I'm immediately rocketed back to reality and what's happening between us.

I push her away and jump up from the bed. Hurt is written all over Wylla's face at my abrupt change in behavior, and my heart and my wolf both want me to run back to her. But I fight them both. This can't go further. My father would never approve of it. *Gosh dammit, I need to shake this daddy won't like it shit.*

"I'm so sorry, Wylla. I shouldn't have. I need to go run." It's all I can manage to get out before I turn, running across the room to the door, grabbing the handle, and rushing out. Never once looking back because the hurt I saw on her face at my rejection will be forever etched in my memory.

I race past the elevator, straight for the stairs, and rush down them. The only thought running through my mind is how my stupid emotions have fucked up everything. Pushing open the door, I run into the night, straight to the woods. Tossing my head over my shoulder, I look back, but no one follows, and I'm struck with both happiness and sadness for it. I make my way deeper into the woods until I find a tree with an opening in the trunk's bottom small enough to hide my clothes that I was still wearing from the party tonight before I shift, allowing my wolf to take over.

We run for hours as I replay all the events that happened since I left home this morning over and over in my head. My wolf whines for me to quit being a bitch and shut up. Begging to be with her mates, and hoping that what my father doesn't know won't hurt him.

Mates! What the hell is this crazy wolf of mine talking about? We have one mate. One that we can't even be with as it breaks all our pack rules.

My wolf runs until she is exhausted, finally finding a large pile of leaves by the base of a tree and curling up in them. We lay there, exhausted as sleep overtakes us, and I dream of the three men I've met here and my gorgeous roommate.

Waking with the bright sun beaming down on me, I realize I'm still in my wolf form. I know I need to get back to my room and deal with the fallout from last night. My wolf, the fucking bitch, is perfectly content to lie here in the pile of leaves and bask in the sun's warmth. She never cared for the pack rules and longed to be free of them, so she sees this as the perfect opportunity to do it.

"We need to head back now!" I command her.

"To be with mates?"

"No, we can't be with him. Father would never allow it. If he caught wind of it, he'd have us on the first plane back to him, and we'd never be allowed to leave pack lands again."

She lets out a low growl of defiance, but slowly complies, getting up onto all four legs and leaning back, so her front paws are extended out as she stretches. Finally, feeling loose, she takes off at a slow pace back to the tree that houses our clothing.

What must be about forty minutes later, we reach the tree. *Fuck, I didn't realize we'd run that far.* Releasing her control, I call forth the shift. For me, the transition never hurt the way others described it. To me, it was an enjoyable change, almost euphoric, a special bond shared between me and my wolf.

I take my time walking back to my dorm. When I ran last night, I didn't take the time to put shoes back on, so my feet are now riddled with tiny cuts as I step on the twigs and branches. They're irritating as fuck, but once I shift, they'll be healed. So the minor burning tingle they have right now is just that, an annoyance.

As I walk, I decide to turn my phone back on, and I'm shockingly surprised when it pings with notifications. There are over ten voicemails and twenty texts all from Wylla, worrying about me. Needing to know if I was okay. Apologizing if she was too forward.

Could this woman be any better? Fuck me for being born into the Exodus Pack.

I ran out of the room like a raving lunatic, and she was worried about me. Allowing my fingers to fly across the screen, I shoot a text out to her.

Me: I'm fine, shifted, ran, and fell asleep. Coming up to the dorms now.

I've barely sent the text when I see tiny little bubbles popping up by her name, letting me know she's replying.

Wylla: Thank fuck! My ass has worried non-stop about you all night. We need to talk. I'm at the library right now looking into that matter we talked about. I'll message when I'm done.

Wylla: I'm sorry too if I came on to hard for you and you're not ready for it. If you have second thoughts, not interested, just know I'm here for you. I'd rather have you as a friend than not at all.

I move my fingers to type a message, then erase it, over and over, as I walk across the grounds between the woods and the building. I want to say so much, but the words aren't right. My heart and my head are disputing what the other wants, or feels, is right.

I'm so lost in my own ramblings with my eyes on my phone I'm not aware of my surroundings and for the second time in less than twelve hours, I run into a brick wall.

One that smells of musky citrus. Looking up, I see him, the guy from the bathroom, the deliciously hot jerk.

"Oh... it's you again. I'm so sorry for the second time, I'm not watching where I'm going." A light giggle comes from me like a silly little schoolgirl.

He just looks at me, his chocolate eyes scanning the length of my body from top to bottom, stopping at my bare feet.

"Where are your shoes?" comes gruffly from him, but it's mixed with what sounds like concern.

"Oh, I... well... ummm, I ran out of the building last night and forgot them, I guess," I confess, not knowing why I feel this overwhelming need to tell him everything.

He reaches out, taking my hair and skimming it behind my ear before quickly pulling his hand away. "You should be careful; you could've cut them by stepping on something."

I'm drawn back to those eyes, ones that look so familiar to me, more than just being on the man I'm lusting over.

"Umm... I'm okay, just a few scratches on the bottom. They'll heal." Why the hell am I so nervous around him? "About last night, I really am sorry for running into you like that."

He looks at me, stunned, his dark hair falling over his eyes. Ones that I don't want to be covered.

"I should apologize for acting like a dick. I... It's not an excuse, but I have a lot on my mind. Shit I need to figure out."

He tilts his head down, and I don't know what comes over me, but I reach out, hesitantly pushing the hair out of his eyes. He pulls away, which causes me to jump. Fuck, he's pissed. I shouldn't have touched him.

"Sorry, it's just you look so familiar like I know you, but I know I don't. Your eyes..." I don't even get to finish what I'm saying before he's cutting me off.

"Sorry, I got to go," he takes off in a sprint around the building.

My heart plummets because I feel like a piece of me has been ripped away. What is it about him that seems so familiar? Those eyes are all I can think about.

Looking up to make sure no one is in my path, I climb up the steps to the back door of the dorms, open it, and step inside. It's only when I get upstairs, I fucking realize I don't have my key yet again. I go to message Wylla but notice there is a message from her I haven't read.

Wylla: I know you didn't take the key when you left last night, so I left the door unlocked.

She is truly an angel because I didn't want to go back down those stairs, praying that by chance someone was at the front desk. Opening our door, I step inside, walk over to the desk by my bed and grab my shower caddy, towel, and robe. I stink and desperately need a shower. I stop only long enough to grab my key off my nightstand before heading down to the communal bathrooms.

Zeke

Fuck, she smelled good. All I wanted was to pull her into my arms and kiss her. But I can't. She's Blaine's fucking mate, a wolf herself, and I'm a fucking ferret. Any chance I had with her is shot, especially when she finds out it was me in the woods. When she went on about how I felt familiar to her, I thought I was going to shit my pants. *Could she tell?*

I knew the guys were in the cafeteria waiting on me, so that's where I took off like a mouse running from the alley cat. Walking in, I go through the line and grab some food before taking my seat at the table across from Blaine. He still has a pissed-off look on his face as he scowls at both Jude and me. Jude, the fucking goof he is, simply laughs and keeps eating like it's not phasing him a bit.

"Umm... I just ran into your... mate... when I left the dorm." God, it still pains me to say that word. He quickly shoots his head up at me with a panicked, worried look on his face.

"Is she okay? How the fuck did she look? Is she still there?" he barks out in rapid succession.

"She looked okay, tired. She, umm, didn't have any shoes on. Said something about running out and forgetting them."

"What?" He drops his head into his hands, then runs his fingers through his hair. I can tell this shit is tearing him up. Hell, it is me too.

"Look man, what happened in the woods that day never would've if I knew she was your mate. We've been friends, fuck, best friends for so long, there's no way I would ever do anything to fuck up our friendship. Hell, you guys have been there with me when others wouldn't after finding out what I am." He lifts his head and stares at me; hell, even Jude is paying attention now.

"I know," comes from him softly.

"I just want you to know I understand the mate bond, that's why I'm keeping my distance, even though I feel like there's this force pulling me towards her. Each time I've left her, it feels like there's a dagger stabbing right through my heart, slicing it in half. So, I'm promising you I'm doing my best to stay away from her, even at my expense."

"You're a fucking idiot, Z, and you too, Blaine. I'm telling both of you right fucking now, I will not stop. I'm attracted to her too, a draw to her just as intense as both of you dicks claim to have. But it's not only her, it's her rainbow bright roommate too. Hell, if it wasn't for you coming in like a macho fucking prick. '*You mate, mine*'," Jude rants, his voice growing louder and ending with a Tarzan impersonation before continuing, "I would've gotten lucky. So I'm telling you right now, I'm following through and figuring out this pull I have to them."

Blaine reaches his arm out, sending his plate flying across the table onto the floor, before standing and storming out of the cafeteria. His pissed-off antics catch the attention of everyone seated around us.

"What the fuck is your problem, Jude? That's his fucking mate. You need to get over it and step back just like I am," I say through gritted teeth.

"No, you can be a fucking pansy but I'm not. I'm fed up with this shit. I have to back away because she's his mate when I have a connection too? Fuck that, man. You can be a sorry ass, whiny bitch if you want, but I'm fighting for what I want, and I want both of them," he stands from the table, taking his plate in his hands.

Reaching out, I take hold of his arm, "Jude..."

"No, fuck you, man. Hell, I was even going to talk to the two of you about sharing. We're fucking supes, man. The two of you are so caught up on her being his mate, that y'all have forgotten that it's common to have more than one mate. The two of you need to take your heads out of your asses long enough to think about each of us having a pull to her. She could be mated to more than just Blaine. So screw him and screw you, Z." He storms off in the same direction as Blaine.

Could it be? Could I be drawn to her as well because she's my mate?

What would she see in me? I'm a fucking prey animal, and she is a predator. She would only want to surround herself with strong mates who could protect her, like a demon and an Alpha wolf, not a ferret.

I don't have a chance in hell.

No longer wanting to be a show for those seated around us who've heard bits and pieces of our conversation, I get up, leaving my plate on the table, and walk out of the cafeteria. Needing to blow off some steam and knowing the cages aren't open at this time of the day, I head to the gym. I need to punch something, and I don't want to run into my roommates while I have this rage burning through my body. I love them like brothers, and I've never been jealous of them, but right now, I am. I wish like hell my shifter was one worthy to be with the goddess I'm drawn to.

Walking into the gym, I look at the boxing ring, and my spirits lift a little. *Fucking Jesse Davis is in the ring.* The asshole went to the same school as the three of us and took any shot he had at reminding me how weak of a shifter I was after he caught me mid-shift when I was fifteen. Since that day, he took joy in belittling me, reminding me of how weak I was. Little did he know, I may be a prey shifter, but no one can fight like me. I hold back all my strength for the cages, but he's caught me at the right time, and he's the perfect person to take my frustrations out on.

He turns his head to the left, just as I'm stepping into the ring.

"Well, if it isn't Mr. Itty Bitty. What the fuck you doing here?" he mocks.

"Same as you, Jesse. Looking to spar. Want to take the little prey shifter on?" I bait him, knowing he wouldn't turn it down.

"Your fucking funeral. Let's go."

Well, this will lift my spirits some. Time to show this fucker what a prey animal can do.

He doesn't see my fist coming until it hits him square in the face. Fuck yeah! There's no one to stop me from beating the ever-loving shit out of him.

Blaine

What the fuck is wrong with my friends?

What part of '*she is my mate*' are they not understanding? What am I going to do? It's normal for wolves and other supes to have more than one mate. I know that, but I'm not ready to share her. Not yet anyway. I just found her. I haven't even had a chance to apologize for how strong I came on, kiss her properly, or introduce her to my wolf.

Zeke, at least, was willing to back off. I wish he was more accepting of himself. I don't think Magnolia would have an issue with him being a prey animal. She might have an issue though when she finds out about their rendezvous in the woods. Jude, on the other hand, is being a fucking douche. Not wanting to back off at all and announcing that not only is he going to try his luck with my girl, but her roommate as well. How can he have an attraction for my mate like he claims, but wants to get with her friend too? Not to mention, she's her roommate. How is that going to end well for anyone?

Sharing her with my two best friends would be ideal. We've been together since we were kids and work well together. I mean, we live together by choice. How much closer can you get than that? There couldn't be a better set of men to share a mate with. Her sharing with another female, though, would be unheard of. Yes, females mate together, but females are usually very protective of their mates, so I'm not seeing Magnolia being okay with Jude being with her roommate, too.

My wolf isn't on board with any of it, which is odd. *Why don't you want to share Magnolia?* I'm met with a deep growl and *MINE!* I need to sort this out. *Lots of wolves share mates, so why not us?* He snaps his teeth together as he growls out more forcefully, *MINE!* None of this makes sense, but I'll put that on the back burner for now.

I'm pissed the fuck off as I storm down the hall toward the library, needing to clear my mind. The library is the perfect place. No one else should be there yet since school is just starting, and it's quiet, no matter if it's full of people.

Finding out everything I can about this Exodus Pack is the number one thing on my to-do list right now. I doubt Magnolia is going to be very forthcoming with information, especially to me. So, the library will distance me from my friends, and I can do research. I want to know more about this designation suppression. Why would they not want their wolves to know what they are before nineteen? It makes absolutely no sense, and why does Magnolia think mating bonds are a thing of the past? Why couldn't she sense that Z was a shifter in the woods? To top it all off, why did she act like she didn't recognize me as her mate?

I head to the back of the library to begin my search. Rounding the corner of the shelf dedicated to wolf shifters, I run head-on into someone else. Knocking this poor soul down, I freeze and compose myself before seeing who the hell else is in here with me.

Wylla.

Reaching down, I grab her hand and help her up, and as she straightens out her clothes, I pick up the books she was carrying. Electricity passes through me at her touch. She pulls her hand back in shock. Did she feel it too? What the hell was it, even? Something else to add to my to-do list, but Magnolia is more important right now. Handing her an ancient but large brown book, she is quick to snatch it from me and clutch it to her chest.

"YOU!" she says accusingly while giving me a death glare.

"Me?" I answer her in confusion. Not sure why she's still acting pissed. I was under the impression we had worked out our shit last night, mostly. I need to talk to Magnolia.

"You need to come with me. You need to hear what I found, too. I'd rather only say it once, so come along, puppy; let's go!" She grabs my hand and drags me behind her, the slight tingle of electricity still there.

Following behind Wylla, I can't help but stare at her ass as she makes her way to their dorm. *I hope that's where she's leading me. Why am I staring at her ass when I'm mated? Why is my wolf not protesting?* She could be leading me to my death or torture for all I know. My wolf isn't raising any alarms, though, so she must be safe. Looking inside myself just to double-check, I see my wolf curled up in a corner, snoozing. *Interesting.*

Noticing we are indeed headed to our dorm, I shake off all the curious thoughts running rampant inside me. Wylla enters the building and shoves me into the elevator before hitting the button for the third floor. We make the short ride and the doors slide open.

Once again, I'm shoved out and grabbed. *Why the hell am I getting turned on by her manhandling me? Fuck, I'm so confused.* She leads me down the hall to a door I don't recognize. I don't know many in this dorm, so this must be her room. *I hope Magnolia is in there.*

She digs a key out of her pocket and unlocks the door, blindly shoving me inside before her. *My goddess, is she worried I'll run off on her?* I stumble into the room, and I'm snapped from my thoughts when I hear a sharp intake of breath.

Sweet mother of the goddess! My mate is standing in front of me with not an ounce of clothing on. I rake my eyes up and down her body before she quickly throws an arm over her tits and a hand down to cover her pussy. *Well, fuck me, my girl has a blonde little landing strip.*

My mouth waters at the sight of her, and I want nothing more than to run my tongue over every inch of her delectable body. To lay her down on the bed and feast on her pussy like it's my last meal.

"What the fuck, Wylla!" she snaps out, still covering her bits.

Wylla whips around, completely unaware of the situation she has put us all in. Her eyes are blown wide, and she's staring at Magnolia like she also would like a taste. *Fuck me, not the witchy roommate, too!*

Magnolia grabs a shirt off her bed and quickly throws it on, covering herself. Her hands are on her hips, and her face is tinged pink, but she's still looking pissed.

"What are you doing with him, Wylla?" she demands.

"I ran into him. Literally. I found a solution to what we talked about before the mixer," Wylla announces and crosses the room without a care in the world and sits on the bed Magnolia just grabbed the shirt off.

"You look good in my clothes, Magz, baby," Wylla purrs.

I'm growling before I can even stop myself.

Wylla

I was up all night talking back and forth with my grandmother and researching. After being pushed away and Magz running out of here like *Ghostface* was chasing her, I had to get out of the room. Not being able to handle her rejection, I went to the library.

I wish the strong-willed, sassy Magz I've met would stay around. It seems every time she does something for herself, she goes back to the docile girl her daddy sent here. I'm wondering if she'll even get the damn tattoo at this point or if I have the whole thing set up for nothing.

Why doesn't she see her worth? Why doesn't she push back on her dad and her pack like she has with Blaine and now me? Goddess, I hope that what I found tonight helps push her to be the badass bitch I know she can be.

She doesn't even need to go back to her pack if she doesn't want to. I could keep her safe. She just needs to tell me what's going on in her pretty little head. Not to mention, something tells me there are three guys upstairs who would be at her side as well.

Shoving Blaine into the room after running into him in the library, I hear a gasp and groan. I whirl around and see the tastiest little morsel naked in front of me. Magz is glaring at me, covering her tits and bits with her hands.

"What the fuck, Wylla!" she hollers, her face turning red in embarrassment. Or is it anger? I'm not sure, and honestly, I don't care as long as she keeps standing there looking like a perfect morning snack. One that I desperately want a taste of.

Hurrying to turn back around, we get a good view of her round plump ass before she grabs a shirt off her bed and puts it on, snarling as she stands with her hands on her hips. She looks as mad as a hatter.

She seems pissed that I'm with Blaine. Not wanting to upset her, I let her know I literally ran into him at the library and brought him here because I think I found what I was looking for to help her. With him being her mate, it's important he knows as well.

She relaxes, and I stride across the room, sitting on the bed in front of her.

"You look good in my clothes, Magz, baby," I purr at her. The wolf growls and stares daggers at me. I give him a shrug. There's no way I'm wasting any chance with this woman. He can just get on board with it or be a pissy little puppy.

"Down, Fido. We have shit to discuss, and I need you to be calm and not all growly. Do we need a shock collar or a rolled newspaper, so we learn to share?" I tease him.

He rolls his eyes at me but stops growling as he falls down into the chair at the desk. Twirling the chair to face us, he crosses his arms and stares at us, a pissed-off scowl on his face.

"I think I found a solution to your problem, but after talking to my grandmother, it's not a one-step fix. According to her, I need to perform a scanning ritual first. It—"

"What?" they both say in raised voices, simultaneously interrupting me, then look at each other, blushing. *Goddess above, this is awkward even for me.*

"It's a simple ritual; the hardest part will be sneaking into the locker room in the sports complex, so we can use their tub."

"Done," Blaine grinds out.

I look at him, but he just gives me a shrug, so I continue, "Then I'll just need some salt and herbs, two black candle sticks, and holders. The rest is just some focus and fancy words. Easy, I told you."

"What exactly will this spell do to my ma—I mean Magnolia?" Blaine demands.

I roll my eyes at his guard dog behavior. "Nothing. It will simply reveal to us if any other spells are in place besides the designation suppression. The spell can only be done once all other spells are removed. So the scanning ritual is a must just for safety."

"Do it!" Magnolia bursts.

"Magnolia, we need to discuss this. I don't want to go in blind on something like this. We don't need to rush," Wolf boy pleads.

"This is my choice. I am sick and tired of males telling me what to do. I would like to take my life back. So Wylla, let's get what you need and go."

Blaine goes ahead of us, rounding the corner of the sports complex, making sure the coast is clear. Looking back, he waves his hand at us, motioning us forward. *Guess the coast is clear.* He never told us how he knew how to get into the locker rooms.

All three of us hurry to the door where Blaine knocks three times fast, then knocks twice again, this time spreading the knocks farther apart. We're looking at him like he's batshit crazy when a guy shows up in the window next to the door. He looks out, noting it is us, then we hear the lock click.

Stepping back, the guy opens it and lets us in. In what can only be described as a bro hug, Blaine claps him on his back.

"Blaine, man, you owe me big for this." He cocks a brow at Blaine as he finishes.

"Thanks, Brick. We owe you. You should come over this weekend. I'll get some drinks, and we'll order in." Blaine looks at Brick for his response. I can't help but notice as he keeps skirting his eyes over to Magz and me. He's cute, but he needs to back the hell up. She already has three dicks and a pussy to keep her busy. She doesn't need him. Plus, he has a weird smell, one that turns my stomach.

Brick fits him. This dude is built like a brick shit house. He's every bit six feet tall, which is shorter than Blaine and the guys. However, Brick is thick with muscle and mass. Light brown hair, piercing gray eyes, and he has a beautiful black bear tattoo covering his shoulder and biceps.

Catching me staring, my nose turns up in distaste, Blaine chuckles and I quirk an eyebrow at him.

"Brick is on the Rugby team. He's a year ahead of us, but we're old friends. His cousins live on pack lands, and he's visited often. His parents actually requested to move to our lands, and I think the board is ready to finalize their acceptance. But you didn't hear that from me." Blaine looks at Brick and winks.

"Nice to meet you. I'm not trying to be rude, but can we go?" Magz whispers softly. I wonder if she wants to get away from the bear as much as I do.

Blaine reaches out, taking one of mine and Magz's hands in each of his as he leads us down the hallway. Whispering softly, he tells us, "The athletic director's office is where the tub is, and it's right down here. We need to be quiet though, just in case someone is around."

Stepping into the director's office, we see the lights are out and it appears to be empty. We shut the door behind us once we're inside, making sure to lock the door. We make our way over to the tub and I pull a table over to it. Looking over my shoulder, I see the bear following us. "What the hell are you doing?"

"I'm responsible if anything happens here. So whether you like it or not, you're stuck with me. Plus, you might need my help," he announces boldly.

Shaking it off, not even wanting to deal with it, I continue what I'm doing before turning to Magz to let her know what she needs to do.

"Magz, go ahead and get undressed, then turn the water on, and let it run over your hands," I tell her as I begin laying out everything I brought in my bag on the table.

She removes her shirt, exposing the forest green bikini she put on before we left our room. Sitting down in the tub, she runs her hands under the water as directed.

"Okay, focus all your attention on your negative thoughts and feelings. Let the water wash them off and down the drain," I tell her as I light a candle and set it on the floor next to the tub.

"Now imagine the flame of my candle and use it to guide your inner thoughts toward your goal for this ritual." I reach into the tub, plug the drain, and allow the tub to fill up.

Turning the faucet off, I hover over the water, willing it to wash away any unwanted spells, curses, or enchantments. "*Skan pro malem entya eelare eorim secreta,"* I chant as I pour the salt and herbs into the bath, mixing them in the water.

We continue in this manner; me chanting the ritual words over and over and Magz just soaking in the tub, quietly focusing. Blaine and Brick are somewhere in the room watching. Brick refused to leave us, saying he was responsible if anything happens here.

Once the candle has burned out, I chant loudly, "*Metum et ostenday nobus!"* The ritual is now completed. I look at Magz and she is staring at me curiously before she lets out a scream and her body contorts; her back arching. She looks like she is the main character in an exorcism. Reaching out to her, I'm caught off guard as intense pain rakes down my body. I scream and can hear Blaine behind me doing the same.

Then the world goes black.

Magnolia

"Wake up. Come on, Magnolia. Wake up, baby." I hear through a haze. What the fuck happened? My arms feel like lead when I try to move them. What the fuck kind of spell did she cast? Because that's the last thing I remember other than bone-wrenching pain.

Strong arms embrace me and help me to sit up. Inhaling deeply, I smell the most delicious cedarwood scent. *Blaine.* But there's another scent assaulting my senses. *Mango?*

My eyes finally come into focus as I scan the room. True to what I thought, Blaine is holding me, and being in his arms feels like home. Confusion fills me with why I feel so comfortable in his arms as if I were meant to be in them. Could my wolf and him be right when they say he's my mate? I don't know...maybe.

Wylla is looking intently at me, concern etched on her face as Brick helps support her standing body. My wolf immediately begins to growl, not liking the sight of it, but unsure of why it bothers her. Hell, it's even bothering me.

She breaks free from his grasp and rushes over to me, dropping down to the floor with me and Blaine. "Fuck, Magz, I didn't know that was gonna fucking happen. Are you okay?"

"Fuck, the way her back arched back like that, it looked like a fucking exorcist. Hell, she even looked like those kids from that horror movie *Mama.*" Disbelief and shock coat Brick's features as he talks. "Then the three of you screamed and knocked the fuck out, dropped to the floor with a splat."

"Shut the fuck up, Brick," Blaine shouts at him as he and Wylla help me to stand.

"Fuck you, Blaine. I let you do your asinine spell here, and I get freaking psycho shit instead. Look, the three of you need to get out of here. Ain't no way no one else felt that power surge, and I don't want to be here when they track it." Nervously twitching as he speaks, Brick's eyes flick between us and the door.

"C-c-can we just go back to the room, please, Wylla?" I beg her, my body weak, knowing I'm going to need help.

"Can I come with you guys? What were y'all trying to do with that spell?" Brick bounces around like a kid in the candy store, eager to get the new flavor.

"No, and shut the fuck up. Speak about this to anyone and I'll kick your fucking ass," comes from Blaine in a voice so forceful and commanding I want to drop before him and worship his body. *What the hell is going on with me?*

"Let's go," Wylla whispers as she begins to lead me toward the door. My steps falter as we go, feeling like rubber underneath me.

"I got you." With his words, Blaine takes me from Wylla and swoops me up in his arms, cradling me close to his chest. The beating of his heart soothes me as it beats a melodious rhythm. Snuggling deeper into his embrace, I allow the music of his heart and the swaying of my body in his arms to lull me.

I feel content in his arms. But there's an urgency in me that needs to know if the spell worked and what Wylla senses now.

They talk back and forth in hushed tones, words I should've been able to hear, but I can't. All I can think of is cedarwood and mango.

We are moving, but time seems to stand still until suddenly Blaine comes to a halting stop, which has me lifting my head. *The dorms.* Wylla opens the door, allowing Blaine to move past her and enter with me in his arms.

"Where are you going?" I hear her ask when he turns to the left, in the opposite direction of the elevators.

"Stairs. I don't want to run into anyone."

"Ohh," is all she replies, soft and short.

We move up the stairs in complete silence, no one uttering a word, the only thing you can hear is our breathing and beating hearts. Once we get to the third floor, Wylla holds open the door for us, and once again, Blaine steps through it into the hallway, not stopping until he reaches our room. I almost forget for a moment how he knows it is ours until I remember he walked in on me in the nude earlier.

Wylla opens the door, and we step inside.

"Set me on the bed, please." His large strides have us across the room in no time, and he sits down with me still in his arms. "Not quite what I meant. Please, let me down. I need to think, and I have some questions."

Wylla takes a seat on her bed as Blaine places me on my bed beside him, but doesn't move away.

"Magz, I am so..." Throwing my hand up, I cut her off.

"I know, Wylla. Can you do that scan thing again and tell me what you see now?" I ask, holding onto the bed and feeling as if I've been on an all-nighter drinking binge. Well, what I think one would feel like after doing it anyways. *Bucket list: get drunk and find out what a hangover is like.*

She stands, moves over to the bed, and begins to rapidly chant words so quickly that I can't understand them. Her eyes go white as she speaks, which is something I really need to ask her about because it happened last time as well.

Her eyes come back to the beautiful shade of deep green that has quickly become my favorite, Wylla's face is drawn, and her eyes are wide with worry.

"What is it, Wylla? What did you see?"

"Umm, the designation block is still there. That means we can do the spell to remove it and find out what you are. It's strong, so I need to research to make sure we do it right. But umm..." She stutters the last part as if she is afraid to say it.

"Well, there's a couple of other blocks as well. One I can't tell what it's trying to block out, it's weird. I'm not getting a clear read on it. But the other thing I see is a mate bond block."

"We already know who the mate bond goes to, and that's me. We are mates. So now you see it's true. We should be able to easily remove it." The pride in Blaine's words makes it seem like it's more important for him to be proven right than the fact that he is my mate.

"No, it's not that simple. The mating block is powerful, really powerful." There's a hint of awe in her voice mixed with bewilderment. "The spell isn't hiding one mate bond. It's hiding five or six, at least." *Five or six mates?*

"What the fuck did you just say?" Flies from my mouth as I stand quickly, causing my balance to falter and fall into Blaine. "You're saying I have multiple mates, not just one?" *Holy fucking guacamole!*

"Yes, the power on the block is far greater than what would be needed for just one. I can't see who the bonds lead to. It's hazy and just out of my sight. So sorry, Blaine." She directs her gaze to him as she speaks. "I can't tell if she is indeed bonded to you."

"I don't need you to confirm shit for me. I feel the bond pull and so does my wolf. Magnolia is our mate," he growls out.

"So if it's multiple, then I could be mated to the Alpha's son and his Beta's, and everything is going as planned by my pack. I am supposed to be with them. So even if it's true and we're bonded, it really doesn't matter. My father won't allow it, my pack will make me bond to who they want no matter if there is a bond or not, and it won't be with anyone outside of our pack."

"No!!!" Both Wylla and Blaine shout out in unison.

"Over my fucking dead body are you bonding with anyone else. I'll kill them first. You belong to me and my wolf," he snarls viciously.

"I am not a piece of meat. I'm no one's prize to covet. I may feel a pull to you, and my wolf may claim you're her mate but I don't know for a fact that you are my bond. I won't know until this block is removed." Stepping in front of him, I stick my finger out and poke him in his chest. Fucking men thinking because they have a penis, they can fucking control you. Blaine's little outburst proves it isn't exclusive to the Exodus pack.

Wylla must sense my rage as she steps in between the two of us, pushing Blaine away. Oddly, he doesn't respond aggressively to her, instead, he allows her to back him up to the door.

"Blaine, I think it's time for you to get out of here and cool off. Go run or lick your balls, whatever it is you wolves do. Let me and Magz talk, and we'll see you tomorrow, so we can try to figure this shit out." He looks between the two of us as she speaks, opening and closing his mouth over and over until finally, he relents.

"First thing in the morning, I'll be back. But Magnolia, I am your mate. And I will fight to the death for you." He turns quickly, opens the door, and steps out into the hallway, allowing it to slam shut behind him.

I drop down on the bed, picking my feet up and placing them on the comforter as I slide my body back to the headboard. Wylla moves over and crawls up beside me. Her body is flush with mine as she reaches her arm around me, placing it on my shoulder. God, why does my body tingle with just her touch?

"Wylla, you don't understand. My life was planned for me. I have no control over it. I either do what my father and the Alpha want, or I risk being exiled. Hell, who knows, they may even kill me if I go against their plans. So maybe what you're seeing with the bonds are them, and when I go home I'll see them and feel it." Tears slowly stream from my eyes, hoping like hell I'm not mated to them.

"It's going to be okay." Her words comfort me as she pulls me closer to her.

"How do you know?" I know I sound like a spoiled bitch at the moment, but I don't want lies, I want the truth. Because if I'm forced to mate, it's not going to be okay. I will live the same miserable life as my mother behind a false facade.

"We will do everything we can. I will do whatever it takes. First, we will find out what you are and who the bonds are to. If they are to the wolves from your pack, I'll contact every elder in my coven to see what we need to do to break the bond. Fuck it, if they exile you, then you can come with me." God, I love this woman, but she doesn't understand. Without a pack, I'll go rogue; I'll be a wild, feral animal. If I was to even think of joining another pack, mine would declare full out war on them, and that's not something I could ever live with.

"Wylla, do you know what happens to wolves who aren't part of a pack?"

"Honestly, no," is all she says, turning her head to gaze into my eyes. I could get lost in her deep, emerald eyes. I have no clue why I'm drawn to her. Prior to the spell, I had a pull, but now, it's even more intense.

Could I be mated to her, too?

No, that's fucking insane. Wolves only mate with wolves. In all the books I've read, there's never been one story of a mate bond between different species. "We go mad if we aren't in a pack. We lose our ability to think logically until we finally shift and our wolf takes over, becoming feral. Once that happens, we can never shift back."

Tears stream down her face as she pulls her arm from around me and shifts her body. "Look here, Magnolia Holloway, that will never happen to you. We'll find you another pack to be with. Just please don't give up yet, let me find a solution. There has to be one, you are not giving up your will or who you are, to be one of the mindless women of your pack, no offense to your mother."

Laughter erupts from me at her words, and it only increases with the confused look Wylla tosses me. "Funny you should say that. My mother left me a letter without my dad knowing, hoping I never came back. She wants more for me than to be trapped in our pack."

"Well, I take back what I said, she's not so mindless. Maybe we can find a way to get her out, too."

I jump at her, wrapping her up in my arms. Hope radiates through my body that we could potentially save not only me but my mother from the hell we were born into. "Do you think you really can?" I ask when I pull back from her.

"I'm not promising anything, but I can try. I will do my best." She holds her hand out in front of her, sticking out her pinky. "Pinky promise."

Doing the same, I interlock my finger with hers. "Pinky promise."

"Come on, lay down beside me, and let's get some rest. Something tells me a wolf is going to be beating down our door in the morning," she tells me, standing up and pulling the comforter back, climbing underneath it. Following her lead, I do the same and curl up to her body.

She reaches across, allowing the tips of her fingers to trail up and down the exposed skin of my arm as she places a soft kiss on the side of my forehead. Warmth pools in my stomach at her touch, it's familiar and wanted. Turning my head to face her, I lean in and kiss her lips. She eagerly returns it as she lets her tongue dart along the seam of my lips. Without thinking, I part them, allowing her entrance.

Reaching out, I wrap my arm around her and slip my leg between hers, grinding my pussy against them, causing me to moan softly. She reaches her arm around me, cupping my ass in her hand, squeezing it as she aids in grinding my heat against her.

"Magz, are you sure? I don't want to scare you again. You're everything I could want, and I can't fight this intense feeling I have for you. We can do this and just sleep in each other's arms."

"I'm so confused with my feelings and everything. There's a pull to you, I can't deny and don't want to fight, but can we take it slow? Can we just hold each other and sleep?" There's so much more I want, but I need to take it slow. What if these mates she says I have wouldn't approve of this? What happens if my feelings grow, and I have to give her up?

"Stop worrying, we'll figure it out together. I can hear your mind running a hundred miles a minute. Sleep. These are questions for tomorrow, not tonight."

And that's what I do. I sink into her arms, horny as hell from not getting an orgasm, and dream of mates I can't see clearly.

Jude

"We've got to talk some fucking sense into Blaine. He can't seriously think he can be the only mate Magnolia can have, right? I mean, none of us have ever felt the pull to anyone before like we do for Magnolia. He expects us to just back off? To let her go without a fight? No way! No fucking way! You might, Zeke, but I'm not. I have to see what's there. Ya know?" I'm rambling in a chaotic rage to Zeke as we sit on our beds. Zeke's working on something in a notebook, but I'm just sitting on my bed, throwing a ball in the air and catching it repeatedly. I'm so fucking irritated with my best friend right now. All I want to do is wring his damn neck until he sees reason.

"Zeke! Are you even listening to me? Fuck, man, pay attention!" I scold him as I chuck my ball at his head, missing it entirely, and it smacks the wall behind him.

He looks up from the notebook he's working in and sighs, "Dammit, Jude, I'm listening, but what do you want me to do? I don't want to lose Blaine as our brother over this girl. I've never felt this way about anyone, and she's already going to fucking flip her shit when she finds out I'm the ferret in the woods. Her scent was so intoxicating that I couldn't stop myself."

I'm about to tell him to just come clean to her about the woods and who he is, but our door flies open, smashing into the wall behind it. Blaine storms into the room, looking like hell, might I add. Flinging open the closet door, he grabs some sweats he discarded there earlier and changes quickly. Storming across the room, he throws himself face-first down onto his bed, groaning about bitch witches, spells, bathtubs, and Brick. *How the fuck does Brick fit into this shit?*

Getting up, I move to shut the door and see that there's a doorknob size hole in the drywall from his antics. *Oh, for fucks sake, who is gonna pay for that to be fixed?* I move toward my bed and sit back down and stare at Zeke, who is glaring at Blaine, who's now just laying there, growling with his face buried in his comforter. *What the fuck is going on?*

"What the fuck's your problem, Blaine? And you're paying for that fucking drywall you just damaged, you asshole," I rage at him. He rolls over and sits up, leaning against the wall his bed is pushed up against. He rubs his hands over his face and sighs loudly before he looks at me, then at Zeke.

"Tonight, I went with Magnolia and Wylla to the sports complex to do a ritual that Wylla found to help Magnolia," he tells us. Zeke and I are off our beds and on our feet, yelling at him and demanding he start from the beginning. He motions for us to sit back down, and begrudgingly, we obey.

"Earlier today, after I left the cafeteria, I ran into Wylla in the library. She was doing some research for Magnolia. Anyway, I followed her back to their dorm room, and she said she can do a scanning ritual on Magnolia that would show her any spells or other shit she has on her. I tried to convince them to wait, but Magnolia went all alpha female on me and said she was doing it. So we went to the sports complex, and Brick let us in. Then Magnolia got in the tub there, and Wylla did the ritual, and we all started hollering in pain, then the world went black. Wylla and I came to first, while Magnolia was still out cold. She woke up, and then we carried her back to their room."

Zeke and I are looking at him like he has two heads. This is batshit crazy. What the hell were those girls thinking? "What happened when you returned to the room? But first, why the hell was Brick with you?" I question him, and Zeke nods in agreement.

"Well, Brick, as I said, let us in the complex. Then the big bastard insisted he come with us to do the ritual, so we wouldn't get caught and he would get in trouble. So when we woke up, he was there just frozen, mouth gaping like a guppy. He led us out of the complex, and we told him to keep his lips shut on what he saw."

"So nothing happened to him, but did to you, Wylla, and Magnolia?" Zeke asks, curiously

"No, nothing happened to the fucker. No gut-wrenching pain, or blacking out. He was awake the whole time. But enough about him. When we got back to the room, Magnolia asked Wylla if she could see anything now that the scan was complete. Wylla said she could see the block on the designation still in place, but she was going to talk to her

Grandmother to see about getting it removed. Then she said she could see mate bonds, but they were faded and from what she can see, it's likely Magnolia will have five or six mates, possibly more."

"Holy shit!" Zeke and I whisper-shout.

"Yeah, so then I was pretty much kicked out of the room and told we would reconvene on this matter later. You guys, that shit was crazy. I've never experienced pain like that before. FUCK! Her body was arched like it was an exorcism, and she was screaming in pain. It was terrible," he tells us softly.

"I almost forgot that Magnolia still denies our bond. Actually, that's not true. She said we could be mated, but that the other bonds could be the Exodus pack Alpha heir and his Betas that her Father said she's mating."

Snarling is heard from around the room and it's coming from all of us. I look at Zeke, and he looks shocked that he's snarling over this woman. "We can't let her mate with those awful men. No way in fucking hell," I tell them through clenched teeth.

"I don't know what to do. This woman is infuriating. She's strong, but then you mention her fucking father, and she does what he says. Does she not know that if she was mated to me, she would be part of the Stonehaven Pack? She wouldn't be feral or packless. But she's still so sure she has to do as her pack says. It's fucking infuriating," Blaine fusses.

"Well, it seems as if our girl is a hot commodity. We have to lock her down first, so she can't mate with those bastards," I demand. Blaine is across the room and on my bed straddling me, giving me a good hard hit to the nose. I instantly feel the blood leak from my nose and the crunch I heard had to be him breaking the bone.

"Goddammit, Blaine!" Zeke exclaims as he comes and pulls Blaine off of me.

I'm holding my nose to avoid soaking my sheets in blood. Once he's totally pulled off of me, I shift into my demon form. I can feel my two horns push through my skull and my tail pop out and wrap itself around Zeke's leg. Last, my wings spring from my back and nearly knock my two friends over as they take up much of the space in this room. I look over at Blaine and Zeke; Zeke's chuckling and Blaine just rolls his eyes. "Okay, you've made your point. Now shift back, asshole," he grumbles.

Quickly shifting back, I resume my human form. "Sorry, but someone decided to be a dick and break my nose. I wanted it to heal quickly and properly," I argue. We're all back to sitting on our own beds in awkward silence. No one is willing to break the tension in the room while we stare at one another.

"We need to talk about what she's doing to us. Might I add unknowingly at that," Zeke, of all people, declares. When neither Blaine nor I add anything, he continues, "Look, we all obviously have a pull toward her, and you are sure she's your mate, Blaine. So what do we do? Also, Jude, I thought you liked the witchy roommate?"

Blaine shoots me a look that's giving me 'yeah, what about her?' vibes. "Umm, I'm an Incubus. We often have more than one mate or partner to satisfy our energy needs. Maybe Magnolia will let me play with Wylla while she watches or we could get back to the Jude sandwich idea I had." Ignoring the growling my best friend is raging with, I babble on. "I don't know what the deal is with the wolf, okay? I have this extreme pull to her, and I have a slighter one to the roommate. I just don't get it. I've never felt a connection with someone before. So maybe it's a mate thing with Magnolia and just an attraction to Wylla? But I can't just let it be. I want to pursue it and see what's up."

"Listen, what if we just let things play out? Blaine, you said yourself, you're her mate, and that she has five to six other mates. What if they are Jude and me? Wouldn't it be easier and better to share your mate with your best friends than strangers? Especially if she's part of this Exodus pack. I mean, we all want her and are protective of her. No matter what, she's your mate for sure, so we would die to protect her, but wouldn't it be better if she was our mate, too?" Zeke asks. What he says is making sense, and I'm open to it. Sexuality and sharing aren't new to me. I'm a fucking lust demon, so I feed on sexual energy. But it would be fucking amazing to share my partner with my friends.

We're both looking expectantly at Blaine, who appears to be deep in thought. "Fine," he grits out. "But I want it to be natural, and that goes for me, too. I want her to want us and to fall for us, and not be pushy or force her into anything. She's had enough of that already. I'll try to calm my wolf, but he's been very snappy lately. I'm hoping once Magnolia accepts us as her mates, he'll relax. Wolves also share mates, so I'm thinking he's just bristly since we haven't been accepted one hundred percent," he admits.

"Okay, so we're going to share her if we're all her mates, and even if it's just you that's her mate, I'm good with that. I think we should back off and just be helpful to her. Let her find her footing at the school first. See who she wants to be and 'can' be outside of that cult of a pack she comes from," I plead. Blaine and Zeke are looking at me like I've lost my marbles or have shit on my face. "What?" I demand.

"Nothing, man, that's just, uhm– very unlike you to be serious and not a jokester or incubus–y. HA! Is that a word? If not, it's definitely what you are." Blaine cracks up at his description of me.

"Laugh it up, assholes. Something about the gray-haired wolf has caught my attention. I just want her to be here, and I don't like what I've heard about this pack." I bristle, shooting daggers at both of them.

"Now that we are all on the same page and not trying to murder one another, let's go to sleep. You have to see them tomorrow to finish talking about what happened tonight, and I know we want to be there, too. Classes start tomorrow, and I have a feeling it's going to be very interesting with Magnolia and Wylla around," Zeke says as he stretches out on his bed and slides under the covers. Blaine and I agree, and we slide into our beds. Zeke claps twice for the lights to turn off.

Fucking ferret...

Magnolia

Waking up, I try to stretch my arms above my head, but I can only lift my right arm, my left is weighed down. Looking over, I see Wylla, her arm draped across my stomach just mere inches from my breasts as her head rests on my arm. We stayed up into the wee hours of the morning just talking, getting to know each other better, anything to put the events that transpired out of my mind. I could have six freaking mates. I don't even have that many places for them to stick their dicks in.

Fuck my life! It has to be the Alpha's son and his Betas, there's no other choice. Blaine has to be wrong, even if he's not, my pack will never allow it. He's an outsider.

I carefully try to pull myself out of her grasp, but as I do, her hand moves upwards and cups my breast, and she begins to knead it, rolling my nipple between her fingers. I can't hold back the gasping moan that comes from me.

I'm so caught up in how good it feels and why I'm not pulling away that I don't notice she lifted her head and is smiling at me. "It feels good, doesn't it?" she asks as she pushes up my shirt, exposing my bare breasts. She lowers her head and begins flicking her tongue across my pebbled nipple, before taking it into her mouth and sucking on it as she twists the other between her fingers.

I've done this to myself so many times I couldn't begin to count, but it's never felt like this before. I'm drawn to her so badly, the guys too, but I don't understand why. I crave them, I want them, my wolf wants to dominate them. But I can't. This can't happen.

My brain wants to protest, but when she slips her fingers underneath the waistband of my sleep shorts, sliding them through my wet folds, I can't push her away. "Fuck, Magz, you're so wet. So responsive," she tells me as she lets my tit pop out of her mouth.

"Wylla," I say breathlessly before I moan out again in pleasure. She starts rubbing circular motions on my clit as she alternates between sucking and nibbling on my nipple.

"Yes, baby. I want you to come for me, all over my fingers. Your pleasure is all I want right now, the rest we'll figure out later. So just get out of your head and enjoy what I can do for you."

My legs part for her as I begin to roll my hips, increasing the speed as she's rubbing my clit. Her hand slides lower to my folds and her slender fingers slide into my tight hole as she pumps in and out of me. She curls the tips when she pulls out, hitting my g-spot as her thumb applies pressure to my clit.

I'm so close I clamp my legs together, eliciting a chuckle from her and spurring her to pump in and out of me faster until I erupt all over her hands in an orgasm unlike I've ever felt before.

My body is still shaking from the aftershocks as she pulls her fingers out of me and sits up, smiling almost lovingly. Then it hits me what we just did and how badly I've broken the pack rules. She must notice the change in my facial expressions as she slowly stands, hurt in her eyes before confidence and desire replace it.

"Whatever you're thinking - - stop, Magnolia Holloway. There was absolutely nothing wrong with what just happened between us. Your pack is full of bigots and freaking control freaks. They've brainwashed you into their way of thinking about what is right and wrong. You need to think for yourself now. I loved every minute of what we just did. I want you and I want to see what we could be together. I'm going to shower for class." She walks over to her dresser, grabbing her shower caddy.

Making her way to the door, she looks back over her shoulder one final time, taking the fingers that were just knuckle deep inside my pussy and sticking them in her mouth, sucking them as if they were a popsicle. "You taste delicious; cotton candy. My new favorite flavor." She opens the door and steps outside the room, before shutting it behind her.

I let my head fall back against the pillow, taking a minute to process what just happened before getting up myself and heading for the shower. Today is the first day of classes, and I still need to go see the counselor.

Forty minutes later, we're dressed and headed out the door to class. I have just enough time before my first class to stop by the counselor's office. Hopefully, it isn't too busy and I can get in and out, adding the introductory courses for my Psychology major. It's going to be a lot of studying, being a double major, but it's what I want.

"So you have Mr. Godrickson for Supernatural History? You lucky bitch! I heard he was fine as fuck. I have some old hag, at least her name sounds like it, Myrtle McVorken." Wylla croons, I swear I see fucking hearts in her eyes.

"Have you ever seen him?" Curious if the rumors she heard were true.

"No, but one of the girls from my coven had him, and she told me. She said when she graduated she tried to hook up with him, but he turned her down, something about saving himself for his mate or something to that effect. Hell, maybe he just wasn't into her," she says, shrugging her shoulders, before lifting her energy drink and taking a large gulp.

"Wylla, Magnolia!" We hear from behind us, and we stop dead in our tracks, turning in the direction the familiar voice came from. "I went by your room, but y'all were already gone, thought I wouldn't see you for a while. We were supposed to talk about what happened with the," Blaine lowers his voice with the last word as he gets closer to us, "ritual."

"Well, I have class in thirty minutes, and Magnolia needs to go by the counselor's office before her Supernatural History class at ten. We don't have time to sit around and wait for a boy." Then she catches sight of the two other boys standing behind him, "Excuse me, boys." Wylla gives them a wink and a silly schoolgirl giggle.

"We were just headed to the cafeteria for something to eat. We all start at the same time today with Supernatural History with Mr. Godrickson," Jude says in his intoxicating, sexy as sin voice.

"What time? I have him, too." Excited about having someone I know in my class.

"Ten, and I can go with you. I need to go by the counselor's office as well. I need to drop off an approved class change," the giant who I seem to keep running into, literally, offers to take me. "I'm Zeke, by the way," he tells me.

"I'd like that, Zeke. Wylla was going to rush to her class after showing me, but this would save her the trouble." I nervously chew my lip, hoping he's serious.

"Well then, I'll catch you later, Magz, and you too, boys." Wylla shoots me finger guns with a wink, before turning and dashing off in the direction I suspect her class is in.

I just laugh, there's nothing much more I can do. When I turn back to face the guys, I find them all staring at me. Like they see me and not just the shell of a body I'm in, which makes me nervous. "Well, I need to get to the counselor's office." Glancing at Zeke, "Ready?"

"Yeah, let's go. See you in class, guys." Zeke tosses his hand up in a pseudo-wave.

"We'll save the two of you a seat," Blaine calls out.

"Sure will. You can have the one beside me," Jude belts out, just before Blaine jumps on his back and they begin to wrestle, laughing the whole time. *Well, I think it was laughter.*

"Let's head over, so I can turn my paperwork in and you can do what you need to do," Zeke begins, gesturing his hand in the direction we need to go. "Umm... Magnolia, I really am sorry about how rude I may have come off the last couple of times. I just have a lot going on, and I ran into you during a time I was trying to process it all. I'm normally not that terrible of a person."

"You're fine. I haven't exactly been the best person to be around, either. Dealing with family, pack shit, and apparently a mate that's not going to make my dad happy," I mutter the last part of it under my breath, hoping he didn't hear it. For some reason, I didn't want it to get back to Blaine.

"Cool and sorry you're having pack issues. My family is actually a part of Blaine's father's pack."

"So you're a wolf shifter too?"

"Umm... no, I'm not. Oh, here we are," he says, reaching out, and pulling the door open for me. "I need to go to the third floor and drop this off. Meet you back here when you're done," he says as he takes off towards the elevator, leaving me curious as to what type of shifter or supernatural he is.

We walk into class at the stroke of ten, well, if there was a clock showing the time. The fucking counselor I got gave me the hardest time changing my schedule until her supervisor came over and took over, then it went smoothly. I was so close to saying fuck it and just sticking with what I had. Maybe it was destiny telling me I just needed to do what my father and Alpha had commanded me to do. But fate is a fickle bitch and someone intervened.

Looking around, I see Jude jumping up and down, waving us over. Could he be any cuter or more embarrassing? "Everything go okay?" he asks, gesturing towards the empty desk he's standing behind.

The classroom reminds me of a classroom in high school. Rows of seats, eight across and probably about ten deep. In the middle of the center rows is a projector pointing straight at the white screen that's been pulled down. I'm about to answer when I hear all the chatter in the classroom come to a screeching halt as the door slams shut.

Standing in front of the classroom is the most gorgeous man I've ever seen. I say man because he is definitely not a student. He looks to be about thirty, with long brown hair and a full beard. Dropping the bag that was over his shoulder on the desk, he turns to face us, "Good morning, class. I'm Mr. Godrickson." His voice is deep and rough, capturing me in its melodic tone.

He's unlike any professor I've ever seen before. Instead of a suit and tie, he's wearing black, skintight, leather pants, a black t-shirt, and, goddess help me, black Harley-Davidson boots. Picking up a stack of papers, he heads to the far side of the room and begins handing out a pile to the first person in the room and continues across the room. "Welcome to Supernatural History. If you are not supposed to be here, now is the time to leave. This class will be fast-paced with weekly assignments due, a midterm exam, and a final." He stops at the row I'm in, lifting his head up, his eyes meeting mine. At least it felt like his gaze lingered on mine, and if the growl I'm hearing is coming from Blaine, I think my assumption is right.

"This semester we will discuss the history of the supernatural world and supernatural species." Stepping back over to his desk, he picks up a controller from it, hitting a button that fires up the projector. On the screen is a picture of the gates out front with the gargoyles, and I'm instantly drawn in, so much so, I almost get a paper cut on the face when the girl in front of me hands the paper he just passed out back.

"Are gargoyles real?" I blurt out loud, causing the class to erupt in laughter.

"Quiet class," he booms out.

"Come on, Mr. Godrickson, I mean she's hot and all, but how stupid is she? They're long extinct," a burly blond sitting in the back calls out, as he garnishes high-fives from his posse.

"It seems both of you are in the dark. Yes, Miss?"

"Magnolia. Magnolia Holloway," I say nervously, now that I'm the center of attention for the class.

"Miss Holloway, gargoyles are real. And Mr. Draighton, I would have hoped you would've paid better attention the last time you took this course, but that's why you are here again. As Mr. Draighton pointed out, they were thought to be extinct, but are not," he begins to explain, and my jaw drops at his revelation.

"You're a gargoyle! I knew they were real," I blurt out excitedly before I throw my hand over my mouth to keep from spurting out anything else.

He lets out a muffled chuckle as his gaze stays focused on me, a small trickle of electricity beginning to flow across my skin. "Yes, I am. We are small in number, with tiny clusters of three to four grouped together across the world, often holding sentinel positions guarding over places of importance, like this college. We are the oldest of supernatural creatures, second only to dragons." He clicks the button through images of other pictures as he explains what they are. "We have numerous supernatural types. Even amongst shifters, you couldn't count the different breeds on two hands. We have the common types: wolf, bear, panther, lion, and tiger. But also the more unique prey shifters: mice, housecats, ferrets..."

His words are now just an audible sound in the background as I begin thinking about what he just said. *Ferret! Could it have been? Nah. I didn't even feel the sensation of another shifter being around like I do with wolves. If it was a shifter, why would he just watch me at that most intimate of moments? Ah fuck, he saw me tiddle my bean, my big O, and then I held him while he licked my fingers.*

"Are you okay?" Blaine leans into me to ask, concern laced in his voice.

"Umm... no... I just didn't know there were ferret shifters." Looking between the guys, I see Zeke has gone pale and looks nervous as fuck as his face turns red.

"Yeah, there are. Actually, I know a few of them." Blaine's words seem to hide a meaning behind them.

My thoughts are running wild with this new information and the need to know if it was a ferret shifter or a real ferret. I try to control them, pulling out a pen and paper from my bag, and taking notes.

Alpha Johnson

My receptionist's voice crackles through the speakerphone. "Alpha, there is a Mrs. Alderman on the line from Arcayne University requesting to urgently speak with you." If she wasn't easy on the eyes, she would have been gone by now, not to mention she sucks a mean dick and is discreet about it.

"Thank you. Send it through." I drop my pen on the desk as I prepare to hear what is so urgent, knowing it must have something to do with Magnolia Holloway. When the call clicks over, I immediately answer. "Alpha Johnson, how may I help you?" Kind words that make my stomach want to hurl, but it's a pretense I must keep up.

"Yes, Alpha, I'm Janice Ovelton, we met when you came here for the national pack meeting a year ago." Ahh, yes. I remember now, she was a fun roll in the sack.

"Yes, I remember. How can I help you?" I repeat, wanting to get this call over with.

"Oh, yes. I was calling about the female wolf from your pack. When she came into the office today, I saw you had handled scheduling all of her classes, so I thought you'd want to know, she changed her schedule."

"She did what?" comes out in anger, and I know by the shrill scream she's shaking in her boots, and I'm not even there. It's just how far-reaching my power truly is. People quiver in fear at the mere mention of the Exodus Pack.

"Yes, sir, she added Psychology as a secondary major and added a couple of introductory courses. I wasn't going to let her, but the head counselor came over when she started making a commotion and did it for her. I even got in trouble for refusing to let her. I knew this change would be something you'd want to know," her voice becomes more sultry as she speaks. I know an Alpha climber when I hear one, and right now, I already have a wife, one who is of this pack and knows her place. An Alpha climber is only looking for the power that the position of being my wife holds.

"Thank you, and please keep me updated with any other information you find out about her." I quickly hang up the phone, dialing the number of the next person I need to talk to.

It rings four times before he picks up the phone. "Alpha Johnson, how can I help you?"

"You can explain to me why your daughter is going against the plans we laid out. You can tell me why she's changing her schedule," I growl out angrily. There is no way this little slip of a girl is going to make a mockery out of me.

"I have no clue what you're talking about. She knew the rules to be able to attend school there. If she's broken them, I'll go there myself and drag her home." We're both quiet for a few moments. I believe him when he says he didn't have a clue. But it's not an excuse. He should have more control over his females. "When is she due to come home for a visit?"

"Two weeks, Alpha."

"You are to notify me as soon as she gets in town and then she's to come and meet me. I think it's time for me to have a private chat with your daughter, my son's future mate."

"Yes, sir, as you command." I hang up the line as I sit, seething in anger. This is what happens when you give a woman just a little bit of leeway, she thinks she can do whatever the fuck she wants. Magnolia Holloway is about to learn a lesson.

Zeke

Fuck! Fuck! Fuckity fuck! I'm dead. Deader than dead once she finds out what I am. That it was me in the woods. She's going to hate me. Any chance I had with her is gone for sure now. I can tell she's putting the pieces together now that this little bit of information has been made known to her. If only I had known she didn't have a clue about all the shifter types that day, I wouldn't be in this fucked up situation.

When she looks over at me, I can feel the color drain from my face, and even without seeing, I know I've gone ghostly white. I can't make out the whispers back and forth between her and Blaine, and immediately, I feel frantic that they're talking about me. He's spilling my secret to her before I even have a chance.

Slow down, Zeke. Just breathe. Your best friend wouldn't do that to you. You need to get yourself in check and calm down.

I have a plan. When class is over, I'm going to bolt from this room. Just get through classes today, then I'll go to her room, confess and pray she forgives me. I mean, it was a total misunderstanding.

The more she looks at me, the more jittery I become. Mr. Godrickson keeps going on, showing slide after slide as he talks about the different supernatural species. I just wish he would shut the hell up, so I can bolt. My prayers are answered fifteen minutes later when he announces class is over and the assigned reading for our next class. It's my chance. Standing quickly, almost knocking my chair over, I snatch my bag from the floor and the books off my desk and run.

"Where's the fire, man? Wait up, where the hell are you going?" Blaine yells out to me.

"Bathroom!" I call back to him, throwing my one free hand up in the air, brushing him off. I glance over my shoulder just long enough to see a look of hurt, or is it concern, on Magnolia's face. Blaine, well, he knew why I was running and was fighting hard to hold back the laughter.

I do stop by the bathroom, long enough to throw some cold water on my face. I need to get my shit together. But most of all, I need to think long and hard about how I'm going to explain this to Magnolia.

Heading to my next class, which of all things was freaking English. I mean, do we really need to take a mundane course like this? We're shifters, not humans, when will the proper tense in a sentence, pronouns, passive voice, or any of that shit be of any importance to us.

What was going to be the only bright spot of the class has now become nothing. For a week, I was excited when I found out that even though I had to take this course, Professor Carlson was teaching it. I met her at orientation and let's just say she had my dick hard the entire time, it may have been because she was a succubus, but still. She was tall, almost six feet, with curves in all the right places. Unlike most women who want a flat stomach, hers was soft with a little pooch. Her emerald green eyes and fiery red hair had me begging to have her looking up at me as she sucked my cock. That was pre-Magnolia, though. Professor Carlson doesn't hold a candle next to the beautiful white wolf that's torn my world apart.

I make my way to a seat in the back of the class and drop down into it, letting my bag hit the floor, then place the books in my hand on the desk. Looking up, I see Jude walking into the room. He looks over to Professor Carlson, and I wait for him to hit on her like he normally would any woman he saw that was drop-dead gorgeous. He looks, but only for a second, with no wink or flirty smile, before he heads to the empty seat beside me and sits down.

"What's up with you, man?" Jude's look tells me he wants to know why I ran the way I did.

"Dude, you heard, so don't act dumb. She knows about ferret shifters and is thinking back to the day in the woods. The better question is what's up with you? You walked right by the professor and nothing," I whisper to him, not wanting anyone to overhear.

"First, just talk to Magnolia. Explain everything, she may be mad at first, but then she'll understand and forgive you. Second, I already have the two women I want. That lady is nothing, hell, any other woman is nothing."

"Easy for you to say, man. You didn't do what I did and kept it a secret from her. I've run into her enough times that I could've told her if I wanted to. But I didn't. So I don't think she's just going to be 'aww, that's okay, I forgive you'. Add to that, I've been a fucking dick more than once to her."

"Class, I am Professor Carlson, and I will be your English professor this semester. Many of you are probably wondering why you need this course. Well, I'm here to tell you. English..." she continues on, but at this point, I've tuned her out and opened my notebook, writing down my different options of how I can tell Magnolia my side of things.

Class went on, and I prayed to hell Jude was at least taking some notes. The girl in front of me giggled as she turned in her chair to place the syllabus on my desk. That quickly changed to fear when she saw my death glare and abruptly turned back to the front.

"Ease up, man. Just grow some balls and talk to her," Jude leans over, whispering to me.

"Whatever, just take notes. I'll need to copy them later."

"Good luck then. I was counting on your ass to take notes. Guess we're both in deep shit." Jude says nothing new. I should've known his notes would be shit. It's one of the reasons he was excited he was in this class with me, so he could copy mine.

Focusing back on my notebook, I continue writing down quick notes and different ways I could explain this clusterfuck of a situation. This class can not end soon enough.

I opted to skip lunch with the guys, and instead, I grabbed something from the vending machine and headed out to the quad. I found a deserted spot under a tree to go over what I'd spent the day writing down. Rehearsing, as if I were talking to her and going through what her responses could potentially be. I want to be ready.

I lean my head back against the tree as I gaze up into the branches and see a squirrel scurrying across the branch, its mouth is swollen from the acorn it's holding. Why the fuck didn't I just tell her that day? I know why. It's because I thought she knew and was putting on a show. Just a tease, waiting to see what I would do. But the more I thought about it after it happened, I realized she didn't, especially when she cuddled me in her arms and spilled all her inner thoughts.

Looking at my wrist, I freeze when I see the time. Class starts in twenty minutes. Standing up, I slap the dirt and leaves from my pants. Reaching down, I stuff the book I had into my bag and pick it up from the ground.

Last class of the day, Introduction to Psychology, then I need to fess up to what I did.

It takes me ten minutes to walk across campus to the classroom. It's empty when I get there, meaning I get the pick of seats. I head to the back and take the last one in the row, which just so happens to be in a corner. Perfect.

I slide into my seat and place my bag on the floor before pulling out my notebook. None of the guys were in this class, so I need to stay focused. All attempts at that are lost the second she steps into the classroom, smiling when she looks around the room and her eyes land on me. She beelines straight to the empty desk beside me, dropping down into it, and breathing heavily as if she'd run all the way here.

"Missed you at lunch, Zeke. Blaine said something about you having to work out or practice something. At least, I think that's what he said when I asked about you. He was being kind of dodgy with answers though."

She asked about me. Shock and excitement overtake me. "Yeah, I needed to work on something, to make sure I know exactly what I'm going to do."

"Ohh, okay. Well, I missed you. I was worried about you after you ran out of Supernatural History class like that." Her voice is soft and tender, as she speaks, filling me with warmth. She cares.

"Yeah, I've got some stuff on my mind. Umm... Can I talk with you after class about something in private? Just you and me." I can't believe how nervous I am, asking that. I can't even imagine how it's going to be when I tell her the truth.

"Of course. Is everything okay?"

God, can this woman be any better? I just give her an 'I don't know' shoulder shrug, as the instructor for the class begins to lecture.

It was hard focusing with her beside me, her cotton candy scent swirling around me, driving me mad with desire. Her sneaking glimpses at me throughout the class didn't go unnoticed.

Looking at my watch, I see there are only a few minutes left of class. The instructor finishes up discussing the group project we would be working on over the semester.

Turning to Magnolia, I give her a forced smile, knowing the potential outcome after I spill the beans to her.

So engrossed in my thoughts, I miss the instructor ending class until I hear the clamor of the others in the class stirring as they go to leave. It's now or never.

"So you wanted to talk after class. I'm free now," her voice chipper as she speaks.

"Yeah, perfect. Let's grab something from the vending machine and then find somewhere to sit down where we won't be disturbed." I stuff my papers and notebook into my bag, placing the strap over my shoulder as I stand. Magnolia does the same. Reaching out, I take her bag from her and place it over my shoulder as well.

"Thank you. To the snack machine," she says with a jump, pointing her fingers toward the door.

We stop at the machine at the end of the hall, get a variety of snacks and some sodas, and head out to the door. We walk around aimlessly in quiet, neither saying a word before she finally breaks the silence.

"There's a bench over by that big oak tree over there, no ones there, how's that spot?"

Casting my gaze over to where she mentioned, I see it's indeed how she described it. "Perfect." Taking her hand in mine, basking in the feeling of happiness that spreads through my body, I lead her over to the bench.

She sits down, taking her hand and patting the spot beside her. "Come on, talk to me. What's wrong?"

Moving and taking the spot beside her, I take a deep breath and tell her my story.

"Okay, first though, promise to listen and not interrupt."

She raises her eyebrow, giving me a curious look. "Okkaayy," she drawls out.

"So, first, I want to apologize for acting like a dick to you more than once. When you hear my story, you'll understand even though it doesn't place me in a good light."

"Ze..." she starts to say, reaching out, I place my fingers over her lips, stopping her from finishing what she had to say.

"No, you promised. Are you going to be quiet and listen?" With my fingers still in place, she can't answer but nods her head yes.

"Okay, so. The time I ran into you by the bathroom wasn't the first time I saw you. I'd run into you before, except you didn't know it was me. I was in my shifted form, and I assumed you sensed I was a shifter, and when you did what you did, I thought you were putting on a show. It wasn't until after that I realized you didn't know, but it was too late. I was so drawn to you, and then when you cuddled me to you, I caught wind of the delicious scent of your arousal on your fingers, and I couldn't help it. I stayed in my shifted form and nibbled on them. I never thought I'd see you again."

She pulls back from me, as everything I said sinks in. "You're the fucking ferret from the woods?" she asks, her voice quivering like she wants me to say it wasn't. All I can do is nod my head confirming it was me.

"You fucking watched me finger myself and didn't say a word. Fucking christ! What the hell is wrong with you? Did you get a good show? Laugh about it with your buddies afterward when you knew who I was." I'm letting her yell everything at me, taking it all in. I don't know until her hand slams across my face that she's slapped me.

"It wasn't like that, Magnolia. I didn't know, I thought you wanted it. Forgive me, please," I plead with her, taking hold of her wrist trying to keep her from rushing away.

She places her hand on my chest, pushing me away from her, causing me to let go of her wrist, so she doesn't stumble.

"Fuck you and your friends. Tell them their time of making fun of the ignorant wolf is over. I never want to see any of you again. So stay the fuck away from me." She takes off, running as fast as she can away from me. The sound of her crying rings in my ears. She was strong the whole time, never shedding one tear until she took off. Walking back to the bench, I drop down onto it, noticing she left her book bag.

Pulling out my phone, I start a group video call to the guys. Each of them picks up within moments.

"What's up?" Blaine asks.

"So, I fucked up. I told her everything. About being in the woods. How I thought she knew and was playing a game until I realized too late she wasn't. About being a dick to her and how I never thought I'd see her again."

"And she was mad but forgave you right?" Jude asks hopefully.

"No, much the opposite. She hates me and the two of you as well. She thinks we were playing some game with her, and she was the butt of the joke."

"What the fuck!" they both scream out in unison.

"I tried to explain there wasn't a joke, but she wouldn't listen, she slapped me and ran off, leaving her bag."

"So she pulled a Cinderella," Jude smirks.

"What the hell are you talking about?"

"You know she left something behind, so we'd have to find her," he finishes explaining.

"Whatever, I'll see the two of you back in the room, so we can figure out how to fix this shit. And before you say anything, you're part of this bullshit, so yes you will be helping me."

Finished with the whole day, I end the call and take a deep breath. Picking up my bag and hers, I throw them over my shoulder and head back to the room.

Being a ferret shifter fucking sucks. If I was a wolf, I wouldn't be in this fucked up situation.

Magnolia

I couldn't believe what he told me. He saw me in the most intimate of moments and never told me. Bet him and the other two got a big laugh out of it. Just thinking about it has my blood boiling. I'm not paying attention to where I'm going and run smack dab into a wall. Well, a human wall. No, that's not right either, it's a gargoyle wall.

"Whoa now, be careful, Miss Holloway, wouldn't want you to fall and hurt yourself," he says as he reaches out, gripping my arms and holding me steady.

"I'm sorry, Mr. Godrickson."

"Nonsense. Are you okay? Did someone hurt you?" He lets go of me once I'm steady and wipes the tears rolling down my face. His voice is so dominant , thinking someone hurt me. Like he's ready to hurt someone for offending me.

"No, just upset. No one hurt me physically. Let's just say it's what I get for being uneducated on supernatural species, which I can now thank you for informing me about."

"Ahh, are you from the Exodus pack?"

"I am. Why does everyone ask me that and look shocked when I say yes?"

"History doesn't have them letting their females leave pack lands to go to school. They're normally taught by one of the teachers if they are of a higher stature or intended to be the mate of a high-ranking Beta or the Alpha. It's also uncommon knowledge, but with my age, I know they're not educated on other shifters, especially some of the more uncommon ones such as myself," he explains. I can't help but notice how his nostrils flare and his face looks disgusted when he mentioned being mated with someone.

"Yeah, well, that would be me; uneducated and dumb. I'm sorry for running into you, but I need to catch my friend when she gets out of class." I take off running, not even waiting for his answer.

I make it to Wylla's English class just as they are letting out. She stopped at the teacher's podium, pointing to something on a paper while talking to her. I stand to the side so as not to block the door, wiping the last of my tears and waiting.

Shifting back and forth on my feet, I keep looking down the hallway in both directions, wanting to make sure I don't run into the men who live above us, who were in on the big fuck with Magnolia joke.

"Hey, chica, what's up?" Wylla sings out as she comes up beside me, reaching up to run her fingers down my arm. She stops when she sees my face. "What's wrong? What happened?"

I go through the whole story, telling her first what I learned in Supernatural History class, then about Zeke wanting to speak with me privately. I went through the whole sordid story of his explanation as we walked back to the dorms. She never interrupted, listening to every word I said. Once I'm finished, she stops in her tracks and turns and looks at me.

"What?" I cry out.

"Okay, first, I am so sorry, Magz, that this happened to you. But first off, it sounds like an innocent mistake. You didn't know about ferret shifters, and also how fucking cute is that? I could just cuddle him and stick him inside my shirt and walk around with him."

"WYLLA, FOCUS!" I scream out, before realizing there are people around when they turn to stare at the commotion I just made.

"Sorry. You've got to admit it's cute. Anyway, he thought you knew and were doing it on purpose, a simple misunderstanding. Plus, he's a dude, and what guy wouldn't react like that? Hell, if I was in his shoes, I'd have done the same thing, and I'm a girl. He could've never told you and kept it a secret, but he didn't. He came clean with you. That says something right there."

"You mean you're siding with him. He only confessed because I learned there were ferret shifters," I remind her.

"No, he could have never told you what he was or denied it was him. I doubt he's the only one at this school."

"You know, I thought you were my friend, but you're siding with him. I can't right now. I'm going for a walk, I'll see you back in the room," I tell her as I take off toward the woods. My wolf crying to go run.

I need to process how my friend can be on his side. To say it was just a misunderstanding.

What the fuck is she thinking?

Wylla

I'm in shock, watching Magz storming away after dropping all her emotions on the table about what happened with Zeke. She's pissed with me because apparently, I didn't give her the answer she was looking for. Heading to the quad, I decide to also take a walk, so I can clear my head and think about what the hell just happened. I need to come up with a way to explain to that infuriating woman that I wasn't taking sides, but merely trying to explain to her that it's not quite as bad as she is making it out to be. He's an asshole, don't get me wrong, but I honestly think it was a simple issue of miscommunication.

Walking around the campus, taking in the fresh fall air, I'm listening to music on my Airpods while thinking about what I'm going to say when I get back to my room. Since I arrived here at Arcayne and met Magz, my life has been a freaking whirlwind. It feels like we've been friends or fighting her pack issues for years and not just a week. Which brings me back to the question of how the hell I can feel so strongly for someone I've only met a short while ago? But from the moment we locked eyes, it was like I knew we were meant to be, she was part of my soul.

Not to mention now I have the three assholes upstairs to deal with. One insists he is her mate and the other two seem hell-bent on being with her in some way, shape, or form. Are we all just supposed to share her? Are we supposed to make her choose? I don't see those three alphaholes sharing their girl with me. Not to mention, Jude has also been flirting with me. At least it seems like it. *ENOUGH! We need to stop with the what-ifs and just take this day by day. Moment by moment.*

In the meantime, though, it's time to head to my room and face the firing squad.

I get to our room, and I'm just about to open the door when I look down and see Magz's bookbag sitting on the floor. Grabbing it, I turn the knob and head inside. Entering our room, I'm stunned when I see Magz sitting on her bed reading a magazine.

"I see you saw the traitor and got my bookbag back for me," she bites harshly.

"Umm. Slow your roll with the attitude. No, I found it sitting right outside the door. So either he left it and didn't knock or you were a chicken shit and didn't answer if he did. But here you go, you're welcome," I tell her, walking over to her bed and dropping the bag down on it.

"Whatever," she huffs and goes back to reading her magazine, pretending as if I never entered the room.

Okay, so I'm getting the silent treatment. Not being one to let anything slide, I grab my lady balls and decide to be the bigger person and speak first. "Hey, Magz, can we talk? I feel like I need to better explain myself."

She sighs loudly, slamming her magazine shut, before looking up at me. Moving to the edge of her bed, so her legs are dangling off the side, she crosses her arms over her chest and glares at me. "By all means, please, tell me how you're going to right what you said this afternoon." *Okay, so we are gonna keep that bitchy attitude. Good to know.* Well, here goes nothing. *Goddess, help me.*

"Okay, umm– first of all, I love this energy from you; very Michelle Rodriguez in The Fast and Furious. I love this for you. Second, this afternoon, I wasn't trying to say what Zeke did was fine and good. It's just that you just started getting to know the guys, and I think they really have the best intentions toward you. Zeke fucked up, but I don't think it was an intentional intrusion or attempt to deceive you."

She opens her mouth to interrupt me, but I cut her off before she can utter a word, causing her to huff and puff like a kid. "Now just wait and listen. You went into the woods and flicked your bean where anyone could have come across you. You saw the ferret in the tree, and if I remember right, picked it up and cuddled it up to your buckass naked body. Which, just in case you didn't know, is kinda a big deal in the shifter world. He licked your fingers while you talked to him about your life. I really think he thought you knew, and by picking up and chatting with him, you were okay with everything that was happening. Do you really think the Zeke you know so far would take advantage of you like that?"

"Well, no bu–"

"There is no but, Magz, you have got to give people the benefit of the doubt. I'm sorry, but it's pretty fucked up that you are so willing to believe and follow your dad and Alpha of your 'wolf cult' but you learn one thing about someone here and want to be a B-I-T-C-H. I love you, girl, you're my bestie, but figure your shit out," I rant at her.

She looks at me with her eyes and mouth gaping open. I slap a hand over my mouth, stunned that I just talked to her like that. I'm still in shock at what I just did when she starts giggling. I can't keep up with this girl's mood swings. Exhausted, I walk over to the chair at my desk and fall back into it. *She's laughing because she's about to fucking lose her shit. She's snapped.*

I'm sitting here just staring at her while she laughs before finally composing herself. "You're right, Wylla. I didn't expect you to yell at me like that. However, I have been unfair, and I'm lenient with my pack stuff, so it's only fair to give Zeke the benefit of the doubt. He did look like he was about to cry or melt into the floor when he told me."

Trying to lighten the mood, I nod and agree with her. "Plus, if anyone should be upset, it's me! I should be mad that the dang ferret got a taste of you before I did!" I quip, getting up and walking over to her, where I wrap my arms around her.

She's laughing, but hugging me back. "You're so crazy," she says as we pull apart.

"I know, but you love me this way. I'm sorry we fought," I tell her, and mean every word of it. I'm glad we got it all out between us, but not glad we had our first argument. She leans back on her bed, and I move to sit on mine. We work silently on our homework for forty-five minutes. I'm just about to pull out my next book to do the assigned reading when Magz throws her book across the room to the floor. Looking at her with a raised brow, she doesn't let me ask what the hell her deal is before she's up off her bed and standing in front of me.

"Any chance your guy's tattoo shop is open right now?" she asks.

"Ummm, yeah, he's open till ten on weeknights. Why, what's up? We have your appointment Saturday."

"Take me there?" she begs.

I agree, and she jumps up and down, clapping her hands like I just told her we are headed to Disney. We throw on our shoes and sweaters and head out. Stepping out of the building into the crisp evening air, we link arms and walk in sync while talking about anything and everything as we make our way to the shop.

We arrive at *Inked Ya*, an easy twenty-minute walk later. The bell above the door dings as we enter, and right away, I see my artist, Hex. Waving to him, he comes strolling over, checking Magz out as he approaches. When he gets to us, he licks his lips and crosses his arms. "Naughty bird," I admonish him as I slap his chest.

He's laughing, but Magz looks like she is about to pass out. "Relax, Magz, this is Hex, my artist. He knows I'm a bitchy witch. He's a crow shifter and loves all the pretty shiny things, which today, apparently, includes you." I cross my arms and pout my lips a little to give Hex a bit more attitude.

"The bi– I mean witch is right." He winks at me, and I glare back at him. "We've been buds for a few years now since I did her first piece. I know she's harmless–well, to me at least." He laughs. "Anyway, what can I do for you fine ladies tonight?"

I look at Magz since I have literally no idea why we are here. She chews on her lips before looking at me and then back to Hex. "Ummm, I'd like to get a piercing."

I gasp and look at her in shock. *She wants to get a what?* "Yeah, I have been letting everyone else boss me around and tell me what I can and can't do in my life so far, and my friend here so eloquently told me I need to stop. So I'd like to get my septum pierced," she says boldly, holding up a crescent moon hoop jewelry piece.

"Magz, girl, are you sure? You're visiting your dad in a week, and you can't take it out. You can't really hide the septum with the jewelry you have picked," I tell her. I am all for her being defiant and standing up for herself, but I also know she has to go home in a week, and I want her to be safe.

"Yup! Let's just call this my first act of rebellion against my dad and Alpha. I want to be in charge of my own life and especially my body. I love your piercings and tattoos, so I'm doing it," she says firmly.

"Okay! You heard her, crow boy, let's pierce her septum!" I give Hex a push to head toward his chair. He turns and leads us to his area. He tells Magz to take a seat, then he gets all his tools open and sterile.

He picks up the needle to make this shit happen. Magz's eyes go wide for a second, then she schools her reaction.

Holy hell, she is really going through with this. *Hell yeah! My girl is starting to stand up for herself!*

Magnolia

I'm going to do this!

"Okay, Magz, just sit still, and I'm going to clean the area and mark it. Okay?"

"Yep," I quip, but I'm nervous as hell. He picks up the needle, then smiles down at me, showing me his pearly whites.

"Good, we're ready. I need you to take a deep breath. Good, now blow out, slowly and steady." I do as he says, and he sticks the needle in.

The pain lasts only a moment, then it's gone. He's still doing something, but all I can think is I fucking did it. I went totally against anything my pack would allow me to do, hell, any woman to do.

"Okay, Magz, ready to take a look?" Hex asks, handing a mirror to me. Reaching out with shaky hands, I take it from him. I can feel it in the middle of my nose, but seeing it still has me nervous. Immediately, my emotions are all over the place, not knowing which one they want to settle on; fear, joy, nervousness, or love. Taking a deep, calming breath, I lift the mirror and gaze at my reflection. Love wins out, because, holy hell, I love it.

"I love it!" I cry. Really it was more like a shriek because Hex had to cover his ears as he laughs. "How hot do I look, Wylla?" Turning to her, I give her a cheeky grin.

"I didn't think you could get hotter, but seeing you with piercings has me creaming my panties. Well, if I was wearing any." I catch a glimpse of her rubbing her thighs together, which has my pussy throbbing with desire.

"Okay, great. So make sure you keep it in for two months, otherwise, it's going to close, and you'll have wasted your money. Are we still doing the tattoo on Saturday?" He looks between me and Wylla as he asks, but all I'm thinking about is how screwed I am now.

"Two months. I can't take it out at all, not even for a couple of days?"

"Sorry, babe. It has to stay in." He raises his eyebrow at me curiously. No doubt he's wondering why I would want to take it out after just getting it.

"Don't mind her, crow boy, she's trying to figure out how she's going to explain this to her strict daddy," Wylla pipes up, saving me from the uncomfortable answer.

"Baby, you're in college. It's time to get rid of the daddy issues or get a daddy to help ease those frustrations." Hex has a smirk on his face, and Wylla is dying laughing, while I'm left in the dark, clueless as to what he's insinuating.

Wylla sees my confusion. "I'll explain later. How much do I owe you, Hex?"

"This one's on me," he says with a wink, just as the bell over the door jingles, letting us know someone else has come in. "There's my next client. See you beauties on Saturday."

"Let's get out of here," Wylla says as she reaches out, taking my hands in hers, and helps me stand. Linking her arm with mine, we head out of the shop and make our way back to the dorm, stopping along the way for some coffee.

I've been quiet, only giving her the occasional 'uh huh' or head nod when she asks me something. Truthfully, I don't even know what she's saying. I've tuned her out, focusing more on how the hell I'm going to hide this piercing from my father. Don't get me wrong, I know I need to grow a pair of massive lady balls and stand up to my pack and my father, but it's hard to toss eighteen years of conditioning out the window.

My body is pulled backward as Wylla stops dead in her tracks. I stumble a bit since our elbows are still entwined together, barely keeping myself from falling on my ass. Her heated words pull my attention to her. "Okay, spit it out. What the fuck is wrong?"

"Nothing," I whine back, not even convincing myself.

"Screw that. Something's bothered you ever since we left. You've barely said a word, and when you did, it was only to agree to anal bleaching, and trust me, I only asked that to see if you were paying attention, which obviously you weren't. So spill it." Her voice gets louder with each word she speaks.

"Fine! I know I shouldn't be worried and I shouldn't care what he says, but I'm freaking out about how I'm going to hide this from my father," I tell her as I point to my nose. "The tattoo, it'll be on my arm. I can handle hiding that. This I can't."

"Magz..." she begins, but I'm not done.

"NO! I don't need a lecture. It's hard. Trying to break how I've been raised to think and act. It's not something I can wave my hands at and poof, it's gone."

"Magz, I get it. We can figure something out, and if we don't, I'll be here to handle the aftermath. If I could go home with you, I would, but I have that meeting with my grandmother and I think it would just make matters worse with your father. Just know if you need me, I'll come running." She pulls me into her arms, causing me to almost spill my coffee on both of us, and hugs me tightly.

"Thank you," I whisper into her ear.

"Anytime. Besides, we have time. Let me research and look at some spells. I can probably find a concealing spell that could work to hide it from your father."

Linking our arms, we continue on to the dorm, the weight on my shoulders lifted slightly as she goes on and on about how Hex was eye fucking me the whole time we were at the shop. With the dorm coming into view, we're both hysterically laughing at Wylla's thought that my dad would simply be okay with it. *Yeah, the funniest thing I've heard all day.*

As we approach our building, we see Blaine, nervously pacing back and forth out front. When he sees us coming, he takes off at a sprint toward us.

"Magnolia, can I speak to you for a moment?" he asks, before glancing over to Wylla and then back to me. "Privately?"

"Yeah," comes out in a drawn out voice, curious as to what it is he wants to talk about.

"I'm going to run inside and pee, and then I'll meet you back down here, so we can go to dinner," Wylla says, before heading up the steps to our dorm and disappearing inside, but not before throwing her arms up in a what the hell motion behind his back.

"What did you need to talk about?"

"Zeke."

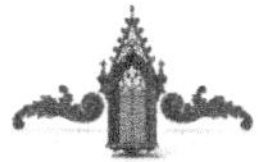

Blaine

Okay. I might have panicked when I saw Magnolia and just screamed at her that something was wrong with Zeke. I mean, while I do need her help with him, I'm acting as if he died. And well, he's not dead, at least not yet.

"What's wrong with Zeke? Is he okay? Where is he?" She shoots her questions at me in rapid fire.

"Well, he didn't handle your reaction to his confession well. He's been a mess all afternoon and evening. Then about thirty minutes ago, he stormed from our room saying he was headed to the cages for tonight's fight," I report.

"What the heck are the cages, and what do you mean fight?"

"Magnolia, the cages are an underground fight ring hosted just outside of campus grounds. Zeke sometimes goes there to blow off steam, but he was really upset, and I don't think he's in the right frame of mind to actually fight. I'm pretty sure he went there to get his ass beat, like he thinks he deserves it or something," I explain.

"Take me there right now, Blaine!" she screams at me, stomping her foot on the ground. *Goddess, she's fucking adorable.*

"I can–"

"Yes, you damn well can, Blaine! You take me to my ferret right now!" she cries. Then immediately slaps a hand over her mouth, realizing what she just let slip from her delicious mouth.

"Alright," I sigh, grabbing her hand and start heading toward the cages. Reaching into my pocket with my free hand, I pull my phone out and shoot a quick text to Jude to let him know what's going on. He's at the fights already, keeping an eye on Zeke, while I came to talk to Magnolia. Just as I pull my hand free from sliding my phone back into my pocket, it's enveloped by a small, warm hand. Looking down, then up, I see it's Wylla. *When did she come out of the dorm?*

"If you thought you were taking Magz to some cage fights without me, Fido, you are sadly mistaken. No way in hell would I miss an underground cage fight. That shit sounds violent and hot as fuck," she purrs.

"Wylla, it's not funny. Zeke could get seriously hurt. He's a ferret, for goddess' sake. OH NO!" she shrieks. "Blaine, do they fight in shifted form? They can't, right?" Magnolia starts to panic.

I can't help the laugh that slips out, spurring her to slap her delicate hand across my chest. Stopping dead in my tracks, I stand there staring at her, shocked by what just happened, in disbelief that she just swatted me. It was playful, I know, but she's never really been playful with us, always keeping herself a safe distance from us.

"Babe, you're in for a treat watching Zeke fight. They fight in human form, and well, I'll let you see for yourself. Hopefully, he actually fights back when he notices you're there," I tell her, smirking. "Enough about Zeke; you'll see him soon enough. I want to talk about that cute little ring that's new to your already gorgeous face."

She blushes as we start walking once more. "Wylla took me to her guy today, and I got it done. I had a rough day, as you know, and someone so kindly put me in my place." I notice the wink she tosses in Wylla's direction.

"Kindly? HA! More like yelled at you and called you a bitch," Wylla cackles.

I snap my head in Wylla's direction. "You called her a what?"

"Oh, relax, Blaine. I deserved it for how I treated her and Zeke. Anyway, I decided to do something for myself and no one else. So here we are. I'm anxious enough about it, so please just drop it," she begs.

Not being one who can let things go, especially when they have to do with my mate, I push her for more. "Why are you anxious? It's just a nose piercing."

She sighs loudly but doesn't answer me. Looking at her, I see she's scrunched up her face like she's trying to find the words for what she's about to say. I look at Wylla with a raised brow, and she rolls her eyes.

"Pretty much, Magz here decided to give a big *fuck you* to her daddy and her Alpha, which is totally badass by the way. But then she remembered she has to go home next weekend as promised and has no idea how to hide her new jewelry. Which kinda takes away a little bit of the badassness of it." She looks around me and stares at Magnolia with a yeah-I-said-what-I-said look on her face.

Surprising the hell out of me, Magnolia laughs and flips Wylla off using the hand I'm not holding. I throw my head back in a deep belly laugh and keep leading these fine ladies to the cages.

We walk in silence for another six minutes before we reach the building where the fights are held. Walking up to the door, we're stopped by the guard, who just glares at us in silence. "Petunia," I say, and he steps aside and opens the door for us, allowing us entry.

"No fucking way is the password petunia to get into a fucking cage fight," Wylla whispers while trying to hold back laughter.

"Sure is. You have to admit no one would guess it, right? So it's perfect." I shrug.

She nods in agreement, and we walk to the main area. The cheering of the crowd gets louder as we get closer. We make it to the crowded space that holds the ring surrounded by a cage, just as they're hauling a body on a stretcher. The DJ starts playing *Girlfight* by Brooke Valentine.

I look over to Magnolia, and her eyes are wide as she takes everything in. Wylla is looking like the cat who got the cream. She's vibrating with excitement.

Well, let's see if we can find our ferret.

Zeke

One hour earlier

"Snap out of it, man. Just give her time to process, and she'll see it was just a simple misunderstanding," Blaine barks out at me with the superiority of being a wolf shifter. *Wait, make that an Alpha heir wolf shifter.*

The fucker can talk shit because he wasn't the one it happened to. She's pissed at me, and it feels like my heart is being ripped from my chest. Standing up, I begin to pace back and forth across the room, trying to calm my nerves. Jude and Blaine think I don't see the knowing glances they're shooting back and forth between each other.

I need to get out of here and beat the shit out of someone. Pulling my phone out of my pocket, I shoot off a text to Timur. The word through the grapevine was there was a fight tonight, that's exactly what I craved. I just needed to see if I could get on the docket. It takes no time for me to get a message back.

Timur: FUCK YEAH!!! Shit dude, the crowd is gonna go crazy when they see you're fighting. When can you be here? Fights start in thirty minutes.

Me: OMW now. See you in 10-15 min

I slide my phone into my back pocket, move over to my bed, kneel down, and reach under my bed to pull out my gym bag. It has my fight clothes, hand wraps, and anything else I may need. Standing up, I pull the strap up on my shoulder and head to the door.

"What the fuck, man? Now is not the time," Jude chastises, stopping me dead in my tracks with my hand on the door handle. I know he does it out of concern, but it's fucking annoying. "And to just walk out of here and not say anything. Bitch move, man." He's already standing from the bed and moving toward me.

"Look, I'm going to explode if I don't release some of these emotions I'm feeling. I got this. Besides, even if I didn't, I'd deserve to get the fuck beat out of me. I should look as bad as I made her feel." Turning the knob, I open the door and step out into the hallway, leaving it open knowing one, or both of them, will be following me.

My thoughts are confirmed when I hear Jude speak, "I got him," before running out the door behind me.

He catches up to me at the stairs, and I know he's wanting to say something but is fighting to keep his mouth shut. He keeps glancing at me as we walk over to the rings, but finally, I can't take it anymore and let out a deep sigh.

"Fucking spit it out already," I bite out, fed up with the sideways glances.

"Come on, man, don't fight. You're upset and not thinking clearly. You made a mistake, it's a misunderstanding, it's not your fault. Listen to Blaine, just give her time." Jude tries to reason with me, but he's only pissing me off more.

I stop and glare at him. My skin is boiling, and I work to rein in my anger before talking to him. Once I have it under control, I lay into him. "Look, if you're adamant about coming with me to babysit, then keep your mouth shut. I don't need or want your advice on the issue. I'm fighting. So just be my friend and shut the hell up." Turning away from him, I start walking again. I can hear his footsteps behind me but refuse to turn and look at him again.

Walking up to the abandoned warehouse, my adrenaline starts pumping even more erratically. I love the fights. I thrive for them. They're the one place where I feel strong, better than any of the other fucking supernaturals around me. Here, as a human, I am stronger and better than any of them. I'm the predator, and they're my prey *for once*.

Saxon is standing outside the building tonight. I don't have to give the ridiculous ass password, instead, he nods for me to go inside. Reaching out, I open the metal door and step inside with Jude right behind me. The thumping of the bass music playing can be felt through my feet as it vibrates the floor.

Slash is working behind the counter, and a cocky ass grin covers his face when he looks up and sees me. "Well, well, Bone Crusher. Timur told me you were added to the docket tonight. Elizan jumped at the chance to have a match with you. He's still a little bitter about the loss to you a few weeks back. You're in the dressing room to the left."

Internally, I'm laughing because the fucker was too cocky for his own good. When he made the comment about making me a pet for his niece, I lost it. I left him in a puddle of blood, reminding him not all 'housepets', as he so eloquently called me, are docile.

"Looking forward to it," I throw back at him as I head through the doors. This puts me in a little bit of a pickle, though, because I wanted to let someone beat my ass tonight, but there's no way in hell I'm going to let him win.

I head to the back, but I'm stopped by Jude when he reaches out and grabs my arm. "I'm gonna get a drink from the bar. Do you want a water?" he asks, finally accepting that he's not going to be able to talk me out of it.

"Yeah, I'm gonna go get changed. See you in the back," I tell him before heading off.

Thankfully, the dressing rooms are out of the way, and each fighter is designated an area based on the matches for the night. This keeps you out of the crowds and opponents apart from each other while they're getting ready. Wouldn't want to have any fighting happen that's not in the cages. That would prevent Timur from raking in the cash from the eager supes betting on them.

Heading inside, I see about eight other guys in there getting ready. From the amount of noise when we came inside, I knew a fight was already taking place. Some of the guys give me a nod, but I'm not here for conversation, I'm here to fight, and right now, I need to get my head in the game.

Moving away from the others, I head to the locker with my name on it. Yeah, I'm that good. I have one assigned to me on either side. I set my bag down on the bench and open the locker door. Slipping out of my shoes, I pull my shirt and pants off, hang them on the hook inside, then set my shoes on the bottom.

I slip my shorts on before I sit down and tape my hands up. Once that's done, I pull my hair up into a tight bun before putting on my fingerless leather gloves.

Sitting there, I allow all thoughts to leave my mind. I breathe in and out slowly, calming my nerves and running through any possible scenarios that could happen with the fight. It's how I prepare before every match. I'm so lost in my pre-fight routine, I don't hear Jude come up behind me, until he places the cold as fuck water bottle on my back, causing me to jump.

"Are you ready? That crowd's fucking crazy out there!" Jude exclaims as he drops down on the bench beside me.

"Staying back here or going out front?" I look over and ask him, his eyes focused on his phone. "Waiting on something?"

"Huh?" he asks, as I point my hand at his phone, clueing him in. "Nah, just thinking. I'm going out front when you head out. Gonna watch the fight like all the common folk unless you want me outside the cage acting as your coach," he says with a forced laugh as he slides his phone into his pocket.

"I'm good. You can head out. Should be about time for me to be up. I know I'm not the featured fight tonight. Just don't get trashed; I don't want to have to carry your ass home."

"Whatever, man. You know you want to give me a piggyback ride. But now that you mention it, another drink sounds good. Catch you on the flip side after you whoop that fucker's ass." He reaches out with his hand, giving my shoulder a firm squeeze before standing and heading out of the dressing room.

Now I can go back to my routine without any further interruptions.

Magnolia

I'm fucking fuming!

The whole way to this crap-looking warehouse, all I could think about was Zeke getting the fucking shit beat out of him. For all I knew, he could've already had his fight and be dead. The only moment my anxiety dropped a little was when Blaine gave the giant out front the code word: *Petunia*. I mean really big bad fight club and that's what you choose to use?

Stepping inside, we pass a counter with another guy who tosses his hand up in a wave to Blaine while giving me and Wylla an appraising once over. "Who we got here, Blaine?" the guy asks, while he eye fucks us.

"Friends from school," he says curtly, before taking me and Wylla by the arm and leading us inside. We pass by a hall, that leads to the left and right, and head straight ahead down a small hallway that opens into a massive room that has two-tiered floors. A staircase to my right leads up to the second floor.

The room is packed, and the music is pounding. I'm anxiously scanning the room for the ferret I'm going to kill for being stupid. My poor little guy is going to get killed. There should be a fucking rule in a place like this about letting prey animals fight.

Where the fuck is he?

"Let's get something to drink, then find a seat?" Blaine yells out over the music as he leads us to the bar. There are tables scattered throughout the room, but they look to be all packed. I'm able to see up to the second floor, which is open in the middle and forms a circle. A large metal cage sits in the center. *That must be where the fights are held.* From the cheers and boos filling the room, it sounds like there is one going on now.

We make it to the bar, with Wylla jumping around in excitement like a kid in a toy store. "What can I get you, handsome?" the slutty bartender behind the bar asks. Leaning forward, she places her forearms on the counter, smashing her tits together, causing them to spill out the top of her low cut t-shirt.

He looks at me and Wylla to see if we want anything. I shake my head no while Wylla shouts out, "Tequila shots!"

"Shot of tequila and a pitcher of beer. Give me four glasses with that," he tells her, turning his focus back on us, which infuriates her. She turns away from the bar with a frown and begins to make our drinks.

"Why four glasses?" I ask, confused.

"Well, for the three of us and Jude," he says with a cheeky tone. "He's around here somewhere."

"Here ya go, baby," the slutty bartender says as she places the shot and pitcher on the counter. She reaches down and writes something before grabbing four glasses and putting them on the counter by the pitcher. "And this is for you. Call me later." Reaching forward, she slides the folded up piece of paper into the front pocket of his flannel shirt.

My wolf instantly wants to rip her fucking head off for being so bold with him. I shouldn't care, but I do. "Slut," I mumble out, sending Wylla into hysterics.

I see Blaine take the number out of his pocket and rip it in half before sliding it back to the bartender. She glares at him in amazement before she shrugs her shoulders, "Your loss."

"Here, let me take that shot off your hands, Fido." Wylla picks up the shot glass. She licks the salt lining the rim of the glass before swallowing the liquor down, shaking her head and hollering out, "Fuck yeah! That's some good shit," as she slams the empty glass down on the bar.

"Let's go, I need to find Zeke." Turning, I head away from the bar into the crowd. They can act like it's no big deal, but I need to stop him before he makes a mistake. I don't even care if they follow me or not.

I'm moving through the crowd, making my way to where the cages are, when I feel a hand slide around my waist and pull me into a large body. I stumble slightly, falling deeper into the intruder's grasp. His body is large, and the smell of rancid cigarette smoke fills my lungs. "Lookie what we have here, ain't she a pretty little thing," he says. Looking up, I see his face. His eyes are pitch black, and a long jagged scar runs the length of the right side of his face from the temple to the edge of his angular jaw.

"Let go of me!" I scream out, struggling to push away from him but failing miserably.

"Oh no, little girl. You're the finest thing up in here. What's that saying, finders keepers, losers weepers?" His putrid breath blows on my face as he speaks.

"Well, I wasn't lost, so I can't be found. Now let go of me."

"I'd do as she says," comes from a deep, pissed-off voice directly behind me.

"Fuck off, demon. We ain't got no need for ya," he spews, but his grip loosens, and I'm able to wiggle away at the same time muscular arms grab me, pulling me out of the way. *Jude!*

"Like I said, she's not for you," Jude says again, standing toe to toe with the man.

"I see we're causing trouble. You wouldn't want Bone Crusher to know you're fucking with his girl," Blaine says as he steps up, making sure to keep Wylla tucked behind him.

"Aww fuck, she didn't say she was with him. Sorry about that, we don't want no beef with him," the fucking coward says at the mention of whoever the fuck Bone Crusher is.

"Come on, Magnolia, let's go get a table. Zeke should be up soon," Blaine says as he leads us over to a table right off the bar separating the cage pit from the rest of the room.

The table has a perfect view of the bloodbath taking place in the ring. The poor soul on the floor isn't even conscious, and they still haven't called the fight. The six-foot-four man is lording above him, gloating, before finally sending a kick to his gut. Turning to the crowd, he holds his hands up in the air as the music goes off and Viking is announced the winner.

Wylla is giddy, her eyes wide as she takes in the scene before us as she bounces around in the chair screaming out, "Hell yeah! You fucked his ass up."

The winner leaves the cage as three men with red shirts on with medic written on them rush into the cage with a stretcher, load the crumpled form on the floor onto it and rush him out.

"How about that, ladies and gentlemen? *Club KO* has a special treat for you tonight. A fight that wasn't on the docket. So get out your money, it's one you're going to want to bet on. Just a few weeks ago, these two were in this very ring. One walked out and one crawled out crying, '*wah wah wah all the way home*'. First up, we have Elizan," the emcee announces as a six-foot-four man comes out from the hallway to the right of the ring. He bounces around on the balls of his feet as he makes his way down the aisle. His body is covered in tattoos, and his hair is cut close to the scalp. Thumping hip-hop music plays until he steps inside the cage and shakes hands with the referee standing inside. "Next, we have a man who needs no introduction. Bone Crusher." *Bodies* by Drowning Pool begins to play over the speakers as both Blaine and Jude high-five each other.

"Just watch. You've never seen anything like this," Blaine leans into me and whispers in my ear.

I'm looking frantically around, waiting to see who Bone Crusher is when I see Zeke step out of the hallway to the left. He has a stone-cold look on his face as he takes his time making his way down the aisle to the cage.

"Zeke, Zeke!!" I scream out, but he can't hear me over the roar of the crowd. He steps into the cage and shakes the ref's hand. Zeke and Elizan stand toe to toe, with the latter towering a good four or five inches over Zeke.

My heart drops into my stomach. My poor Zeke is going to get hurt, and it's all my fault. Blaine said he's only here because of how I treated him this afternoon when he confessed to me.

The ref moves out of the cage, slamming the door shut behind him. Zeke's opponent takes that as the perfect time to attack. Zeke is quick though and drops to the floor, sweeping his leg around, and kicks Elizan's legs out from under him, sending him slamming down to the floor.

The man quickly recovers, doing a kip up, landing firmly on his feet at the same time, throwing a punch, and catching Zeke across the jaw. Zeke fucking laughs.

"Zeke," I scream out again. This time he hears me as he turns his head and locks eyes with me. My stupidity in calling him causes him to lose focus of the fight, and he's caught with another punch, catching him right in the eye.

"FUCK!" Jude screams out

"Get your head in the game, Z! Show him who you are," Blaine screams out.

"Shit, that had to hurt, but fuck, if this isn't exciting," Wylla cries out as she wraps her arm around my waist, pulling me into her. "He's going to be okay," she says comfortingly.

I bring my hand to my mouth and start to nervously chew on my nail. Zeke regains his composure, and the two of them begin to throw punch after punch at each other. This seems to go on forever, both of them bleeding from their face until Zeke jumps up doing a roundhouse kick that lands against the huge fucker's temple, and he flies backward, hitting his head on the mat. Zeke uses this opportunity to jump on top of him, straddling his body as he begins to lay a series of punches to his face.

I can't just sit here. I need to get to him. Looking around, I find a gate that leads to the area around the cage and take off in a sprint to it.

"Sorry, lady, you can't pass here," the guard tells me as he stops me from entering. I've lost track of what's going on in the ring, but from the screams, it must be coming close to an end.

"You're not fucking keeping me from him," I growl out, baring my teeth to the jerk, before calling on every ounce of strength I have, pushing him away, and running to the cage.

"And the winner is Bone Crusher," the emcee announces, and I can see Zeke stepping out of the cage.

"Zeke!" I scream out, getting his attention, as I barrel straight toward him, jumping into his arms, and slamming my lips onto his. His hands grip my ass as he deepens the kiss.

Blaine

Is this how life is always going to be with this woman? Chasing her ass around because she just runs off? This is becoming a habit of hers, and the only good thing about chasing after her is getting to watch her plump ass bounce with each step she takes.

Following her through the crowd of people in the pit area surrounding the cage, I can see every man and woman's lust-filled eyes on her. I make sure to keep an eye on Magnolia as she so recklessly runs toward the fight, the crowd parting for her like the sea. I'm not taking any more chances on someone grabbing her like that asshole did before the fight. I thought Jude was about to shift and go full demon on his ass. People think that his only power is sex, but his demon side actually has increased speed and strength, along with the fact that he can suck a person's soul out of them with his kiss of death.

He doesn't use it unless he's sent to do something for the demon court, but I think he was about to change that when scar face touched our girl. Luckily, at *Club KO,* all we had to do was mention who she was here for and he unhanded her quickly. No one around here will dare fuck with Bone Crusher. Our girl is about to find that out firsthand.

It's been adorable watching her worry about him. Thinking, since he's a ferret, he would be injured or killed. She was chewing her nails, fretting over him being hurt. As if anyone stands a chance in a fight with him. When he took that hit to the face when he noticed her in the crowd, she turned ghostly white and jetted from our table to get to him, acting as if her worst fear had come to life.

So here I am, following her through the crowd until we come to an abrupt stop. I look up from her delectable ass to see why we halted our journey. We've made it to the gate that leads directly to the cage. The guard is informing Magnolia she can't get through, but she shoves him away like he's a piss ant, and barrels toward the winner, Bone Crusher, otherwise known as Zeke.

He catches her in his arms and their lips connect. *MINE!* My wolf growls, watching our mate so easily kiss Z when she has continuously rejected us. I soothe him by telling him she'll be *ours.* We just need to be patient. He settles slightly, but I can feel him pacing inside me as we watch our friend taste our girl.

They're too wrapped up in each other to notice the rest of us standing here watching them make out. I clear my throat, "Can you quit eating my mate's face, Bone Crusher?"

Magnolia breaks the kiss and climbs off of Zeke, his eyes widening in recognition of what just happened. Magnolia wastes no time in spinning around and chastising me, "You don't own me, wolf boy." I raise an eyebrow at her, silently asking her if she's sure about that. Paying me no mind, she turns her attention back to the ferret.

"So Bone Crusher, huh?" she asks Zeke while putting a hand on her hip.

He rubs the back of his head with one hand, looking bashful of his nickname here. "Ugh, yeah, I didn't pick it. Timur gave it to me, and it just kinda stuck," he tells her as his cheeks redden. She just nods her head in acceptance.

There is an awkward silence between them before Zeke breaks it with his voice in a stage whisper, "So not that I didn't enjoy your lips on mine, Pretty Wolf, but what was that about? You were ready to bathe in my blood at school today."

Magnolia runs her shoe in front of her on the ground while looking down, not answering. Then, after a brief silence, she looks up and takes a deep breath. "I'm sorry, Zeke. It was wrong of me to react so poorly without listening to your side of the story in its entirety. I just wanna move past it and start over. If that's what you want?"

"The ferret thing doesn't bother you, Pretty Wolf?" he asks, and I roll my eyes. If I had a quarter for every time my best friend worried about his shifted form, I'd be a fucking billionaire, I swear.

Surprising the fuck out of me, Magnolia pulls back and socks him right in his shoulder. "No, what you shift into doesn't matter to me. Do you think I'm that shallow?" she asks demandingly.

He blushes, and Jude smacks him upside the back of the head, "Told ya so!"

That comment has Magnolia whipping her head Jude's way and glaring at him, "And just what is that supposed to mean?" Jude reddens to the color of a strawberry before pulling his composure back, then with a cocky-as-hell grin on his face, he wraps an arm around Magnolia, pulling her close to his side.

"Means we all have the hots for you, Maggie."

"Maggie?" she asks at the new nickname.

Jude just shrugs, "I like it. Magnolia is too formal for our woman, babe, and I plan to try to make you our woman."

Her eyes widen, and her mouth is open in shock as she quickly looks between all of us. "Oh, don't worry, babe, we all agreed to pursue you since we are all best friends. Right, guys?"

Magnolia pulls away from him quickly and wags her finger at him. "There can be no pursuit. I am promised to another." Another feral growl leaves my body as I snatch her up, bringing her nose to nose with me. Or as close as I can get since she's so much shorter than me. "Over my dead body," I say through clenched teeth. Jude and Zeke voice their agreement with me.

Then suddenly a flash of rainbow slips in between us and is stealing our girl away. "Sorry, fellas! But this is how it has to be," she hollers back to us. Then mouths 'for now' and with that, she turns and drags a giggling Magnolia back through the crowd toward the exit.

Jude chases after them, calling, "Wait up! I'll walk you two fine ladies to the door." I'm glad he piped up and went with them. I wouldn't want anyone else thinking they could put their hands on her or Wylla like that fucker from earlier. I watch them until I can't see them anymore.

FUCK!

That woman is so infuriating; Magnolia, not the witch. Why can't she just see what is right in front of her? Why does she continue to hold on to this '*I have to do what my Alpha says*' mentality? She's so fucking hot and cold. One minute she is flirty, and I think she is ready to court us, then the next she is all 'I'm promised to another'. It's driving me insane.

Jude comes strolling back up to us, preening like a peacock. "I got them to the door with no issues. I think they were just going back to the dorm to call it a night," he tells us. I look from him to Zeke and can see my friends are feeling the same way. So I do the next best logical thing, wrapping an arm around each of their shoulders. "You guys wanna get shit-faced? I hear the *Elixir* is having a half-off on any beer on tap."

"Yeah, let me go clean up, and I'll meet you fuckers outside," Zeke answers. Jude just claps me on the back, and we part ways with Zeke, heading out front to wait for him.

Three hours later, we're sitting at the bar in *Elixir,* half in the bag. *Counting* by Volbeat comes on, and the three of us are singing some bad off-key karaoke while sloshing our drinks together in cheers. *Half-priced tap beer was a great idea!* The drum solo hits, and I slam my drink down and begin drumming my hands on the counter to the beat, while Zeke and Jude cheer for me.

But I read you like a letter lyric is sung when I feel a hand run from my shoulder down my chest. Looking down, I see long red nails clawing at my chest. I turn around to see who the fuck is touching me. *Fuck me, it's the bartender from the fights. Did she follow us here?*

"Hey, baby, you left *KO* too fast and didn't call. Don't you wanna play with me tonight?" the fake, high-pitched voice purrs at me.

Grabbing her hand, I pull it from my chest and drop it midair in disgust. I hear the guys snicker behind me. "No, thank you–Ava, was it? I have a girl. Now leave us," I growl at her.

"That girl with the old-lady colored hair? Come on, she looks like a prude nun. Let me take you home. Tell ya what, I'll bring some friends for yours, and we can switch later if that's what gets you going," she whispers seductively in my ear.

Looking her straight in the eye, I fake gag. "I said no thank you. Now move along, and if you talk about my girl like that again, I might just break my rule of putting hands on a female."

She stomps her foot and gives a shrill shriek before turning and storming away. She meets up with two girls who look as desperate as her, then turns and eyes me from across the bar. "You'll see, wolf baby, it's me you need. Not her," she says before grabbing both of her friends' hands, and they leave the bar.

I turn back to the guys, who are trying to hold back their laughter. "What?" I snap at them. They burst into a fit of giggles like two little girls who know a secret.

"Nothing, we just... We don't know, but that gagging? Then she stomped at you? It was fucking hysterical," Jude cackles. *Goddess above, we are shitfaced.*

We resume our boys' night while drinking beers when a brilliant plan smacks me straight in the face. "Guys, I just had an idea. One that will show that sexy little mate of ours how good it can be to be ours," I tell them, vibrating with how good I think this idea is.

They stare at me on pins and needles, waiting for me to tell them this epicness. I say nothing, keeping the wheels turning in their heads. They say nothing as they wait and Jude shakes his head at me in a 'well go on then' gesture.

"Okay! Damn. No need to yell at me. We need to show that little wolf how good we could be for her. We spoil the hell out of her. We would anyway, but we start now, not when she accepts us as her mates. Are you fuckers in?" I slur.

They nod ecstatically, and we raise our glasses, cheering to our new plan to show that irritating but sexy creature just what it would look like to be with us. Beer sloshes all over the bartop, and the bartender comes over, cutting us off and sending us on our way back to the dorm to sleep it off. We wibble wobble all the way home, arms around one another's shoulders as we brainstorm how we are going to get this plan rolling.

Watch out, Magnolia, your mates are coming for you.

Wylla

Last night was insane! It was fun, but then it turned into a damn nightmare. *At least for me.* The fights were fucking awesome. I love a good, bloody fight as much as the next dark magic bitch. Watching Zeke beat the hell out of that tiger shifter was glorious. I wonder if the tiger went home and licked his wounds. *Pun intended.* He was annihilated by a ferret, that was the fucking best thing I've ever seen.

Then afterward, Magz ran through the crowd like a wild woman trying to get to Zeke. Once she knew he was okay, she jumped into his arms as soon as she was close enough, locking her lips to his. It was adorable, and I actually had no jealousy over watching him taste her. The nightmare started when the kiss broke.

Jude informed Magz that Zeke, Blaine, and himself would be pursuing Magz to be their girl. They want to share her with each other, which is cool, fine, whatever. However, they didn't mention sharing her with me, and she didn't mention me either. She just said there could be no pursuing her, she was promised to another. *Again, not me.*

We leave, and I placate the guys in their love fest for her, thinking once we're away from them, we can talk and she will clarify her feelings about what Jude said. *Nope!* All the way she talked about them and what they said. What this means for her, and how can they want her still, when they know she's promised to the pack heir? *Blah blah blah!* The topper on this nightmare cake? She asked me how they could want to share her, to watch each other with her intimately. *WHAT!*

We've shared kisses, and I finger blasted her into next week. She's not concerned about that at all. Or that I watched her kiss Zeke and didn't freak out? No, it's all about the cocks swinging between those imbeciles' legs. So what, the kisses and orgasms were just drunken mistakes? *That shit fucking hurts.*

I need to call my grandmother and ask again about undoing these blocks Magz has on her. I'll do what I promised and help break the designation and bond spells. But then? I think it's time I stop playing cat and mouse with my roommate. Either she admits she has feelings for me and wants to be with me as bad as I do her, or I'm going to dip. My feelings are already growing so strong for her that I couldn't bear watching her with them. I like some pain, but not heartbreak pain.

This whole week has been long and boring. I don't know how people actually enjoy classes. Like, who wakes up in the morning and thinks, *'I can't wait to see what I learn today'*? Not me. I'm only here because my grandmother thought it would be good for me to take a break from the coven. Those bitches are always giving me the side eye because of who my dad is.

Your mom goes off and hoes it up one night and ends up knocked up by a warlock from the *Matilda Coven.* They met on a night out drinking and hit it off, only sharing their names and nothing else, and wham-bam-thank you-ma'am, nine months later the most badass witch who ever lived was born. *That's me, by the way.*

The Matilda Coven is known to be a bunch of ruthless, take no prisoner people, so I've never met my dad. In fact, I don't think he even knows he has a kid. *A fucking epic one at that.* Anyway, I'm getting off track. I'm part of the Samara Coven with my whole maternal side of my family. They're fucking awesome, but the rest of the coven? *Bitches.* All because of half my heritage. It's whatever, but it's why Grandmother pushed so hard for me to come here.

I mean, all in all, I met Magz, and she's been worth the whole learning thing. Until this week, all of a sudden the guys have been up her fucking ass. Even Jude. We've always been flirty, and I thought we had a connection, but he's even pushed me to the side. If she wasn't a virgin, I'd swear someone turned them all into one giant anal plug, walking with her to class, carrying her books, and getting her meals in the cafeteria for her.

They'd probably wipe her fucking ass if she asked. The best part, or maybe the worst, is that my girl is totally oblivious to it all. She's eating the attention up. I'm sure that's because she doesn't receive it much in her pack, and especially because the guys don't wait on the women hand and foot. There it's all 'men good-women bad', so she thinks it's sweet and adorable. They want to be so caring. *GAG!*

All this week has done for me is shown me that I'm a big fucking fifth wheel. Magz has been amazing at including me and so have the guys, actually. I'm not blind though, their attention is all on Magz, and hers has been on them. *Thanking them, chatting with them, them, them, them!* No way am I going to stick around and get closer to them; especially Magz, for my fucking heart to break when she decides she wants to be with only them.

Grandmother told me over the phone last night that after we video chatted for the meeting with this council, she'll advise me on breaking both spells for Magz. Her bonding block and designation block. After that? I'm marching my thick ass down to admissions to talk about moving dorms or at least rooms. I can't be this close to Magz, continuing to fall for her more until she drops me like a hot potato.

She slept in my bed again last night, which just makes this whole thing so much harder. We fell asleep in our own beds, then I woke up in the middle of the night, hotter than hell. When I opened my eyes to see what the heck was going on, Magz was in my bed, cuddled up to me, sound asleep. The woman is a fucking conundrum, I just don't know what to do anymore.

Which brings me to today, it's Saturday, thank goddess. We are headed back to *Inked Ya* to get her tattoo. She has been vibrating with excitement since she woke up two hours ago. *Speak of the wolf.* Magz comes skipping into the room, humming *Not Your Barbie Girl* by Ava Max. She's wrapped in only a lavender towel, and her hair is dripping down her neck. She shuts the door behind her and spins, facing me. When she catches me smirking at her, she freezes. "Can you believe I'm getting a tattoo today? I am so flippin' excited!" she squeals.

"Are you still getting the wolf design you talked about?" I ask.

She raises a brow at me. "Are you serious? Of course, I am!" Then she turns her back to me, heading to our closet to pick out some clothes. She pulls a spaghetti strap tank over her head, then shrugs on a zip-up quarter sleeve sweater. Look at her like an old pro already, wearing something so Hex can easily access her bicep.

Stepping into some yoga pants, she whirls on me. "Are you still not going to tell me what you're getting done today?"

"Nope," I tell her, popping the 'P' at the end. "A total secret, at least it is to your cute ass. Hex knows what he's doing and I have no doubt he's going to kill it as usual."

"Okay, but like can you at least tell me where you're going to put it? Where is there room left?" She grins at me deviously. *Little brat.*

"For your information, Magz, I am getting it as my boob chandelier," I sass back.

"Boob chandelier?"

"Yes, it's the space on the sternum like right between but under the breasts. Right here," I tell her, lifting my shirt to show her.

Her cheeks turn pink as she stares at my exposed skin. Then she just nods her head and turns her back, slipping some socks onto her feet. *See! A fucking conundrum.* What she doesn't know is that I'm getting the glass dome from *Beauty and the Beast*, but instead of a rose inside, I'm having Hex draw me an intricate Magnolia flower.

I'm on the fence about if I'm staying in this school, let alone this room with her. So I want the tattoo to memorialize my first love. After I disappear from her life, I want to look at my chest and know that even for a short while my heart was hers, even if she never knew it.

I also can't wait to see her face when she tries to pay Hex, and he tells her it's covered. I've been keeping a secret from her. I paid for her tattoo already and want it to be a surprise. She's going to be so annoyed, then hopefully she is all swept up in the sweetness of the gesture.

Snapping my attention from my inner turmoil and back to the woman standing in front of me, I see her impatiently tapping her booted foot on the floor with her hip popped at me. "Earth to Wylla! Are you ready?"

"Shit! Yeah, sorry, Magz, I was daydreaming." I stand up, sliding my feet into my rubber clogs. "Let's blow this popsicle stand." With that, I grab her hand and drag her from the room, heading to the elevator, so we make it to *Inked Ya* on time.

Magnolia

I'm sitting in the chair as Hex cleans my arm, then places the stencil of the tattoo I picked on my outer left bicep. It's going to look fucking amazing when it's done, an outline of a wolf and girl, both howling at the sky. It's the perfect first tattoo, representing the two parts of me.

"Okay, you are positive you want this?" he asks, as he picks the gun up from the table.

"Positive." I've never wanted something more in my life, other than freedom from my pack. I know Wylla and the guys said I would always have someone, but I'm afraid. I've only just met them. What happens if their feelings for me change, and I'm left all alone after leaving the only pack I've ever known? My real fear is that something far worse could happen, and my pack retaliates, causing the people I've come to care about to be hurt. I couldn't live with myself if that happened. *Fuck! I have so much to think about and figure out.*

"Alright then, let's get started." He turns on the gun, the sound easing my anxious nerves as the first prick of the needle hits my skin.

The humming mixed with the vibrations lull me into a calm as I cast my gaze around the room. My sight catches on Wylla as she talks to the gorgeous female artist who'll be doing her tattoo. She's a beautiful, busty blonde covered in the most colorful art that seems to tell a story. Confusion hits me at the jealousy I feel when she playfully swats at Wylla's arm as she hands her a folded up piece of paper. It's the same one she hurriedly shoved in her back pocket back at the dorms when she denied my request to look at it.

She looks my way, and I duck my head, trying to avert my attention elsewhere, so it isn't so obvious I was blatantly staring at her. My face grows hot when the girl gives Wylla a seductive smile just before she begins to bite on her lip, allowing her teeth to drag across it. I know for a fact if Wylla was doing that to me, my panties would be soaked. I wonder if Wylla's are? Is she attracted to this girl? I shouldn't be worrying about it or feeling so jealous. I'm apparently mated to multiple people according to Wylla, and even if I wasn't, I've already been promised as a mate to members of my pack.

Wylla takes a seat and lies back on the bed, as the artist begins to ready her tray, moving her chair in my line of sight, blocking my view of Wylla. As time passes, they continue to talk in hushed tones that I can't hear. *That's fucking odd.* Being a wolf, I should be able to hear everything they're saying, which leads me to believe that Wylla cast some type of spell. Is she into this girl and doesn't want me to hear? Is she talking about me? The tattoo? Fuck, why am I feeling this way?

"Hey, Magz," Hex shakes my arm, attempting to gain my attention.

"Fuck, I'm sorry. What did you need?" Looking down, I can see the tattoo is outlined but not finished.

"I was letting you know I'm taking a quick break to get a different shade of gray ink, I really want some contrast in the shading. So if you want to stand and stretch or use the bathroom, now would be the time."

"Okay," is the only thing I can manage to say.

Looking around the room, I fight the impulse, urging me to move closer to Wylla to try to eavesdrop on their conversation that she is obviously keeping masked from me. My strength is dwindling as my will to know what's happening between them grows stronger.

Glancing around the room, I take in all the different designs for tattoos plastered on the wall before I catch the girl lying on the bed in the far corner. Her shirt is laying across her legs, leaving her breasts exposed to all who can see. Her nipple is held captive in these metal clamps the piercer is holding.

"It's hot, isn't it? A woman with her tits pierced always makes my cock rock hard," Hex's deep voice rumbles in my ear as his hot breath skirts across the rim of my ear.

"Does it hurt? Umm... with... you know sex..." God, I feel like an idiot talking to him, not even able to express a complete thought without stumbling over my words.

"Well, some say it hurts for just a bit while it's being done. While others say it hurts like hell after. But everyone says it's fucking amazing sexually. Having their partner tug on them, hook chains to them. The things you could do are endless." His eyes are staring right at me, burning a hole right into my soul.

"I want to do mine," I announce boldly. It's time I do what I want with my body and stop worrying about my father and the pack. Plus, what they can't see won't hurt them.

"Then hop that fine ass back in the chair and let's get you finished. We don't have much more, just some shading, then we'll be done." Doing as he says, I sit back down as he resumes working on my tattoo. My mind drifts, thinking of how it'll feel having my nipples pierced, having them pulled and tugged on as shocks of pleasure explode through my body. The thoughts are so vivid in my mind that a small moan escapes my lips before I can even stop it. A deep rumbling growl echoes through the air. "Keep that up, little wolf, and you'll have a crow descending on you ready to feast on the greatest meal he's ever had. Your moans have my cock begging to bust free from my pants and trust me, I don't think Wylla will like that one bit." He looks over his shoulder, causing me to follow where his line-of-sight ends. *Wylla*. "And by the look in her eyes, if I act upon what I want to do, she'll have me tied to a stick roasting over a fire."

He gets back to work on my arm, finishing up the shading, leaving me to mull over his words while stealing glances at Wylla. Once he's done, he cleans the area before placing some *Sorry Mom* balm on it along with some clear cling wrap as he goes over the care instructions with me. Once he is sure I understand, he guides me over to the woman who I watched pierce the other girl's nipples.

"Jewel, this is Magz, and she wants to get her cute, little nipples pierced." He lets her know.

"Cool, are you comfortable out here or do you prefer a private room?" she asks, as she finishes cleaning the bed she just used.

"Private!" I announce quickly and without thought. There's no way in hell I'm ready to expose my chest to anyone, much less a room of people.

"No problem, let me finish up here, and we'll head to the room right over there." She gestures to the room, where the door is open to the left of her.

Hex places his hand on the small of my back, before letting it slide around my side and pulls me closer to him. "Need any help with taking care of your tattoo or piercings, just give me a call. And if you want help with the other," dropping his eyes to my crotch, "I'm your man, I'll fly there in a minute." He gives a small squeeze before letting his hand fall away, and he turns and walks away, heading over to his work area to clean up.

"Okay, Magz, let's get you taken care of." She motions towards the room, heading inside, and I quickly follow behind her.

Twenty minutes later, I'm putting my shirt back on, still in shock that I not only got a tattoo but two, no wait technically three piercings since getting here. *Who the hell am I?* Now it's kicking in what I've done and fear and worry take over thinking about how the hell my father is going to respond.

Magnolia

Wylla and I strolled back to our dorm linked arm-in-arm the next morning with our large cups of coffee in hand. She has me giggling, telling me about the girl from yesterday at the tattoo parlor and a story she had told her about a guy who came in and got his junk tattooed. I'd nonchalantly mentioned in a conversation on the way home last night how it seemed like the girl was into her, and all she could do was laugh. *"Magz, no! Why the hell would you think that?"* she had balked, but never gave me a legitimate confirmation that she wasn't. After not getting any clarification, I dropped it, feeling like she didn't want to tell me.

"So how are the nips today?" A devilish grin crosses her face as she gives me a slight hip bump that almost makes me spill my coffee.

"Umm... A little tender and sensitive as hell. I couldn't wear a bra today because it kept rubbing on them, hence the oversized sweatshirt," I confess, looking down at my body, as visions fill my mind of Wylla, tongue out, teasing them, as she straddles me on our bed.

Where the hell did that come from?

"So where are the guys this morning? Figured they'd be attached to you like flypaper," she asks coyly.

"Probably asleep. Why?"

"Just surprised to get you all to myself. They seem to be stuck up your ass lately, and with the way your eyes light up, it seems you're enjoying it. If I'm being honest, I just kind of feel in the way, like a fifth wheel on the Magz bus. To me, it felt like we had a connection, that there was something between us, and I kind of feel used right now." I go to speak up, interrupting her, barely getting the start of her name out, but she stops dead in her tracks, untangling her arm from mine and places her finger on my lip.

"No, listen to me, please. There are some things I need to get off my chest before they eat away at me. I know the pack you're from, and you feel you have to obey them. Honestly, I think you suffer from some type of Stockholm Syndrome, but we'll talk about that another day. From the first time we met, I felt a connection, a draw to you, and I thought you felt the same. Then we do the spell and find you have multiple mates, and I was like 'fuck yeah, this explains shit'. It could be me, and I know Blaine already says his wolf screams to him about the mate bond between the two of you. Then there are the other two meatheads who want you, but isn't there space for me? Fuck, I wouldn't mind having some of them too. Hell, from the first time I met Jude, I wondered what it would feel like to have his demon cock slamming into me as I'm bent over a desk. Just tell me, honestly, do you have feelings for me or am I imagining them? The stuff with the guys we can figure out later." A deep sigh escapes her as she stares at me, wide-eyed and anxious, awaiting my answer.

I pause, staring in awe. I do like her, there's no doubt about it. "Wylla, I do like you, and I mean really like you and the guys. I have this pull to each of you that I can't seem to explain. Crap, it's just I've had eighteen years of being told I had to be one way. Even though I have always wanted more, I'm scared of going against my father, and the pack. What would happen to me, to you guys if I did? There are so many emotions running through me, and I'm trying to process them all, to find that strength in me to stand against my father and become the person I want to be." My heart races as I bare my soul to her about how I feel.

"You are being a badass. Look at you! Tattoos, piercings, you're already finding that strength and rebelling. Just keep it up and don't be afraid. The Exodus pack is not the only place for you, and you'll always have us in your corner." She takes her hand and wraps it around me, pulling me closer to her as she rests her head in the crook of my neck. "You will always have me, Magz, just don't push me away anymore. I need to feel like you want me around."

"Okay, can you give me some time and not give up on me yet?" I ask between sniffles.

She pulls away from me, a smile gracing her face. "Yes. Now let's get back to our room. I still need to work on my English assignment." She links her arm back with mine, and we continue the walk back to our dorm.

We chit-chat about what she wants for her next tattoo the rest of the way. When we enter our room, I head straight for my desk, knowing I should really go ahead and knock out my assignment for Mr. Godrickson's class. He told us to pick a supernatural type to learn more about and write a two thousand-word essay on what we found. I picked a ferret. Surprise, surprise.

Placing my cup of coffee on my desk and taking a seat, I power up my laptop, wishing I hadn't when I get the email notification popping up. I see who it's from and dread fills me.

Magnolia,

I hope you are following all the rules as we discussed. Your mother and I look forward to seeing you at home this Friday for your weekend visit. Attached is your travel information for your flight that is leaving on Friday.

Father.

My heart sinks, and I feel sick. I knew it was coming, it just seems to have come too quickly. My panic grows when I realize I now have tattoos and piercings to cover, both against what I was allowed to do. He's going to fucking kill me.

Wylla must sense my attitude change, as I've gone quiet and rigid. "Magz, what's wrong? You look pale as shit like you've seen a ghost or something. If you did, it's okay; they're cool as fuck. I had a friend back home that would have me laughing so hard I thought I was going to die. She used to fuck with the humans non-stop, scaring the shit out of them. This one time this snotty ass bitch actually shit herself, she was scared so bad. Best day of my life until I met you."

Turning to face her, I let out a long sigh. "No. It's an email from my father reminding me I'm to come home this weekend, no ifs, ands, or buts. I'm scared, Wylla. What's he going to say when he sees me, the changes I've made? Oh no, the spell. He's going to know what we've done. Oh fuck, oh fuck!" I begin to breathe rapidly, hyperventilating.

When I feel a sharp sting across my face, I look at Wylla. *She freaking slapped me!*

"First off, I'm sorry about that, but I had to get you to calm down. Second, we didn't remove any spells, so he'll never know. While you're gone, I'm meeting with my grandmother, and I'm going to talk about the spells we need to do. So stop worrying about that. Third, we'll find a way to cover up your sexy ass modifications to your body. Just act like you normally would at home and everything will be okay. It's just a couple of days, you can do it." Her pep talk helps, and I feel my heart slow as I calm down.

"You're right, just a quick trip in and out. I can do this."

A knock at the door draws our attention as Wylla makes her way over. The rhythmic sway of her hips calms me even more. She grips the handle and opens the door. "Well, well, if it isn't my second favorite scent, smoke and honey." A scent that overtakes me as well, my body calling out, wanting to be near it.

Jude

Standing at the girls' door, I'm nervous for goddess knows what reason, but here I am. Well, really it has more to do with the fact that I came to invite them up to our room for pizza and drinks. Lifting my hand, I knock swiftly on the door. It doesn't take long before it's swung open to reveal Wylla standing there looking frazzled.

"Well, well, if it isn't my second favorite scent, smoke and honey," she says loudly, before mouthing, '*help me*', and moves her eyes quickly over to Maggie who's sitting on the bed about to cry.

Stepping inside the room, I rush right past Wylla and kneel down in front of Maggie. I lay my hands on her thighs. "What's wrong, babe?"

"Nothing, it's stupid. I'm fine." I can tell she's fighting hard to hold back her sobs.

Reaching up, I grab her chin and turn her, so she can look into my eyes and know how serious I am. "No way, Maggie, I'm here to listen and be your friend. Tell me how I can help."

She wipes the tear that left her eye and sighs before straightening her spine and looking over my shoulder to where Wylla stands, watching us. She must give her a look or something because Maggie nods her head, then sighs. "I got an email from my dad. He wanted to make sure I was behaving and living up to the standards and rules given to me before I came to school. Then he gave me my travel arrangements for my trip home this weekend, and I, well, I just started to panic."

I stand up and sit on the bed with my back against the wall and reach out to her, pulling her into my lap. Wrapping my arms around her, I kiss the top of her head. "What are you anxious about? Let's see if we can fix some of the issues."

"Jude, I'm not supposed to have any jewelry or tattoos, and I went and got both. If my dad or Alpha see them, I'm as good as dead. They'll mark me as not mate-worthy, then what will I do?" She starts crying again.

"Okay, first of all, it's Fall, so you can wear long sleeves and no one will see the sexy little ink you got. As for the piercings, depending on where they are you can get some tape and cover them up. I will get a roll and drop it off to you Friday before you leave," I murmur into her hair as I hold her.

"But how can I hide the one in my nose? I think they'll notice the tape there. I can't take it out yet, and it's a hoop, so I can't just flip it up in my nose like the internet says you should be able to do," she rushes out without taking a breath. I can tell her anxiety is rising again.

"Yes, you're right. If we can't hide it with tape, and Wylla can't cover it with some type of spell, then you simply say you made an error in judgment and ask for forgiveness. See, taken care of."

She nods in approval, and I rub my hands up and down her arms in comfort. I look up to Wylla who is leaning against the wall by the door, watching us. She mouths thank you, and I wink back at her.

"Anyway, babes, I came here to see if you little hotties wanted to come up to our room for some fine dining. In case you were wondering, the chef will be serving pizza and beer."

Maggie turns, so she's facing me as she listens to my request, and she looks undecided. Meanwhile, Wylla stays silent. I'm assuming she's going to follow her girl's lead on this. But I need them to come upstairs; the guys have no idea what I'm up to. Before I left I just told them to clean our room like our parents would want and sent Zeke to get supplies. My goal here is to surprise them and have a chill but fun night with our ladies. Knowing I haven't paid as much attention to Wylla as Maggie lately since we are trying to show her how serious we are, but I need to. Though I don't think Wylla is the type of witch who needs constant reassurance of my interest. I really fucking want them to come upstairs, so I need to butter them up.

"Now, I know you're still iffy on some of the things involving the two fucks upstairs, but let us wine and dine you ladies with the finest beer we could find at the gas station." I wiggle my eyebrows suggestively at Maggie.

Maggie giggles. "Sure."

I turn to Wylla to get her answer, but she just rolls her eyes at me. "Alright, demon boy, you win. Let us get cleaned up a bit, and we'll come up for your greasy pizza and shitty beer."

Standing up, I pump my fist in the air. "Fuck yeah! I'll wait here while you two do what ya need to get ready. Perhaps a little changing of clothes? Ehhhh? Or you two could massage lotion on one another's backs," I tease. "I could supervise or be a spare hand if needed."

Maggie laughs some more as she stands from the bed and heads toward the closet. I'm watching her ass in the sweats she has on, so intently I don't see the pencil cup thrown at me until it smacks the side of my head, "Lotion? On each other's backs? Really? I thought as an Incubus, you'd have a wilder imagination than that. Besides, I think we can handle that ourselves. I'm well versed in massages and don't need to be supervised by a horny ass demon," Wylla says as she crosses her arms and quirks a brow at me.

"Baby, I have quite the imagination. You'd be shocked at the filthy things I could dream up to do to your body."

A tiny gasp has both of us whipping our heads toward the closet. Where Maggie is standing in a new shirt but has her legs clenched, rubbing her thighs together.

I stroll over to her, making sure to allow the lust to waft off me in waves, and wrap my arms around her, bringing my lips close to her ear, "That turn you on, Maggie? Hearing I want to do filthy things to your roommate and you?"

A quiet whimper is all I get in answer. Wylla, being the annoying but sexy little witch that she is, comes over and grabs Maggie's hand, pulling her out of my hold. "Come on, lovebirds, let's go upstairs. I'm starving."

Maggie looks back at me with her bottom lip between her teeth but lets Wylla pull her from the room. I follow behind them as we get to the elevator, and we are all silent as we ride up one level to our floor. Leading the way out of the elevator to our door, I turn the knob, then kick the door open, so it flies against the wall. "Surprise, fuckers! We have guests."

Blaine

Jude, that smug, sly little bastard, saunters into the room with Magnolia and Wylla behind him. This explains why he had Zeke and me clean our nasty ass room. Also, why he asked Zeke to go down to the gas station to get beer. We thought maybe he was trying to have a party. This is a much better idea, though. Just the girls and us. It's all the party we need, and it gives me a chance to get a little closer to Magnolia.

Wylla plops down on the bed next to me. Jude snags Magnolia around the waist as she passes him and pulls her down into his lap in the computer chair he likes to sit in. She's giggling, and the sweet sound has my cock jerking in my pants. *Mate!* My wolf must like the sound of her sweet little giggles, too. I settle him with promises that I'm working on getting her to believe she belongs to us. I'm staring at Magnolia in awe when our door once again opens, and Zeke stands in the door frame frozen with both hands full of beer.

He swiftly composes himself and puts the beer in the mini-fridge. "You guys all want one?"

"Yes," comes from everyone. Zeke pulls them out and, one by one, hands them to us. There's a knock on the door as he grabs one for himself. Cracking open the lid to the can, he takes a drink, ignoring whoever's at the door, and takes a seat on his bed.

"I got it," I call out, a little annoyed, as I stand from my bed and head to it. Opening the door, I see it's the pizza. I grab the pizzas and set them on top of the fridge when my ears pick up the rumbling of someone's stomach. Turning, I see Magnolia wide-eyed in embarrassment.

"Sorry, I must be hungrier than I thought," she whispers. Her face turns the cutest shade of pink, hiding her face in Jude's shirt. I quickly give my attention back to the pizza boy and throw him a ten and shut the door without another word. I don't have time for pleasantries with the delivery driver. My mate is hungry, and my wolf wants her to eat.

"Magnolia, you come get your slices first. The rest of these delinquents can wait," I tell her as I hand her a paper plate. She accepts it as she stands and grabs two slices of the veggie pizza. I throw another on her plate as she turns back to her seat. She quirks a brow at me, but I just shrug, "Sorry, babe, my wolf wants you good and full."

Her eyes widen a bit before she composes herself and sits in the extra chair next to Jude and starts eating. I catch a glimpse of Wylla and what looks to be hurt on her face. Not wanting to upset my mate's best friend, "Wylla, you're next." She jumps up, grabs a plate, and places two pieces of meat lovers on it. For some reason, my wolf screams out to me that she needs more. Doing the same as I had with Magnolia, I add an extra slice to her plate, earning a curious look from her that I quickly brush off.

We've all had our fill of pizza, and I think each of us is feeling tipsy from the beers we've drunk while eating and chatting about our lives. I'm also feeling slightly annoyed that Jude is monopolizing all of Magnolia's time. He keeps directing all his questions to her and touching her every chance he gets. I love him and all, but I'm kind of thinking about breaking a finger or two if he doesn't start sharing.

"Blaine, why are you growling?" Magnolia asks, pulling me from my fantasy of snapping my best friend's fingers while laughing about it. *Shit! I didn't realize I was growling.* I try to think of a response that won't upset our sweet little mate, but I come up with nothing. I open my mouth to apologize when Wylla saves the day. Or should I say saves my fucking ass?

"We should play truth or dare!" she squeals in delight as she claps her hands together. I look at her baffled. Where does she get this shit? No one says anything, we all stare at her silently. "What? Are you worried you won't be able to handle playing with me, boys?" she quips, and Jude cackles.

"I'll play," Jude says as he catches his breath. Magnolia just nods in agreement.

"What about you, noodle rat, you wanna play?" she asks while looking at Zeke. This causes Jude to fall out of his chair, laughing, and Zeke quirks a smile at her brazen mouth.

"Yeah, sassy witch, I'll play," comes from him gruffly. But what surprises me is that he didn't come back at her with something worse.

Wylla then snaps her gaze to mine. "Come on, Fido, we're waiting on you." I have to say her term of endearment is growing on me.

"Fine, Magnolia, truth or dare?"

She worries her bottom lip between her teeth before whispering, "Truth."

"Is it true that if you weren't terrified of the Exodus Alpha and your Dad, you would date someone in this room?" I ask. The guys' and Wylla's eyes snap to me, and I'm definitely getting some glares and some what-the-fuck looks, but I want to know the answer. Deep down, I'm sure they do too.

"Yes," she says, and I just nod at her answer, not wanting to push her any further. "So now it's my turn to pick someone, right?" she asks quickly, no doubt to keep us from asking anything further about her response.

"Fucking hell! You've never played before, Magz?" Wylla asks, her tone laced with shock. Magnolia shakes her head and giggles. Damn, that sound has me hardening again.

"No, but I get the gist of it. So I get to ask, right?" she asks again. Wylla nods, and Magnolia wastes no time. "Wylla, truth or dare?"

"Dare."

"Hmm. I dare you to kiss one of the guys." She laughs, and my eyes bug out of my head as I look at her. She wouldn't dare Wylla to do something bold unless the beer loosened her up. Wylla stands up and straightens her outfit as she moves to the center of the room. She freezes there for a second, looking at each of us guys, then she moves toward me.

"I want to try something," she says as she gets to me and leans down, pressing her lips against mine. She moves her tongue against the seam of my lips, and I open for her, allowing her entry. Sliding her tongue in my mouth, we deepen the kiss, fighting for dominance. I can feel my cock growing hard with this kiss. This shouldn't happen with anyone but my mate. *What the fuck is happening?*

A small growl from the side of us has me gently pushing Wylla away. We both look over to where the sound is coming from and see a confused and slightly hurt look on Magnolia's face. "I guess maybe you do wanna date someone in this room, huh, Magz? Maybe your mate or someone else?" Wylla purrs as she settles back into her spot next to me.

Magnolia quickly recovers, putting a smile on her face as she flips Wylla off before quieting down so Wylla can pick her victim. This girl has to be more than tipsy at this point. She's acting way more fun and free than she has ever before in front of us. Minus the night at the mixer, when we were dancing, but she was with Wylla that night mainly.

"Jude, truth or dare?"

"Dare, babe, there ain't no way I'd pick truth after the show I just saw the last dare get," he teases.

"I dare you to kiss Magz." Magnolia gasps but turns her gaze to Jude next to her. Jude leans in and sucks her bottom lip into his mouth. I growl and quickly receive a hard punch to the arm. Snapping my attention to the little witch who just hit me, she's giving me a death glare, so I take that as my 'stop fucking growling, you just kissed me' lecture. Groaning has my attention, so I refocus on my best friend and mate kissing. She whimpers slightly as they kiss, which has Jude breaking the kiss, and he chuckles.

"Well, Z man, you're the only one left, so truth or dare?" Jude asks.

"Truth," Z says, which shocks the shit out of me. I thought for sure with all his issues with his ferret, he'd pick dare.

"Chicken shit!" Jude yells. "But fine, if you could be any shifter, what would you be?" Goddess above, Jude would ask the one question that would cause the most issues. No one else would ever ask Zeke that because he has enough self-doubt about his shifted form.

Zeke winces as Jude finishes his truth. "Um, I'd be a dragon; they're powerful and most feared."

The room is quiet as we sit in awkward silence. I'm sure like me, nobody really knows what to say after that. Deciding I have to say something, I just hope I don't make an ass out of myself. "Zee–" I'm cut off by an angry gray-haired wolf.

"No! I like you just how you are, and you shouldn't be ashamed of it. I know I'm not ashamed to be close with you knowing what you are," she scolds. At some point, she stood up and is in front of Zeke, shaking her finger at him like an angry school teacher.

Zeke's eyes are wide in shock that she's so upset with his choice of words. He says nothing, staring at her in admiration. Me? I fell in love with her the moment I saw her and knew she was my mate. Now? I fall for her even more. I fucking hope we can figure out her pack and dad situation because I need this girl more than air.

Taking a quick look around the room, I see I'm not the only one feeling that way. Zeke and Jude are both staring at her with pure heat in their eyes. All of us are waiting for the other to make a move. Hell, for her to make a move. Wylla stands suddenly and claps.

"Well, it's been fun, fellas, but it's time to say goodbye." She grabs Magnolia's hand and pulls her, rushing from the room.

"What the fuck?" Jude barks out at her just as they reach the door. Wylla whips around and smirks at him with a shit-eating grin.

"Calm down, sexcubus, it's late and we have class tomorrow, ya know." She gives us a wink and opens the door, pushing a giggling Magnolia out the door.

What the fuck? I think all three of us were just cock blocked by a necromancer. Isn't she supposed to raise bones, not kill them? *Ha! I just made a necromancer sex joke.* I suppose it's a good thing she dragged my mate from this room. I was ready to ravage her, and Goddess knows she's not ready for that. I can't wait for this spell to be done, so she knows who her mates are and that it's not anyone from her pack back home. I'm as sure of that as I am of my next breath. Until then, I just have to be patient and play it cool.

Zeke

I wait for the door to shut behind the girls before reaching down, picking up my shoe from the floor, and chucking it across the room, right at Blaine's head. "What the fuck, dude!" he barks out, barely holding onto the beer in his hand.

"What the hell was that shit with Wylla? You claimed relentlessly that Magnolia was your mate, then you go and kiss her best friend like that. Dude, I could see your hard-on from here, imagine what Magnolia saw and how she felt about it. If you screw this up for me now that we are finally heading to a good place, I'll fucking kill you."

"Dude, it was a game. I thought we were all playing and having fun. She didn't seem mad, especially when she turned around and kissed this fucker over here," he says, pointing in Jude's direction before running his fingers through his hair.

"Yeah, I get that it's a game, but you fucking enjoyed it." I mean, really, who the hell does he want to be with?

He lets out a deep sigh, falling back on the bed as he lifts his hands and begins rubbing his eyes. "Fuck, man, it was weird as shit. I know Magnolia is my mate, and I can feel it so intensely, my wolf feels it, needs it. But there's this pull to Wylla as well, not as great as the one I have to Magnolia, though. The kiss was so fucking good, man. It went straight to my cock, and at no time did I or my wolf feel like it was wrong, or forbidden." He sits back up before continuing, "Goddess, this is fucking confusing as hell, but you're jumping down my throat. What about the sex demon over there practically fucking my mate in front of me? What the hell was that shit, Jude?" he growls out as he clenches and unclenches his hands. I have a sinking feeling he's trying to reign in his anger and not go flying across the room toward Jude.

"Fuck you, Blaine, you're being a fucking hypocrite. You want to bitch at me for playing the game and kissing the girl who I also have a fucking pull to. Yeah, you heard me, I have a pull to her as well, and you heard what Wylla said just as good as me, she has multiple mates. You just seem to have selective memory when it comes to that little fact. So if you and your wolf are smart, you'll know you need to get used to it. For all we know, I might be one of those other mates. I plan to kiss her just as much as I fucking can. Wait, let me rephrase that, her and my rainbow sprite. Hopefully soon, I can make sweet love to them," Jude fucking croons, and I want to barf. Imagining him having sex with anyone, let alone the girl I want, makes me feel ill.

"Both of you cocksuckers need to get your cocks in check. Just make sure you don't fucking screw shit up. She's finally over what happened in the woods, and I don't want to make her upset again. Shit, you heard her, she's okay with me being a ferret. No one's ever been okay with it before. Once chicks find out what my shifted form is, they bolt. Magnolia accepts me, and I know she is my future, the one." I pour my heart out to them. I've never felt for someone like I do Magnolia, and it's scary. I've fallen for her fast and hard. "We just need to make sure we're not fucking with their feelings. I like Wylla, and I have a pull to her just like you guys claim, but not the way I do to Magnolia. But leading her on, making her think there are more feelings for her than there really are, is wrong."

"I get it. Really, I do, but I don't feel like I'm leading her on because I genuinely have feelings for her too. It's hard to explain, maybe it's because I'm an incubus, and we have the ability to love or care for more than one person with more ease than most." Jude stands slowly from his seat and walks over to the trash can, dropping his empty bottle in it before heading to the mini-fridge and pulling out another.

"And it seems like our pretty little wolf has caught the attention of the witch too. I think they're friends, but if my intuition is right, Wylla feels more than just friendship toward Magnolia. She might feel a pull too and be a mate, it might be why we all feel pulled to her as well, just not as strongly. We need to be mindful of Wylla and her feelings for Magnolia too, not just ourselves. The four of us could be the mates she will be looking for once that fucking spell is lifted." He lifts the bottle to his lips, swallowing down the liquid.

Looking over at Blaine, I see his face turned down to the floor. He feels it as well, even though he may not want to admit it. "Okay, so we continue to get close to Magnolia but be mindful of how we're treating Wylla. We don't want anyone's feelings to be hurt."

We all nod in agreement and drop the subject. We spend the rest of the night drinking and bullshitting before we finally call it quits and go to bed.

Wylla

We stumble down the hall, ping-ponging from one wall to the other, holding hands and giggling. *Shit, we drank a lot.* I thought the pizza would help absorb some of the alcohol, but either I didn't eat enough or drank way too much for it to work. Probably the latter, since wolf boy put an extra slice on my plate. Not that I'm complaining because I ate it, but still, *WEIRD!*

"Wylla! How much further till our door? I wanna sleep," Magz slurs from beside me. My girl is drunk too, and she is adorable like this. Giggly as hell, her pupils are blown, and she has a tinge of red covering her chest. She has been so fun and like a normal run-of-the-mill college student tonight, not worrying about what her father or her pack would think. I'm glad we decided to go upstairs.

"We're almost to the elevator, baby, then just a few more steps."

She turns to me with heat in her eyes, wagging her brows at me and biting her bottom lip between her teeth. *Fuck me!* I can't believe I just called her baby. She seems to have liked it, though. I'm just as confused as ever. Magz just told me she has feelings, but she needs time to work through them, but then she's wagging her brows as her pussy pretty much drips for me in the hallway? This wolf needs a therapist or an Exodus Pack exorcism.

I seriously think if she was free from the fear of her pack and Dad, she wouldn't think twice about being with any one of us. Her stupid ass pack has so many rules on mating though, no same sex, no non-Exodus wolves, hell no non-wolves at all. It's insane. Why, of all people, did I have to fall in love with someone from that pack? *Karma is a fucking bitch!*

We step inside the elevator, and Magz hits every single button trying to hit our floor number, but somehow seems to miss it. I laugh as I reach around her and hit our floor, amusement filling me at seeing her so playful. She sighs and leans against the wall, murmuring her thanks. I smile and wait for the ride to end now that we have to go up to the top and back down.

Getting to our floor, the doors slide open, and I step off, grabbing Magz's hand and pulling her behind me. We get to our room in a few strides, and I unlock the door, letting us in. Magz rushes past me and strips down to her bra and panties. She plops down on her bed, laying face down on top of her blankets. Chuckling, I move to my closet and grab a shirt to sleep in and quickly change into it. Once changed, I grab my clothes and pick up Magz's discarded ones from various places on the floor and shove them into our hamper. *Damn, we are gonna have to do laundry soon.*

I sit down on my bed and look over at Magz who is still face down on her mattress. "Magz, girl, are you still with me?" I see her stir when I call her name, and she rolls over and stares at me. "Hi, friend. You okay over there?" She smiles and nods at me, pulling a blanket up over her body. "Did you have fun tonight?" I question.

"Mmhhmm, so much fun."

"You seemed upset when I kissed Fido. Are we okay or do we need to talk?" Now probably isn't the time for this conversation, but I want to know where we stand if that game damaged our friendship.

"NOPE!" she says, popping the P.

"Okay, well you were growling, so are you sure?"

"Yeess, Wylla, I'm sure. The growling was for both of you." She hiccups and gasps at her admission. I smile at her, letting her know it's fine for her to be honest with me. "Also, it was hot."

"Well, okay, if you say so. How was your kiss with the demon? Was that hot?" I ask, laying down and pulling my blanket up to my chin. She is giving me radio silence. Did I ask something wrong? Did she not like it and doesn't want to admit it? I open my mouth to ask again, then I hear her soft snores. *This bitch passed out on me!* I'm cackling on the inside. I don't want to wake her up, ya know?

Laying in bed, I close my eyes to try to sleep, but I'm plagued with thoughts on how it felt to kiss Blaine. I felt my magic call out to him. The urge to leave my magic mark on him was not as strong as it is with Magz, but it was definitely there. Watching her with the demon was sexy as hell. All I could picture was me between them as they kissed and explored each other's bodies.

Also, it was nice to be included tonight. Magz has been better since we had our talk this morning. The guys tonight though were way more inclusive to me, and I had a good ass time. I didn't feel like their fifth wheel at all. I hope the last week was just growing pains, and this is how it is from now on. Tonight's events make me want to stay and not ask for a new room. I feel like this could be the start of our own little pack.

Magnolia

Ugh... my head's pounding. I struggle to open my eyes, only to be assaulted by the brightness of the room that makes my stomach turn. Why the hell did I drink so much last night? I know why; I wanted to cut loose for a change, be me, and not worry about who anyone else thinks I should be. Waking up this morning to my first fucking hangover ever, I'm seriously rethinking my choices. The only thing puzzling me is why the hell I didn't feel like death warmed over when I drank wine with Wylla.

I manage to open my eyes long enough to lift my head and look over to see that Wylla's bed is empty. I wonder where she is and if she feels like shit also. I slowly sit up, having to reach out and steady myself by placing my hands on the bed because the room is making me feel like I'm on the tilt-a-whirl ride at the fair.

Swinging my legs off the side of the bed, I start to stand, but immediately drop back down when the room begins to spin. Fuck me! I'm never drinking again in my life! Once I think I've gotten the room to stop turning, I stand again. *Success!* Moving over to my desk, I decide to open my laptop and check my emails, just to make sure I didn't do something stupid like send something to my father that I'll live to regret.

Dropping down into my seat, I type in my password–it's a simple one, *password*–then I open my email. Before I do anything else, I check my sent folder. Nothing. Thank you, Goddess, for keeping me from doing anything stupid last night. Well, other than the game of truth or dare that I vividly remember. That's something to think about at another time. I just want to bask in the fact I won't have my father or the Alpha beating down my door and dragging me out by my hair.

Clicking back over to the incoming mail, I open it to a message from Professor Godrickson.

Miss Holloway,

Sorry for the early email, but I need to speak with you during my office hours today between 4 and 5 PM. If this does not work for you, please let me know and we can discuss a time that would be more feasible for you to come in.

Thank you,

Professor Godrickson

What the hell does he want?

I'm still stewing over it when I hear the bedroom door open and shut behind me. "Oh, you're awake," Wylla says softly, making me think either she also has a hangover, or she's pretty confident I do and is taking pity on me. Either way, I'm one hundred percent okay with her toning down her bubbly ass self this morning.

"Yeah," I muster, still worrying over what Godrickson wants to see me about.

"What's wrong? You look like someone's pissed in your cornflakes. You just woke up. What could have happened between the time I left the room to take a shower and now?" she asks as she sits down on the edge of her bed, looking at me intently. I can see how concerned she is, but when she speaks up, I know what has her looking at me the way she is. "Did your dad contact you? Or your Alpha? Are they making more demands of you?" she rattles off in succession.

"Umm... Professor Godrickson wants to see me today during his office hours," I mumble nervously.

"You lucky ass bitch, fuck me. I mean, I wish he would fuck me." She cackles in excitement as she fans herself with her hand. "I'd kill to be alone in his office with him. Your fine tail better wear a short ass fucking skirt and no underwear and make sure to bend over and show him that tight, pretty pussy of yours." I feel my face growing warm and my panties becoming damp at the image her words create.

"Wylla, stop. What if it's serious? I can't be failing because school just started. I'm freaked the fuck out, and you're over here making sex jokes."

"Girl, you're worrying about nothing. Maybe he just has an extra credit assignment for you," she says, tossing me a flirtatious wink as she spreads her legs wide, allowing her towel to ride up and bare her naked pussy to me.

Fuck me, this woman has my hormones on overload. I've never been drawn to a woman like I am to her. Seeing her there, freshly showered, legs open with her clean shaven core on display, I want to sink to my knees on the floor in front of her and have a taste.

"Magz... Magz..." She pulls me from my erotic fantasy. "Where did you go? Look, it will be okay. Go shower, get dressed, and we'll go grab some coffee and something to eat."

"Fine, but Wylla, seriously, have you seen my silhouette? Geesh!" We both let out a laugh, happy to break the tenseness of the situation for a moment before I continue speaking "But really Wylla, what could he want?" I whine to her as I gather my clothes and get my shower caddy to go take a shower.

"Magz... stoppppp! You're not going to know until you meet with him. So shut up, get dressed, and stop stressing, for Goddess' sake." She stands from the bed, and in a few graceful strides, she's standing in front of me. Reaching her hand up, she takes the stray strands of hair that have fallen into my face and tucks them behind my ear. "Trust me. Everything is going to be okay, and if it's not, you got me and the lugheads upstairs. We got your back, with everything, baby." She leans in, places her lips on mine, and kisses me. A kiss so soft and delicate, but so intoxicating. "Now, go shower." She turns and heads to her closet, looking for something to wear.

Bringing my hands to my lips, I touch them, savoring the way hers felt against mine. *I long for them to be back on me.* Fuck, help me. Between the three cocks upstairs and the pussy in my room, my virgin ass is scared. How the hell do I handle all this? Are they even going to really want someone as inexperienced as me?

Opening the door, I step into the hallway and head to the shower, my pussy begging for some attention. Goddess, I hope no one is there because I really need to take care of myself.

Standing in front of Professor Godrickson's door, my nerves are on overload. All I can think about is how he looked at me during class today. Every time I looked up, I saw his eyes on me, the heat of them burning a hole right through me, but he never spoke directly to me.

Jude must have sensed my unease, reaching out and covering my hand with his, squeezing gently. "What's wrong, Maggie?" he whispered as softly as he could with his deep voice. I shake my head no, hoping he takes it, but no such luck. "Nuh uh, spill it." His voice was deeper and more forceful.

Leaning in closer to him, keeping my voice low so I don't draw attention to myself, I explained what was wrong. "Professor Godrickson wants to see me in his office today during his office hours."

"Want me or the three of us to come with you? It's probably nothing." He tried to comfort me with his words.

"Nah, I'm a big girl. I can do it alone. I've just got myself worked up."

Hell, I'm still worked up. Taking a deep breath, I lift my hand and knock on the door.

"Come in!" he shouts out from the other side. Opening the door, I step inside to see him seated behind his desk with a laptop open in front of him.

"Magnolia, thank you for coming in today. Please, shut the door and take a seat," he tells me as he motions towards the plaid-patterned, wingback chair in front of his desk.

Moving nervously over to the chair, I slowly sit down on the edge of it, keeping my back rigid as I let my bag fall to the floor and cross my hands in my lap. He cocks his eye at me in confusion for a moment before speaking again, "You look nervous, Magnolia. I assure you there is no reason to be. I simply wanted to discuss a couple of things with you."

"Oh, okay." I know it sounds like I'm a bumbling idiot, but I truly don't know what else to freaking say to him.

"First, I just want to make sure you're okay. The other day when we ran into each other, you seemed upset. I just wanted to check on you." He pauses, staring at me intently, no doubt waiting for my response. I'm caught off guard. I've never had a teacher concerned about me being upset. *Why is he?*

"Yeah, I'm fine. Had a misunderstanding with a friend, but we're working through it. Is that all you wanted to discuss with me?" I ask as my shoulders relax a bit, knowing it wasn't anything too serious. I slide back in my chair and get more comfortable.

"Great, I'd hate to see you upset." I couldn't help to feel there was some underlying message in his words. "Now, the second thing I wanted to talk to you about. Your knowledge of the supernatural world is limited, through no fault of your own. Sadly, your pack is one that feels women should be ignorant of the world around them. What I want to do, if you're in agreement, is offer some private tutoring to get you up to date. We can meet two or three times a week at this time, or whatever is more compatible with your schedule." He pauses, his eyes laser-focused on me, as he sits in silence.

"Y-y-y-you want to tutor me? That's what the email was about?" Confusion and relief overwhelm me at the moment.

"Yes." His response is short and simple. "I feel it would make this semester's course load easier for you, as well as increase your understanding of the various types of species out there. I imagine it must be confusing for you to encounter species you never knew existed." He shuts his laptop, placing his elbows on his desk as he leans forward.

"Oh, that sounds good. Would it just be you and me?" Fuck, he already has me on edge. How could I handle what I assume would be an hour a day for three days a week?

"Yes. You are the only one at a disadvantage with the knowledge. Is that okay? I promise I won't bite." He opens his mouth to say more, but quickly clamps it shut. Fucking great, now all I can think is about him pinning me down and sinking his teeth into me. My panties are damp from my arousal, and I wonder if he can smell it. *Shit, I'll be so embarrassed if he can.* I need to hurry this along and get the fuck up out of here.

"Okay, when do you want to start, Professor Godrickson?"

"How's tomorrow? Same time, same place." He smiles hopefully at me, and goddess, it makes me want to swoon.

"Perfect. Anything else? If not, then I need to go and take care of my homework." I bend over, pick my bag up from the floor, and stand as I slide the strap on my shoulder. The whole time I'm doing it I mentally replay Wylla's words about me doing this very thing except in a skirt and no panties. He stands as well and reaches out to shake my hand. Placing mine in his, I'm stunned by the electrical shock that passes between us. I immediately drop his hand and bolt for the exit, stopping momentarily to wave an awkward goodbye as I open the door and step out into the hallway. *What the hell was that?*

I'm surprised to see Wylla, leaning against the wall with a book open in her hands and intently reading. "Waiting for me?"

"Yeah, you were pretty worked up this morning, so I figured I'd be here just in case it was bad, which by the absence of tears on your face, I assume it went well?" Pushing off the wall, she quickly closes the book and loops her arm in mine as we walk down the hallway.

"Well, you were right. It wasn't anything bad. He just wants to do some tutoring sessions to catch me up on the supernatural world and to make sure I was okay from when he saw me the other day. You know, after the whole Zeke in the woods thing. What were you reading? You had a huge ass smile on your face."

"Can I say it now? Fuck it, I don't care. *I told you so. I told you so,*" she sings out to me like a kid before finally calming herself enough to speak again. "Lucky ass bitch, getting to be alone with that sexy ass man. I wonder what he's like in bed. Is he the dominant take charge, whip me around and tell me what to do type, or is he the sweet, cuddle bunny type? I'm down for either. As for what I'm reading, it's this spicy little number about this girl who goes undercover to find her childhood friend who she believes killed her other best friend. Think criminal minds meets mafia. You should read it, we could have a book club."

"Sounds amazing, let's go back to the room and order it, so I can read it too, but we need to wait until after dinner. Jude made me swear we would meet him after my meeting. But before we go, can I tell you something?"

"Of course."

"When I touched Professor Godrickson's hand, I felt a shock run through me. It wasn't the first time either, it happened before. What do you think it means?"

She's silent for a moment, almost like she wants to be careful in how she responds. "It could be anything, especially with your unique ass situation. You throw everything we think through a loop. I'll do some research and see what I can find out."

"Perfect. Now about that book..."

Jude

Moving my ass across campus, I'm trying to make it to the girls' room before they go to bed. I have the tape to cover Maggie's piercings. I meant to get it to her on Monday, but she was so nervous about her meeting with Mr. Godrickson it slipped my mind. Then it became a crazy whirlwind this week and I totally forgot to give it to her. Classes really picked up with the workload, so we've barely managed to even see Wylla and Maggie outside of class. We made sure to have dinner in the dining hall every night this week, so we could eat together. It was the highlight of each day for me but it was hardly the place to give her piercing tape.

Listening to both girls recall their day and how each class was for them should have been boring, but I felt hooked on each word. Maggie has been attending tutoring with Godrickson, and while none of us guys are too thrilled that she's alone with a male teacher for an hour each session, we've sucked it up and not bitched and moaned about it. Well, not in front of her, that is. We've definitely done it when she's not around. We've even gone so far as to come up with a plan to sneak Zeke inside the room in his ferret form so he could spy on them. Maggie has already learned so much, and hearing her excited about all the *normal* shit she now knows is amazing. *It's also a tad bit sad and super fucking infuriating.* I'm glad she's getting educated on everything she was clueless about, but I've just got this nagging feeling in my gut there's something more with Godrickson. I just can't put my finger on it.

Reaching the girl's door, I knock and Maggie yells, "Come in." I turn the knob and let myself in, seeing Maggie alone and packing a suitcase that's sitting on her bed.

"Where's Wylla?" I ask her. I thought for sure since she leaves tomorrow, the sexy witch wouldn't stray too far from her.

"Wylla went to the library to do some last-minute research before she calls her grandmother this weekend." She sighs while continuing to pack basic solid color, long sleeve shirts in her bag followed by a pile of black leggings. "I wish I didn't have to go back there," she whispers, barely loud enough for me to hear. Her head is downturned as she stares at the clothes sitting in her suitcase.

"It's only a weekend, Maggie. You got this. Once we have the spells broken, you won't have to if you really don't want to. But until then, we can't let your dad or Alpha know that we know about the blocks. You need to appear clueless about them," I encourage her, reminding her why she's going this weekend.

She sits on the bed. "I know, Jude. I've just really started to enjoy my life here and the freedom to be the real me. I have to go back there and dress and act how they want a good, obedient female wolf to act. Fuck, my dad even plans the meals my mother cooks."

Nodding, I listen to her, and when she's finished, I cross the room and squat in front of her on the bed. "Baby, it's going to be fine. Two days, that's all you gotta get through. You survived them for eighteen years. Two days ain't shit."

"You're right. I'm overreacting. It will be fine," she says as she shakes her body out like that somehow will shake the anxiety out of her too. "Now tell me how to use this tape, little demon."

Grinning, I hold it up in front of her. "It's really easy, Maggie. You legit just rip or cut a piece to size and put it over the piercing. You want it to wrap around the jewelry itself, though, so it's not touching the skin. Then it can't just peel off the skin and make any awkward lumps or bumps."

"That sounds easy enough." She snatches the tape from my hand and shoves it into the front of her suitcase.

"Anything else you need from me, Maggie?" *Like maybe a kiss or my fingers caressing that beautiful clit of yours, easing all this tension built up inside of you.*

"No," she says as another sigh leaves her body. "I'm just hoping it works. If he sees all the *sins* I've committed against my body, he'll flip his lid. I'd be locked up, or worse. I'm hoping to the Goddess that he doesn't get too worked up over the nose."

Standing up, I grab her under the arms and pull her to her feet so that we're looking at each other eye to eye, our noses touching, my arms wrapped around her. "I'll make you a deal. If you don't return on Sunday night like you're supposed to, hell, even if you are five minutes late, we will come for you. No matter what, the guys, Wylla, and I will come to those forsaken pack grounds with guns blazin' to get our girl back. Okay?" I ask as I kiss the tip of her nose.

A lone tear escapes her eye, and I pull my right arm from around her, lifting my hand up to her face, so I can run my thumb over her cheek and capture it before sticking the digit in my mouth. Tasting her tear, I close my eyes and groan. "I'm serious, Maggie. The Terminator won't have anything on me in demon form. We can't forget Bone Crusher, either."

A giggle escapes her lips at the thought of the ferret's ironic cage name. "You're crazy, Jude. But you got yourself a deal."

I spin us around, so my back is to her bed, and sit down, moving her so she is straddling me as I perch on the edge. Leaning in, I kiss her pouty lips, eliciting the sexiest little whine from her, which drives me to continue the kiss but with more gusto. I lick the seam of her lips, and she opens for me. I take that as my opportunity to thrust my tongue into her mouth, tasting her as she runs her tongue over mine like she's fighting for dominance in this kiss.

Taking my chance, I run my hands under her shirt and rest them on her sides as we continue to battle for control of this kiss. I slowly creep my hands up to her full tits and cup them softly. I don't want to get too rough with the new accessories each perky nipple is now rocking. Wylla let it slip at dinner this week about the nipple piercings. I'm a hundred percent sure not one man at the table that night left with a soft dick.

Just as I start to slide under the band of bralette, she pushes a hand against my chest and breaks the kiss. "We can't," she tells me with her now red and swollen lips. "Maybe things will be different after this visit. But until then, I have to be smart and cautious. I know I'm drawn to all of you, Jude, just as you're drawn to me, but I have to do this on my terms, and I'm just not sure what those terms are quite yet," she tells me.

I open my mouth to tell her what I think about her terms and pack, but she doesn't give me the chance. "Jude, it's frustrating and maddening as hell. I can't even imagine. While I know I've always wanted more for my life than being a mated wolf, it's also hard to think that my entire life I've been lied to and magically modified so that those lies were more believable. Not just me, our whole damn pack. I have to wrap my mind around that, and it's harder than it seems."

I nod, because, well, who am I to argue with her about that? I'm sure growing up sheltered like she was, then coming here and finding out your whole life is pretty much a lie, is life altering. Add in three sexy men and a rainbow death witch, and she actually has a point. *HUH? Maybe I should pass on this new wisdom to Blaine and Zeke.* Or *I could let them suffer until they reach the same conclusion.*

She stares at me, waiting for my response. *SHIT!* I was so lost in my thoughts, I didn't give her an answer. She probably thinks I'm pissed. *DAMMIT, JUDE!* I kiss her gently once more, "I'd wait an eternity for you, Maggie," I murmur against her lips.

She nods and I stand, still holding her, and set her down on her own two feet. "Well, I guess I should let you get to it. I'll see you in class tomorrow morning before you leave. But remember, babe, Sunday night or–" I make my fingers into little finger guns and shoot them into the air mentally thinking '*Pew pew, mutherfuckers!*'.

She giggles and shoos me from her room. "I'll miss you, Jude Goodman!" she hollers down the hall behind me. I laugh and wave at her over my shoulder.

Getting to my room, I find Blaine and Zeke doing homework on their beds. They both look up as I come into the room. "What took so long? I thought you were just dropping off the tape?" Blaine questions me. Fucker should have known I was going to try to get as much time with her as I could.

Smirking, I wag my eyebrows at him. "Have you met our girl, Blaine? It's kinda hard to just drop things off and go. She's addicting, like a habit I never wanna kick," I tell him. "She also tastes fucking delicious, like a sugary treat of cotton candy." I laugh at his reaction.

His face turns a darker shade of red every second as he glares at me. "You tasted my mate?" he demands, and his wolf's claws pop from his fingertips. A growl leaves his throat, and he stands, moving closer to me. Zeke stands to interfere if need be.

"Calm your wolf down, Blaine. I simply kissed her, but Goddess, are you easy to rile up." I laugh as I move to my bed and grab my literature book, so I can start the essay we were assigned. Blaine moves back to his bed and once again starts on his homework, mumbling about stupid fucking sex demons. He's so fun to work up. I can't wait to see how he is when we are mated to our girls. *Wait... our girls?*

Today has dragged on. I'm assuming it's from the knowledge that after classes, Maggie's headed home. We are all dreading her having to go back to that cesspit of a pack. However, it's necessary. Her not showing up on the first weekend home would send all kinds of red flags to her dad and Alpha, and we need them to think she is still clueless. At least until Wylla can remove the blocks. We all, well, at least me, are having a hard time knowing we won't be there if she needs us, and we won't have a goddamn clue what's going on with her.

I'm praying to the Goddess that this weekend when Wylla talks with her grandmother, she gets the missing information she needs so we can get this shit done ASAP. Blaine is even more eager than me. He's ready for Maggie to accept him as a mate and complete the bond. I am too, but demons mate differently than wolves, especially incubi. We don't go crazy without our mates like wolves do. More than anything, we just have to fuel our energy with more and more people. However, if Maggie and I mated, I'd only need to fuck her maybe once a week to stay at full power.

It's something I've been meaning to talk to her about. I haven't fed off anyone by fucking since she arrived. Only fueling up on others' lust as I come across it. Needless to say, I've been spending a lot of time near popular hookup spots on campus. It won't continue to be enough, though. I'm going to have to tell Maggie and see what she thinks. *Fuck, I'm dreading that! But just feeding off of the lust of others isn't going to sustain me. Hell, I don't think I have much longer before it's not enough at all.*

Now that classes are done for the day, we are headed to meet Maggie in her room to say our goodbyes. She doesn't know we're coming, but we wanted to surprise her and send her off the right way. I get to her room just in time to see her lugging her suitcase off her bed as Blaine and Zeke stand on opposite sides of the door frame.

"I wish you'd let me help you, pretty wolf," Zeke says.

"I'm fine, Zeke. I don't need a man to carry my bags for me. I got this," she sasses him.

He just rolls his eyes but grabs her around the waist when she steps closer to him. He gives her a bone-crushing hug. *HA! Get it?* Kissing the side of her head, "Bye, pretty wolf, be safe."

Blaine steals her away from Zeke and holds her to him, so their foreheads are touching. "Just stay calm, little mate. Come back Sunday and we'll figure it out from there." He kisses her forehead and steps back from her. She looks over and moves the few steps it takes to cross the room to me.

"Hey, Jude."

I grab her, picking her up, and spinning around in a circle. "Be good, Maggie, and remember what I said, Sunday night, or we're coming for you." I use my best Terminator impersonation. She laughs as I set her down, and I lean in to kiss her cheek. But she's pulled abruptly away from me.

"Come on, ya lovesick fools. It's two days, not a lifetime. Let the woman get going," Wylla scolds us, laughing. We say our final goodbyes and leave the girls to it. As we make our way to the doorway to the stairwell, I turn and see the girls walking toward the elevator holding hands. *Sunday can't come fast enough.*

Magnolia

The whole plane ride, I've been sick to my stomach. Wylla wanted to accompany me to the airport, but I convinced her it was best for me to go alone, never knowing if someone was watching and reporting. *My paranoia is on overload today.*

"*Ladies and gentlemen, we are beginning our descent. Please, put your seats back in the full upright position and fasten your seat belts. We want to thank you for flying with Maltan Airlines today.*" The airline attendant's voice rings out through the cabin of the plane from where she stands with the intercom in hand.

Fuck, I feel like I'm going to hurl those pretzels they gave us for the in-flight snack. Doing as directed, I fasten my belt, letting my head fall back against the seat's headrest, and close my eyes. Taking deep breaths, I try to calm my nerves about seeing my father for the first time since leaving. I was able to cover everything but the nose ring. Wylla would have done a spell but she didn't want my father or the Alpha to catch a scent of magic on me. Hopefully, he doesn't flip his lid too badly or demand I take it out. Luckily, he won't see the others, and they can stay safely intact if I need to remove the septum piercing to appease him. Instead of focusing on what's to come, I let my mind drift to that kiss with Jude last night, then each of the guys' and Wylla's goodbyes to me today. Those memories of them are what's going to get me through this trip. Thank Goddess, it's only until Sunday.

After disembarking from the plane, I head straight to baggage claim to get my suitcase, stopping only long enough to use the restroom. I dig my phone out of my purse and power it on. It immediately begins buzzing, alerting me to messages. Opening it, I see a slew of messages from the guys and Wylla telling me how much they miss me and that everything's going to be okay. They make my heart smile, and I even catch myself cradling my phone against my chest, pretending that it's them. I make a group chat, including them all, and send them a message that I'm here and okay and I'll text them later tonight.

I take my time reading their replies, knowing my lollygagging is going to piss my father off. Well, that is until I see his message.

Dad: I'm in a meeting with the Alpha. Get an UBER and head straight to the house. Your mother will be waiting for you. No stopping anywhere else.

Yes, sir! Guess it was too much for his fucking ass to come pick me up. Maybe it's a good thing he didn't. It gives me more time before he sees the new me. Gathering up my suitcase when I see it come around the carousel, I head outside and order an Uber to come pick me up.

Once everything is confirmed, the app informs me that Han will be here in fifteen minutes. I open my texts and send one to the group chat for Mom and Dad, letting them know I've arrived and I'm waiting on my ride to get here. According to the app, I should be there in about forty minutes. I wonder if I could get there in wolf form faster, but then I have to worry about people who might see me as well as the struggle of having to carry a suitcase in my mouth. Nope, not happening. I'll just wait for the ride, plus I'm in no hurry to get home, anyway.

I decide to spend my time doing this jigsaw puzzle app I downloaded as I lean against the column in front of the airport. Wylla suggested it last night to help calm my nerves, giving my brain something to focus on. At the moment, it's working. Let's see if it continues to distract and settle my nerves. True to the app's notification, Han pulls up in front of me in his black 2020 Toyota Camry. He jumps out of the driver's side, confirming who I am before taking my suitcase and putting it in the trunk. Opening the back passenger door, I slide into the car after thanking him. He's not bad looking, about five-foot-eight, with shaggy black hair that's falling into his eyes and dimples in each cheek when he smiles. If I had to guess, I would say he's in his early twenties and apparently, by the looks he keeps sneaking in the rearview mirror, he likes what he sees. I mentally choke on a laugh, thinking how my guys would react to that. *Wait, my guys? Where the hell did that come from?*

"So, you from around here?" he casually asks, looking up into the mirror.

"Yeah, just here for the weekend, visiting my family." I drop my phone in my lap and twiddle my fingers together nervously.

"Oh, do you have plans for the whole weekend? My friend is having a birthday bonfire tomorrow if you'd like to go. I could pick you up; I already got your address." I wonder if he realizes how stalkerish his words sounded.

"Umm... Thanks, but I'm not sure what my family has planned. So I'd hate to say yes and not be able to," I say, hoping this stops him from prodding any further.

Coming to a stop at the red light, he picks up his phone and types away. He no sooner returns it to the cradle on the dash, than my phone is pinging with a message. He grins at me mischievously in the mirror as I check the message. *It's fucking him! What the hell!!*

He must see the confusion etched on my face. "The app automatically gives us your number in case we need to message you for any reason. Now you have mine if your plans change, or, if you decide to go, just let me know." He gives me a wide shit-ass grin, putting his perfectly straight white teeth on display for me.

"Oh... thanks." Shocked by his boldness and honestly, a little fucking creeped out, I don't know what else to say. He doesn't smell of wolf, but with my senses not being as strong since I don't have a designation, it's harder to be able to detect supernatural beings due to the fucking blocks on me. I can't honestly say he's a hundred percent human. If he is a wolf, my address would give off what pack I belong to.

He tries to make small talk for the rest of the ride, and I only nod or smile, giving short answers. For all I know, this is some kind of test from my father, and there is no way in hell I'm going to fail it. We finally make it to my house, and he pulls into the driveway, puts the car in park, and jumps out, heading to the trunk. I exit, pulling the strap of my purse onto my shoulder, and step to the back of the car, taking my suitcase from his hand.

"So just shoot me a text if you decide to go, or even if you just want to chat." He winks and rushes back to the driver's side of his car. I take a deep breath and turn, heading inside the prison I call home.

Opening the door, the house is quiet except for the faint sounds of music playing, coming from the kitchen. "Mom, I'm home," I call out loudly, so she can hear me, something I wouldn't have done if I knew my father was here.

I hear her scream of delight and the patter of her feet on the linoleum floor. "Magnolia, darling, I've missed you so." She stops dead in her tracks when she sees me, all the color draining from her face as her eyes go large in fright. "Magnolia, no, you have to take that out right now. Your father will be furious when he sees it."

"I know, Momma, but I can't. Don't worry about it. He probably won't even notice it. What were you doing in the kitchen? Let me put my suitcase away, and I'll come help."

I quickly try to change the subject, knowing she's going to keep fretting over the nose piercing.

I head up the stairs, leaving my mom standing there, wringing the dish towel in her hands. Taking the steps two at a time, I make it to the second floor in no time. Moving swiftly down the hall, I take hold of the door handle to my room. I feel a war raging inside me. This was once my escape, the one place I could be by myself, even though I wasn't who I wanted to be.

Once I step inside I shut the door behind me, taking a moment to look around, noticing everything is just as I had left it. Even my pillow is still lying askew on my bed. Moving over to my bed, I sit my suitcase down on top of it, deciding to unpack later, or maybe I'll just live out of it for the weekend so that way I don't have to repack it on Sunday. *Yeah, that sounds like a plan!*

What I really want to do is snatch my mom by the hand and run right back out that door and back to school, but I know I need to face the firing squad, and I'd rather have a few moments of quiet time visiting with my mom before he flips his fucking lid. Heading back downstairs, I come up short, seeing my mom on her hands and knees on the kitchen floor scrubbing it with a fucking sponge. I clear my throat, so she knows I'm there. "Got an extra sponge so I can help you?"

She smiles sweetly at me. "I've got this, but if you want to take out the trash, I'd appreciate it. I'm almost done here, anyway."

"Okay." I pull the bag out, tie it in a knot, and quickly replace it with a new one before heading outside.

I take a little longer, wanting to prolong having to step back into the house that sucks the life out of me. Opening the door, I hear my mom talking. She must be on the phone because I don't hear another voice. "Yes, Alpha. I'll do it now. Goodbye." That's all I catch of the actual conversation before she's hanging up the phone.

"Who was that?" I ask, startling her. She turns to face me, and I see she's ghost white.

"It was Alpha Johnson. He wants you at his office right away. Magnolia, baby, please take out the nose piercing. I'm begging you." Tears begin to roll down her face, and if I was still that girl who left here just a couple of weeks ago, I would, but I'm stronger, and I refuse to go back to that person.

"It will be fine, Mom. Let me go. I don't want to keep him waiting. Can I borrow the keys to your car, or do I need to ride my bicycle?"

"Magnolia, you know I can only use the car to run errands for your father and the home, nothing else," she tells me like I don't know.

"Yeah, but Alpha Johnson wants to see me, and I really don't think he wants to be kept waiting. If they say anything, I'll say I took the keys without you knowing." She just stares at me for a minute before she walks over to where her purse is hanging on the hook and pulls her keys out, handing them to me.

"Please, Magnolia, take it out. Don't bring their wrath down upon you," she pleads with me. I know she cares for me. But I just wish she would find her own backbone, like Wylla and the guys are helping me find.

"It will be fine. I love you, but I need to go. We don't want to keep him waiting." I give her a smile as I turn and head out of the house.

The Alpha's office is maybe twenty-five minutes from my house, but I take the long way, even stopping to fill Mom's tank, so it ends up taking me a good forty minutes to get there.

Pulling into a vacant spot, I turn the car off and sit there for a moment, gripping the steering wheel so tightly my knuckles turn white as I build up the nerve to step inside. I know once I do, all hell's going to break loose.

Exiting the car, I stand tall, pull my shoulders back, and head inside. Of course, being who he is, the Alpha's office is on the top floor, so I head for the elevator. Once the doors open, I allow the people inside to step off, their lingering gazes and shocked faces when they see me almost break through the tough exterior I've built up around me. I won't let them get to me. Keeping my face blank, I step inside and push the button for the top floor. I don't worry about anyone getting off with me since his office is the only one on the floor.

The elevator dings and I take a deep breath, stepping off the elevator and making my way over to his receptionist's desk. She's a Beta, a busty one at that. Hell, her tits are popping out of the very low-cut tight shirt she's wearing. She glares at me as I step up to her desk. "Magnolia Holloway, Alpha Johnson requested my presence." She just leers at me as she gets an evil glint in her eyes as they slowly travel the length of my body.

She picks up her phone and hits a button. I hear someone's muffled voice on the other end before she speaks. "Sorry for the intrusion, sir. There's a Maolia Holloway here for you."

"Magnolia," I angrily growl at the cunt.

"My apologies, Sir, Magnolia. She didn't speak clearly. It may be due to the hideous thing she has hanging from her nose, interfering with her speech." She smiles wickedly at me as I hear a growl over the line before she hangs up.

Before she can say anything else, the door behind me flies open and heavy steps come pounding up behind me before I'm yanked backward by my hair. I'm dragged into the Alpha's office, barely able to keep my body upright, and tossed down in a chair. My father stands angrily before me, as he glares at me. "What the fuck have you done to your face? It's disgusting. You look like a fucking whore with that shit in your nose," my father spits out vilely to me.

I'm so distracted by my father I don't even notice the person who steps up beside the chair until his fingers are trailing down the side of my face, allowing his fingers to flip my nose ring when he reaches it. "I don't know, Beta Holloway, I find it sexy as hell. There's just something about a bitch who doesn't conform to the rules. It makes breaking them down to obedient little women that much sweeter. My cock's already hard thinking about it and all the dirty things I want to do to this body. Seems college life has been good to her. She's filled out a little, nothing better than a bitch with some meat to grab onto while I'm ramming my dick into her greedy ass cunt," Reid, the Alpha heir's Beta croons. I want to vomit at his words.

I can't fucking mate with him; he's psychotic. Wylla needs to come up with a plan to get these blocks off me, so I can get far away from this pack. Even if I have to leave them behind and go somewhere on my own where no one knows me.

"Reid, chill. We don't want to scare our little mate before the bonding ceremony now, do we? Imagine how fun it's going to be to break a fucking virgin in, in front of the others." I shoot my eyes to Max, the Alpha heir. *What the hell is he talking about?*

The Alpha, my father, Max, and Reid all start laughing outlandishly. The only one not seeming to take glee in my distress, though he's good at covering it, is Jeremiah, my other intended mate. His face has a hardened look to it, void of emotion except for his eyes which are full of compassion.

"Oh, you didn't know? Since you are to be mated to the Alpha heir, our bond will be completed in front of every male in the pack. It shows you belong to us and no one else is to touch you. So make sure you don't gain any more weight. Reid may like them on the chunky side, but I don't," he whispers into my ear, leaning down. "If there are any other piercings on your body, I'm going to take great pleasure in ripping them out."

I'm fuming, but I can't show it. I keep my eyes down and sit there since I haven't been excused as my father and the Alpha discuss the union between me and the three men in the room, laughing about memories of breaking in their own women.

I don't look, but I know there are three sets of eyes burning a hole through me, my intended mates. It seems like forever, but the Alpha finally speaks to me.

"Magnolia. I strongly suggest you clean your act up and get rid of that disgusting jewelry on your face. You are to be the mate of the next Alpha of this pack, and you need to represent yourself as such. At the moment, you look like a trashy whore. There were stipulations to you attending school off pack lands, and at the moment, you are not living up to them."

"But Alpha Johnson I am..." I start to say but I'm quickly cut off as Max, places his hands on my shoulders, digging his nails into my skin as his father starts to speak.

"Since when are you permitted to speak without permission? This is the unacceptable behavior you are learning at that school. Which brings me to why I called you here today to begin with. I have learned you've made adjustments to your schedule. You will correct it back to the way it was and if this rebelliousness continues, you will return and never leave again. Samuel, get her home, and I expect you to get better control of your daughter." His voice is dark and powerful, sending waves of fear coursing through my body.

My father nods in reply, yanking me so hard by my arm it feels as if he is going to rip it off, as he drags me from the room in silence.

This isn't going to be fucking good for me!

Wylla

I've been a nervous wreck since yesterday afternoon when I walked Magz out to her ride to the airport. It's just two nights, that's all, yet here I am, worrying myself to death. She better be back tomorrow evening as planned, or her dad and that pack will be dealing with me. I may look fun and come across as sweet and playful, but don't cross me. I like to say I'm a really nice bitch, but the truth is, I'm an evil bitch when you mess with what's mine. And trust me, that gray-haired goddess is mine and the three cocks upstairs.

With two of the most powerful covens' blood running through my veins, I'm also extremely powerful. I like to play it down because telling someone I could literally kill them at the snap of my fingers makes it hard to make friends. Also, being able to raise the dead and control them fully is not really a cool hobby and tends to scare even the worst of supernaturals away.

It's almost lunchtime, which means I have just enough time to get presentable for this meeting and grab a snack before video chatting with my grandmother and this wolf pack board. I'm not sure why we're moving the whole coven there, but Grandmother is our head elder, and she said the Goddess gave her a vision, and we're to be bound to this pack. Otherwise, she's been very tight-lipped about the whole thing, not even telling me what pack it is. I promise if it's Exodus, Goddess be damned, it's not happening.

Slipping into a black dress with a white Peter Pan collar and sleeve embellishments, I smooth the fabric down my chest. Grabbing my favorite fishnets, I roll them up one leg, then the other before slipping my feet into a pair of black-heeled combat boots. I head to the desk and turn on the little mirror I use to get ready. Plugging in the curling iron, I set it down and start on my makeup while I wait for it to heat up.

A swipe a little pink blush on my cheeks and then pick up my well-loved eyeshadow palette, smoking my eyelids out with the perfect shade of gray. The final touch is the lipstick; Nightshade is my go-to color, and today will be no different. I coat my lips in the black paint and smack them together in the mirror. Happy with my face, I hurriedly rush through giving my rainbow hair a slight curl so it has some bounce to it. Finally pleased with my look, I stand and head out the door.

I barely make it back from the dining hall in time for this video chat. If I'm late, my grandmother will have my ass, and she is one woman I never try to piss off. Rushing up the stairs of our dorm building, I shove the key in the door and kick it open. Grabbing my laptop, I sit back at my desk and power it on. Once it comes to life, I move the cursor over to the video chat icon and click it, scrolling down to my grandmother's contact.

The computer rings only once before my grandmother's face fills my screen. "Salutations, Wylla. How are you today?" she asks.

"I am fine, Grandmother. I'm just worried about the roommate I told you about. She had to go home to her pack for the weekend, and I'm concerned about her being back with those wolves," I tell her, and my voice starts to break.

"Well, child, I told you I would give you the information you needed, so what I'm about to tell you might help ease the worry once she is back on school grounds."

I nod and move closer to the screen, eager to know the info she has come across. "You will need to remove the block on her designation first. For the info we seek will tell us if the wolf is meek. What she discovers might have her second-guessing having mates. But that decision will greatly affect her fate."

"Grandmother, what does that even mean? Why does it always have to be in riddles? Why can't you just say 'Hey, Wylla, you should do this before this so that the world doesn't end'," I snark. I should have known she would deliver the information that I need in riddles and clues. Whatever, I will remove the designation block, then Magz can decide if she wants the mate block removed.

"Wylla, you seem upset by this news."

Sighing, I rub my hand down my face before answering, "I'm not upset, Grandmother. It's just I think we might be mates, so that little nursery rhyme you just shared might affect me as well."

She nods, giving me a half smile. "Yes, my child, but would you want your mate to come to you willingly or with a push?" *Damn her!* She's right, even though I want, in the worst way, to be mates with Magz. It has to be on her terms. I don't want her to resent me forever, so I'm going to keep my lips sealed and remove the block and go from there.

"Now enough, Wylla, we have to meet with this pack board. We need to be able to move there and time is of the essence." She looks at her keyboard and I can hear the click-clack of keys as she types. My screen is then split, and I see my face, my grandmother's, and two squares that are empty waiting for our guests.

After a few rings, a middle-aged man's face fills the screen. "Good afternoon, Morticia, it is great to see you again. This must be your granddaughter, Wylla. Nice to meet you. I am Alpha Gray of the Stoneridge Pack."

"Good afternoon, sir. I'm pleased to answer any questions you may have for me. My grandmother said there were some concerns with our application due to my paternal lineage being the Matilda Coven. I can assure you, sir, I have never, nor do I ever, plan to be in contact with my father. If he wanted to know me, well, he'd have done it before now."

Alpha Gray nods his head. "I appreciate your candor. We are just waiting on my son, then we'll talk it over more and give you our decision before this call is over. Since he is Alpha heir, I want him to be involved in these decisions from here on out, you understand?"

I nod once and sit in silence, waiting for our last guest to join the call. Grandmother and the Alpha are making small talk, but I'm just sitting with my mind continuously circling back to Magz. Damn, I can't wait for her to be back tomorrow, then she's never going there again. The blank square in the corner of the screen flashes, then a face I recognize appears. "What the fuck?" I whisper, but not quietly enough.

"Wylla Moon Michaelson! You will not speak with such language in front of the Alpha and his heir!" she chastises me, and I flinch at the tongue-lashing.

"Sorry, Grandmother and Alpha Gray, it's just that Blaine is actually a good friend of mine from here at school. I had no idea he would be a part of this meeting." It's the truth. Blaine never mentioned having a video chat or I would have linked the two together. Instead, I'm shocked and confused about why we would need to move to Blaine's pack lands.

Blaine laughs, then turns his attention to his father. "Wylla is part of that situation we were discussing earlier, Dad, with the Exodus pack." His father nods in acceptance, then everyone is silent as we wait for what this means for our move.

"Well, I meant to interview you further, just to double-check things since Wylla has Matilda ties. However, it seems we may be more connected than we think. Welcome to Stonehaven Pack. Please bring yourselves and your belongings to pack lands within the next thirty days." I look at my grandmother, and she has a beaming smile on her face.

"Thank you, Alpha. The Goddess is ever pleased with this decision. We shall prepare and be at your lands within the month." With that, the screen flashes, and she is gone, without saying bye to me. Dang. That woman is intense.

"Well, I should be going too, Son. I have things that need my attention. Wylla, nice meeting you, and I'm excited to see what this new endeavor brings," Alpha Gray says, and he nods in Blaine's direction, then hangs up. I look at Blaine and glare at him before hanging up on him.

Slamming my laptop shut, I stand from my desk, grab a water from our fridge and exit our room. I have a wolf to find, and he has some Goddess damn explaining to do. I mean seriously, what the fuck was that? He's the Alpha heir for the pack we're moving to? *Oh, shit!* That means I will now be living on the same pack lands as all three of those dimwits. Fido, the noodle rat, and the sexcubus all live there with their families.

This could be a great thing, though. If we are already all together, then it will be easier to convince Magz to leave her pack and join Stoneridge. I step onto the elevator and hit the button for their floor.

Blaine better be in his room and ready to talk. I have questions for the asshole.

Magnolia

My father spent the rest of Friday and most of today harping about my looks. I escaped to my room, claiming I had an assignment for school I needed to work on. He kept going on and on about how I embarrassed him in front of the Alpha and the pack. But did I really? Only a couple of people saw me. He followed behind me all the way to the house to make sure I didn't stop anywhere. Once we made it back, he made it abundantly clear I wouldn't be stepping back out of the house until I left for school.

I stood firm, though, and haven't removed the piercing. Well, I may have lied and said I would once I returned, as it required a special tool to unclasp it, which he actually believed. I thought my father was a little smarter than that. I guess I was wrong.

The only saving grace getting me through this hellacious weekend was the texts back and forth between Wylla and the guys. We decided not to call each other, not wanting my father to overhear any conversations, so we kept to text messages. They even managed to send some pictures, some that had my core hot with desire with the amount of flesh they were showing. *Goddess, help me when I finally have sex! They are going to break me!*

I came up to my room around two in the afternoon. Now looking at the clock sitting on my nightstand, I see it's getting close to five, dinnertime, and my father hasn't been up once. I have a nagging feeling in my gut that this isn't the blessing it should seem to be. It feels more like the calm before the storm, and lightning is about to strike me hard. The only question is, will I survive it?

Lying on my stomach across the bed, I let my legs sway back and forth in the air while I read my Supernatural History book. I'm so engrossed in learning about ferrets that I'm caught off guard when my door flies open and my three intended mates step inside. I jump up, sitting back on my haunches as my book drops to the floor.

"How the hell did you get in here?" It doesn't dawn on me until the words are out of my mouth, and I see the angry look on Max's face that I realize what I said.

"If I were you, I'd mind your place. That is not how you speak to your intended mates or your future Alpha. In fact, that's not the response to be given to any male in this pack by a bitch."

"I don't know, Maxie, I kind of like the fire in her. I especially like seeing her ass up in the air like that, giving me the space to move in behind her and fuck her like I would in wolf form." His tongue snakes out of his mouth, licking across his lips, a hint of metal in his mouth flickering in the light. *Fucking hypocrites.*

My eyes jump back over to the last of the three, Jeremiah, who's leaning against the door frame. He just stares at me, his eyes seeming to be fighting a battle. "You guys are crazy. She's a virgin; the fun will be in taking it from her." The other two howl in laughter as they all move inside the room.

Reid moves over to my dresser, opens it, and begins to run his fingers through my underwear. Pulling out a pair of my lacier ones, he brings them to his nose, sniffing them before licking the crotch. *I'm going to be sick!* My eyes immediately flip to my discarded clothing from last night, my used underwear lying on top. Reid moves quicker than me, snatching them up in his hand, and sticks both pairs into his jeans pocket. "These will serve me well, little bitch."

My wolf growls, pissed at the way they are talking to me, for being in my space, and at me for allowing it to happen. She needs to be patient. We just need to get through this weekend and make it until the day we can break free from this heinous pack. My mother may want to live a life of misery, but I don't. I won't.

"Sorry for my choice of words." Goddess, it makes me sick, to feign niceness and say those words. "You just caught me off guard, being in my room alone with me. I'm surprised my father allowed it, as well as shocked as to why you are here." I move to sit on the edge of the bed, swinging my legs off so that my bare feet rest on the floor. I make sure to keep my eyes downcast as a proper female wolf should.

"Oh, didn't your father tell you? Of course not, you're just a bitch. You don't need to know shit, but we're here for dinner. Call it a chance for us all to get to know each other better, seeing how we will be mates soon. Now, get presentable and meet us downstairs. I wouldn't dawdle either. My father is already pissed with you and rethinking allowing you to go back to school," Max declares before turning and heading out of the room. Reid tosses me a flirtatious wink as he brings his fingers up to his mouth with his pointer and middle finger spread and waggles his tongue between them. *Ugh, gross!*

Jeremiah is the last to turn and leave, staring at me long and hard before finally saying, "I'd hurry if I were you." He turns quickly, racing from the room, I assume to catch up with the others.

I bend over and pick up my book from the floor, letting my hands rub across the cover. There is no way I'm doing anything to make them keep me here. I will play the dutiful future mate of the Alpha heir and his Betas during dinner, then I'll make sure when I leave tomorrow that I never come back here again.

I place the book on my bed and stand up, straighten out my clothes, run my fingers through my hair, making sure it appears to be brushed, and head down the stairs. I can hear the loud, obnoxious voices of both Alpha Johnson and my father as I near the bottom step. Plastering a smile on my face, I step into the dining room.

"There she is. You've kept us waiting long enough, Magnolia. Come take a seat between Max and Reid," my father announces as he gestures towards the only empty seat at the table.

"Sorry, Father," I meekly say, moving towards the empty seat.

"I'll have to teach her to be more punctual once we are mated. I think I'm going to have my work cut out with her. Father, what do you think? Maybe she should spend more weekends at home so we can work on the skills of being a mate she is lacking." Max sneers at me as he speaks, placing his hand on my leg under the table and squeezing tightly. He's using so much force, I know there will be a bruise there.

I try to tune them out, keeping my head down and only speaking when spoken to as the dinner drags on. The men carry on a conversation, going on about this pack and the other. My ears perk a little when they mention how disgusting the Stonehaven pack is by letting in non-wolf members. I try to keep my face neutral, not wanting to show that I have any interest in what they're saying, but to me, a pack that is accepting of all species sounds amazing.

Dinner finally draws to an end, and my mother places coffee down on the table for my father and the Alpha. "So, Magnolia, your father informs me your return flight to school is tomorrow. One of your mates will be taking you back to the airport. What time is your flight?" Alpha Johnson questions me.

"It's at three, Sir," I respond, making sure to keep my tone even and eyes down.

"You will need to change your ticket. The boys have training at that time, and your father has a meeting with me."

"Sir, I can just take an Uber to the airport if my future mates are busy. I wouldn't want to impose." See, I can be sweet because I sure as hell don't want to be alone with them, especially Reid, that fucker creeps me out.

I hear a throat clear across the table from me. "Alpha Johnson, I can take her. I'm not in the training as I'm finishing up the hard drive update to our security systems. I can take time from it to run her over to the airport to ensure she gets there and remind her what will happen if she doesn't clean up her act," Jeremiah announces, not even glancing my way.

"Good, we have that taken care of, then. It's time we head home. Samuel, I urge you to keep your daughter in line. We'd hate to have to announce my son's renouncement of her as his mate, before the official announcement in two weeks' time." My eyes shoot back to Alpha Johnson, confused by his comment about an official announcement in two weeks, the same time my father would expect me to be back here.

"Yes, Sir. Magnolia, excuse yourself and head upstairs. Make sure you are packed. We do not want to keep Jeremiah waiting tomorrow when he comes to collect you."

Pushing back my chair, I stand up. "Yes, Father. It was a pleasure seeing you tonight, Alpha and Luna Johnson. Max, Reid, Jeremiah, it was a pleasure to see you as well." I'm going to need to clean my mouth with soap to clear out all the shit I just spoke.

Leaving the room as quickly as I can without seeming to be running, I rush up the stairs to my room, closing the door behind me as I let out a deep breath. Sliding down the door, I land on my butt, stretching my legs out in front of me, and pray for an escape from this pack.

Waking up this morning, I only leave my room long enough to get something to eat, then escape back to it. I made sure to pack my bags last night, so all I've been doing is twiddling my thumbs when not messaging back and forth with one of the guys or Wylla. Each of them told me how excited they are to have me home.

The biggest question I had was for Wylla, wanting to know what she found out from her grandmother, but all she would say is we would talk about it in person when I get back to our room. The fucking wait is going to kill me. Looking at the clock, I see it's one thirty, and I pick up my suitcase and head downstairs. Jeremiah informed me by text message this morning he would be here around one forty-five to pick me up. How he got my number still has me puzzled, unless my father gave it to him.

I place my suitcase by the door and go in search of my mother, finding her once again on her hands and knees on the floor, scrubbing it with a sponge. It's my father's favorite way to punish her when he feels she's been disobedient. I wonder what she could have done.

"Momma, I just wanted to say goodbye and I love you." She turns her head up to look at me, and I can see how red and puffy her eyes are, telling me she's been crying for a while.

She stands slowly, dropping the sponge on the floor, and wraps me up in her arms. "I'm going to miss you, baby. Please, do as your father and the alpha have asked, and be sure to remove that from your nose once you return to campus," she whispers into my ear.

"Yes, Momma." It's a lie, but if it makes her feel just the tiniest bit better, then it's a good lie. The doorbell rings, pulling both of our attention. "I'm sure that's my ride. I'll message you to let you know I got back safely." She just nods her head and hurriedly returns to cleaning the floor.

Heading to the living room, I pick up my suitcase before opening the door, and sure enough, there stands Jeremiah. "Let me take that for you, Magnolia."

What? Was that kindness? I just stand there, stunned, waiting for the bolt of lightning to hit me or the asteroid to come barreling from the sky, landing directly on me. But neither happens.

"Sure," I mumble as he reaches out, takes my luggage, and heads back to his car, with me following behind.

He puts the suitcase in the trunk while I open the passenger door and get inside. It's only a moment before he's sliding into the driver's side and we're backing out of the driveway. A small sigh of relief comes from me. I'm one step closer to getting back to freedom and away from the suffocating pack lands.

The ride to the airport is filled with deathly silence, neither of us uttering a word to the other. It doesn't mean I didn't catch him glimpse my way when he thought I wasn't paying attention. He's a curiosity to me. While he tries to play the part of the bad boy Beta, he has a glimmer of kindness hiding in his eyes.

Pulling in front of the airport, he puts the car in park and jumps out, rushing to the trunk. I follow suit and meet him there. He hands my suitcase to me, holding on slightly longer than he needs to as he stares at me before releasing his hold on it.

"No hug goodbye for your mate?" he asks.

Stepping up to him, I wrap my arms awkwardly around his waist as he pulls me into him. He reaches around me, sliding his hands into the back pockets of my jeans. "Read it when you are away from here, Magnolia." His words are a riddle to me.

Slipping my hand into my pocket, I feel a small folded-up piece of paper. Pulling my hand back out, fighting the urge to pull it out and read it, I turn and head inside, eager to get the fuck away from here.

Once I've finally boarded the plane and we've taken off, I unfold the paper and read it.

Magnolia,

Please do not come back to pack lands, it's not safe for you here. I'm working on a plan. I'll have a package delivered to your dorm later. Until then, don't speak or show this letter to anyone. Your life is in danger. Once I'm able, I'll explain everything.

-J

I fold the paper back up and slip it back into my pocket. The words are so confusing, and I don't know whether to trust him or fear this is some trick, and if I don't react the right way, it will end badly for me.

I spend the rest of the flight both excited to see Wylla and the guys and worrying about what this letter means. Maybe talking to Wylla about it will help give me some clarity. The airline attendant coming over the speaker pulls me back from fretting as she begins her landing speech. One I already knew all to well.

Once I've gathered my suitcase, I head outside to order a ride, stopping short when I see who's waiting for me.

Blaine

Mate! My wolf growls as we lean against the truck, waiting for our girl to exit the airport. She doesn't know I'm coming, but the guys and Wylla agreed someone needed to be here to pick her up. We all wanted to be the one, so a serious game of rock-paper-scissors decided for us, and I came out victorious. No way was our girl Ubering when she has four mates. Even if she hasn't claimed us yet.

Looking up, I see her making her way toward me. Damn, she's beautiful, her gray hair floats side to side with each step she takes and her tits bounce, clueing me into the fact that she's not wearing a bra. And now my dick's hard. I casually reach down and adjust it with my hand. The woman is perfect if she'd just accept how strong she is. She needs to stop living in total fear of her father and pack. It's a work in progress, and I have no doubt if we are patient, the reward will be immense.

She's just a few steps away from me when she finally looks up and realizes I'm here. Dropping her bag, she runs toward me, and as soon as she is close enough, she leaps onto me, wrapping her arms and legs around me. Her head is buried in my neck, and I can already feel the warmth of her tears soaking my shirt. Wrapping my arms around her tighter, I hold her as she cries in my arms. *What the fuck did they do to her?*

When she finally has herself composed, I set her down and nuzzle my face into her shoulder. "I missed you, babe." As she's about to respond, I feel my nose twitch, and I push her back gently, still holding onto her shoulders. "Why do you smell strongly of another wolf, Magnolia? I know your dad wasn't there to bid you farewell, and this scent is very strong and very fresh. What happened? Is this why you were crying? Tell me who upset you!" I'm all but yelling at her. My wolf is pacing inside, growling and snapping in rage, ready to tear whoever the scent belongs to limb from fucking limb.

"Probably Jeremiah, one of my intended mates. He's a Beta and offered to drive me to the airport," she tells me as if it's no big deal.

"Why didn't you take an Uber?" From what she messaged us over the weekend, that's how she got to her house from the airport.

"That was the plan, but last night, my father surprised me at dinner with the Alpha and his son with his two Betas. He all but demanded I change my flight unless one of my intended could drive me. So, thankfully, Jeremiah offered to take me. He's not that bad, actually. Something is different about him. I just can't put my finger on it."

What the fuck? Not that bad? What is this woman smoking? That whole pack is rotten from the bottom to the top. Now she comes home and one of the Betas she's supposed to mate isn't that bad. Is she going to change her mind about everything and go along with their arranged mating? Was this all a joke to her? Was she brainwashed while she was there?

Annoyed by her words, I quickly walk to where she left her bag, snatch it up and storm back toward my truck, dropping it in the back roughly. She looks at me in shock, then walks silently to the passenger side of the truck and gets in. I make my way to the driver's side, open the door, and slide in. Turning the key in the ignition, I hear the truck come to life. I look over to Magnolia, who is just silently sitting, staring out the window. I grunt before reaching over her and grabbing her seat belt to buckle her in.

Leaning over to buckle her was a mistake, but I want her to be safe in the vehicle. However, it gave me another potent whiff of the other male wolf, who had to have touched my mate for his scent to be that strong. She smells like rain mixed with cotton candy and rain is not her signature scent.

We drive in complete silence for the first ten minutes of the trek to campus. I keep looking over at her, and each time, I catch her staring at me in confusion. "Blaine, can you please tell me what's wrong? I know I smell like another wolf, but I don't understand. I told you I got a ride," she says, breaking the silence that filled the cab of the truck.

"I'm sorry, Magnolia. If anything bad happened, I trust that you'd tell us instantly. I just don't like you smelling like someone who isn't one of us." Sighing, I try to settle my wolf, so I don't keep upsetting our mate.

"Us?"

"Yeah. Me, Jude, Zeke, and Wylla... us."

“Oh, okay,” she responds softly. Why would she question it? Who else would I be talking about? She has been gone forty-eight hours, and she’s acting like she’s forgotten we’ve all told her how we feel about her. I fucking hate her father and her pack. I will destroy them if it’s the last thing I do.

Arriving on campus, I park the truck and jump out, hurrying to her side and opening her door for her. She slides out and gives me a beaming smile as she follows me to the back of the truck, so I can grab her suitcase. I pick it up and head toward the dorm building, with her following close behind me.

“Blaine, I can carry my own suitcase,” she scolds.

“Yeah, but with a mate who very much wants to take care of you, why would you?” I snark back. She is silent and continues to follow behind me as we make the small journey to the dorm building. Once we get to our building, I open the door and let her in first, then I follow her, watching the sway of her hips and ass as she leads us to the elevator. She huffs as I reach around her to hit the button, and when we get inside, I hit the floor number before she can. She growls at me quietly, and I chuckle at her annoyance with my over-caring.

When we get to her door, she unlocks it but doesn’t open it. Instead, she turns to me and gives me a once over with her eyes from my hair down to my shoes. “Thanks for coming to get me, Blaine. I was ready and willing to take an Uber or taxi.”

“Well, if we let you do that, then how would we know if you got home okay? How would we have known if we were declaring war on your pack to get you back?” I tell her, and I mean every single word. I would raze the world for this wolf standing in front of me.

She looks shocked at the seriousness in my tone. “I ju–”

I lean in and kiss her softly. “Magnolia, you’re still confused about things, I know. I’m trying like hell to give you whatever you need to figure things out, but you are my mate. I would go to hell and back for you. You need to realize it for yourself. You’re so worried about leaving that pack and being packless or going feral, babe. Did you ever think that you could be a part of my pack? We wouldn't let you be alone because you'd be with us at all times."

She gasps, and I see her eyes start to glass over. Hopefully, she's listening to what I'm saying and not just hearing me. I mean every word, and I know Wylla and the guys feel the same. I don't want to see her cry after experiencing a weekend from hell, one that she hasn't shared anything about yet, but I'll soon get details. I grab her shoulders, turning her body, so she is facing the door. Leaning down, I whisper into her ear, "Now get in there and talk to your best friend, then go take a shower and wash that wolf's scent off you. I'll see you tomorrow."

She turns the knob, and I smack her ass. "Good girl." She quickly looks over her shoulder as she gasps at my words. I throw her a wink and saunter off back toward the elevator. I check behind me when I'm a few feet away to make sure she got in the room, and sure enough, she's not standing there anymore. Stepping into the elevator, I adjust my cock in my pants as the doors close. Her little gasp and the way her pupils were blown after I called her a good girl has me hard as fucking stone in my jeans.

Getting to my room, I walk in and see the guys sitting on their beds playing some zombie video game. They look up as soon as I enter and shut the game off. "Well, how was it? Is she okay?" Jude asks right away.

"Yeah, she's fine. She didn't tell me much about the weekend. Which is probably for the best, so she can tell us all at once. But she did smell like another wolf, and it was strong, almost like he had his hands, his body on her. My wolf and I were not happy. Luckily, the little minx is so sweet and innocent, she soothed him easily enough."

"What do you mean, she smelled of another wolf? Did they touch her?" Zeke shoots off the bed, coming close to me.

"Relax, man. I'm serious, she was fine. No visible marks, but she did cry when she saw me. I think it was more like a 'thank Goddess you're here and I'm not there anymore' reaction, if you know what I mean. She did tell me the scent was probably Jeremiah, one of the Betas she is promised to. She had two choices: change her flight or get a ride with him, so he took her. She also said, which ticked me the hell off, that he seemed different and not so bad."

They both say nothing but stare at me in confusion. *My thoughts exactly, friends.* I cross the room and change into a pair of sweats and pull my shirt off. "Tomorrow, we ask a few questions about what happened this weekend. But I don't want to push her so much that she feels like she's being interrogated. We'll go from there. Until then, I have some homework I can finally focus on and get done, now that our girl is back where she belongs."

I sit on my bed, Zeke returns to his, and we work quietly on our homework. Seems I'm not the only one who couldn't get shit done this weekend with Magnolia at *home* with the cult.

As soon as I finish the last assignment, I stand up. "I'm finally done, fellas. I'm going to go take a piss, then I'm headed to bed for the night. What do you two have planned?" I ask them.

"I'm with you, I need sleep. I barely got any this weekend. I was so worried," Zeke replies as he's shoving his books back in his bag, his bed now cleared of debris, and he looks to Jude for his answer.

I see Jude stand from his bed and stretch, "I think I'm going to go for a run and clear my head, then hit the hay. I'm hoping to find a couple or two hooking up along the running trail, so I can fuel up my energy reserves."

I nod, understanding this is how he has to feed right now until he talks to Magnolia. He turns and quickly exits the room, and I finish packing the stuff in my bag I'll need for class tomorrow. I head to the bathroom to do my business, then I need to go to sleep. Good ol' fashioned beauty rest now that I can be at peace, knowing my mate is just a floor below me and not being held captive by a crazy wolf cult.

Magnolia

Stepping into the room, I drop my suitcase to the floor, shutting the door behind me. Lifting my fingers, I let the tips glide along my bottom lip as thoughts of the kiss from Blaine replay in my mind. Not to fucking mention how him calling me '*good girl*' has my pussy wet and begging for attention.

I'm lost in my thoughts for a moment, well, more like my daydreams of Blaine with his head between my legs as he feasts upon me, my hands gripping his hair when my eyes scan the room, the very empty room.

Thank goddess, I would have been so embarrassed to have been caught in the middle of a sexual daydream. But where is she? I could have sworn she told me she'd be waiting for me. Actually, I was hoping she'd be here; I fucking missed her. I know some would say it's only been a couple of days, but I've gotten used to seeing her every day.

I begin to panic, fearing that my father and Alpha Johnson sent someone here to hurt her, holding her responsible for my change in appearance. Or even worse, they had somehow discovered my attraction to her. My eyes scan the room again, eagerly looking for any clue that would give me some kind of information about where she is. Then I stop, my gaze lingering on the empty spot on top of her dresser where she keeps her shower caddy. A deep sigh of relief escapes me. She's just in the shower.

Picking my suitcase up, I carry it over to my bed and lay it down on top of it, debating whether to unpack now or wait until later. Later wins out when I slip my hand in my pants pocket, once again finding the note that I fretted over and read multiple times while on the plane. At this point, I have each and every word memorized, forever committed to my memory. But still, I sit down on the bed, gripping it in my hands as I read it yet again, praying to the Goddess that this time some answer will jump out at me. What is he trying to tell me? Can I trust him or is this just a game?

I'm still scouring my brain, trying to figure it out when Wylla steps back into the room. Her hair is wet, and she's wearing only a towel. She literally looks like a wet dream come to life. I give her a forced smile because I'm so racked with anxiety I can't generate a genuine one. "What's wrong? Did something happen at home? Did the puppy do something to you? I'll neuter his ass if he did." She drops her caddy on the floor and rushes over to me, taking a seat on the bed beside me and wrapping her arms around me.

I can't hold it back any longer. I burst into tears as she strokes her hand gently up and down my back, whispering soothing words to me. I sob for ten minutes while she holds me until I have no more tears left to shed. Pulling away from her, I just stare at the woman I am so lucky to call my friend. The woman I care for far more than that, though, one I want to call my lover.

"Now tell me, who am I placing a curse on? Who are we sending the house pet after to lure them into a false sense of security before he rips their heart out and feasts upon it? Who is our sex god depriving of any sexual desire, and who can we sick the puppy on? Whoever did this to you will suffer. I will raise every dead beast I can think of to end their life." Her eyes are laser-focused on me, and I know for a fact she means every word and these aren't just mindless threats, but what she will make a reality.

"No, Blaine didn't do anything, and well, the trip home was more or less what I expected. The Alpha came to dinner at our home Saturday with my intended mates and mandated that one of them would be bringing me to the airport or I would have to change my flight. Jeremiah, the nicest of them, volunteered, and slipped this note into my pocket." I hand the note over to her, allowing her to read it.

"This is crazy," she finally says. "What the hell does he mean by this?"

"I don't know, Wylla. It's so confusing. Do I take this as the truth and he's trying to help me, or is this a ploy to see if I fuck up so they can come snatch me? What should I do?" I ask in exasperation, letting out a deep sigh as my shoulders sag.

We just sit there for a moment, her eyes gazing back at me as she chews on her bottom lip. She keeps opening her mouth to say something, only to clamp it shut again. Slowly standing up, she begins to pace back and forth between my bed and the door. I can almost see the steam escaping from the top of her head as she thinks.

Finally, she stops dead in her tracks and turns abruptly, so she's facing me. "This is what we're going to do. You're going to go along with what he says, but you're not going to give him too much information. If he asks you something, be vague or avoid answering altogether. We're going to ride this out and see if he turns out to be a friend or foe. For all we know, this is a test from your pack's Alpha to see if you will comply and be obedient to your intended mate. So for now, do nothing. We'll wait to see what his next step is, let him put his cards on the table, so to say."

"Okay," I say meekly, gaining the nerve for the next part. "Wylla, I've thought hard about it over the weekend. I don't want to ever have to go back to my pack. I want to do the spell, to leave my pack and be with you and the guys. I even want to talk to Blaine about possibly joining his pack once I'm free from the blocks that are on me. Did your grandmother have good news? Did she give you the spell that would do it?" I'm eager and ready to be free of my past, and I want to move toward a future with my new friends, my family.

Wylla

Eyeing my roommate, my best friend, my mate—*I think*—pure fury takes over me, and I'm shaking. I'm so freaking mad. The Exodus pack has no clue who they're dealing with. To them, I'm sure we're a bunch of young supernaturals who are subpar to them. While I may play down my powers, I'm not one to push. I have a feeling Jude is the same, and the dog and noodle rat are strong as hell and stealthy.

Whatever this Jeremiah fellow has up his sleeve will be met with kindness or death. Magz doesn't see it yet. She's still naïve to the world around her, but she has a powerhouse of supernaturals behind her. Not to mention the people who would follow us if we said the word. I'm snapped out of my inner thoughts when Magz calls my name, asking about my grandmother and the blocks.

"Yeah, I know what we need to do. She said I'll need to remove the block on your designation first. '*For the info we seek will tell us if the wolf is meek. What she discovers might have her second-guessing having mates. But that decision will greatly affect her fate.*'

Like really, she just couldn't tell me in plain English." Magz looks at me, confused, and I sigh. "Grandmother always delivers in riddles and rhymes; it's infuriating. Pretty much, we need to remove the designation block first, then we can do the mate block."

She nods. "Okay, whatever you say, but I'm not sure why. I'm going to be a Beta, and so I'm not sure how that would affect my mates."

"Well, however it turns out, I can do it ASAP. And we'll be there with you the whole time, no matter what." I grab her chin and look her in the eyes so she can see just how serious I am. I want her to know the guys and I are with her for the long haul.

"You can do which one? You weren't clear there, Wylla," she asks in a whisper, staring deeply into my green eyes.

"Both, Magz. Both are relatively simple, so I can do both on the same night actually, as long as you still wanna remove the mate block once you find out what you are. Umm, both blocks really just require a few simple supplies and enough bodies to form a circle around you, one body at each point, north, south, east, and west, with you placed in the middle. See? Simple." She nods, and I leave it at that. It's the truth, and for the most part, the most difficult thing is acquiring the hell honey. I'm hoping our little incubus can help with that.

"Okay, so can we do it this weekend?" she asks, and I can see the hope sparking in her eyes.

"Yup!" I respond, popping the p. "I will get everything I'll need together and we'll do it Friday night."

The room is instantly filled with awkward silence, which is weird and very unlike us. Usually, we chatter like two squirrels fighting over a nut. I look at Magz, and she's chewing on her fingernail. I see it's already been chewed down past the skin. Goddess, she's close to gnawing the whole thing off.

I walk toward her and pull her finger from her mouth. She snaps her head in my direction and gives me a glare that would make a lesser woman nervous. "You need to relax, Magz."

"I can't stop thinking about that note and what Jeremiah's game is. He seemed nice and totally different from any other males in our pack. However, he's still a Beta to the Alpha heir, and I just don't know what angle he's playing at."

"I have an idea to help you relax, Magz. Are you open to my theory?" I ask, my tone dripping in flirtation, as I wag my brows at her.

"What do you have in mind?" she whispers, before sucking her bottom lip between her teeth. I don't answer her with words, instead dropping my towel, letting it fall in a puddle at my feet. Magz gasps, and I move so that I am standing directly between her thighs. Putting one hand on each shoulder, I push her backward, so she's laying on the bed with her legs dangling off of the edge.

"First, you're wearing way too many things, babe. I'm going to take these off, okay?" I ask, grabbing the top of her leggings. I don't move them yet, though; I wait for her to give me the green or red light. This is at her pace. She nods, and I rip the leggings down her legs, taking her panties with them. Grabbing each of her cute little feet, I push each leg up onto the bed, bending them at the knee and setting her feet on the blanket that she's laying on.

Her perfect pussy is open and on display for me. Dropping to my knees, I'm now at eye level with the dessert that is about to be my feast. Bringing my right hand up, I use two fingers and run them down her folds, moaning, "Goddess, Magz, you're soaked for me." She whimpers in response, and I use my left hand to part her pink lips while simultaneously using my right to rub up and down on her clit.

"Ooohh, fuuuck!" she cries out, and I grin, enjoying the effect I have on her. Her hips thrust, making me giggle but I decide to stop torturing her clit with my fingers and lean in, giving it a kiss. Her hips thrust up once more, chasing my mouth as I use my right hand to wrap around her waist, holding her in place. Leaning back in, I run my tongue from her hole to clit and am about to suck her pretty little nub into my mouth when someone knocks on the door.

I growl, "I swear it better be the goddess herself." Magz whines as I get up and head to the door. "Who the hell is it?" I yell through the closed door.

"It's Jude, babes, let me in." Well, fuck me. The incubus is on the other side of the door and wants to see his girl. Looking back at Magz in question, she nods her head, and I swing the door open.

"The fuck you want, demon boy?"

Jude

Rainbow Sprite swings the door open and stands there in her birthday suit. And what a suit it is; she's just as delectable naked as she is clothed. Looking past her, I see Maggie on the bed with no pants on, laying there with her weight on her elbows as she sits up looking at me with her legs spread wide, baring her beautiful pussy to me.

I knew something fucking naughty was happening in here because I felt the lust as soon as I stepped off the elevator. Getting off and heading down the hall, I was surprised to find it was coming from the girls' room. Not as fucking surprised as I am to see it's coming from a situation between Maggie and Wylla.

Reaching down, I adjust my hard-as-iron cock in my pants and walk past Wylla into the room. "Well, what do we have here?" I ask as I cockily stroll through the room and up to Maggie, sitting on the bed beside her. Wylla shuts the door and stands in front of it with her arms crossed.

Maggie chews nervously on her bottom lip. "Wylla was helping me relax. I was stressed after the trip home, and she said she had the perfect way to do that." She giggles at the last part. I raise an eyebrow at her and wink before turning to the naked rainbow.

"I bet she did. Do you want me to leave, Maggie? Leave you to be with Rainbow Sprite?"

"No." Her cheeks redden bright like a tomato. It's fucking adorable and makes my cock even harder, if that's possible. I reach down, adjusting myself, groaning at the contact of my jeans touching my cock. He's painfully hard, and I think it's only going to get worse tonight.

Leaning down, I pull her shirt off before pushing her back flat onto the mattress, kissing her sweet lips. Running a hand down the side of her body, I make sure I graze the side of her perky breast. My eyes catch on the sparkly rings in each nipple. *Those are new!* I don't want to cause her new piercings pain, they're not ready for fingers or tongues yet so I leave them alone.

Getting to her pubic area, I cup her pussy in my hand, making sure I don't touch her clit or entrance. Just holding her mound in my hand has her whining into my mouth. I tease a finger through her slit and play with the rim of her tight hole, rubbing over it, never penetrating. "Maggie, are you a virgin?" I ask. Her eyes widen, and she bites her bottom lip like she's embarrassed. "I have suspicions, but I need to know for sure, babe. Nothing bad. I just don't wanna hurt you, that's all," I tell her, reassurance dripping from my tone.

She nods, and I groan at the thought of how pure and innocent and fucking tight she is. Pushing my middle finger into her pussy, I pump slowly in and out of her, allowing her time to adjust to my thicker finger. A minute or two go by, and I add another finger. She mewls, and I feel her clamp down around my fingers.

I take my free hand and undo my jeans before reaching in and pulling out my cock. Good thing I went commando today, or well, most days, because it makes it easy to access him. I give my cock a few good tugs and pre-cum drips heavily from the tip. Maggie turns her head, her eyes locking on her prize, and she moves up, trying to reach for it. I pull back away from her, so she can't touch me just yet.

Wylla takes that as her cue to join the festivities again. "Magz, baby, do you wanna learn how to please *our* demon?" she asks as she grabs my cock and gives it a firm tug with her soft hands.

"Yes."

"Get on the floor on your knees, Magnolia," Wylla commands, and Maggie jumps up off the bed and sits on her knees on the floor, staring at the two of us and waiting for her next command. Wylla pulls me to standing, then drops to her knees next to Maggie. Reaching up, she pulls my pants the rest of the way down. I easily step out of them and kick them off the side. "Now taste him."

"Wha– how?" Maggie asks, and she looks ashamed that she is asking such a question. I start to reassure her, but Wylla beats me to it.

She takes my cock in one hand and moves her face closer to my groin. Leaning in, she licks me from the base all the way up to the tip. I groan at the feel of her hot tongue on my shaft. "Just like that, Magz. Treat his enormous cock like a popsicle. You got this," she promises Maggie.

Maggie shyly moves so that her tongue is positioned right by my balls, then she lets her little pink tongue run firmly up my shaft before swirling around the head, lapping up the pre-cum that was pooled at the slit. "Mmmm," she hums, then sucks my tip into her mouth.

"That's so good, baby. Now take him to the back of your throat as far as you can, then bob up and down. If you choke, don't panic. Some guys like that and some girls do, too." Then she winks, and both Maggie and I catch it. *Oh, so the witch is a filthy girl.*

Maggie takes my cock all the way to the back of her throat and gags. She looks up at me through her thick lashes. "It's okay, babe. You're doing so fucking good, sucking my cock." I tell her with a moan. She raises up and drops her mouth back down, taking me a bit further this time. She pulls back again and is about to slip her hot little mouth back down when Wylla grabs her hair and holds her still while whispering in her ear. Maggie lets my cock pop from her mouth, and I'm about to curse the fucking rainbow death witch, but Maggie moves to the side just a tad. What the hell are they up to? I'm looking down, watching, when they both latch onto either side of my dick, sucking it together.

I look at them in surprise at first, but then how fucking sexy this is hits me, taking over my mind. I watch Maggie closely to make sure she is okay with this because I'm almost positive we are mates and I don't want her upset with me for letting Wylla touch me. However, she seems to not have a care in the world as she and her best friend suck my cock.

Wylla reaches up and squeezes my balls, putting one finger of pressure against my taint. They suck my cock in tandem, pumping up and down in sync like this was a practiced event.

"I'm gonna come!" I cry. Wylla grabs Maggie, and they sit side by side on their knees, looking up at me. I reach down, grab my cock, and start stroking hard and fast. "Goddess... fuck... yes!" I groan and pump jet after jet of hot cum onto their chests. My horns and tail pop out as I come, and I blush. Fuck! *That hasn't happened since I was thirteen.*

The girls start giggling, taking in my dark blue horns with red accents and my blue tail whipping around behind me. I leave them out, not ashamed of them but kind of embarrassed at how they just popped out. "You think that's funny, ladies?" I purr as my eyes turn black, feeding on their lust.

"Yeah, what are you gonna do about it? Tickle us with that cute little tail?" Wylla asks as she focuses on my swishing tail.

"Up on the bed, both of you. NOW!" I growl, and they both scramble up and onto the bed side by side once more. Maggie nods her head as she looks at Wylla, and grabs her hand so their fingers are interlocked. I take the two steps it takes to get to the bed and stand at their feet, looking down at them.

"I see two little women the big bad demon wants to eat up. What do you think, Maggie? Should I eat you both up?"

She whimpers, and I take that as my cue. Dropping to my knees, I push Maggie's feet up onto the bed like she was when I walked into the room. I lean in and run my tongue from her ass to her front before sucking her clit into my mouth hard. She cries out, and I murmur against her pussy, "You even taste like cotton candy, baby."

Moving to the left, still on my knees, I lean in and do the same to Wylla but keep my eyes on Maggie. My tongue flicks against something solid, freezing. I flick my tongue against it again and right away know it's piercing. *Holy fuck, this filthy slut has her clit pierced.* While I play, I'm watching Maggie to make sure she is okay with what I'm doing. "Jude," she whispers, and I freeze, thinking she's about to tell me this is too much. "Next time, can you teach me how to do that?"

Wylla and I groan at the same time, and I stand, positioning myself in between their legs. I slide my left hand up Wylla's thigh and thrust three fingers roughly into her wet pussy. "Fuck... Jude... Ahhh," she moans as I fuck her roughly with my fingers. I look over at Maggie and wink as I let my right hand hold her knee to Wylla's, so she can't slam them shut.

Then I sneakily run my tail up her leg, starting at the ankle, and let the feathery tip brush against her skin until I make it to the apex of her thighs. I flick my tail back and forth against her clit quickly, making her cry out. I circle one... two... three times before I let the skin at the tip cover the little wisps of hair, making it a hard tip, and gently ease it into Maggie's tight pussy.

Moaning at how she grips me like a vice as I fuck her vigorously with my tail, I never go so deep as to tear that soft tissue of her innocence. I want to save that for when she decides we're her mates. Both girls are a quivering, panting mess, and I grunt before removing my right hand from Maggie's thick thigh and start jerking my cock in time with my tail.

Soon the room is filled with cries of pleasure as I cover my hand in my own release. Wylla and Maggie arch off the bed, crying out and shaking as they both cum all over my fingers and tail. Pulling out of them at the same time, I bring both to my mouth and suck one finger and the tip of my tail between my lips. "Mmmm, you taste like citrus sugar together. My new favorite snack," I purr, and they giggle.

Walking to the shower caddy that was left abandoned on the floor, I reach in and grab out a pack of wipes and pull one out, cleaning up my tail and cock. I throw the used wipe in the trash before grabbing another and cleaning both girls up. They climb off the bed and trudge to the mirror to fix their thoroughly fucked hair.

Hearing the noise of furniture moving, Wylla spins. "The fuck are you doing, demon boy?" Then she sees me moving the beds together to create one huge bed. "Oh, good idea, incubus."

When the beds are moved to my liking, I crawl in, and when the girls are done, they join me. Maggie is in the middle, and Wylla is on the outer edge. I wrap an arm around Maggie and pull her close to me. Wylla reaches up, grabbing her hand, and they stare at each other like they're having a silent conversation.

I leave them be as I close my eyes and fall asleep in my girls' bed in a state of pure bliss, my energy reserves overflowing. Tonight was a good fucking night.

Magnolia

I awake, burning up, not believing the fucking erotic dream I had about Wylla, Jude, and myself. It was so good, I'm getting hot and bothered just remembering it. I go to roll out of bed, but I'm stopped by the very feminine, tattooed leg draped across my thighs and a very masculine arm cupping my breast. Also, might I add, it's a very naked feminine leg over my very exposed crotch.

Fuck, it wasn't a dream! It really happened! My first freaking sexual experience with a guy. Wylla and I have messed around, but it's never gone as far as it did last night. Then Jude and what he did with his tail, my center immediately clenches as heat rushes to it.

I need a shower, a nice long cold shower to calm my lustful body. Carefully lifting Jude's hand from my breast, exposing my pebbled nipple, then easily guiding Wylla's leg off of me, I slither down the middle of the bed like the snake in the Garden of Eden.

Once I'm at the end of the bed, I slowly sit up, looking back over my shoulder to see the two of them have gravitated toward each other. A beaming smile covers my face at the sight of the two of them as memories of last night flood my mind. It was truly a wonderful experience I wouldn't have wanted to have with anyone else. Well, maybe a few more. But I already have a delightful suspicion that I'll have some amazing moments to make with them as well.

Standing, I tiptoe over to my dresser, taking hold of my shower caddy, robe, and room key, and move toward the door to quietly exit the room. "Where are you going, Maggie?" comes from the sex demon in my bed, his gravelly morning voice sending tingles across my skin.

"Shower, go back to sleep," I whisper to him, not wanting to wake Wylla.

"Okay, I love you, Maggie," he whispers back before scooting closer to Wylla and draping his arm over her waist as he nestles his face into her rainbow hair.

Did he really just say that? Did he mean it that way, or was it just a casual word of affection? My mind is on overload as I step into the hallway and shut the door behind me, making sure to close it softly, so it doesn't make too much noise.

Making my way down the hall to the communal bathroom, there's nothing but silence. Very unlike a typical Monday morning. Either we really slept in or something crazy is going on. But it does warrant me some freedom in the bathroom to ease this ache between my thighs without anyone hearing me.

I make sure to check every stall and once I'm satisfied I'm alone, I hastily undress, placing my discarded clothes and robe on the bench outside the stall. Turning on the water to full blast, I let the heat from the spray soothe my aching muscles as my hands slide down over my breasts, along my stomach, to my aching heat. I allow my finger to slip through my folds, teasing my little bundle of nerves as I replay last night in my mind. I'm so aroused, it doesn't take long before I'm exploding all over my fingers, as I reach out with my free hand and brace myself against the wall. Not even a minute later, I hear the bathroom door slam open as it hits the wall and muffled feminine giggles. Thank fuck, I finished in time.

I lather myself up with some soap and quickly wash my body. I'm hoping Wylla is up when I get back to the room because we need to do this spell sooner rather than later. If my betrothed gets wind of what happened last night, not only am I being dragged out of here but Wylla and Jude are as good as dead. Alpha Johnson and his son are cut-throat, and there's no way they will let us off with the shame of what we did. Not with the way it would look for his son to be shamed by a mere woman of no standing. I'd probably be shunned by my pack, locked away in some dank, mildewed cell in some underground tavern.

I took longer than I planned in the shower and rushed back to our room, opening the door slowly, I step inside, keeping my head down as I tiptoe over to my dresser and place my caddy on it, before tossing my clothing into the overflowing laundry hamper. We really need to do some laundry, otherwise, I am going to have to go commando.

"Umm... why are you sneaking around?" Wylla asks from behind me, which makes me jump out of my skin, and let out a startled shriek, not noticing that she was awake.

"Fuck, you scared the ever-loving piss out of me." She's doubled over laughing as I scan the room, noticing that Jude is missing. "Where's Jude?"

"Oh, the demon sex freak headed upstairs to wake up the rodent and the puppy for class. They're going to be back down in a few, so we can head over and get something to eat," Wylla tells me as she slides her shirt over her head.

"Oh… okay." I open my drawer and pull out a pair of panties and step into them, sliding them up my body. Taking off my robe, I hang it on the hook on the dresser before pulling out a bra and putting it on, fighting with trying to hook it in the back.

"Let me help you with that, babes," Wylla croons. I feel the air shift as she steps up behind me, taking the clasps from my hand and hooking them. Reaching around my waist, she lets her hands slide over my bare stomach as she leans in and begins to pepper soft kisses along my shoulder.

"Thank you," I mutter softly. "Wylla…" I pause, waiting for her response.

"Uh-huh," comes out muffled against my skin, as she continues, moving across my skin to give some attention to the other shoulder.

"Do you think we could do the spell sooner than later?" I pull away from her, moving over to the closet. I slide the hangers across the pole until I find the dress I want. Slipping it over my head, I allow my hands to smooth out all the wrinkles before I turn back to face Wylla.

"Is there a reason you're in a hurry now? Has something changed?" she asks as she moves over and takes a seat on her bed.

Letting out a deep sigh, I head over and take a seat beside her. Reaching out, I grasp her hand in mind before I continue, "I don't want to go back to my pack. There's no way I can do another weekend visit. I'm afraid the next time I go back, they won't let me leave, and I'll be stuck there and never see you again. Do you think Blaine would talk to his father and see if I can join his pack and swear an oath of loyalty to them? If not, then I'm going to have no choice but to go rogue and leave here to go somewhere my father and Alpha Johnson can never find me," I rush out, maintaining a tight grip on her hand as a lone tear slides down my cheek, falling onto our joined hands.

"I'm sure Blaine would jump at that chance," she tells me, the corners of her lips turning up into a smile

"Even if we're not mates, because we still don't know for sure, and if I am mated by a bond to the Alpha heir and Betas, my joining their pack could end in a war. Would they really want that? I've just got so many questions and fears, Wylla. If someone got hurt because of me, I don't know that I could live with myself."

She shifts her body on the bed so that she's facing me. "Listen to me, Magnolia Holloway. Blaine is your mate, and I have a sinking suspicion who the others are as well, and it's not the Alpha heir and Betas of your pack. Plus, your becoming a member of the Stoneridge pack is a win, especially since I just found out over the weekend my family is joining it as well. So, you see, we would all be together."

"What! Really? Seriously, you're going to be a part of Blaine's pack? Holy hell! Do you think Blaine will talk to his father for me?" Suddenly I'm excited about the plan.

"Couldn't hurt. But I have no doubts about what his answer will be. Give him a call and tell him to get his ass down here with the other two stooges," she says, her voice sounding as giddy as I feel.

Letting go of her hand, I stand and walk over to the dresser, where my phone is plugged into the charger. Picking it up, I debate on calling or texting him, but with the way my nerves are eating me up, I decide to just text.

I type, erase, type, erase on repeat before I decide on something simple and send it out to him.

ME: I need to talk to you in my room. You can bring Zeke and Jude. They should hear it as well.

BLAINE: I'll be there in 20 minutes or less, just waiting on Mr. Suave to finally realize he doesn't need to take 5 hours to do his hair. If he doesn't hurry up, I'm grabbing him by the tail and dragging his ass out of here.

ME: K

Turning back to Wylla, I let out a deep breath. "They'll be here in a little bit."

True to Blaine's word, they were downstairs in less than twenty minutes, ten to be exact. Jude gives me a sly grin. "How are ya feeling, Maggie?" he asks as he moves stealthily across the room, scooping me up in his arms and swinging me around before burying his face in my neck and beginning to nibble on it. A menacing growl comes from behind us, sending him into laughter that vibrates against my skin before he pulls away. "Calm your wolf, man."

"Then stay the fuck off my mate like that."

"Stop, you two. There's plenty of our girl to go around and make no mistake when I say our girl, I'm meaning she's all of ours. Now get your muscle-head caveman thinking out of here. Our girl has something to ask Blaine, and I think he's going to like it." Wylla steps in, putting them all in their place.

"You have something to ask me? Is that true, princess?" Blaine turns, looking me in the eyes with so much intensity.

"Yeah, um... I was wondering if you would talk to your father about me joining your pack. I know you think we're mates, but we don't know that for sure, so if it turns out we're not, he may not want me to." "Stop right there." He makes it over to me in three large strides, taking my hands in his. "First, Magnolia, I don't just think, I know you're my mate. My wolf knows you are. Your wolf screams out to me like no other. So we have nothing to worry about there, but my father would welcome you into our pack even if you weren't my mate. To be honest, I've already been talking to him about it, praying to the Goddess that you would finally decide to do it." The sincerity in Blaine's voice is so strong, but I need to hear it from his father.

"Really? Is there any way you can ask him, though? I just want to be sure. If he says no, then I'm going to have no choice but to leave school and go somewhere far away from here."

"The fuck you are. There's no way you're leaving me, leaving us. Where you go we go," Zeke belts out, anger mixed with fear lacing his words. "Blaine, call your dad so she can hear it for herself or we go pack our bags because I know for a fact if she decides to leave, I'm going with her."

Everybody turns to look at Blaine to see what he's going to do. Instead of responding to Zeke's gruff words, he pulls out his phone, placing it on speaker as he dials a number. We hear the phone ring before an older, deep voice rings out into the room.

"Hello, Son. I wasn't expecting to hear from you so soon."

"Hey, Dad, I have the guys, Wylla and Magnolia, my mate I told you about, here. Magnolia has voiced her desire to relinquish her bond to her pack and move to ours. She has some concerns that if it were to come out we're not mated after the blocks on her are removed, that you wouldn't let her be part of our pack."

"That's nonsense. Can she hear me, Son?"

"I can, Sir," I say meekly. The power radiating from him, even across the phone line, makes me imagine how strong it would be in person.

"Firstly, it's an honor to meet you, Magnolia. I have no doubt in my son or his wolf when they say you're their mate. You are welcome in our pack no matter what. We can start the process now. Knowing the history of your pack, I'm afraid once they find out you're planning to defect to another pack, they'll come to take you back, potentially locking you away. So I will

begin working on a plan for that and let Blaine know. Just know, you are always welcome in the Stonehaven pack. Does that ease your worries?"

"Yes, Sir, it does. Thank you so much."

Blaine takes him off speakerphone and says a few more things to him in hushed tones.

Wylla walks up to me, lifting her finger and letting it travel along my jawline. "See, told you that you were worrying yourself for no reason." A heavy knock at the door stops her from saying any more. Being the closest she turns and takes the three steps to the door, opening to see a man dressed in a matching brown shirt and pants with a small package in his hand and an electronic pad.

"I have a delivery for a Magnolia Holloway. Are you her?" he asks, as his eyes travel the length of Wylla's body, setting off a rage in me that someone else is looking at what's mine. *Why the hell did I just think that?*

"That's me," I call out, stepping forward in apprehension.

He hands the package to me and I take it in my hands. "If you could just sign here for me that you got it." He never once takes his eyes off of Wylla. Pissed, I snatch the tablet from him, immediately scribbling my name on it, and shove it back at him before slamming the door in his face.

If the looks on their faces weren't concerned for what was just delivered, I think every single one of the fuckers including Wylla would have died from laughter at my reaction. Ignoring them all, I walk over to the bed and look at the box. There's no return address to give me a clue as to who the hell it's from. Taking a seat on my bed, I begin to open the box slowly, feeling four sets of eyes burning a hole right through me.

Taking a deep breath, I peel the tape off and open the flaps to find a cell phone with a charger and a note on white stationary paper with the logo of my pack on it. Taking the note out, I set the box to the side as I open and read it.

Magnolia,

Once you are in a safe location where you can talk freely without anyone overhearing, call the saved number in the contacts. We have a lot to talk about and not much time.

-J

Immediately, I know who it's from; the note is in the same handwriting and the signature used matches the last note he gave me, Jeremiah. But what is his game? Can I trust him? Blaine storms over, impatient as ever, and pulls the note from my hand, reading it. "Is this the wolf that touched you, whose scent was all over your body? The Beta who thinks he can take what is mine?"

"It's Jeremiah, yes. What should I do? Should I call it and find out what his angle is?"

"Yes, but remember, don't give away too much information until we know whether or not we can trust him." Wylla moves over and sits beside me as Blaine stomps back and forth across the room, steam fuming from his head as he crumbles the note up in his hand.

"The fuck she is. There's no way in hell, my wolf or I are going to let her speak to him. Fuck that shit, I won't allow it."

"Excuse me. I will do what I want. I'm done being controlled by men. If he knows something that may be important, I need to find out. For all I know, Alpha Johnson and my father could be on their way here now to drag me out of this school, kicking and screaming." I've finally grown a backbone, and there isn't a man who is going to tell me what to do any fucking more. I immediately click over to the contacts, seeing the only one saved, J, and text that I'm free to talk.

Ten minutes later, Blaine is still sulking in the corner while Jude, Zeke, and Wylla find humor in his wet dog attitude. When the phone rings, I jump at the sound and immediately lift it to my ear and answer, "Hello."

Jeremiah

Sitting in the meeting with Alpha Johnson, Max, and Reid is fucking awful. Max is just as bad as his father, with his views on women and any supernatural who's not an Exodus wolf. The Alpha truly brainwashed his son to the pack's beliefs. Reid is the same as any other male in this pack, thinking he's Goddess's gift to the earth since he has a cock swinging between his legs. *Makes me sick.*

I could've been just like them if my sperm donor- *I refuse to call him father* -didn't betray our whole family, waking me up from the cult views we're practicing. I should have run, but where would I go? I can't leave my sister. No way in hell would I do that, she needs me.

We were called here at the ass crack of dawn because Solomon's spy, well one of them, reported Magnolia was seen at a fighting pit. She apparently was there with her roommate and three males and she kissed one of them, even wrapped her shapely legs around him. My wolf, for some reason, growls in anger at the thought of her pussy rubbing on another male. Solomon and Max are pissed and have been droning on and on about it.

Personally, good for her. I meant what I wrote in that letter. She can't come back here. Every time she steps foot on pack land, she's risking not returning to school or leaving here ever again. Her father is so far up Solomon's ass he can probably taste what was served for dinner last night.

This news on top of the nose ring she had when she came here last weekend has Solomon furious. Reid is agreeing with everything they say, like the moron he is. He doesn't have two brain cells to rub together, so it's easier for him to just nod his head and keep being the fucking creep he is. The only reason he's Max's Beta is that he can fight like no other in our pack, and he'll follow every order given to him with no complaints. If it wasn't for that, his ignorant ass would just be another menial pack member.

"I'm told the male she put her lips on is a ferret shifter, of all things. Disgusting! Snakes with legs and fur who are far beneath us and everything we stand for," Solomon spits.

"Yes, Father, we'll have to teach her a lesson when she returns for her next visit," Max agrees hurriedly. Goddess, he's such a little ass-kisser. He was one of my best friends, but once things went south with my sister and he didn't help me but agreed with my father, I knew he wasn't who I thought he was. Fuck, he could've at least fought for her freedom. He showed his true colors to me that day.

"We could paint her lips in bleach to clean her from any other foul beasts she puts them on," Reid pipes up as a suggestion from his place at the table. *What the fuck?* Where does he even think of these things? The things I've heard him say he wants to do to Magnolia make my stomach revolt at just the thought and imagery.

"Excellent idea, Beta. I will leave you in charge of that once we get her back on our lands," Solomon sneers.

My phone dings in my pocket. Discreetly, I pull it out to check, and sure enough, it's the alert I've been waiting for since Magnolia left Sunday. The package I mailed and told Magnolia about has been delivered. Now I only have to pray she listens and contacts me, so I can warn her about the nefarious things Reid, Max, and even Solomon have planned.

"Son, let's discuss the mating ceremony and the plans to mate the bitch in front of the pack. What are your thoughts?" Max leans forward, smiling like the Cheshire cat, giddy at the fact that someone wants to know how he plans to assault Magnolia.

"I'd like her to be kept at her house and prepared there. Then I'm thinking she should be brought to me wearing nothing but a white nightgown. I plan on bending her over the mating altar and fucking her from behind. Once I feel her innocence drip onto my cock, I've spoken to Reid about grabbing her and forcing her pussy down on my cock as I lay on the altar, he will then push her, so we are chest to chest and he can take her asshole. After that, I think we'll just all fuck her until she's full of our cum. I was contemplating making an offering to you as Alpha and her father for securing this bond for us. Thoughts?" Max slumps back in his chair with his arms crossed, proud of the rape he just detailed.

"What kind of offering, Son?"

"Well, I was going to give you two options: the new Luna's blood or pussy. It would be an honor to have my Alpha and his best Beta fuck my mate's pussy. But if you'd prefer to cut her and taste her blood, that would also be an honor," he answers, and my stomach revolts at what he just said. I can't believe these people sit and plan this shit out. What the fuck is wrong with this pack?

"Hmmm, I'll have to think on that, Son. Both ideas sound magnificent. I'll let you know when the time gets closer. Have you spoken to her father about this? Has he chosen?"

"Yes, Father. Reid was sent there this morning to tell him and to get his choice. Reid, would you like to tell our Alpha what his Beta has decided?" Max informs us as he looks at Reid and motions for him to stand and share his findings. What is this? An episode of Criminal Minds? We all stand and tell the team what we've learned? Newsflash, we're the bad guys!

"'Kay, so I went to talk to your Beta about Max's plan for his daughter, and let's just say he was ecstatic. He said that if it is decided he gets an offering, which would be an honor, he chooses to fuck Magnolia. It's what she deserves after flaunting her tight ass around him all these years. He did ask if it would be pushing the envelope to taste her after you've filled her with your seed, Alpha." He runs his fat tongue over his lips like what he just described isn't the vilest thing ever spoken.

"If I decide to go that route, then no, I don't think that will be a problem as long as my heir is open to it." Solomon nods. Max just grins and shrugs. I don't even understand the thinking behind this. Why would you want your dad and hers to fuck her? It's not even that, though, you'd be letting them rape her after you did.

If Magnolia doesn't heed my warning and comes back here, I'll have to make another plan because I won't sit by and watch this happen to her. But I need time to come up with an alternative if she does come back. I have to make sure Magnolia and my sister are free from here, no matter the cost to me.

"Enough of that. First things first, we need to teach that bitch her place. Maximus, I want you to take Reid and Jeremiah to the school and remind her of who she is, where she comes from, and who she belongs to. Drive that rat and whatever grotesque creatures she's gotten close with away from her. I want results by the end of the month. Do I make myself clear?"

"Yes, Father," is all Max says before Solomon storms from the room, leaving just the three of us left in the study. "I'll meet you guys back at our place in thirty minutes."

"Where ya going?" Reid questions.

"If you must know, I'm going to visit my flavor of the week. Sadie needs to be taught to respect her brother, and I was asked to be the one to do it. My cock is weeping at just the thought of her protests. See you guys in a few." He shoots us a wink and strolls from the room.

At least this way, I only have to ditch Reid in order to let Magnolia know anything. Hopefully, she answers when I call. Leaving the room, we make our way outside and start the quick walk two houses down to our place. It's just Reid, Max, and myself living there right now, but soon, Magnolia could be imprisoned there if she doesn't heed my warnings.

Getting inside, I immediately go to my tech room and close the door behind me. As soon as the door shuts behind me, I pull out my phone and call Magnolia. She answers on the first ring.

"Hi, Magnolia."

"Hello," her sweet voice purrs from the other end of the line. If only she wasn't who she was and I wasn't who I was. I would pursue her to be mine. She's the most beautiful woman I've ever seen and so strong, even if she doesn't know it yet.

"You're in danger, Magnolia. You need to stay at school and not come back here. Forget your parents and everyone else who's here that you might care about. The plans Max, Reid, and the Alpha have planned for you aren't for the faint of heart. We've been instructed already to make a plan and come there to remind you of your place after you were seen kissing a ferret," I vomit out. That wasn't exactly the plan, but panic took over when she answered, and all the gentle plans of telling her flew out the window.

Someone in the background pipes up, "What the fuck does that mean?"

"I'm not sure. We were just told this maybe ten minutes ago. Max is supposed to be back soon and come up with the plan. I'll tell you when I know more, I swear."

"And why should we trust you? You're to be mated to her too, so why help us and prevent that from happening?" That same voice demands, and just from the tone and the way I feel, I know it's another Alpha wolf. Good, hopefully, he's strong, so he can protect Magnolia.

"Daisy, my older sister, is locked away in our basement. She's my father's dirty little secret. She presented as an Omega, but he beat her into her rightful place pretending to be a 'Beta' instead of the whore she turned out to be. Currently, he's been thinking about letting older pack members who lost their mate sample her to see if they want to throw their hat in the ring to mate her. I don't want that for her or Magnolia. I hate this pack, but I can't leave Daisy," I admit. A tear slides down my cheek as I think of my sister chained to the basement floor.

"Fine. We will trust what you say. If I find out you're playing us, I'll rip your throat out," the Alpha growls.

"I understand and would expect nothing less."

"Now what are these plans that Max and his father have planned? You say they're not for the faint of heart but that is very vague. We need more than that so we can plan accordingly." One of the men pushes, but I don't want to repeat what the plan is. It's too fucking disturbing to bother repeating especially with what Magnolia's dad said he wanted. "We're waiting."

"I won't give you every gory detail because quite honestly I don't think I could let those vile words leave my lips. They plan to rape you repeatedly Magnolia; Reid, Max, Alpha Johnson, and even your father. He knows and agreed to the whole thing." Magnolia gasps and I hear snarling from her end of the conversation. "Just promise me you'll stay away from here, Magnolia." With that I hang up, stashing my phone, and just in time too, since the light inside the room lights up red, signaling someone has come to the door. Opening it, I'm met with Max's mean glare.

"What the fuck are you doing? It's time to make our plan, let's go," he growls and turns on his heel, leaving me standing there. Well, I guess it's time to get this shit show on the road.

Max

Leaving the meeting with my father, I head straight to Calvert's to get this over with. I need to make plans to get my bitch back in line. Where I would normally let my punishment go on for hours, I want to get this shit over with and get back to the guys. It takes me no time to get to his home, and he's opening the door before I even have a chance to knock, already knowing how I hate to wait.

I have Sadie bent over on her hands and knees on the bed like a good little bitch as I fuck her senseless. She was such an obedient little girl when she was informed I was coming, much different than the disobedient whore Calvert made her out to be when he asked if I would come to remind her of her place in the pack. She'd become mouthier with him, wanting to rebel against the norm.

Stepping into the room, she's already assumed the submissive position she knows I crave. Nude on her knees with her legs spread, putting her bare pussy on display, her hands on her thighs palms up with her head bowed. "Sadie, you know why I'm here?" I ask her as I walk over to the bed, already seeing the whip lying there. Picking it up, I feel the weight of the handle in my hand, and my cock hardens knowing what's to come.

"Calvert tells me you've been a disobedient bitch, speaking back to him like you're more than a willing hole for one of our men to fill when they have the need. I thought our last session would have reminded you of your place, but I was mistaken. This time, I won't treat you with as much kindness." Cocking back my hand, I bring the whip down, slicing through the air as it cracks on her skin, cutting through and allowing her delicious red blood to spill as her body lurches forward, and she screams in agony. *Perfection!*

Her screams pierce my mind, shooting right to my dick, hardening against my pants as my balls become heavy. "I'm so sorry, Max. I-I-I..." she whimpers, just the way I like, and I let the whip crack again against her milky white skin, as I add more scars to the ones already littering her back. If I didn't love her screams so much, I'd cut her tongue from her mouth, ensuring her vile words against our pack would never cross her lips again.

She's bent forward, her hands on the floor as she sobs, and I'm pissed, she's out of the position I want her in. Reaching down, I yank her up by a handful of her hair and drag her across the floor to the bed. When I was getting the whip, I noticed Calvert had done as I instructed and added the restraints to the bed. Dropping the whip, I pick her up and toss her on it, quickly latching her limbs into the cuffs, with her face down.

Bending over once more, I take the whip in my hands and begin to strike it against her skin, starting at her feet and going up to her neck. I take no breaks, only stopping when she's flowing crimson. Her screams have quieted, and when I lift her head, I see she's passed out. Another indiscretion to add to her list.

Fully aware of everything I planned to do today, he already has a blade waiting for me, and I get to work carving my ownership into her back. She doesn't move with the first slice, but the second sends her jerking up and screaming out, begging my cock to fuck her, which I fully plan to do. It takes me about five more minutes, but her back is finally marked to give any other male knowledge of who she belongs to.

Property of the Alpha.

From this point on, it will be decreed to our pack she belongs to the Alpha and Alpha heir until her death. I hope she enjoys the comfort of her bed today, she'll never see it again. Once I'm done, my father's guard will storm upon her and drag her bloody, naked body through the center of town to our dungeon. If an infection happens to ravage her body from her delicious wounds, then she simply wasn't strong enough to be part of this pack, and she should welcome death willingly.

Reaching down, I undo my pants and pull out my dick. Wrapping my hand around its thick length, I stroke it from base to tip, giving it a little pull at the end. Reaching into my back pocket, I pull out the condom I'd slipped into it this morning before heading to my father's, using my teeth to rip open the package before placing it at my tip and rolling it down the length of my shaft. There's no way in hell I want any bastard heirs running around the pack thinking they can fight my true heir for the rank of Alpha when it's my time to step down. My father made that mistake, and I made sure to rip his throat out when I came into my wolf, never giving him the opportunity to challenge me.

I don't want to see her when I fuck her, but first, it's time to let all men know who she belongs to when they take her tight, sweet pussy. Taking her by her hips with my hands, I yank her ass up, putting it on display for me, her ass and pussy calling for me to rip it to shreds. I was going to take her sweet hole, but now that her body is bleeding with my handiwork, I've decided to take her ass, no prepping. She's just a whore and doesn't deserve the prepping my future bitch will.

Taking my hand, I spread her cheeks wide, as I take my cock in my other one and line it up with her glory hole, before slamming inside of her. Her screams drive me on as I fuck her, slamming in and out of her with enough force that my condom-covered dick is painted red. Normally, I would take longer to come, but I have things to do. I envision my Magnolia underneath me, taking her sweet virginity as the men in my pack watch on. The sweet images running through my mind send me over the edge, and I scream out my orgasm as my cock shoots its load.

Pulling out quickly, I pull off the condom, discard it in the trash, put my dick back in my pants, and zip them back up. Leaving her in a sobbing mess and covered in blood, she'll stay restrained until the guards come to collect her. I pull out my phone and shoot off a text to the guys that I'm on my way and to be waiting in the living room for me, we have plans to make. Sliding it back in my pocket, I don't even wait for a response, they'll do exactly as I ask.

Ten minutes later, I'm walking into the home I share with Reid and Jeremiah, ready to make our plans. My mate needs to be here, not at some school around the trash she's associating with. Stepping into the living room, I see Reid sprawled out on the couch, cock in hand as he watches porn on the sixty-inch television mounted on the wall. This isn't an uncommon sight, and we've become so accustomed to it that it doesn't surprise us anymore. Soon, our new plaything will be here to soothe those cravings of his.

"Where's Jeremiah?" I ask him.

"In his office, I think. I saw his keys on the table, so I know he's here," he tells me, without stopping or slowing down his masturbation.

"I'll get him, finish that shit up fast, we'll be right back. We've got plans to make." I motion toward his cock as I speak, anxious to get started. The sooner we get to that school, the better.

Storming all the way to Jeremiah's office, I lift my hand to bang on the door, but before I can, the door flings open, and I glare at him. His ass should have been waiting for me just like Reid, well, not masturbating, but waiting nonetheless. "What the fuck are you doing? It's time to make our plan, let's go," I growl out at him as I turn and head back to the living room. I can't wait to plan out the fun I'm going to have with my mate once she's back under our thumb, just like my father taught me to handle a mate when I was younger.

Stepping back into the living room, I see Reid licking his fingers with his cock put away. Jeremiah steps in behind me and takes a seat in the recliner.

"Good, we're all here. Let's solidify what we're doing and how we are going to get our mate away from that school," I command with malicious delight.

Magnolia

My mind has been on a rollercoaster with what happened yesterday when I left home, last night with Jude and Wylla, and then this morning. Getting the okay that I could join the Stoneridge pack was a relief like a burden was lifted from me. But then the delivery came from Jeremiah with yet another warning not to return to the pack I grew up in.

I don't know what to think, what to do. Do I trust him, or is it just a trap? I have so many questions and no answers. With everything going on, I almost took the day off from classes, but Wylla suggested I go to keep my mind busy and to make it look like I didn't know anything, in case Alpha Johnson had more spies here watching me. I know there was one at the fight, and they saw my kiss with Zeke, but were there more?

The guys and I barely made it to Supernatural History on time, and I could see the frowning look on Professor Godrickson's face as we came rushing into the classroom after it already started, causing an uproar of laughter and muffled comments, especially the guys who think we were in the throes of a gang bang that made us late. Blaine must have heard the same as he growls at them all, baring his teeth.

I slide into my seat, hastily pulling my book from my bag, before setting my bag on the ground and turning to the chapter I knew we'd be discussing from the syllabus. My mind is still playing everything on replay as I work to try to find an answer for what to do, who to believe, and who I can trust. Jude reaches out across the aisle and rubs his hand along my thigh, attempting to comfort me, but all it does is spiral me into memories of last night and his tail. Fuck, that was the most erotic thing I've ever experienced. Which isn't a lot, I know.

"Miss Holloway... Miss Holloway!" I swear I hear my name being called, but I can't seem to focus on it. It seems like an echo in my mind, maybe a memory.

A gentle shake of my shoulder brings me back to reality, and I look to my right to see it's Blaine. "Babe, the professor's been calling you, are you okay?"

"Huh?" comes out more loudly than I'd anticipated.

"Ahh, good, it seems you've rejoined us, Miss Holloway. I was asking you your thoughts on the supposed extinction of some of our older supernaturals like Unicorns, Minotaurs, and Dragons. Do you believe they are truly extinct or merely hiding in plain sight for the day they can return to the public?"

"Oh... umm... I... Well, I think, since this is all so new to me, that maybe they're still around. Some might even be our best friends. What made them go into hiding? I guess we'll just have to hope that one day they'll tell us when they feel comfortable enough to rejoin the world."

"Well said, Miss Holloway, and please stay after class, so I can speak with you for a moment," he says before continuing on with his lecture. The class was so busy acting like high schoolers with their oohs and ahhs that I don't think they caught the wink he gave me, but the angered growl beside me tells me someone did.

Thirty minutes later, class comes to an end. I go to reach down for my bag, but Jude beats me to it and hands it to me. "Thank you," I whisper to him.

"Welcome, babe. Wonder what he wants to talk to you about? He can't be all tied up in knots because you were spaced out. Hell, most of us were, not just you."

"It's okay," I tell him as I hang back, knowing Professor Godrickson wants to speak with me. What I wasn't expecting was for the guys to stay with me. "Go, I'll meet up with you when I'm done," I tell them as I try to shoo them off.

"NO!" Blaine growls out loudly, crossing his arms over his chest as he glares in Professor Godrickson's direction.

"Come on, man, she'll be okay. See you at lunch." Zeke leans in, giving me a chaste kiss on my cheek as he shoves Blaine out of the room, with Jude doubled over in laughter as he follows behind them.

Shaking my head at them, I head to the front of the room to talk to Professor Godrickson. "You wanted to see me? I'm sorry about spacing out during class..." He raises his hand, cutting me off before I can finish.

"You're fine, I just wanted to see how you've been since our last meeting. I know you were a little anxious that day, and well, you seem to be very distracted in class lately."

"Yeah. There's just so much going on, and I don't know what to think or do," I tell him, really wishing I had someone I could trust, outside of everything, that I could spill my guts to and get their unbiased opinion. *Could he be that person?*

"I'm here if you need to talk, and I'll give you the best advice I can," he volunteers as he pulls a chair up to his desk for me to sit in, then takes a seat himself.

"Really. You'd do that for me, a student?"

"Of course. But only if you feel comfortable talking to me." He reaches out, putting his hand on my knee, giving a slight squeeze, and electricity shoots through me, causing me to jump in response.

I regain my composure quickly as he pulls his hand away, and I spend the next half hour spilling my soul to him. Telling him about my home life, the plans to mate me to the Alpha heir and his Betas, what happened over the weekend, Wylla and the guys. Everything. Finally ending with the note and call from Jeremiah. He listens intently to every word, never once interrupting me. Not until I let out a deep breath at the end, just before the river of tears begin to fall from my eyes.

He reaches out, using his fingers to wipe them away, and then embraces me in a hug that's not normal for a teacher to do. It causes tingles of electricity to float along my skin, making my hair stand on end. Not in a 'psychotic killer is after me', or 'my skeevy uncle is making a pass at me', but more of an 'I need more' kind of feeling.

Releasing me, he leans back, then takes one of my hands in his. "I think your friend Wylla has given you some good advice. Listen to what this Jeremiah has to say, but keep your guard around him and don't divulge too much information. Stay with your friends and be aware of your surroundings and who's around you. Can I see your phone?" I pull my bag into my lap. Reaching inside, I rummage around until I find it and hand it to him. He takes it from me and begins typing away, then hands it back. "Now you have my number. If you need me, call me. Night or day. Do you understand?"

I nod my head yes as I slide it back into my bag.

"No, Magnolia, I need to hear your words." His voice is deeper and more commanding, causing my center to pool with heat.

"Yes," comes out with a breathy moan that has me embarrassed.

He grins at me. "Good girl, now go meet your friends. But remember, I'm here."

I scurry from the room with a need between my legs, begging to be taken care of.

Garth

It took everything in me to not take her in my arms and claim her. To place my mate mark on her, warning everyone she belongs to me, one of the most powerful gargoyles. Not that anyone would know that, since we've kept our presence unknown. The majority of the supernatural world once believed us to be extinct except for the limited few we brought into our inner sanctum of confidence. But after a number of years, we decided to announce to the world that we will still exist, omitting that our numbers were greater than what they thought, wanting to maintain some level of anonymity.

I'd long given up hope of ever finding my mate. After six hundred and seventy years, I'd assumed she was a mythical unicorn, who by the way are also not extinct. Unknown to the masses, one enrolled in the school this year. She's actually a hybrid, witch and unicorn, a witch-icorn if you will.

The first time I saw Magnolia in class, I knew right away that she was my mate. But I couldn't understand why she didn't feel it as well, but now knowing about this block on her, it makes perfect sense. I thought I was going crazy, that my gargoyle was as well, projecting a bond to a girl who wasn't ours. I still don't know if she feels the connection between us, the spark. I feel it every time I touch her. It's why I try to do it at every opportunity.

My gargoyle pleads with me to tell her who we are, what we are to her, to claim and protect her from the pack she was born into. Thank goodness she managed to finagle a way to come to college here, or we would have never found her. I finally manage to appease my gargoyle that we will once she breaks the block, but until then, we need to keep it a secret. She's already so overwhelmed with just knowing she has multiple mates and the new information about her pack, we don't want her to have a breakdown. Our saving grace will be when the block is removed, and it comes to light I'm her mate. She will simply think she was masked from me as well.

Putting my number in her phone wasn't my plan, nor was sending myself a text, so I would have hers, but I needed to be able to contact her. For her to be able to reach me if everything goes sideways and her pack comes for her. When she mentioned her desire to join the Stonehaven pack, as well as their Alpha heir claiming to be her mate, my fear for her safety lessened, not a lot but some. Blaine's father and I have been friends since he was just a pup. He keeps the secret of my species not being extinct, and I'm ready to fight for him at his call. Blaine doesn't remember me, nor his wolf I suspect, but I used to bounce them both on my knee when he was just a pup only a few days old. We knew he would be coming here one day, so I stopped visiting him when they were about three. My heart swelled with pride when I saw what an amazing young man he's turned into.

Pulling out my phone, I texted my brethren, needing to update them on the change of events and the possible war coming to us. We need to call all the gargoyle clans and have them on alert. I fear the worst for my mate if the whispers are true that anyone who attempts to leave is met with a disastrous end.

I pray to the Goddess that this Jeremiah is true of heart and can be trusted. Otherwise, he will be food for our hounds. The scuffling of feet draws my attention to the gaggle of girls coming through the door. Their need to sit in the front and flirt, like I would ever want anything to do with them, is revolting, especially when I have my mate so close.

Wylla

Lounging on Jude's bed, we all get comfortable before we start this meeting he demanded we have in regard to Magz. Once all of us are seated and ready, Jude looks at me. "I officially call the meeting about Magz to order. Rainbow Sprite, the floor is yours." I glare at him because what the fuck? He called the meeting and insisted we get our asses here, but now it's up to me to lead it. *Fucking sex demon.*

"Actually, I lied, let me tell them about the night Maggie came home. Prepare yourself, Wylla girl, they're going to be jealous as hell." He wags his brows at me. I throw a pillow at him, and he catches it, cackling before opening his mouth again to speak. "Well, boys, I got a taste of our girl and her friend here."

"The fuck does that mean?" Zeke yells.

A deep, menacing growl comes from Blaine's chest. Goddess above, his wolf is pissed. Jude is going to be lucky if he leaves here with all his limbs still attached.

"Yes, Jude, what the fuck does that mean?" he manages to grit out between his clenched teeth.

"It means that I went to see Maggie, and when I knocked, the little witch here was naked and so was Maggie. I entered the room and asked if I should stay or go, and Maggie said stay, so I joined them. Oh, goddess above, my friends, Wylla taught, no more like showed Maggie, how to suck a dick. Let's just say Rainbow Sprite would have a gold medal if cock sucking were an Olympic sport. And well, she's a damn fine teacher too, and my little Maggie, she's a prize pupil. They worked me together with their mouths, and hot damn, I'm getting hard just thinking about it." He reaches down and adjusts himself. "Then a little situation presented itself when I came on them. They laughed at me, so I had them on the bed side by side and tasted each of their sweet pussies before Wylla rode my fingers like the pony express and Maggie girl took my tail like a champion. Don't worry, Blainey boy, I made sure to keep her hymen intact." His eyes are full of lust. I'm pretty sure he's fueling himself just thinking about the other night.

"You're telling us that you and you played together, and Magnolia was there and enjoyed it?" Zeke asks.

"Yup," Jude replies, popping the p.

"Wylla, you were okay with being with Jude and Magnolia at the same time as well?" Blaine asks, his teeth still clenched, as if he is fighting back what he really wants to say.

"Yeah, I have a pull to each of you. Nothing as strong as Magz and me, but my guess is that Magz will be the center of our group, and we will all be mated to each other through her. Like brother mates, but I have a vagina."

"I'm not fucking either one of these shitheads. No way, no how. I'll watch, but no way could I let one of them fuck me. We've been brothers for too long," Zeke says, looking at his friends with horror written all over his face.

Cackling, I curl onto my side, holding my stomach. "Not mated to them in that sense. I mean like mate brothers, as in our life forces will all be connected. If my suspicions are correct, we will be able to communicate and feel each other the same as if we were all actually mated, just some of us without the sex and mate marks."

The guys are looking at me like I've grown a third tit in the center of my forehead. "It's extremely rare. Actually, such a bond hasn't been seen for hundreds of years, according to my grandmother. It would be nice to know who these other mates are besides us though. Do you three have any ideas?"

They all shake their heads no. "The most important thing is to remove the spells on her. First, I have to remove the designation spell, then after she finds out what she is and if she still gives the go ahead, I'll remove the mate block. Grandmother said they have to be done in that order. And no, I don't know why, but she told me some riddle that made absolutely no sense to me, but I don't see the harm in doing one before the other."

A phone ringing breaks the tense silence filling the room after I told them what I know.

"It's the food. I'll go down and get it and be right back," Blaine says as he strolls from the room, his phone to his ear.

After we've all gorged ourselves on pasta and soda, it's time to get to business. I need to task them with a few things for the breaking of the blocks Friday night, and we need to make a plan to keep Magz safe.

"Okay, boys, so we want to do the ceremony to remove all blocks Friday. That gives us two days' time to be ready and prepared for whatever the hell happens that night. Magz doesn't wanna wait any longer, and quite frankly, I don't think any of us do either. However, I need a few things. Jude, can you go to hell and get us some honey? It has to be hell honey. It's the strongest and best thing to use when breaking spells or curses."

Jude nods. "Sure. It's been a while since I've been to my old stomping grounds, but I can pop in to get some and morph back to you. It'll be tight though, so you'll have to tell me where we're doing this so I can just pop right to you."

"Perfect, we'll be doing it on the school's field. We need a large outdoor space, and the team has an away game that night, so no one should be around. Blaine, if I give you a list, can you grab a few things like candles and such?"

"No problem, anything you need, I got you," he says without hesitation.

"Okay then, I'll see you all Friday night ready and prepared to see what the fuck is going to happen with us and our girl."

"What about me? You don't need anything from me?" Zeke pipes up, seeming annoyed I didn't give him an errand.

"Well, little noodle rat, I'm glad you asked. Since they know you were the one she kissed, and they somehow know you are a ferret, I thought the perfect place for you to be was with our girl, shadowing her and making sure she's safe. I think one of us needs to be with her at all times. Zeke, I think you can be the least suspicious, though. Her pack is so ass backwards they probably think you're a weak, meek ferret. It seems, from what I can tell since it hasn't been mentioned, they only saw the two of you together and not you fighting. We however know differently, so I think it's best you stay with her more than the rest of us."

He rubs his hands together and bites his bottom lip. "I like this plan so much that I'm going to give the noodle rat thing a pass."

"I agree with Wylla. I think we need to stay close to her. Especially since it seems her betrothed is planning on coming here and doing Goddess knows what. As much as it will kill me to do so, if they do show up and just wanna lurk from the shadows, we need to play it off like we're just friends. Like we have a project or something we need to work on, and she's helping us or some shit like that. That way she's safe from them without alerting them too much. We will know more once that Jeremiah fuckhead calls again with more information. We need to play this smart and on the down low till we know all the moving parts. Unless shit goes south, then we protect our girl, no holds barred. You all with me?" Blaine asks.

A string of yeahs comes from the rest of us, and I get up, making my way to the door. "Bye, bitches, I'm going to go cuddle our mate," I tease and hear all three growling behind me. Paying them no mind, I open the door and make my way to the elevator.

Getting to our room, I find Magnolia sound asleep with a book still in her hands. She must have fallen asleep while studying. Goddess, she is fucking precious. Plucking the book from her hands, I slide it into her bag and move it over by the door, so she has it for tomorrow. Quickly changing out of my clothes and pulling a t-shirt over my head, I crawl into bed with Magz, pulling the blanket up and over us. Reaching out and wrapping my arm around her waist, I move her body closer to my chest. Placing a soft kiss on the side of her head, I close my eyes, allowing my mind to stop racing. Tomorrow starts our new plan, and we have to be aware of what's going on around us at all times. No way am I letting any of those Exodus fucks harm my girl in any way. Even just their sharp tongues will get them on my shitlist.

I fall asleep to dreams of my zombie creations, ripping her old pack to shreds and feasting on their insides.

It's Friday night, and I'm standing here in the middle of the football field, waiting for the rest of this rag-tag group of Magz's mates to get here. My heart feels like it could beat out of my own dang chest. Nervous would be an understatement to what I'm feeling right now. I'm not nervous about performing the removals or their success. No, I'm nervous about what happens afterward.

Our main man, Brick, is once again the lookout for tonight's festivities. At this rate, the dude might as well just join our little gang. Not as a mate, though! Oh! Maybe there is a sweet little someone at the school here that we could hook him up with. Definitely going to ask the guys if Brick has anyone he's interested in or if he has an idea of who his mate could be. We owe the dude a solid for sure.

I'm snapped out of my thoughts by the mouthwatering scent of cotton candy that I catch in the wind. Jerking my head up, I lock my gaze on Magz and Zeke as they stroll onto the field hand in hand. Quirking an eyebrow at her and flashing my eyes down to their hands and back up, she just shrugs and gives me an eye roll. So the ferret won't let her go and she's too soft-hearted to be bitchy. I chuckle quietly about how sweet and empathetic our girl is.

"Are you ready for this, Magz? No going back after tonight," I say, but we all know her answer. She's been ready since she came home from her visit, especially after we

spoke to Jeremiah. Magz has now made it her mission to help him free his sister, if he doesn't betray us, that is. Because I'm still iffy on the rabid dog myself.

Blaine comes jogging onto the field with a bag over his shoulder. He sets it on the ground in front of me. "Sorry, I'm late. The little witch here had me out shopping for supplies. You wouldn't believe how hard it is to find specific colored candlesticks." Magz giggles at him, and he smirks at her while she blushes and chews on her bottom lip. He walks over to her, picks her up, and spins her around before setting her down and giving her a sweet but quick kiss on the nose. A *whoosh* has us turning around immediately on our toes ready for war. Jude morphs in, fully shifted into his demon form. He holds up the jar, and I hurry to grab it from him.

"Sorry, took me a minute to get to hell and back, woman. Dang, you're demanding as hell. Ha! The irony in that statement." I ignore him and start pulling everything we need out of the bag Blaine brought with him.

"Okay, let's fucking do this. Is everyone ready?" Everyone nods in agreement, so I take that as my signal and get to work. Taking the gold candles out, I hand one to everyone. "Magz, go stand over there in the center of the circle I drew. Menfolk, take a candle and stand at each directional point around Magz; South, East, West. Once the guys are repeating what I say, Magz you then chant with us looking at the stars, eyes closed, and asking the Goddess to remove the designation block."

Taking my own candle, I head to the North position. Taking the lighter, I light my candle before passing it to Blaine. He follows suit and passes it to Jude, who follows our actions before he hands it off to Zeke.

"Now repeat after me. *Dirige viamo, sternen viamic. Nisi in sinute servat designationem."* The men chant with me when I start again. At the beginning of the third round, Magz can be heard along with us. Once we've all completed the third round, I pull my snuffer from my skirt pocket and extinguish my candle's flame.

The wind gusts around us, putting out the guys' and Magz's candles. Magz then lifts into the air, a bright golden light exploding from around her. She's suspended like that for a minute or so before she falls to the ground in a heap. Power explodes from the center of the circle, blowing the rest of us to our asses. Sitting up, I look around and see Blaine up and moving toward Magz first. The rest of us are up and running toward her as soon as we are on our feet.

Blaine grabs her, helping her stand. He gasps, and his eyes widen to the size of saucers, staring at our girl. "Blaine, why are you staring at her like that?"

"Can't you feel it? She's a fucking Alpha. Holy Shit!" He's yelling at us, but you can tell by his tone and how wide his eyes are, he's shocked.

Magnolia

'*Finally! I'm free. Now I just need to get back to full strength.*' My wolf howls as I just stand there in shock.

I'm a fucking Alpha! What the ever-loving hell is going on?

'*Yes. We are Alpha. We're powerful. Our people will bow to us.*'

"*HOLD ON!!*" I scream out to her. I need to wrap my mind around this. This changes everything I've ever been told. A female Alpha is unheard of among wolves, or at least that's what I, we, have always been taught.

"Blaine, have there ever been female Alphas before?" I ask with a need burning in me to know. Has my pack hidden even more from me? From all females? What if I'm not the first in our pack this has happened to? Where are those females now?

He just stares at me, slack-jawed. Does my being an Alpha change the way he feels for me? Does he hate knowing that he's mated to a wolf of equal standing? My anxiety washes over me, and I feel a panic attack building. Casting my eyes around at the others, I see them gawking at me, their mouths and eyes wide as well. Do they feel differently about me now? Have I lost them before ever even claiming them as mine?

Blaine moves straight toward me before abruptly stopping in front of me. Reaching up, he takes my chin in his hand and tilts my head upward. "First, I want to address something else, and then I'll answer your question. You being an Alpha changes nothing. You are my mate, and honestly, I feel even less worthy of you now. So drop all those doubts I can see racing through your mind. They're wrong. Nothing will change how I feel about you. You and your wolf are ours. Now, about what you asked. Yes. There are female Alphas; though I will admit, they are extremely rare, but not unheard of."

"So I'm not a freak, and my pack lied to me all these years, telling me that women could never be an Alpha, have power, or be strong." Just saying the words 'my pack' makes me want to puke. I'm convinced now more than ever that I'm making the right decision. My mom may want to continue to stay there, but I can't. "I'm so sorry." Why I'm apologizing, I don't even know.

"Don't ever fucking apologize for feeling how you do and speaking up about them. In fact, I'd be more pissed if you didn't. We're a bond, one you'll know for certain soon, as well as these guys..." He throws his hand over his shoulder, waving his arm at the others and clearing his throat before he begins to speak again, "Excuse me, guys and girls. We're all bonded in some freakishly crazy way that I'm down for. My wolf and I will learn to accept you being with the others. I just ask for your patience. In fact, we're already imagining seeing you writhing in pleasure from the others, so I think we're going to be perfectly fine with it. So we may not need you to have much patience," Blaine says with a chuckle before he leans in, placing his lips on mine and kissing me deeply. My lips part for his, allowing his tongue entrance as he tangles it with mine.

I feel a soft hand touch my arm, pulling me from the lust-filled haze overtaking me with Blaine's kiss. "Magz, sorry to interrupt this make-out session, but do you want to continue? We can do the spell to remove the mate block another time. I know this has been a lot and not what you expected to find out." Wylla's voice soothes the rage building inside of me at the lies I've been told my entire life.

"No, we can continue with the spell. I need to, no, I want to know who I am mated to, if for nothing more than my own sanity. If I'm mated to the Alpha heir and his Betas, I want to see if we can find a way to break the bond, severing it forever. Is that possible, Wylla?" My wolf feeds me the strength to say the words.

"Even Jeremiah?" she asks, which sets Blaine and the guys in an uproar.

"Of course she fucking does. Is that even a question that needs to be asked?" Blaine growls out angrily, his hands already beginning to shift into claws.

"You can calm it down, puppy, and put those claws away. It's a question that needs to be asked. Magz herself said she felt something different around him, and he is showing himself to be a better person than the others. At the moment, he's showing himself to be a standup guy," Wylla announces as she looks to me for an answer.

"I want to say yes, break the bond to him as well if there's one. But you're right, I'm conflicted at the moment. He's showing me he's not like the others, and if he is true to his words and he is bonded to me, then I want to give it a chance to grow. But also, I know I want to help him save his sister, regardless if I ultimately decide to sever the bond."

"Babe, are you sure?" Zeke comes up behind me, wrapping his arms around my waist as he kisses my neck. I nod my head yes. "Okay then, I'll support your decision."

"I will too, Maggie," Jude pipes up as he steps beside Wylla. "You know I always have my bitch's back," Wylla sing-songs.

"Fine, but one step out of line and my wolf is eating him," comes from my grumpy wolf mate.

"Okay then, everyone back into the same position as the last spell. Time to find out once and for all who our girl is really mated to," Wylla announces with joy, but I can hear the slight trepidation in her voice. Fear that she may not be mated to me. *Goddess, please, let these three men and this one amazing woman be my mates.*

Turning around, I see Brick on his knees, sitting back on his haunches, eyes wide, glued on me.

"Brick, are you okay?" I move over to him, kneeling down before him. "Earth to Brick, do you hear me?" I ask again when he doesn't respond.

"I just- I can't- Fuck me sideways, you're an Alpha. That's freaking amazing. Wait until I tell all my friends," he says with such glee and pride. Sheer happiness for me radiates off of him.

"No! Brick, promise not to say anything yet. Not until I figure out how to handle this with my pack. My life depends on it." I add the last part, knowing I can be honest with him, that if he knew how important it was, he'd keep his mouth shut. Honestly, I don't know how we're going to hide it. I can feel the power radiating from me now, and from what my wolf says, we're not even at full strength.

"I promise, Magnolia." He stands slowly. "I'm going to move back out of the way while you do the next spell. But I'm here if anything freaky happens." He gives a genuine smile before turning and walking over to the sidelines of the field.

"Thank you," I whisper-shout to him, knowing he heard me. Turning back around, I look around at the guys and Wylla. Taking a deep breath, I move to the center of the field. It's time to find out who my mates are.

Wylla

I head back to my bag to grab the items needed for the next spell, feeling completely fucking shocked that my girl is an Alpha. I definitely didn't see that coming. I thought Beta, maybe even Omega with how many mates I saw, but nope, I was wrong. My Magz, our Magz, is a full-blown fucking Alpha bitch. I'm both excited and scared as shit. What happens when her pack finds out? We know they have someone here watching, but what happens if they spill the beans? Shaking the thought from my mind, I need my brain to be clear when I do the spell.

Grabbing the cream sheet of paper and the crow feather—thanks crow daddy—I snag the honey Jude brought and hold it up to admire the gold liquid with swirls of black moving gracefully inside the jar. *Fucking weird as shit!* It feels like the honey is alive! This specific honey is only found in the second circle of hell, where incubi and succubi live. Thank the Goddess we have Jude; otherwise, I don't know how we would've gotten it.

Making my way back to the circle, the men are standing around again with Magz in the center. I hand them each a black ribbon. "Once again, friends, repeat after me. As soon as you've been passed the jar of honey, take a finger full of it and draw a cross over your heart. This signifies we all have good intentions of removing the block. Keep chanting until Magz shows signs like before that the spell has worked." Well, at least I hope she reacts the same way and nothing bad happens.

Opening the honey, I take a glob out and smear it over my heart, right on my shirt. *"Aufers hunc scandalumy sociorum eius. Sciats verots amores fasti."* Handing the jar to Blaine, he mirrors me, then Jude, and finally Zeke.

When everyone has drawn over their heart, I pull the feather out and write on the paper the names of those we're hoping Magz is mated to. Begging the Goddess that this doesn't lead to her being mates with Max and Reid. I shove the paper into the jar of honey and seal it before slowly squatting and setting it on the ground in front of me. I pull a ribbon and scissors from my bra. I begin to cut the ribbon, letting the scissors fall to the ground with the ribbon pieces after I cut the last piece. We continue chanting until Magz lets out an ear-piercing scream. She grabs at her chest where her heart is. Falling to her knees, she's panting as tears run down her cheeks.

The guys all dart towards her, stopping in their tracks when I scream out, "Stop!" They turn, glaring at me, "We need to let the spell finish. We need to wait for Magz to let us know it's done, that she's okay."

"But she's in pain," Blaine growls out.

"I know, but we need to wait. We can't do anything to interfere with the spell. You need to trust me. I love her Blaine, hell I haven't even told her yet. Do you think I'd do anything to hurt her more?" I plead with him.

"Blaine, man, she's right. We need to trust her. She knows more about this magic shit than we do. Once Magz gives us the okay, we go to her." Jude backs me up, placing a hand on Blaine's shoulder.

"Fine," he growls out as we watch the spell continue to ravish Magz.

I expected lights and power blasts like the other removal, not pain. *Fuck, I would have warned her about pain.* She's just frozen, clutching her chest, staring at the ground, and trying to catch her breath.

"Magz, baby, are you alright? You should be able to feel or know who your mates are now if it worked. Just like Blaine did that night at the mixer when you see them you'll know right away." My words are begging her to look at us, to show us some sign that she's okay.

"Maggie, baby, you gotta do something, say something, so we know you're okay," Jude pleads with her

Zeke bends down, moving an arm out to Magz, but Blaine growls and snatches his hand, not letting him touch her. "Let her be. She needs to come to this on her own terms. Just give her a moment."

"Blaine is right. Touching her before the spell is finished could counteract it. She'll be okay. We need to wait and let her come to us," I reinforce.

Finally, those pretty eyes look up at us, and they pin us all in place with an icy stare and recognition shining through them. Her breathing is heavy as she stares at us, her eyes burning a hole right through our hearts. She gives us a cocky smirk that has me spiraling in fear that I, we, were wrong and she's not mated to us. Looking over at the guys, I see the same fear etched on their faces.

A powerful growl comes from her as her voice becomes husky and the one word she speaks has my heart soaring.

"Mates!" is all she says before she's standing and throwing herself into our arms.

Magnolia

Mates! Oh, my Goddess. I have mates! All four of them belong to me and my wolf.

What the hell have I been doing? Why have I fought this? Crouched around me are four of my mates, but I can feel there are more, just not who they are. All I feel is an intense draw to them unlike anything I've felt before, but there is still an emptiness in my heart for the bonds I don't know yet. Casting my gaze between them, their eyes are locked on me. Movement in my periphery catches my attention, and my wolf forces a growl so strong it comes right out of me for all to hear.

"Magnolia, it's me, Brick. Your friend. Remember me. Umm, I see that you're all okay, so I'm just going to be on my way." He moves closer, holding his hands up in an 'I give up' fashion. His movement halts, but it isn't my growl that stops him in mid-step. It's the angered voices from the surrounding ones. "No worries, guys, and Wylla. I'm leaving, she's all yours." He slowly begins to back away from us.

"Brick, thank you for your help, but that might be the best choice. We're good, and well, we just all want to be alone with our mate," Wylla tells him before he turns and sprints away across the field. She turns back to me. "How are you, baby? Want to head back to our room where we can have some privacy and talk?"

Zeke is still squatted down in front of me, and he reaches out, taking my hand in his, and helps me stand. I stumble at first, but he saves me by wrapping his arm around my waist and pulling my body firmly against his chest. Bending his head down, he places a kiss on my forehead. "My mate. I've waited so long to say those words. Never did I think

I would be lucky enough to have a mate as wonderful as you." His sweet words cause a single tear to escape my eye and slide down my cheek.

"Come on, let's get back to the room so we can sit and process everything and maybe have a stiff drink. Well, puppy, looks like you can give us the ol' 'I told you so,' seeing how you were right about being her mate." Wylla takes one of my hands in hers, tugs me from Zeke's embrace, and starts pulling me across the field toward the dorms. "Hey, Fido, how about you, the wet noodle, and sex god get all this shit cleaned up and meet us when you're done?" She doesn't even wait for a response, just keeps tugging me along.

A pang in my heart grows the further away from my mates I get. Reaching up, I claw at my chest over my heart. "Wylla, why is the pain in my heart growing?" It feels like a blade has been stuck right into my chest and is slowly being turned as it's pushed deeper and deeper in.

"It's okay, baby. The pain will go away once the others are with us," she tells me, leaving me with even more fucking questions. If that's the case, why did we leave without them? Why is she wanting me to feel this pain?

"Then why did we leave them?" I need to know. Surely she can't be so cruel to want me to feel this pain.

"Because I needed time to explain to you what you're feeling without my brother mates hovering. Until the bond is completed, you're going to feel this way anytime you're away from them."

Before she can say anymore, I cut her off speaking up, "But we did. That's what we did tonight."

She lets out a small chuckle that infuriates me. She is slowly moving down the list of my favorite people. Right now, Zeke is at the top.

She stops in her tracks, turning to look me in the eyes. "No, Magz, all we did was move the block, so you would know who your mates were. Until you physically complete the bond and mark each of us with your bite, you'll feel how you are right now. To clarify, you have to do that with each of us. Once you complete the bond with one of us, it won't hurt to be away from that person. I didn't think you knew due to true mate bonds not being a thing with the Exodus pack, so I wanted to explain it to you in private."

I just nod in understanding as we resume walking to the dorms. My body moves on autopilot as I try to process everything that's happened and what Wylla has explained to me. The comfort of her hand in mine as she leads me to the dorm soothes my soul, which is screaming for me to turn around and claim my mates.

Once we've made it back into the room, Wylla leads me over to my bed, helping me to sit before kneeling down in front of me and removing my shoes. "You okay?" Two small words, but the meaning behind them is overpowering.

"Dealing. So much has happened. How do I handle it all? I'm so glad to know the four of you are my mates, but I still feel an emptiness. That there are some who are missing. Is that possible?"

"Yes. Until you have met all your mates, you will have a hole, so to say. It could literally be anyone. You could have met them before, but with the block, you wouldn't have known. Now that it's removed, if you come in contact with them again, you'll know," she explains to me as fear sets in about Max and Reid.

"The Alpha Heir?"

"Not your mate. If they were, then the spell was laced to show a projected image of them. Since there was no image, they are not your mates. Jeremiah, on the other hand, was not included, so we won't know until you come in contact with him." The door opening causes us both to look up as three of my bonds step into the room.

They each walk up to me, taking turns to place a kiss on my lips before finding somewhere to sit.

"Do you feel it? A bond to each other?" I ask curiously.

Zeke clears his throat before speaking, "I feel a closeness, more than I had before, to each of these guys, but not a sexual one. Let me make it very clear I have no desire to fuck any of them, but Wylla is different. I feel a connection, a pull to her, but it's not as great as the one to you. I have the urge to be with her sexually, but again, not as strong as I do for you. How about the three of you?" I whip my head around to each of them, taking a moment to look them in the eyes as I wait for their answer.

Wylla is the next to speak up, "I have to admit, I feel the same as Zeke. I have a pull to them, but unlike him, I have a desire to be with all of them, but not as great as you. I have a suspicion the other two will have the same thing to say, which leads me to believe I was right in assuming you are the center of the bond." Looking at Blaine and Jude, I see them nod in agreement.

"We need to find my other mates," I announce boldly.

"Do you know how many more there are? Can you tell in some way? I know you could make out six, but it was unclear if there were more," Blaine asks eagerly.

"No, I don't know how many more, but it's weird, after you explained about the whole bond thing to me, Wylla, it does feel like my heart knows them, that I've met them. But

I do know that I want to complete the bond with the four of you. I want this, the bond, you." Excitement and love cover all their faces. I know it's weird to say that. We've only known each other for a few short weeks, but it's what I feel.

"Oh, Magz, trust me, we all want to complete the bond with you as well. But you're a virgin, and I think we need to take it slow. Your first time should be special and a one-on-one experience. Since the sex god and I have already had some sexy time with you, I think it should be either Zeke or Blaine. Blaine has known you were his mate from first sight, and well, Zeke, he's the gentle you need. It should be one or both of them if you want more than one. Even though I think you should pick just one of them with this being your first time." Wylla stands from the floor in front of me and sits on the bed beside me, then leans in and whispers into my ear. "Now don't think for a minute, my little wolf mate, that it means I don't want you. I'd take you now in a heartbeat. I want nothing more than to bear your mark."

A smile crosses my face as I look around at them all, feeling a little mischievous as I speak. "Okay then, well, who wants to take my virginity and bear my mate mark first?"

Everyone looks around, their gazes landing on Blaine and Zeke, who are staring at each other.

Blaine speaks up first, "Magnolia, there is nothing in the world I want more than to mate with you. To complete our bond and take your virginity. But this is your choice, and Zeke would be a perfect choice to bond with first."

His words are so kind, but I know who I want.

"I want both of you. My first time should be with my mate who knew and fought for me even when I was in denial and the sweetest, most amazing man I've ever met." I get up and move over to where they're both sitting on Wylla's bed. "I want to bond with the two of you tonight, let's not wait any longer. This is what I want."

"We are going to take that as our cue to give you some privacy. Me and Rainbow Sprite are going to head upstairs." Jude tosses a wink, but I just shoo them away with my hands, eager to be with the two men left in the room.

Once we're left alone in the room, I begin to remove my clothes until I'm standing before them nude and ready. "Shall we have some fun?" I seductively say to them, ready for what is to come.

Blaine

"Shall we have some fun?" Who even is this woman right now? Twelve hours ago she was an innocent, in denial, virgin. Now? She's standing in front of us, buck-ass naked, asking if we're ready to fuck. To bear her mate mark and fuck if I'm not. It's her Alpha behavior mixing with the mate bond pulling on her body. If we were better men, we'd postpone and let her settle in with being an Alpha and knowing she has true mates. I can't seem to find that in me right now, though. I've wanted her since the day I laid eyes on her, and my wolf is ready to rut and mark her.

Magnolia seductively sways her hips as she makes her way back to her own bed. She sits down, leaning back on her elbows, just staring at us, waiting for one of us to move. I stand from Wylla's bed and cross the room to her in two big strides, grabbing her and spinning, so I can sit on the bed and she can straddle my lap. I kiss her softly at first, then she pushes her tongue into my mouth, and I growl while deepening our kiss.

A purr that sounds like a cat shifter fills the room, and I move my eyes, looking around before they settle on the little vixen in front of me. Magnolia is purring; that's fucking adorable. She nips my lip, and my eyes snap to hers instantly. She winks at me before once again tangling her tongue with mine.

Our tongues battle, sliding back and forth between our mouths. She pulls back and her eyes dart back and forth between mine. Gasping, her eyes cloud, filling even more with lust. Two large hands gently run up her sides and cup her full tits. "Pretty wolf, I know these are new, so I'm trying to be gentle. It's fucking hard, though. I want to wrap my lips around your little bars and tug on them," Zeke murmurs into her ear, causing her to whimper, and my cock pushes even harder against the constriction of my jeans.

I hand her off to Zeke, who lays her gently back down on the bed. We're standing side by side, staring down at her. Her chest is panting rapidly, and her pupils are blown with want and longing. We quickly strip our clothes and hold our cocks in our hands, giving them a stroke. Magnolia licks her lips at the sight of pre-cum beading on our tips. Zeke crawls onto the bed beside her, kissing her lips and running his mouth down the side of her neck and back, teasing her with his warm touches.

"I wanna taste your cunt, mate, to feast on you like the sweetest dessert." I drop to my knees and spread her creamy thighs, so I can see the glistening pink prize that is now all mine. *Ours.* I lean in and flatten my tongue as I lick her from ass to clit, collecting as much of her cream as I can and groaning as her flavor bursts against my tongue.

I flick my tongue up and down against her as she squirms beneath me. "Zeke, can you keep our girl busy? I've waited too long for this and don't wanna hunt my dinner down." Zeke, being the best friend he is, gets to his knees with his cock bouncing in front of Magnolia's face.

"Wanna show me those new skills Jude and Wylla taught you the other night, pretty wolf?" Magnolia nods, and I see Zeke feed her his cock slowly before I turn my attention back to this pretty, little pussy in front of me. Spreading her lips, so I can get better access to her little nub, I suck it into my mouth, swirling my tongue around it. Releasing her from my mouth. I lick softly before gently inserting two fingers into her.

I pump my fingers in and out as I lap at her like she's my favorite ice cream. *She's dripping like a melting cone on a hot summer day.* I start to hook my fingers, running them against her inner walls as I pull out, and that does her in. She squeezes my finger like a vice, and her thighs slam shut, holding my head to her pussy. I continue to lick through her release. When she finally stops shaking, she opens her legs again.

"Sorry, Blaine, I almost suffocated you." Her cheeks redden at her apology, and Zeke caresses her cheek in comfort.

"You're fine. It would have been the best way to die, feasting on my mate and drowning in her juices," I tell her, wiping her release from my face before licking it off my hand and fingers one by one.

"Fuck me, Blaine," she whines, and the control I had to take this slow snaps.

"Hold her, Zeke. I want her to be held as she loses her innocence." Zeke slides beside her, so he can kiss her lips once more. I stand and position my head at her slit and run it through her slick pussy. Once I'm good and lubricated with her arousal, I start to enter her tight core slowly. She gasps, and I freeze, not wanting to hurt her.

"Don't stop," she whispers, and I start to move again. I push the rest of the way in, taking her virginity. I don't move, just hold still while I'm bottomed out inside her. "Move, please." Taking that as my cue, I slowly start to fuck her. We continue like this for a few minutes before she wraps her legs around me, her heels digging into my ass cheeks. Looking down, I make eye contact with her. "More," she growls.

Pulling my shaft from her, I look, and my cock has some blood on him. That doesn't stop me, though. I grab Magnolia, spinning her so she's on the bed on all fours. I position my tip at her entrance and thrust in one go, bottoming out in her once more. She mewls, and I start fucking her hard and fast. If she wants more, I'll give her more.

I've been focusing on watching my cock slide in and out of her pussy that I didn't notice Zeke move. His groan pulls me from my new favorite sight, and I snap my eyes up. I see he's in front of Magnolia, and she has her lips wrapped around his cock, sucking him like a lollipop. I slap her ass once, then rub the mark I just left behind. "I'm gonna come, pretty wolf," Zeke moans, and she doesn't stop, just takes him back into her mouth, and he roars his release as his cum shoots down her throat.

When he's drained, he pulls from her mouth with a pop, and I pull her body up so her back is flush against my chest. "Tell me you want my mark, mate. I wanna bite you as I fill you with my seed." She nods in response, and I come undone, jerking violently inside of her as my cum coats her walls. Extending my teeth, I latch onto Magnolia's neck, marking her as mine. She screams her release, and I continue to fuck her slowly through it. Once she's back with us from reaching her orgasm high, she wraps a hand around my neck, dragging it down to her teeth before she sinks her canines into my neck. I feel the mate bond snap into place, and I come inside her again as she licks the mark she just left on me.

Pulling out of her, I sit back on the bed as I try to catch my breath and my heart to stop beating out of my chest. I watch as Zeke moves closer to her and grabs her wrist, sinking his teeth into it. She leans toward him, but he pulls back away from her. I see her wince, and I can feel her rejection through the bond. "Not rejecting you, pretty wolf, but are you sure you want to mate a ferret? You're an Alpha now, pretty wolf." She ignores him, moving like lightning and latching her teeth into the skin of his left pec right above his heart.

Just like that, I can feel Zeke inside me, just like I can Magnolia. *Fucking weird since we aren't mated.* Wylla was right, Magnolia is the center of this bond, and we'll all be connected through her. Zeke and Magnolia are locked in a heated kiss, and I see a tear roll down Zeke's cheek.

Deciding to give them a bit of privacy since I know Zeke really thought this day would never come, I move toward the girls' shower caddies and find some wet wipes. This fucking sucks, I want a warm cloth to clean my mate up and care for her. The communal bathroom isn't going to work for us anymore. I'm going to talk to them ASAP about moving into a house together. Then we can always be together, too.

Moving back to the couple, I clean Magnolia up as she cuddles with Zeke. I clean myself up too before throwing a wipe to Zeke. I toss the used wipes in the trash and lay down next to them, holding Magnolia.

Fucking ecstatic is the only thing I feel right now, like a missing piece of my soul has snapped into place. I still feel like something is missing, and I have a tingling feeling that it might be that rainbow-haired sassy thing upstairs with our demon brother.

Looking at Magnolia, I stare at her as she sleeps, thinking about how much I fucking love her. I'll do anything for her, fucking die for her, and I'll make damn sure she doesn't end up with that Exodus pack. A growl leaves me before I can stop it.

"Same, brother," comes from Zeke, and I look over at him. He's looking at Magnolia and thinking the same thing.

Tomorrow, I need to call my dad. He needs to know I'm fully mated now, and that the future pack luna is a female Alpha. Also that our pack needs to get ready for war. It's time we wipe Exodus from the wolf registry.

Zeke

Waking up with Magnolia snuggled up against my side, and her arm draped across my chest is amazing. Never in my wildest dreams did I think I'd have a mate, I mean other than a ferret. But to be mated to a wolf, an Alpha to be exact, who is also mated to other strong supernatural beings, never crossed my mind. It's still so hard to wrap my brain around.

Her pack will never let her go, and I think we all know that especially after that call from the Beta she's supposed to mate. A war is coming, and we all need to be ready. I'm not much of a threat in my ferret form, but in my human one, I can kill like no other. Hell, they don't call me Bone Crusher for nothing. You just don't get a name like that unless you've crushed a few. If only I could supe up my ferret form, turn it into a superhuman ferret, or some shit like they do in those human Marvel movies where the puny guy gets bitten by a spider and gains power. Something I plan to talk to Wylla about, maybe sooner rather than later.

Lifting my head and looking over Magnolia's body, I see Blaine, deep asleep and hanging halfway off the bed. Looking over the other way, I see Wylla's bed is empty. She must have stayed in our room last night, giving us some alone time. One thing I know for sure, we need a bigger bed for Magnolia, especially with all of us, and if more than one of us plans to sleep with her at a time. This tiny ass bed is for the birds.

Reaching up, I rub my eyes with the heel of my palm before taking my fingers and raking them through my hair. *Fuck! We need to get up!* Our mate needs to eat, we need to formulate a plan on how we're going to handle the Exodus pack, and who these other mates are. Tilting my head down, I kiss Magnolia on the top of her head, smelling the mixture of Blaine and my scent on her. My ferret is chirping with happiness at being mated. Using my hand, I gently shake Magnolia's shoulder as I whisper to her, "Time to get up, pretty wolf. Wake up, sleepyhead."

She nestles deeper into me. "I don't want to. Can't we stay like this all day?" she mumbles into my chest as she moves her leg over mine, grazing against my already hardening cock.

"I'd love to, babe, but if we don't get up, Blaine's going to end up on the floor." She lifts her head as I tell her, looking over her shoulder, and lets out a soft chuckle. Just to prove my point to her, I reach over her and smack him right across the back of his head. Sure enough, he jumps up with a startle and falls down onto the floor with a thud.

Magnolia and I burst into laughter at Blaine's expense. "Fucking asshole!" he growls out as he jumps up from the floor, causing me to cover my eyes, not wanting to see his cock flapping in the wind. But from the gasp our little she-wolf lets out, she's enjoying the show.

Magnolia calms down long enough to lean in and kiss me deeply before rolling out of the bed, moving over to Blaine, wrapping her arms around him, and kissing him as well. He sticks up his hand behind her back and flips me off. Letting them have their moment, I get up slowly, pick up my abandoned clothes from the floor, and get dressed. Pulling my shirt over my head, I decide it's time to break them up. They haven't moved from each other's arms since she went to him.

"Okay, time to break it up. Blaine, you need to get dressed, so our girl can get a shower while we wake up the two upstairs."

Our girl lets out a little whine at us leaving her.

"Oh, none of that now. Z's right. We need to get dressed, feed you, and talk to my dad. He needs to know we're mated now," Blaine tells her, which appeases her for a minute.

"We also need to invest in a bigger bed," I interject.

"Who are you telling? I was the one who was hanging on for dear life and ended up on the floor."

Blaine pulls on his jeans, then reaches down, picks up his other discarded clothing and shoes, and heads for the door. "Come on, Z. Let's wake them up. Magnolia, baby, shower, and we'll be right back."

She gives us a little pout as we leave the room, which makes me giddy inside.

Magnolia

Once the guys leave, I grab my shower caddy off my dresser and head straight to the bathroom, taking the quickest shower known to man. I'm caught up in my memories of the most amazing night, and the ache between my thighs reminds me it was real and not a dream. I've got mates, I'm an Alpha, and I'm no longer a virgin. Stepping into the room, I don't even notice Wylla sitting on my bed, grinning at me like the Cheshire Cat from ear to ear. "I need all the dirty little details now before they get back down here." Jumping up from the bed, she skips over to me, taking my hand in hers, and pulling me back to my bed. "Oh my Goddess, Magz, baby, did they treat you right? Ravish you with orgasms?" Before I can even respond to her, there's a knock at the door.

"That must be the guys, but why the hell are they knocking?" Wylla spits out as she stands and heads over to it. Opening the door, I expect her to have some witty banter for them, but there's silence. "Who the fuck are you?" she barks out at whoever's at the door.

Curious, I stand up and move up behind her, just as a deep voice speaks. "Watch who you're speaking to, bitch. I'm here to see my betrothed. Where the hell is she?" Peering around Wylla, I see Max and one of his Betas, Reid.

"Max, Reid," crosses my tongue in fear. *Why are they here?*

Max's nostrils flare, and he growls out, "We came to check on you. We've heard you've forgotten your place, even after my father, your Alpha, warned you." He lifts his nose, sniffing the air just as the elevator dings. Both Max and Reid turn on alert, growling fiercely.

All I hear is a maddening growl from my wolf mate, "Get the fuck away from my mate!" He charges Max and Reid, with Zeke and Jude hot behind him.

"Fuck you, wolf boy. She belongs to us." Max gets a menacing grin on his face before letting out a burst of maniacal laughter. "I know who you are. I can smell the other wretched creatures on you. You're from that impure pack." Max turns his head over his shoulder to look at me. "It's beneath my mate to be associating with the likes of him.

Expect your punishment to be swift and severe. Reid has many creative ways to make you earn your penance."

Fear overtakes me as I step closer to Wylla. "The fuck you'll lay one hand on her," Blaine says sternly, stepping into his face as they stare each other down, with Jude and Zeke flanking his side and mimicking how Reid stands beside Max.

"No!" I scream out. It's time I put an end to this. I step around Wylla and into the hallway. "I don't belong to you, you're not my mates. There is no way I'll ever be with you. You'll have to kill me first. You, the Alpha, and the Exodus Pack can all kiss my ass. I'm no longer a member. I'd rather be a rogue wolf than part of it any longer." Fear ravages me, but I feel stronger and happy that I'm finally standing up for myself. Maybe it's because the blocks have been removed from me, but I no longer want to be tied to the backward thinking of the Exodus pack. It just amplifies my desire to leave them.

"You heard *my* mate. Get the fuck out of here and take your little fucking Beta with you," Blaine growls at him.

Looking down, I see Max's hands starting to shift. Reid must catch it as well. Placing his hand on Max's shoulder, he leans into him. "Not here. Let's go. The Alpha wouldn't want us to cause a scene, and there's a ban on fighting at this school. She's not going to be protected by them twenty-four seven."

Max quickly stops the shift taking over him, looking over his shoulder at me. "We're not done, bitch." He storms past Blaine, knocking him in the shoulder before they head down the stairs, not even waiting for the elevator.

Jude shoots past Blaine and takes me in his arms. "Are you okay, Maggie? I'm so proud of you for standing up for yourself like that."

Then panic sits in. "Oh, my Goddess. My block is gone. Do you think with everything happening they smelled I was an Alpha?" *Fuck! Fuck! Fuck!*

"If they did, we'll deal with it." He puts his arm around my shoulder and leads me back into the bedroom, swooping his other arm around Wylla as we pass her. "Question is, did you feel a bond to either of them?"

"Nope, nothing at all."

Blaine steps into the room last, shutting the door behind him. "I need to call my dad. He needs to know this shit just happened." Zeke and Jude voice their agreement with him.

Max

I've kept my rage contained, the drive back to the hotel only giving me more time to stew. Stepping into our room, I pace back and forth across the room. How dare that cunt speak to me like that. Each time I pass by Reid, I just glare at him. He should've let me rip those low-level beasts to pieces before taking my mate and leaving. Hell, he could've taken that mutt of a necromancer for his plaything.

"Can you believe how she spoke to me as if she was someone? She's just a fucking bitch who's forgotten her place," I spew at Reid. As much as that's eating at me, something else is bothering me more.

"Chill man, you know if you caused a scene, it would piss your father off more. They can't be with her every minute of the day. We catch her alone and take her back to the pack. Why your father even let her leave to come here is still a mystery to me." Reid takes out his knife and begins carving into the desk.

"It is to me, too. Did you smell her? She's a fucking Alpha. There are not supposed to be female Alphas any longer. My great-grandfather saw to that when the last one was born."

"Better question is, how did she find out before the designation ceremony? My bet is on the half-breed necro. When we snatch our mate to take home and reprogram her, we need to get her as well. When the pack catches a whiff of a female Alpha, there will be a revolt amongst the women. One we don't want."

My anger continues to boil and my wolf craves to be let free. He wants the wolf that was promised to us, wants her to bow in submission before him, as he mounts her, taking what's his. She's going to pay with a far worse punishment than was initially planned for her. I pick up the chair and sling it across the room just as the door opens, barely missing Jeremiah as he steps in, almost dropping the bags of food in his hands.

"What the hell is going on?" he shouts out in surprise.

"The bitch is a fucking Alpha! We need a plan now! The games are over. We're taking our mate and going home."

Jude

What in the hell just happened? The guys came back to the room, giving Wylla and me the all-clear that we could go back to our mate. Wylla flew from our room like her ass was on fire. While the guys changed, I slid on some real pants and not just some sweats. I've no sooner stepped out of the elevator when I hear Zeke and Blaine start snarling behind me and fighting to be out of the doors.

They run past me, bolting toward the girls' room before I even know what's going on. Looking beyond them, I see Wylla at their bedroom door with Maggie, cowering behind her. When I notice the two large wolves getting in Wylla's face it instantly pisses me off. The fear is radiating off Maggie. Blaine starts to shift when the larger one of the wolves in front of him does as they stand toe to toe, fighting over our girl. I'm thankful the other night that the girls powered up my reserves because I'm going to need it if this goes sideways. She quickly snapped into her new Alpha wolf and yelled at all of us to stop and told those two cocksuckers she was not theirs, nor will she ever be.

I want to know how they even got here and what happened to the Jeremiah dude giving us a heads-up. We were just totally blindsided by their arrival and only Wylla was with her. I'm not even sure of her fighting ability or power level. We need to fucking discuss what our capabilities are and strengthen our weak points. Fuck! They could've just snatched our woman.

Jeremiah wasn't with them, so perhaps he didn't know or they found him out. More than likely, his whole spiel was a ploy, and we played right into his hand by trusting him. Blaine pushes the girls inside the room, and we head in behind him quickly before he slams the door. "I knew we shouldn't have trusted that fucking wolf, but we were so quick to side with the girls and now look what happened. Maggie was here with Wylla alone, and she could've been taken, or worse. Thank Goddess, we showed up when we did," I roar at him, anger coursing through my veins. I feel like I'm frothing at the mouth, I'm so upset.

"How fucking dare you think I couldn't protect our mate, demon! You know nothing about me or my abilities. I could kill you right now with a flick of my sexy wrist, so keep talking shit. What were you gonna do? Fuck the enemy into leaving us alone?" Wylla snaps back, clearly pissed that I insinuated she couldn't protect Maggie.

"Everyone needs to calm the fuck down! Fighting with each other isn't going to help anyone. We don't know if Jeremiah betrayed us. Let me find my phone, and we'll know for sure," Maggie scolds us, moving to the corner of the room where her discarded clothes are from last night and pulling her phone out of her pants. She's scrolling through it, looking at it intently as she does, and her head suddenly snaps up to look at all of us. "There are calls and texts from Jeremiah last night, a lot of them. He tried to warn us, warn me, but we were busy with the spells and mating. I knew he wouldn't betray me; call it a gut feeling or whatever you want, but I just knew he wouldn't."

"Maggie, you can't go anywhere without one of us. I'm dead serious, this isn't the last we'll see of them, and you know that as well as I do," Zeke pipes up, his tone laced with concern and love, so she doesn't think he's trying to control her, but I can tell he's fucking worried about her.

"I called my dad when we were upstairs changing, and he said he had a lead on a rental property we could have, so we could all live together if that's what we want. I was going to bring it up later in a better setting after our chat this morning about the beds, but it seems like it might need to be brought up now," Blaine admits. He looks nervous, like he's afraid we might be upset about him jumping the gun and calling his dad about getting a place together.

"I'm for it," I tell him. "It will be safer if we're all together and not floors apart. Plus, now that they're marked, Zeke and Blaine will want to be with you as much as possible, Magnolia. Being apart from each other will be painful at first until you've settled into the bonds."

"I agree, I want to live with you all. Being apart from y'all isn't an option anymore. This bond was fought and denied for too long. Can we go see it tomorrow?" Maggie asks, and I love seeing her smiling and excited about getting a house we can all live in together.

"Sure can, babe," Blaine says, looking around at the rest of us, and we all nod our agreement. We order food to the dorm, not wanting to leave, and head upstairs to our room where we stay the rest of the day cuddled up between our three beds, watching movies and just trying to be together before the shit hits the fan. *Yep, we definitely need to figure out a way to have one huge bed for all of us to share.*

We all wake up stiff and sore, but thankfully since we are all supes, a good stretch and we'll be good to go in fifteen minutes or so, ready to start the day. Our bodies heal faster than humans, so while it wasn't ideal for the five of us to sleep in our room last night, it was worth it to make sure Maggie was safe. After a lot of tossing and turning on our single beds, we decided to push them together, making one semi-large bed that offered slightly more room.

We quickly get dressed, then escort the girls to their room to change, so we can head out to look at the property Blaine's dad has a lead on for us to rent. He apparently has an agent from the pack waiting to show us around and give us the keys today if we decide we want it.

The girls are dressed and ready to go in under ten minutes, so we make our way to Blaine's truck quickly and efficiently. *Guess they're excited to see what could be our new home while we go to school here.* Blaine leads the way with Maggie behind him and Wylla close behind her. Zeke and I are in the back, and all of us have our heads on a swivel, making sure we aren't attacked or being followed.

Piling into the truck, we barely fit, and with more mates out there, we're going to need to upgrade to an SUV, so we can have that third-row seating. Pulling out onto the road, I keep checking behind us to see if we're being tracked. Catching Blaine's eyes in the rearview mirror, I see he's doing the same thing.

Toxic by 2WEI comes on the radio, and Wylla squeals in excitement and reaches in front of her, hitting the volume dial and turning it up. She's singing along and dancing in her seat, and Maggie giggles beside me in the backseat, watching her best friend, now mate, dance to her favorite song. When the song comes to an end, Wylla quickly turns the radio down, and the tension-filled silence once again fills the cab of the truck.

"How much longer until we're there?" Maggie asks.

"Like ten minutes, according to the GPS." She sighs at Blaine's answer, and I see her squeeze her thighs together.

"Maggie, do you need to use the bathroom?" I ask teasingly.

"Yes, I'm sorry. I should've gone before we left, but I was too excited, and, well, drinking that bottle of water didn't help."

Blaine pulls off the main road, following the signs to the gas station. Pulling in, he parks at a pump closest to the entrance of the gas station. "As long as we're here, I'm gonna fill up." He gets out and swipes his card at the pump, pulling the nozzle so he can fill the truck.

Wylla and Zeke jump out, announcing they're going to get snacks since we didn't eat before we left. Magnolia climbs out and power walks to the bathroom, her ass jiggling with every step as she squeezes her legs together. It's funny and cute all at the same time. The bathroom to this gas station is apparently on the outside of the building, very nineties of them. Standing outside the truck watching my woman hurry to the bathroom, I laugh. "We sure are lucky, huh?"

"Sure fucking are," Blaine growls as he reaches down to adjust himself in his pants. We make small talk while waiting for the pump to finish and for everyone to get back to the truck. "We can't let them get her, man, no matter what it takes. Actually, I was thinking this weekend we should take her home to the pack and have my dad mark her officially as a member."

I open my mouth to voice that's a great fucking idea when a blood-curdling scream has me whipping my head back towards the gas station. Wylla's standing at the entrance to the building and the drinks she has in her hands fall to the ground, exploding around her. She's staring off to the other side of the parking lot where a large white pickup speeds out of the lot, and I see Magnolia's gray hair through the back window with the creepy fucking Beta from yesterday petting her hair and whispering into her ear.

Blaine and I jump into his truck, and the other two are right behind us, barely shutting the doors before Blaine roars the truck to life and speeds after them. Tires squeal as we turn out onto the road and gain on them fast. No way in hell are they getting away with our fucking mate. We're hot on their tail on this country-ass road when suddenly they veer right, driving under a large arch that covers the road. Wylla is chanting, and her eyes glaze over as she focuses on the truck in front of us.

Half a mile later, they cross a bridge, and the truck disappears instantly on the other side. "What the fuck?" everyone screams. Blaine hits the brakes, and we come to a screeching stop.

Wylla is out of the truck and running across the bridge, screaming so loud I think my eardrums are about to burst. She turns around, and her eyes are pitch black. She looks absolutely feral right now. "She's gone. Our mate is gone!"

Epilogue
Magnolia

Just minutes before...

I have to pee so badly, and it's taking everything in me to make it to the bathroom. If I didn't have to pee as bad as I do, I'd be turning around without haste and stepping out of the bathroom. It's absolutely disgusting in here. One by one, I open the stalls, looking inside as I hold back the vile that's begging to come up. Giving up hope as I step up to the last door, I push it open anyway, but I'm happy to say it's the best out of all of them, and my bladder isn't going to last any longer. I hurry inside, pull some toilet paper off the roll and make a barrier between the seat and my ass and sit down. A sigh of relief escapes as the sound of my stream hits the water inside.

Hearing the door open, I immediately perk up, but when the sound of feet are lighter, more feminine, I relax. Hearing a stall door open and the scuffle of feet stepping inside of it, I let out a little snort at my paranoia. Just someone else who needed to go, probably as bad as I did.

Pulling up my pants, I step out of the stall and over to the sink to wash my hands, mindlessly thinking about how much my life has changed in just a short period of time. Hearing a door open, my mind instantly thinks it's Wylla. "Did you get me something with chocolate?"

But it's not her voice that answers me. "Did you think you could take the man I've wanted right out from under me, bitch? He's mine and there ain't no two-bit wolf going to take him from me. Looks like you're about to get your just desserts, though." Turning around, I see the bartender from the fight club, Ava, the one who was flirting with Blaine.

"What do you want? He was never yours. He's my mate. How did you find us here?" I respond to her, but she laughs an eerily insane cackle. Fuck, is she that crazy?

"You see, it's you who's wrong. Who would have known how beneficial it would be to keep up with all the different wolf packs? And when a little birdy told me the Alpha heir of the Exodus pack was here to put his bitch of an intended mate in her place..." An evil smirk crosses her face.

"I don't have time for you. He doesn't want you, and to make it more clear to you, we've already completed our bond." To make sure she really gets the picture, I lift my hair and turn my head, so she can see the mate mark newly adorning my skin.

"That means nothing." She lunges for me and shoves me back, causing me to fall into the sink. A burning pain rages through my back at the impact.

The bathroom door opens and hope springs into my heart that either Wylla or one of the guys is here. But the person stepping through the door sends me into a panic. "Well, well, if it isn't our little mate, and she's been left all alone for the big bad wolf to come and take," Reid sneers at me as he spins and twirls a knife in his hand.

I go to scream, but the bitch works quicker than I do and pounces on top of me, taking me down to the floor, then straddling me. Taking my hair in her hands, she begins to slam my head into the floor. I go to scream, barely getting the first yelp out before her hand clamps over my mouth.

"Are you going to help me shut her up before they realize something's wrong?" she bellows out to Reid.

"Always someone wanting to spoil my fun. But bitch, remember your place." Reid moves over to us as I squirm beneath her, trying to break free from her grasp. Kneeling down beside us, he leans closer to me, licking his tongue up the side of my face as he pulls something from his pocket. "I'm going to have so much fun breaking your ass and marking this creamy skin of yours with my knife. Fuck, my cock is already hard in anticipation of your screams, smearing your blood all over my dick before plunging it inside of you, fucking you into oblivion. But we need to go. Maxie boy is waiting for us in the car." He holds up his hand, and I see the syringe, just before he sticks it into my neck.

The room begins to spin as my vision goes hazy.

Noooo! This can't be happening, not now, not when freedom was so close. My body grows heavy, and I'm unable to move it. "Get off her. She's ready, and it's time to go," Reid orders as he scoops me up and tosses me over his shoulder. My vision goes blurry, and I can barely think.

My wolf and I both scream, but our pleas land on deaf ears or I imagined the cries for help as everything goes dark.

To be continued in Destroying the Alpha...

Cassie's Acknowledgments

First I have to thank Chad my husband for supporting this dream. To our kids' Faith, Roshun, Mario, Marshon, Sutton, and Georgia. (Y'all probably thought I was kidding about six kids huh?) Thank you! Thank you for letting me type away while you entertained yourselves and for helping to wrangle your younger siblings when I couldn't. I love you all so much!

To my ALPHA/ BETA readers you all are the bomb! Loving this story as much as us and really making it what it is today.

To Shayna the best PA a gal could ask for. Thank you for answering a zillion questions and putting up with my requests.

Bre for taking a chance on a newbie and co-writing with me. I love our book and our friendship so much. You mean the world to me!

About Cassie Lein

Cassie resides in Northern Illinois on a farm with her husband and six kids. When not writing, she can be found reading, chauffeuring her kids, or showing pigs. Cassie is a huge advocate for foster care and adoption. She enjoys a good horror movie, dark romance, and alcohol. Lots and lots of alcohol. You did just read she has six kids right? To keep up to date with Cassie and all that is new with her please join her group on facebook Cassie Lein Reader Group.

Also By Cassie

Check out all her books here

Vacation Valentine

(2/11/23)

Up In Smoke

(7/25/23)

Beyond the Pack Duet w/Bre Rose

Rise of the Alpha

Destroying the Alpha

Coming 4-1-23

Kindlevella w/Bre Rose

All on the Field

Under the pen name G.P. Darling

Unknown

(8/20/22)

Exposed

(12/10/22)

Collapsed

(coming 2023)

Bre's Acknowledgments

First as always, I want to thank my family, my amazing children. Y'all mean the world to me and I couldn't imagine this life without you. To my bestie Melissa, I love you more than you could ever know. Thank you for being my support when I need it the most.

Cassie, girl, thank you for popping my co-writing cherry. I love what we created together and can't wait to write more stories with you.

Shayna, my PA, my right hand, what can I say? You keep me on track with everything I need to do even when I'm feeling defeated or stressed. You're calming words let me know everything is going to be alright. You are a blessing.

My BETA team: Olivia, Sullen, Sadie, Kim, Tory, Beth, Sandy and Katrina. And to our Fluidity Team: Martha and Joy. I want to thank you for everything and for your love of our book. You guys rock

My ARC readers, what can I say you ladies rock. I am blessed to have each and every one of you. The majority of ladies have been with me since the beginning. Here are too many more books together. And please don't hate me after you read that part.

To my Street team: Thank you all for sharing my books and pimping me out. It means the world to me and I love each and every one of you.

Lastly, to my readers, I appreciate all of you. Without you I'd still be just playing those stories out in my head. It is your support and enjoyment in reading my work that keeps me wanting to write more. I hope to be able to bring you stories for years to come.

About Bre Rose

Bre Rose writes under a pen name and is a newer author with seven published books currently. She writes in the contemporary and paranormal why choose genre primarily but does have works that will not be. Bre is a native of North Carolina and mother to three amazing sons and two feline fur babies more affectionately known as her hellhounds. She's always been an avid reader then progressed to becoming an ARC, BETA and ALPHA reader for some of her favorite authors. After some encouragement she decided to tackle writing the stories in her head and is loving every single minute of it. When she isn't reading or writing she enjoys traveling the world and still has some places to mark off her bucket list. She also enjoys spending time with her family and advocating for the differently abled population. To keep up to date with all upcoming releases and all things Bre then simply join her facebook reader group Bre's Rose Petal Readers.

Also By Bre

Bre's Book Library

Memphis Duet

Finding Memphis (Book 1)

Saving Memphis (Book 2)

Memphis Spinoffs

Unbreakable

Memphis Beginnings:Novella

Prophecy Series

Shay's Awakening (Book 1)

Shay's Acceptance (Book 2)

Shay's Ascension (Book 3)

Beyond the Pack Series co-write with Cassie Lein

Rise of the Alpha

Destroying the Alpha

(coming 4-1-23)

Kindlevella Co-write with Cassie Lein

All on the Field

Anthologies

Love on the Ice: Jingle My Balls Anthology

Memphis Christmas: Under The Mistletoe A Wildone Holiday Romance Collection

In the Heat of the Moment Anthology Cowrite with Cassie Lein